Death by Cashmere

Death by Cashmere

A SEASIDE KNITTERS MYSTERY

Sally Goldenbaum

AN OBSIDIAN MYSTERY

Obsidian
Published by New American Library,
a division of Penguin Group (USA) Inc.,
375 Hudson Street, New York, New York 10014, USA
Penguin Group (Canada), 90 Eglinton Avenue East, Suite 700, Toronto,
Ontario M4P 2Y3, Canada (a division of Pearson Penguin Canada Inc.)
Penguin Books Ltd., 80 Strand, London WC2R 0RL, England
Penguin Ireland, 25 St. Stephen's Green, Dublin 2,
Ireland (a division of Penguin Books Ltd.)
Penguin Group (Australia), 250 Camberwell Road, Camberwell,
Victoria 3124, Australia (a division of Pearson Australia Group Pty. Ltd.)
Penguin Books India Pvt. Ltd., 11 Community Centre,
Panchsheel Park, New Delhi – 110 017, India
Penguin Group (NZ), 67 Apollo Drive, Rosedale, North Shore 0632,
New Zealand (a division of Pearson New Zealand Ltd.)
Penguin Books (South Africa) (Pty.) Ltd., 24 Sturdee Avenue,
Rosebank, Johannesburg 2196, South Africa

Penguin Books Ltd., Registered Offices:
80 Strand, London WC2R 0RL, England

First published by Obsidian, an imprint of New American Library,
a division of Penguin Group (USA) Inc.

First Printing, August 2008
1   3   5   7   9   10   8   6   4   2

Copyright © Sally Goldenbaum, 2008
All rights reserved

OBSIDIAN and logo are trademarks of Penguin Group (USA) Inc.

LIBRARY OF CONGRESS CATALOGING-IN-PUBLICATION DATA
Goldenbaum, Sally.
Death by cashmere: a seaside knitters mystery / Sally Goldenbaum.
p. cm. — (An Obsidian mystery)
ISBN: 978-0-451-22471-2
1. Knitters (Persons)—Fiction I. Title.
PS3557.O35937D43 2008

Set in Palatino   •   Designed by Elke Sigal

Printed in the United States of America

Acknowledgments

*T*he seaside knitters (and the author) would like to acknowledge those who have helped bring the knitters' story to life. My sincere thanks to:

Cindy and the entire staff of The Studio Knitting & Needlepoint in Kansas City, and especially Sarah Kraly, who showed me what life in a knitting shop is all about—lovely yarns, generous help, friendship and laughter, and a cozy place to be on a cold winter day.

Kristen Weber, for gracious, smart, and generous editing; Andrea Cirillo (for *years* of encouragement); and Kelly Harms (whose passion for knitting and life fueled the Sea Harbor women every step of the way).

My dear porch-writing friend Nancy Pickard, who understands it all.

And to my amazing family, the Cape Ann McElhennys: Aria, John, and Luke, who sent books on lobstering and quarry history, walked with me on breakwaters, through museums and seaside towns, and who shared with me their love of the sea. And the KC Goldenbaums: Todd, Danny, and Claudia, who are ever-present, fixing broken computers, building Web sites, and salving the spirit. And a special thanks to Don, for thirty-eight years of reasons.

Web site address: www.sallygoldenbaum.com

Prologue

Late Thursday night, Sea Harbor, Massachusetts

North of the Harbor Road shops, a mile or two up the coast—past the Canary Cove artist colony and the ocean-view vacation homes, some of which had been turned into enviable residences with wide seashell drives and two-story carriage houses—the land curved sharply like a sea serpent's tail.

When the moon was full, the sky a whitewash of stars, and the breeze a warm embrace, the beach on the tail and the stalwart breakwater were perfect places to walk on a summer's night. But tonight the weatherman had predicted rain, and the winds were gusty, discouraging evening strolls and lovers' trysts.

At the far end of the tail, beyond the yacht club and private homes, the wide stone breakwater jutted out into the ocean, protecting the waters from the ocean's vagaries. Not many people would be out on the breakwater tonight, or on the public beach just north of it, no one with good sense at least. Not fishermen or lovers or teenagers with six-packs stuffed in their backpacks. It would be the perfect place to have a drink, a talk, or whatever the encounter required.

On one side of the breakwater, the waves pounded hard against the structure. Foam, like beer from a tap, danced high against the black night. The breakwater—fifteen feet high or more, depending on the tide—was built of wide granite blocks, one on top of another, and it ensured calm waters for anchoring sailboats, small fishing vessels, and the smooth beach where young children built sandcastles on the tended shore.

Tonight no one sat on the beach. The expanse of windows in the clubhouse revealed warm flickering lights, visible from the height of the breakwater. Most of the families were gone at this late hour, but some couples remained, sitting at white-clothed tables and feasting on chunks of fresh lobster baked in crisp, buttery pastry and drinking the club's fruity cocktails. In the lounge, a few couples danced to a local band. Outside, the wind whistled through the needles of the pine trees.

A small sitting area on the edge of the property, across a stretch of beach from the breakwater, held two stone benches and a table—a perfect place for drinks at sunset on a pleasant evening. Or a place to sit in private tonight, with only the low lights of the dock illuminating the lone figure's deliberate stance. Calling her was risky, but it couldn't go on any longer. It had to end. And this would be a smart meeting place to iron out problems, to settle demands in whatever way was necessary.

Two figures sharing a drink, even walking out on the high breakwater, should it come to that, would appear as shadows against the sky to anyone who stepped out on the clubhouse's veranda for a smoke or a breath of air—nondescript, vague, undefined shadows. And the couple's voices would be carried away on the wind.

It didn't have to be like this, of course. Life was about compromises. Negotiations. Forgiveness. Not betrayal and disloyalty and idiocy.

Peering into the blackness but seeing nothing—no one—the lone figure felt a sudden slice of fear, almost painful in its intensity. It began deep in the pit of the stomach and churned painfully up until it was overpowering, an ugly acid taste.

No! A sharp command calmed the body and the mind. It wasn't the time to be afraid, not a time for cowards. Steady, deep breaths, an inner voice dictated. A long drink from the silver glass did its magic. And as always, the fear slowly resided.

And then the sound of footsteps on the rocky shore, just barely heard above the rising, crashing waves, caused a strange relief. A figure walked *slowly and purposefully toward the stone table. Tall and unafraid and brash.*

It was almost as if two friends were meeting for a private talk or a business deal, a drink shared—except for the fierce anger that charged the air, calmed only by a slow, deliberate breath, and a long swallow of scotch.

It was time. Two glasses. A flask. A walk along the breakwater. To talk and reason. Or not.

Chapter 1

Early Thursday evening

Izzy Chambers stood with her hands on her hips, staring hard at the ceiling. Crashing thumps from the floor above sent tiny flecks of paint floating to the floor. The music was loud, too—screeching, unrecognizable words and a freight train–loud bass that Izzy could feel in the pit of her stomach.

Behind her, Nell Endicott, thirty years Izzy's senior, felt the same vibrations, but perhaps with more weight. Had she been back in Kansas, there'd be no doubt in Nell's mind that a tornado was pummeling down to crush her niece Izzy's small knitting shop.

But neither she nor Izzy was in Kansas. They were in Sea Harbor, Massachusetts, and tornadoes were rarely spotted in the sleepy oceanside town.

"Maybe she's Rollerblading," Izzy said. She grimaced at the continuing noise.

"Rollerblading is a lot better than some of the thoughts that passed through my head."

"Oh, phooey. Let's not worry about it," Izzy said, spinning around on her newly knitted socks and facing her aunt. "Angie's rambunctious, that's all. She's usually not so noisy."

A new sound—a series of heavy clunks—caused the track lighting to quiver and brought Mae Anderson rushing in from the front of the knitting store.

Izzy held up her hands to shush her sales manager before she could say anything. "Mae, it's just a little music."

"The *little* music, Izzy, made Laura Danver's baby cry—that's how loud it is up at the cash register. And Laura left without buying the yarn she'd been waiting weeks for."

Izzy sighed. "I'll drop Laura's yarn by her house later, Mae."

Nell could feel Izzy's frustration—the young mom wasn't Izzy's most patient customer, but she was certainly one of Izzy's best, and Izzy couldn't afford to offend her.

The bell above the front door jingled, and Mae hurried off to help a new customer, but her eyes told Izzy that she needed to do something—and soon. Priding herself on her senior status, Mae didn't hesitate to tell her young boss how things should be done.

Nell looked up at the ceiling again. The music was softer now, but heavy shoes—boots, maybe—clunked back and forth across the floor above.

"Thicker carpet," Izzy said, half to herself.

"No, sweetie," a lilting voice from the doorway chimed. "Thicker skin. That's what you need. Angie Archer needs to move on."

Birdie Favazza, the oldest member of the Thursday-night knitting group, stood in the doorway. A diminutive woman of nearly eighty, Birdie stood straight, her chin lifted and her eyes bright. A short cap of silver hair outlined her small, fine-boned face. "Landlords need to be tough, darlin'," she said, and walked on into the room.

"She's a good tenant, Birdie. She's probably just had a rough day at work." Izzy scooped up stray pins and measuring tapes and tossed them into a wicker basket on the table.

Birdie shook her head in clear disagreement and walked briskly across the room to a worn leather couch. Her bulky backpack landed on the floor. A bottle of wine protruded from the top of the pack and Birdie pulled it out, putting it on the coffee table in front of her. "I'm here to knit and snack and share a glass of this very fine Muscadet, Izzy. Not to judge you, dear. But—"

"—you told me not to rent the apartment to Angie."

"And you're not quite ready to admit I'm right," Birdie said in a distinct accent that blended fine breeding with a salty touch inherited from a sea captain grandfather. She tugged her bright yellow cable-knit sweater closer around her diminutive frame and tenderly pulled a ball of qiviut yarn from her bag. She fingered its softness with still-nimble fingers and pondered aloud whether to make a shawl or a scarf out of the luxurious wild-berry yarn.

"A shawl," Nell suggested. She looked around the studio. Nell knew exactly why Izzy liked having Angie living above the knitting shop. When they had turned the broken-down bait shop into the Seaside Knitting Studio the winter before, Izzy had decided to move into a cozy New England cottage a short bike ride away, leaving the apartment space above her shop empty.

"This shop could easily become my whole life," she had told Nell. "I need to build in distance." But she liked having *someone* live above the shop. And when Angie moved back to town and was looking for a place, it seemed a fine match.

Nell had agreed. Birdie was wrong this time. Sometimes she clung to old memories a tad too fiercely, Nell thought. She was remembering a young, wild Angie. But college and graduate school had intervened, Angie had mellowed, and in Nell's opinion, she was a fine tenant.

"Angie loves living here," Izzy said, rummaging around in a side drawer for a pair of scissors and some extra needles.

"And how could she not, sweetie?" Birdie said. "Your apartment is a bit of heaven."

Nell looked out the east windows, the same view Angie could see from the apartment above. A rectangle of mullioned windows framed the harbor and an expanse of endless ocean beyond—wild and churning one day, and a smooth silken blanket the next.

Nell thought the building was worth most anything for the view alone. She remembered standing in that same room the year before, Izzy at her side. The Realtor, brushing dust off her taupe suit, had stepped over broken boxes and bottles and motioned Izzy and Nell over to that same window, smudged and filthy, with a broken pane at the bottom and glass scattered on the floor.

Izzy had recently abandoned a boyfriend and a lucrative law career and was looking for the perfect place in which to sink her savings and begin a new life.

And to this day, Nell swore it was looking out that mullioned window that did it.

The Realtor had tugged and pushed at the latch until the windows opened wide, framing the sea and dozens of small boats moored in the Seaside harbor. She slipped into the background then, in that way that Realtors did, leaving Nell and Izzy standing side by side, seeing new beginnings carried in on the waves.

"See," the Realtor said with practiced excitement. "You can jump directly into the ocean from these windows."

Izzy and Nell had smiled. Neither had been inclined to take the plunge, but they were both lured by the sound of the waves against the stone wall below and the breeze that carried new dreams directly into the knitting room.

Not long after that day, Ben Endicott built a window seat directly below the windows, and Nell cushioned it with a thick blue tufted pad. It was a favorite spot for Izzy's customers and friends.

The back room, as it came to be called, was filled with personal things of Izzy's—Uncle Ben's old leather chair, a table that Nell had found at an estate sale over in Rockport, paintings Izzy had bought from local artists on Canary Cove or Rocky Neck in Gloucester. A bank of bookshelves held knitting books, some dog-eared and smudged with coffee.

With Nell and Ben's help, the space had been transformed

into a cozy, inviting knitting shop, stocked from floor to ceiling with fine hand-dyed yarns and skeins of bright cotton and wool. It drew in townsfolk and summer people alike—a place for friends and strangers to sit and talk and share their knitting passion.

The small rooms grew out of one another like the arms of an octopus. One was filled with patterns and soft old chairs to settle into while picking out the perfect hat or sweater. Another held small cubicles filled with baby-fine cottons and cashmere, and dozens of tiny knitted sweaters and pants to lure even the weekend knitter into a project. A side room—Izzy called it the magic room—housed tiny chairs, a soft rug, and baskets of Izzy's own childhood toys and books, a place for children to play while their moms got help finishing a sweater, picking up stitches, or figuring out the intricacies of knitting a Möbius cowl.

And everywhere, on walls and tables, there were wooden cubicles or large wicker baskets holding every imaginable kind of yarn—alpaca and cashmeres, wool and cotton, linen and silk and mohair.

The first time Nell had walked through Izzy's shop, once the paint had dried and cubes and shelves and baskets were filled with soft plush yarns, she had called it a "sensory overload."

Izzy loved the description. A rich, lovely, sensuous experience. That's what knitting was all about.

Birdie looked up from her yarn. "Having someone here is comforting, Izzy—and I know for sure it helps your aunt Nell sleep at night." She lifted her silvery brows and looked over the top of her glasses at Nell.

Nell knew there was an unspoken "but" at the end of Birdie's statement, but at least she understood the feelings that gave birth to the Seaside Knitting Studio—and her own feelings, too. Izzy was like a daughter to her. And though Nell didn't expect anyone to break into the shop—Sea Harbor wasn't a high-crime sort of town—it made her feel better knowing there was someone living there. And it *did* help Nell sleep better. Birdie was dead-on right about that.

But this evening, from the sounds of things a floor above, no one was—or would be—sleeping.

"Good grief, Izzy—" Cass Halloran breezed into the room. "What's Angie up to?" She pulled off her sunglasses and stared at the ceiling.

"She's energetic," Izzy said.

"Energetic like Muhammad Ali." Cass's thick black hair was shoved up beneath a Red Sox cap, but the damp strands that curled from beneath it announced that she had managed to squeak in a shower after a day of lobstering.

Birdie nodded approvingly, having established the shower rule for Cass months ago. "You are lovely, Cass," she had said. "But the smell of your lobsters should be left at the dock and not ruining Izzy's fine yarns."

Cass lifted her backpack off one shoulder and set it down on the floor beside the fireplace. She walked over to the table where Nell had lined up four brown sacks and leaned toward the steam rising from one of them. "Ah, Nell, life is good."

"We needed a cobbler tonight. There's a brisk wind picking up and something warm and sweet seemed right," Nell said. She slipped off her suede jacket and hung it on a hook by the back door.

Cass nodded. "Nasty winds and probably a little rain during the night." The owner of over two hundred lobster traps, Cass knew the quirks of New England weather intimately. She glanced out the windows at the darkening sea. "It's almost as if nature needs to show us who's boss. Too many warm summer days need a comeuppance." Cass eyed the food sacks on the table again and put one hand on her flat stomach. It growled beneath her touch.

"Cass, you'd starve to death if it weren't for Nell." Izzy picked up a basket of yarn and needles and moved them to the coffee table.

"Of course I would," Cass said. "That's why I joined this group, if you remember, Iz. I hate to tell you, but it wasn't your cashmere yarn. When I spotted Nell walking in there that night, trailed by the most amazing food odors that ever met this nose, it changed my life forever. I swear it did."

Nell remembered the night well. One of those chance events when life's forces line up exactly right.

It happened by accident—Izzy kept the Seaside Studio open until seven on Thursday nights. And Nell often stopped by to bring her niece something to eat—lasagna, scallops and linguini, thin slices of fresh tuna—whatever she had made that day, or the night before.

One Thursday night Cass Halloran wandered in to take a look at the new shop, and she'd smelled the garlic clam sauce hidden in Nell's Tupperware container. Cass had looked at it so longingly that Nell went back home and brought the rest of the leftovers from her refrigerator. On impulse, she'd slipped a freshly baked pie into her sack.

Birdie Favazza happened by that Thursday night, too, on her way home from the Cape Ann nursing home where she taught tap dancing steps to the residents. She spotted activity through the window and decided she needed a few new skeins of merino wool. Surely Izzy would let her in. Eyeing the clam sauce feast spread out on the table in the back room, Birdie suggested that a cold bottle of Pinot Grigio, which she happened to have in the backseat of her car, would complement the "snack" nicely.

And so the Thursday-night knitting group was born.

"Who knows, Nell," Cass said, inching her way over to the food, "if it hadn't been for your clam sauce that night, the world would be short the thirty-seven scarves I've worked up in this cozy room—and just imagine all the fishermen with cold necks who'd be wandering around Sea Harbor." She lifted a plastic lid off one of the containers. The blended aroma of garlic, butter, and wine curled up into the room. "This is just what I needed tonight."

"Bad day, sweetie?" Nell asked.

Cass nodded, her thoughts on sneaking a taste of the sauce without Birdie seeing her. "Someone was in my traps again. The ones over by the breakwater."

"You need to get the police on this, Catherine," Birdie said. "They won't put up with poachers. They'll hang them up by their toes."

"I've talked to them, Birdie. But poachers are hard to catch. I swear, they're like snakes in those black wet suits, slipping into the water in the middle of the night or however they do it." Cass began pulling plates from a cabinet beneath the bookcases and set them, a little too loudly, on the table. "I swear I'll get them, one way or another."

Nell tugged open another sack. "If you need Ben's help with this, Cass, let him know. He'd love to play sleuth—and I don't want you putting yourself in danger."

"Now there's a thought. There's no one I'd rather sleuth with than Ben Endicott." Cass eyed the round of Brie that Nell placed on a wooden platter. "I think if I could find me a Ben, Nell, I might consider getting married someday."

Nell laughed. "Well, that would certainly make your mother happy."

"But think of the loss in revenue to the Church," Izzy said. "Mary Halloran keeps the priests in new albs with all the candles she lights during her 'Please, God, let Cass get married and have seven children' novenas."

Nell laughed and set a bowl of spinach on the counter, picked that day from the garden behind her house. She'd added sliced mango, a handful of sugared almonds, and sourdough croutons.

Another thud shook the room, this one sounding like a boot hitting a wall.

Birdie put her knitting down on the table and looked up. "Oh, lordy. I think Angelina has just nailed the lid in her coffin. I need to have a word with her."

"Oh, shush, Birdie," Nell said. She sprinkled a balsamic dressing on the salad and tossed it lightly. Birdie would fight dragons for her friends—and win. But Angie didn't quite fit into the dragon category—at least not yet.

"Any idea what she's doing up there?" Cass asked.

Izzy pushed a hank of flyaway hair behind her ear. "She's been preoccupied the past couple weeks—probably had a hard day. It happens to all of us. Now give it a rest—we're here to knit, right?"

Before anyone could agree or disagree, the upstairs door slammed shut, and footsteps clicked on the staircase along the outer wall of the shop.

A second later, Angie opened the side door and stepped inside.

"Hi," she said, her carefully made-up eyes looking around the room. She was on stage, dressed for an audience, and all four women were momentarily speechless.

Angie was nearly six feet tall, with thick red hair that framed her narrow face. Trim and fit, she was dressed tonight in a camisole, a gauzy see-through blouse, and a slim skirt that hugged her hips and stopped above her knees. An elegant cashmere sweater was tied around her shoulders, loose and lovely.

Nell looked at the sweater. "Angie, that sweater looks beautiful on you. I volunteered to wear it, but for some crazy reason, Izzy didn't think it'd get as much attention on me."

Angie touched the cashmere with her fingertips. "Not true, Nell, but while it's on my watch, I'll protect it with my life. I promise. And I'll give it back soon. I just wanted to wear it one more time. It's the most beautiful sweater I've ever seen."

"No rush, Ange," Izzy said. "It's a business deal—I get a real-live model for my sweater; you get some warmth."

Nell touched the edge of the kimono sweater. Izzy had worked it up in a saffron-colored cashmere yarn and knit cables along the front and back. It had a lacy, elegant touch, a unique one-of-a-kind sweater.

When Angie had seen the sweater in Izzy's shop, she'd fallen in love with it—and it took one effusive compliment for Izzy to loan it to her. "Just for a while," she'd said. "It's great advertising—people will ask where you got it, then come visit the Seaside Studio."

Angie dropped a set of keys down on the table. A knit square with a big A in the center—an old swatch from a wool sweater Izzy had knit for Nell—identified the apartment keys. "Here's that extra set of apartment keys, Iz. I don't need them."

"Thanks, Angie. I have a master key, too. But don't worry. I certainly won't go snooping around."

Angie's voice was husky, a smoker's voice, though she had assured Izzy that she'd quit. "Nothing to snoop for. My life's an open book, Iz."

Nell watched Angie's self-assured movements as she walked over to the sideboard and peeked beneath one of the lids. Then she turned on boot heels so skinny and tall that Nell wondered how she could possibly remain upright. One slight awkward movement, and she'd surely break a leg.

But Nell noticed something else about Angie tonight—a serious look beneath the mascara and eye shadow. And her smile wasn't right somehow. Angie's smile was just like her mother, Josie's. A full-lipped kind of smile that could turn heads if she chose to use it. It seemed forced tonight.

"I love what you've done to this shop, Izzy," Angie said. "It was a disaster before you bought it, a real pit."

"And you'll take care not to ravage it?" Birdie asked, speaking up from her post near the fireplace. Her brows arched over clear eyes.

Angie brushed off the comment with a wave of her hand. "Of course not, Birdie. I couldn't get these on, is all." She looked down at the tight leather boots hugging her legs. "It irritated me, and I guess I threw one. Frustrating," she said, her voice dropping and her eyes looking at her boots as if they might have the answer to something she was seeking. Her voice was barely a whisper. "Boots can be frustrating."

"Hot date, Angie?" Cass had been standing apart from the group, looking out the back windows at the ocean, one knee up on the window seat. She turned now and looked at Angie, her voice flat.

For a minute, Angie didn't answer. When she spoke, her words were measured and neutral. "Don't worry, Cass. I won't eat him. Pete's a good guy."

Before Cass could answer, the back door opened and Pete Halloran's tall, lanky body filled the doorway. He stepped inside and pushed the door closed against the force of the wind. "Hi, ladies," he said, looking around the room. "You, too, Cass."

Cass made a face at her younger brother.

"What are you doing here, Pete? Taking up knitting?" Izzy asked.

"I hear it has its rewards." Pete eyed the food on the sideboard.

"Not until you learn how to knit and purl, Peter." Birdie looked up from the delicate dewdrop stitch she was working into her scarf. "It's becoming quite popular with men, you know. They're finally catching on. They will never be as accomplished, but they can certainly try."

"It'd be damn near worth it," Pete said, still eyeing the fettuccine.

"Not tonight, sweet Pete." Angie came up behind him and looped one arm through his.

At Angie's touch, Pete's face turned the color of her hair. He turned toward her with a slow smile creasing his tan skin.

He's crazy about her, Nell thought. And they certainly made a striking couple. Pete so tall and sandy-haired, and Angie just a few inches shorter, her cascade of red waves brushing against his shoulder.

Nell had seen Pete outside the Sea Harbor Historical Museum a few days before. He was sitting on a bench in the square, just across the brick road from the library where Angie worked, tossing pieces of a sandwich to the gulls. But his mind was clearly not on birds, and Nell had wondered why he wasn't out checking lobster traps with Cass, helping her with the day's catch.

Pete hadn't noticed Nell, though she had waved as she walked past him on her way to a board meeting. Then Angie appeared, walking down the library steps in pencil-thin jeans and a bright green sweater, her hair flying in the breeze, her head held high. She still had on the earphones that she wore in the library sometimes— bright orange earphones that looked liked daisies and amused the older volunteers.

The look on Pete's face when he spotted Angie told Nell exactly why he was there.

Seeing Pete sitting on the bench, Angie had slipped the earphones down around her neck, then walked across the street, her eyes holding Pete's. She'd squeezed down beside him on the park bench, one hand reaching in his sack for a sandwich with a familiarity that spoke of more than a casual acquaintance.

"Opposites attract," Ben had said when she repeated the scene at supper that night. "Angie needs a nice guy like Pete in her life."

Nell had nodded, but she wondered if Angie could ever be in anyone's life in the way that nice guys needed.

Cass walked back to the sideboard, burying her nose in one of Nell's thick sacks. Cass didn't like conflict. And she didn't like Angie. But she loved Nell's cooking.

And she fiercely loved her brother, Pete.

Cass pulled the remaining Tupperware containers from the sack, lining them up on the countertop and immersing herself in the sensory experience of the food. Angie was instantly forgotten, replaced by spices and buttery hunks of lobster and scallops and big globs of sweet baked garlic.

"Sorry we can't stay," Pete said. He looked longingly at the food. But one squeeze to his arm from Angie, and the roomful of women sensed that even Nell's cooking could be upstaged if the hormones were lined up right.

"Watch out for the weather," Nell said. She bit back a warning to leave the cashmere sweater in Pete's car if even one drop threatened to fall from the sky.

Angie smiled at Nell, then glanced at Cass and hooked her arm through Pete's. "Pete will keep me warm."

Cass kept her back to the couple, blocking out Angie's words.

Nell watched the two young people walk through the door and into the night. The look on Angie's face earlier reminded Nell of a young Angie, upset with the world, determined to right its wrongs. Her shoulders held more than a skimpy blouse, a deep tan—a luxurious cashmere sweater.

Chapter 2

$\mathcal{T}$wo hours later, after Cass and Birdie had helped stash the leftovers in the refrigerator and gone on home, Nell and Izzy locked up the shop and walked out into the night.

"What would we do without these Thursday nights?" Izzy mused.

"Cass might starve to death," Nell said. "And Birdie's wine and wisdom would go to waste."

"And Ben would be huge if he were the only outlet for your cooking. And me? I'd be absolutely lost without you three."

"My sentiments exactly," Nell said, giving Izzy a quick hug.

The summer sky was dark, with only a star or two breaking the heavy black clouds, and a gusty wind tossed loose scraps of paper along the windy road and rumpled the awnings over shop windows.

Nell smoothed down her hair with the flat of her hand, pressing it against her head. At sixty-one, her dark hair was streaked with silver, but rather than clouding her hair, the wavy lines ran through it like carefully placed highlights.

"Wikkid tiger stripes," Ben called them, and he'd smooth them out with the blunt tip of his finger.

"Are you going home, Izzy?" Nell asked, looking up at the sky. "The rain will be here before too long."

Izzy looked up at the sky. "Good. Rain is good for business.

Perfect weather for sitting on the front porch with a ball of soft wool." Izzy hooked her arm through Nell's. "I'm meeting some friends over at the Ocean's Edge for a drink before I head home, but I'll walk you to your car first."

Harbor Road—called Seaside Village by the town brochures, and just plain "the village" by locals—was the hub of Sea Harbor. The narrow, curvy roads were lined with shops and small cafés, a couple of taverns, and a coffeehouse, all shoulder to shoulder and each unique as new generations of owners fixed up the buildings and made them new again. At midpoint, the shops gave way to an open area where Pelican Pier jutted out into the harbor. The long dock housed whale watching and pleasure boats and small commercial fishing vessels, all mixed together because a town the size of Sea Harbor was too small to segregate commercial from private vessels. On the shore, the Ocean's Edge Restaurant and Lounge, lit up like a carousel, offered music, drinks, and late-night meals.

"It looks like Archie still has customers," Nell said as they paused in front of the Harbor Road bookstore, admiring a new display of local-author books in the window. The door was still propped open, and a stiff breeze ruffled the blinds on the door.

Archie Brandley had store hours posted on the glass door of his bookstore just like the rest of the Sea Harbor merchants, but he never asked anyone to leave, no matter what the hour. Instead, Archie or his wife, Harriet, would balance the register receipts or shelve new books until the last guest, as Harriet called their customers, pried himself from a cracked leather chair and shuffled out the door. Sometimes the late-night guests didn't buy books, but it didn't bother Archie or Harriet. Reading was all that mattered, they'd say.

The blustery wind whipped Izzy's hair from the back of her neck. She made a face at her reflection in the bookstore window, the mass of thick wavy hair tangled and flying about her face. "The wicked witch of the north," she said. She grabbed a fistful of hair and slipped an elastic band from her wrist to the bunched hair, fastening it at the base of her neck.

Nell watched Izzy's face in the window and remembered the gangly, pigtailed child with the scattering of freckles across her nose and cheeks that had characterized a young Izzy Chambers. Izzy had thought more about horses on her family's Kansas ranch than how she looked back then. But she'd finally shed her pigtails, and she'd grown tall and graceful, heading back east to college, where people came to remember Isabel Chambers long after meeting her. They might not remember her name, but they remembered the enormous brown eyes that filled her face, the dimples that punctuated a wide smile in her fine-boned face, and the slender figure of a woman whose slightly irregular features fit together in an intriguing way.

"Look, Nell." Izzy pointed beyond her reflection to the small loft above the sales counter. Several chairs and crowded bookshelves filled the cozy space. "I'd know those boots anywhere."

Angie Archer sat on one of the chairs, her face partially hidden in shadow. The cashmere sweater was still around her neck, with one saffron edge draped over the arm of the chair.

Standing above her, his eyes focused intently on Angie's carefully made-up face, was a man. His stance was angry.

"Somehow I hadn't expected Angie and Pete to end up here," Nell said.

Izzy leaned closer to the window, shielding the glare of the lamplights behind her by cupping her hands to the glass and peering through them. "Cass said they were going to have a quick drink at the Gull, then head over to Passports in Gloucester." Her breath painted a circle on the window, and she backed away, turning to Nell. "I wonder what they're doing here, Nell? Pete was so happy earlier—he looked like he'd died and gone to heaven. That's not a happy stance."

Nell stepped closer to the window. Just then, the man turned and walked away from Angie, heading down the loft stairs. "And that's not Pete, Izzy. That's Tony Framingham."

A shadow appeared from the back of the store. Archie stopped at the foot of the stairs, his friendly smile gone and his expression stern. "What's going on up there, Tony?" His voice was low but traveled through the open door, out to the sidewalk.

Rather than walk past the open entryway, Nell and Izzy took a step back, their faces obscured by the display of books. Archie's voice grew louder.

"You're welcome in my store, Tony, just like anyone else. But you're an adult now, and you don't cause problems here like you did when you were a snot-nosed kid. You don't curse and threaten a lady in my bookstore, no matter who you are. You were brought up better than that."

"Lady?" Tony said, but Archie stopped him with the palm of his large hand held up between them.

Tony turned, lowered his head, and headed for the door.

Before Izzy and Nell could move away from the window, he walked out, his brows knit together and his hands shoved in the pockets of his jeans. A gust of wind pushed a patch of dark hair flat against his forehead, and he brushed it back with his hand. It wasn't until Tony pulled out his car keys from his pocket that he raised his head and spotted Nell and Izzy.

For a minute Tony looked startled—and then, with the ease of one used to difficult situations, he forced a half smile across his face. " 'Evening," he said, nodding his head slightly. He glanced over Nell's shoulder and through the store window, his eyes scanning the store as if to gauge what Nell and Izzy had seen, then focused back on the women standing in front of him.

"I haven't seen you much since I've been back in town, Nell," he said. "Are you and Ben doing all right?"

"We're fine, Tony," Nell said, trying to ease the awkward moment. "It's nice of you to ask."

Tony looked over at Izzy, and his preoccupied expression began to clear. "And Izzy Chambers. I hear nice things about your shop on Harbor Road. Kind of a surprise, I must say. But my mother thinks it's the best thing to hit Sea Harbor since the quarries closed."

Izzy laughed. "Your mom is my best customer, Tony. I think she has more yarn in her house than I have on my shelves."

Tony Framingham had been Izzy's first summer love. They'd spent long evenings walking hand in hand along Pelican Pier or over at the yacht club beach, spinning dreams of where they'd be in ten or fifteen years. Izzy was going to live in Italy and paint, though even back then Tony Framingham didn't buy it. A lawyer, he had predicted. "A female Atticus Finch—you can argue with the best of them, Iz, and you'll make the world a better place."

Tony, they'd both agreed, would have a house on the Riviera and travel the world, managing stocks and bonds, buying and selling businesses. And they'd meet each other now and then in magical places, the world at their beck and call.

"We had some dreams back then, didn't we, Tony?" Izzy said.

"And from what I hear, I was right about the lawyer bit. Boston's Elliot & Pagett, no less."

"For a while," Izzy said. "I didn't fit too well, Tony."

Tony nodded. Like everyone else in Sea Harbor, he had heard about Izzy's short-lived law career. "And here we both are, Izzy, back in Sea Harbor. Who would have thunk it?" His laugh was deep and traveled on the night air.

"So you've moved back, Tony?" Nell asked.

"I don't know, Nell. I have things going on in New York and Boston. But I came up to help my mother. Since Dad died, she's tried to handle everything by herself—that house, and my dad's business, too. It's too much for her—she thinks she's still forty."

"Tony, don't ever underestimate your mother. There isn't

much Margarethe Framingham can't handle. She's been an amazing force in this town." And Margarethe had always handled her husband's business dealings, Nell knew, long before Sylvester Framingham Jr. died. She did it as easily as she knit up sweaters and jackets. And she'd probably saved the family fortune once or twice.

"Well, she needs to slow down, sell that damn mansion. Not worry so much about things."

"I don't think she thinks of it that way." Nell held back from telling Tony it might not be his decision to determine what his mother did or didn't do. The Framingham house was certainly huge—and a little ostentatious, in Nell's opinion. Parisian curtains and marble hallways seemed a little out of place in Sea Harbor. But Margarethe loved her home, and she was exceedingly generous in sharing it. It had been in the Framingham family since they began mining the stone quarries on outcroppings of their land. And if that was how she chose to live—and decorate—that might not be anyone's decision but her own.

"You're right, Nell," Tony said. "It's her house." But his face tightened as he spoke.

Just then the light in the front of the store went off, and Archie knocked on the window. He waved, mouthing a good night, then pulled down the blinds on the front door and slid the dead bolt in place.

Nell looked through the window into the darkened shop, half expecting Angie to appear, but the store was dark and silent.

Before she could ask Tony what had happened to her, he mumbled a hasty good-bye and was off across the street, headed toward his bright orange Hummer.

"Where's Angie?" Izzy asked Nell. She looked back through the window into the dark, quiet store.

"She probably went out the back door, like Archie does, instead of walking past Tony." Nell looked back at the Seaside

Studio next door. The upstairs apartment was dark. Angie hadn't headed home. Nell hoped that for Pete's sake, Angie was back at his side.

"I remember Tony's argumentativeness," Izzy said. "There's a temper beneath all that charm." She tucked her arm back through Nell's, and they crossed the road, dodging a group of boys who breezed by on shiny bikes.

"He was cocky in his teenage years," Nell said. "But that's part of growing up." Tall, good-looking, and smart, Tony was sometimes involved in minor scuffles back then, but Nell never thought him a bad boy. He was always gracious when he came to the house, and Ben liked him. He was simply a product of too much indulgence, Nell had always thought.

Once Tony had to face real life, Ben always said, he'd shape up.

And taking care of his mother certainly fit in that category, even though Nell found it hard to imagine that anyone would presume to take care of Margarethe Framingham.

"I never thought Tony would come back here," Izzy said. "He seemed destined for a bigger world than Sea Harbor."

"Maybe he succumbed to its magic, like you did." Nell stopped at the door of her car and pulled out her keys. She was parked in front of the Gull, a local hangout. Yellow light from the bar spilled through the windows, lighting up the brick sidewalk.

Nell opened the door and put her knitting bag on the backseat, then turned toward Izzy and looked at her closely. She felt a familiar tightness in her chest. The feeling she had had off and on since Izzy moved to Sea Harbor.

Izzy searched her aunt's face. Then she wrapped Nell in a tight hug, breathing in her familiar soapy smell. "I love you, too, Auntie Nell," she whispered.

When Izzy pulled away, Nell collected herself. Why was she feeling so emotional tonight? She kissed Izzy on the cheek and slipped into her car. When she looked back to wave, her niece was already walking away, her arms swinging and her hair flying on the wind, headed toward the Ocean's Edge.

Nell slipped the key into the ignition and looked up to see a lumbering, slightly hunched figure crossing the street in front of her. It was Angus McPherron, a long-retired stonecutter who spent his days wandering the harbor and spinning tales for anyone who crossed his path. "The old man of the sea," the kids called him.

Nell wondered for a minute if she should drive him home. Sometimes Angus wasn't quite in touch with his surroundings, and he might not notice the impending storm. But the old man looked up then and gave a small wave. His small beady eyes were clear and bright with recognition. In the next instant, Angus slipped inside the Gull, swallowed up by music and bodies, and disappeared from her sight.

Nell looked after him. He was a kind man, but a bit unfocused sometimes. She looked through the tavern windows, trying to see his rounded shoulders, his lumbering gait. A mahogany counter, running along the width of the windows, was packed tonight with the usual Thursday-night crowd, anxious to get an early start on the weekend. Angus would have his pick of listeners. A good night for him.

Nell squinted, pulling the scene inside the bar into focus.

"Oh my," she said aloud.

Seated on a high stool, his eyes staring off into space, was Pete Halloran. He sat alone, unaware of the jostling activity on either side of him, his elbows planted on the counter. A half-dozen empty beer bottles littered the narrow space in front of him.

Nell slipped out of her car and walked toward the Gull's windows, her intentions unclear, but her body propelled forward.

As she neared the window, Pete's hand lifted into the air and curled into a tight fist.

On either side of him, men and women laughed and drank

beer and picked fried clams from wicker baskets, oblivious of the troubled young man in their midst.

The veins in Pete's forehead pulsed and his jaw clamped shut. He stared through the window, but Nell knew he didn't see her. In the next second, Pete's raised fist swept through the air and slammed down on the pocked wooden counter, sending discarded beer bottles, paper-lined baskets, and bits of clam and French fries crashing to the hardwood floor.

And the next minute, Pete was gone, swallowed up by the crowd of people on either side like a hole in the sand, filled in by a rushing tide.

Chapter 3

Friday was a perfect Sea Harbor day. The night rain had washed the village clean, and a white sun hung over the water, warming bare shoulders and cheeks. A perfect day for fishermen heading out in small boats to check traps. A perfect day for friends to gather on the Endicotts' deck to talk about the weekend regatta or share news from Boston or gush over the shipment of new alpaca yarn that Izzy had unpacked that day. A perfect day for grilled tuna with Nell's spicy herb sauce and Ben's magnificent martinis.

Too perfect, Nell would think later. Beneath the glossy sheen of perfection, tiny cracks could widen in the blink of an eye, taking one by total surprise.

"I'm ready, how about you?" Nell called from her post at the kitchen sink. The open windows carried her voice out to the wide deck, where Ben poked and prodded a pile of coals in the stone grill.

Ben looked up, his thick gray brows lifting suggestively over sparkling eyes. "Ready, you say?"

Nell brushed her hair back behind one ear and smiled. What a comfort this big bear of a man was. Ben knew her so well. And he could still punch the buttons that made her remember what it felt like when they roamed Harvard Square, arms wrapped around each other, totally unaware that there were other people in the world. The desire was mellow now, not that crazy, exhilarating rush of youth. But rich and full, just the same. Ben Endicott still lit fires in Nell—and the fires warmed her to the bone.

Ben was at the door now, wiping his hands on an old towel. "I need to get some ice from the garage for the cooler. But otherwise, my darlin', the bar's ready and the grill will be soon. Some soft jazz and we'll be set."

Friday-night gatherings at the Endicotts were all about relaxing, putting the week to rest and being with friends. Ben and Nell were never sure who would show up, but it didn't matter—there was always enough food and friendship to go around. And if it was just the two of them—though that happened rarely—that was just fine, too.

Nell stood in the doorway and looked out over the backyard. Later in the evening, tiny gaslights would blink on, but now the large yard was bathed in the soft light of day's end. When she and Ben had decided to move to Sea Harbor permanently, they had added a guesthouse behind the garage, tucked cozily into a grove of pine trees. Beyond it was a narrow pathway, flattened into the earth by generations of Endicotts making their way through the pines to the beach beyond. The first time Nell had visited Ben's family vacation home, years ago when his parents were still alive, she thought she would never in her life find a place quite as perfect as 22 Sandswept Lane. And she'd been right.

Ben looped one arm around her shoulders. "You didn't sleep much last night."

"The rain, maybe." Nell leaned into his body, her head just touching his shoulder.

Ben touched her hair, then traced her high, prominent cheekbone with the tip of his finger. "I'll make sure you sleep tonight."

Nell smiled and nodded into his shoulder.

"Anyone home?" The front screen door banged open and shut, followed by sandals flip-flopping on the hardwood floor.

Izzy breezed into the family room, a large wicker basket hanging over one arm.

"You look like Little Red Riding Hood." Ben walked across the room and wrapped Izzy in a warm hug. He took the basket from her arm and carried it over to the kitchen counter.

"Ha," Izzy said, following Ben into the kitchen. "And the wolf's name is Gideon, our new security guard—the guy the shop owners hired to patrol at night. He's kind of creepy, Nell. He was sitting on Angie's apartment steps tonight when I left. Acted like he had a perfect right to be there and gave me the oddest smile."

"Was Angie home?"

Izzy shook her head. "At least I don't think so. I haven't seen her all day, in fact."

"That's odd." Nell unwrapped a hunk of Vermont cheddar and placed it on a wooden platter, then spread crackers at either end. "I poked my head into the research library to say hi when I was over there today for a meeting, but she wasn't at her desk. I wonder if she's sick."

"Maybe she was out late last night and slept the day away. Or stayed at her mom's. I remember a time or two when I crashed at your home in Boston after a night of too much fun." Izzy pulled some aluminum foil from a drawer and began to wrap the bread for the oven. "Pete Halloran is the one I'd worry about, not Angie. Cass said he stayed at her place last night. He came in late and not in great shape. Cass is ready to strangle Angie for ditching him the way she did."

"At least he had the sense not to drive back to his own place. He wasn't in any condition to be on the road."

"I saw him at McClucken's this afternoon buying rope for the boat," Ben said. "He looked a little down in the dumps, so I told him to be sure to come tonight. A chilled pint, good friends, Nell's cooking—that's what Pete needs."

Izzy looked up at Ben and brushed his cheek with the back of her fingers. "You are such a sweet softie, my uncle Ben."

"Soft?" Ben frowned and pretended to flex a muscle. "Not a good thing at my age, Izzy girl."

Izzy squeezed his bicep.

"He's strong as nails," Nell said. And Nell made sure he stayed that way. A mild heart attack a few years back had frightened Nell—and Izzy, too—in an icy, paralyzing way. But the outcome, Nell often said, was a good thing—a reminder of their mortality. And together they decided to work less and enjoy life more. A few months later, to the surprise of the foundation Nell directed and Ben's business associates, they'd sold their Beacon Hill town home and moved permanently to Sea Harbor.

"What time is Cass bringing the tuna by?" Ben asked, deftly shifting the attention away from his sixty-five-year-old physique.

"She should be here by now," Izzy said. "She was baiting traps over at the cove, but planned to drop the fish off before going home to shower."

Nell looked at her watch. "Maybe I'll give her a call. Ben could pick it up and save her the trip."

But before she reached the phone, a rattling and screech of brakes in the driveway announced the arrival of Cass's ancient Chevy truck. Nell headed for the door to help her with the ice chest of fish, but before she reached the front of the house, the screen door banged open.

Cass was dressed for the sea, her muddy yellow waders and baggy bib overalls hiding her shape. The familiar Sox cap was missing, and masses of thick tangled curls were plastered against her wet, red cheeks. But it was the enormous tears streaming down Cass's face that stopped Nell in her tracks.

Nell reached out instinctively for the young woman. "Cass—what is it?"

In a heartbeat, Cass was in Nell's arms, her head burrowing into Nell's shoulder. Her body shook, and Nell pulled her close.

"It will be all right, Cass," Nell whispered. "Whatever it is, we'll make it right."

Cass's head moved from side to side. "No, it won't be all right, Nell." Cass pushed away from Nell and wiped her cheeks with the back of her hand. She took a deep, steadying breath, pulling herself together.

"It's Angie," she said. Her husky voice was reduced to threads.

"Angie Archer?" Nell asked, not wanting Cass to answer.

"She's dead," Cass said, her voice as heavy as the anchor on her lobster boat.

Izzy and Ben came into the hallway just as Cass's words thudded onto the hardwood floor.

"No, Cass," Izzy said, her voice catching in her throat. "Angie's not dead. She's at the apartment, or out somewhere, you know how she does, or—"

Cass lifted her hand to stop her friend's words. She took a deep breath, sucking in the air as if it were her last breath. She let it out slowly. When she spoke again, her voice was unusually loud, the words pushed out with force.

"She's dead, Izzy," Cass said. "I *saw* her. Her hair was tangled up in the warp from one of my traps, pinning her down to the bottom of the sea as surely and completely as a trapped lobster."

Chapter 4

$\mathcal{T}$he story came out in starts and stops, with Ben, Nell, and Izzy sitting quietly on the couch, letting Cass take her time as she took them through the terrible afternoon.

A couple of policemen were on the breakwater—"finally checking out the poachers' turf," Cass said. Since she was in her boat, they climbed in and circled around the shallow cove with her, and she pointed out her lobster buoys to them.

"Since we were out there, they helped me pull up a trap so I could show them what I was finding every day—the bait gone, and the lobsters gone, too."

She paused and sipped the tea that Nell had given her. Her fingers gripped it as tightly as a warp on her traps. "It was the second set of traps we pulled up, the ones closest to the breakwater—" Cass's voice broke, but she went on.

"It wouldn't budge. Sometimes they get mired in the muddy bottom, so the guys tugged at the line until I thought I'd have to pull them out of the water, too. Finally, the trap moved and they heaved it up, just enough for us to see . . ."

Bound into the wire mesh of the trap were the thick red locks of Angie Archer's hair, Cass said, with her lifeless body tangled in the warp.

In a short time, more police arrived, an ambulance, and Angie's body was pulled out and taken away.

"It seemed to take hours," Cass said.

"How horrible for you, Cass," Ben said.

"I felt connected to it," Cass said.

"Because you knew her?" Nell asked.

"No, not that. Not because it was Angie. But it was my trap. My warp. That's what was holding her down beneath the water."

Izzy touched her arm, and Nell nodded, but there wasn't anything anyone could say.

"I feel responsible, you know?" Cass said sadly. "Like somehow I killed her."

After a hot shower in Nell and Ben's guest bath, Cass curled up beneath a soft comforter in the wide guest bed and fell asleep.

Pete never arrived at 22 Sandswept Lane that night, but Birdie, the Brandleys, and a few friends who had heard the news gathered on the deck beneath the full moon while Cass slept soundly upstairs. Nell tossed grilled vegetables into linguini, put out warm chunks of sourdough bread and a spinach salad, and they sat late into the evening, trying to make sense out of the day's tragic happenings.

The *Sea Harbor Gazette* reported little else in the weekend edition. The story of the beautiful redhead carelessly walking out on the breakwater with a storm approaching was spread all over town. A rogue wave was the culprit, most believed, something every Sea Harbor child was taught to respect and fear.

Chapter 5

 $\mathcal{T}$ he bells in the stone tower of Our Lady of the Seas church tolled long and mournfully on Monday morning, rolling down the hill like flood waters, filling homes and businesses and hurrying those walking along the winding side streets or driving through the town on their way to the church.

Josie Archer had told Father Northcutt that she wanted her daughter's funeral held as soon as possible. And though the autopsy would take a few days, the old priest accommodated Josie's wishes, with plans for a private burial later. He cancelled the regular eight o'clock Monday service and scheduled Angelina Mary Elizabeth Archer's Requiem Mass for that time.

Neighbors, friends, and parishioners came, some carrying sweet breads, casseroles, or homemade *malasadas* for the gathering in the church basement afterward. If they didn't know Angie, they knew her mother or her late father. Or some simply needed to attend the Mass to mourn a young life so carelessly ended and to pray that it wouldn't happen to them or those they loved. And a handful, as always, were simply curious.

Nell, Ben, and Izzy walked down the steps to the church basement after the service, talking quietly about Father Northcutt's simple homily. He had known Angie since birth, and he was able to offer her family and friends sweet memories of Angie, avoiding the more colorful aspects of her life.

"I can't begin to imagine the depth of Josie's emotion," Nell said. "Burying a child—it's unthinkable."

Ben slipped an arm around Nell's shoulder in silent agreement.

"And I can't imagine Angie falling off the breakwater," Izzy said.

Nell nodded. She knew that Izzy found it easier to put emotion at bay and address the logic of the incident.

"It doesn't make sense," Nell said. "I agree with you completely, Izzy, but we'll have to deal with that later."

A broad woman in a flowered sundress elbowed her way in front of Nell and Izzy. "What was that crazy girl thinking?" she said, speaking loudly to the owner of the Main Street stationery shop. Her strident voice cut through the muted conversations around her.

Nell frowned at the woman. But it was Izzy who glared the woman into silence before following Nell and Ben into the church hall, where the altar guild had set up long tables for food with stacked plates and plastic forks at either end.

A crowd had already gathered and formed a line.

Ben and Izzy headed for the coffee urns perking on the side table. "Don't let gossip bother you, Izzy. Everyone will have an opinion," Ben said. "But it is what it is—a terrible accident." He filled two paper cups and handed one to Izzy.

"But it wasn't an Angie-like thing to do, Ben," Izzy said. "You know that. For one thing, she was a terrific swimmer—she always beat the bejesus out of me when we competed on those summer swim teams. And Angie was smart. Why would she wander out on the breakwater on such a nasty night? And we had seen her just hours before."

And perhaps could have stopped her?

The thought had plagued both Izzy and Nell all weekend as they replayed the tragedy. But stopped her from what? All they knew was that the evening had apparently soured for Pete and Angie. And Angie and Tony seemed to have fared no better. So why had she gone to the breakwater, a couple miles away? Pete refused to talk to anyone, Cass said, and they all agreed that this wasn't the time to ply him with questions. But their questions hung in the air like gulls waiting to swoop down for an answer.

"There was no way on earth you could have done anything to change what happened, Izzy," Ben said, reading her thoughts. His voice was stern, but not convincing enough to stop the tears that gathered in Izzy's eyes. He put his arm around her and led her back to where Nell was talking with Ham and Jane Brewster, old friends—and founders of the artists' colony on Seaside Harbor's Canary Cove.

"Ham and Jane said Angie had been spending a lot of time recently on Canary Cove," Nell said to Ben as they approached. She saw the tears in Izzy's eyes and tried to channel the conversation to pleasant memories.

"I couldn't figure out why she wanted to hang out with us old geezers," Ham said, scratching his beard. "But we enjoyed having her around. She was interested in the early days of the colony— how we bought the land and the old fishing shacks and turned them into galleries. She wasn't the same bratty kid I remembered years ago, who used to hang around the colony and mess up my watercolors. She was interesting, and knew some things about land acquisitions around here that I didn't even know."

Jane nodded. "She was ambitious, too. Had plans for her life."

"What kind of plans?" Nell asked.

"Oh, what she'd do when she left here. I got the impression it'd be soon. She thought she might travel some, then go back to school and get a doctorate."

"That's odd," Nell said.

"Which part, Nell, more school?"

"The planning-to-leave-soon part. Her job at the Historical Society was a full-time job, not temporary. Why would she talk about when it ended?"

"From the way she talked, she was working on a special project and would leave when it was over," Ham said. "She told me outright she wouldn't be here long."

"Well, we all know that Angie wasn't the most predictable person around," Ben said. He set his coffee cup down on a table and looked around the room. "This is just damn sad." He focused on a small group sitting on folding chairs off to the side. Josie Archer sat still, leaning slightly forward, her face pale and eyes glazed. At her side was Margarethe Framingham.

"It looks like Margarethe is taking care of Josie," Ben said, nodding toward the group.

Nell looked over at Margarethe sitting on the metal chair, her hands covering Josie's, which lay limp in her lap. Margarethe was a handsome, large-shouldered woman, stately, and almost Zen-like in her posture, Nell thought. She looked elegant today in a black designer suit and her hair carefully coiffed in a bun. Her demeanor was one of compassion as she leaned in to comfort the devastated mother.

"She's been a big support to Josie," Ham said. "She offered to have the reception at her own home, but Josie said no. She wanted it in the church."

"Margarethe has been a leader in this town for so long, I think she feels the loss of one of us almost as if it were her own," Jane said. "Is there any part of this town she hasn't helped?"

"That's true. She's very generous," Nell said. Ben's family had always helped Sea Harbor causes, but in a behind-the-scenes way. Margarethe's efforts were large and sweeping. She stepped in to influence zoning laws that helped the thriving arts community that Jane and Ham had founded, and she organized a drive to help build a new park to honor the fishermen. Nell had served on committees with Margarethe and had experienced firsthand her ability to get things done.

"And look who else is here," Izzy said. They all followed the tilt of her head and looked to the wall just inside the door. Angus McPherron, dressed in a white, thrift-shop shirt and dark wrinkled pants, stood awkwardly and alone, his large face washed in sadness.

"I've never seen Angus in a dress shirt before," Nell said.

"Or in church," Ben added. "Poor guy. He looks like he lost his best friend."

"He and Angie were friends," Nell said. "I often saw her sitting with old Angus down at Pelican Pier. She listened to his stories with true interest. Sometimes she had her computer on her knees and typed in things that he said. It gave him great pleasure."

At that moment Birdie Favazza slipped in the back door, her white hair mussed by the breeze. Birdie missed the funeral part in the church, Nell noted, but that was probably intentional. She didn't spend much time in Father Northcutt's church, but her concern for Angie's family wouldn't allow her to miss the gathering after.

Nell started to walk toward her, but just then Birdie spotted Angus standing alone and walked over to his side.

Birdie touched Angus lightly on the arm.

They all watched as Angus looked down at Birdie, whose head barely reached his shoulder, acknowledging her presence with a slow nod. Then he wiped his eyes with the back of his sleeve, and his face grew hard. With one hand grasping the back of an empty folding chair, he leaned over until his eyes were nearly even with Birdie's, his voice thick with emotion.

"She didn't drown, Miss Birdie," he said, the words loud enough to interrupt the hushed conversations nearby.

Josie Archer and Margarethe looked up, startled.

Nell tensed.

"Angus, hush," Birdie said in a loud whisper. "Not now, dear." She pulled gently on the old man's sleeve, trying to move him toward the door.

Angus shook off her hand and stood as tall as his humped body allowed, no longer looking at Birdie. His eyes focused over the tops of people's heads, off into space, and he spoke as if to an invisible being. "Angelina was a good girl trying to help," he said in a husky, determined voice. "That's all. Just trying to make things right. She didn't deserve this. Who did this?"

Birdie reached again for Angus's arm, and, seeing the horrified stares of Margarethe and Josie, she pulled with all her strength until he followed her out of the church hall.

Nell released her breath. "Good grief. Josie doesn't need that."

"Angus is usually such a sweet man," Jane said, "but sometimes he simply isn't all there."

"Sometimes." Izzy nodded, her eyes still on the doorway. "But other times he clearly knows exactly what he's saying."

And Nell knew exactly what Izzy was thinking. But neither of them would say it out loud. Suppose Angie hadn't been alone? Suppose she had argued with someone and been pushed off the breakwater? What solace could that possibly bring to Josie Archer? A part of Nell said to let it go, let Angie rest in peace. Let her mother grieve and begin to put their lives back into place.

But another part of her couldn't block out the feeling that parts of Angie Archer's life—and death—might not have been what they seemed.

Nell looked over at Josie and saw that Margarethe had gestured for Father Northcutt to join their group, and Josie was once again calmly receiving condolences from neighbors and friends.

Josie was a strong woman herself, and Nell knew she would survive this.

Tony Framingham, who had been standing at a distance, approached his mother and leaned over, whispering into her ear. Nell wondered if he had seen the disturbance Angus had caused.

Margarethe listened to her son, then shifted on the metal chair, turning away from Tony without responding. She focused all her attention back on Josie Archer and the next group of people who were waiting to speak to Josie in hushed, sad voices.

Nell caught the look of frustration on Tony's face. He looked as if he were going to interrupt again, but instead, he walked briskly away. As generous a woman as Margarethe was, Nell imagined she might be difficult to have as a mother, even when that child was a grown adult, successful in his own way.

Tony walked over to a metal coat rack near the back of the hall and stood quietly against the wall.

Nell considered going over to speak to him. He had been with Angie so close to her death, a memory Nell was sure haunted him now, just as it did her and Izzy. Nell replayed Archie's harsh scolding of the young man. He accused Tony of threatening Angie. The thought caused tiny goose bumps up and down Nell's arms.

"Tony is all alone," Izzy said, following Nell's gaze. "He seems so much more serious than the Tony I knew."

Nell nodded. "Life does that to you sometimes. But it's nice of him to come to the funeral. Like so many others here, he's known Angie all his life."

"And like Angie," Jane said, "he's come back. They had that in common, too."

"And they are certainly two that no one—their parents included—would ever have expected to settle back here," Ben added.

Nell wondered briefly if Tony's plans were not as straightforward as they seemed, either. He didn't seem comfortable here at the funeral. And when she saw him around town, he was polite, pleasant, but made no efforts to renew old acquaintances. At least not that she could see. He was handsome and wealthy, and caused a stir among the unattached women in town. But as far as Nell could see, he wasn't interested.

"Cass and Pete are over there," Izzy said, tapping on Nell's arm and pulling her attention away from Tony.

Nell followed the nod of Izzy's head and saw Pete standing next to Cass a short distance away. His handsome face was drawn, and Nell suspected he hadn't been sleeping. His blank gaze moved over the crowd, from one small clump of people to the next, as if he'd find what he was searching for somewhere in the closed, warm room. Cass had one hand on Pete's arm and looked, Nell thought, as if she'd rather be anywhere in the whole world than here in this crowded church basement. It had been a rough few days for her, but Cass was a survivor, and Nell knew she'd be fine. Pete, she wasn't so sure of.

Izzy caught Cass's eye and waved her over. Cass waved back, then tugged on Pete's arm and started to walk their way.

Pete glanced over at the group, shrugged off Cass's hand, and stepped back against a wall.

"He'll be okay," Cass said when she reached the group. "He just wants to be alone."

"That's understandable, Cass," Nell said.

"He's eyeing Jake Risso as if he'd like to kill him," Izzy said. "Are you sure he's okay, Cass?"

Cass looked back at her brother.

Pete's body had stiffened, the limp, hunched figure straightening, as if ready to strike.

A few yards away, the owner of the Gull Tavern was talking to a group of neighbors and shopkeepers. Accustomed to speaking over the din of tavern noise, Jake Risso spoke in a big gravelly voice that carried above the clatter of beer bottles and merrymakers in his bar. In a room filled with mourners, it was a foghorn on a still, soupy night.

"She could drink with the best of us, that one could," Jake bellowed to the group.

Archie Brandley and his wife, Harriet, were standing nearby, holding plates of egg casserole and chunks of melon and talking to Salvatore and Beatrice Scaglia. Archie and Sal both looked over at Jake and gestured for him to quiet down.

But subtle gestures went unnoticed by Jake, and he continued. "I liked Angie, make no bones about it. Who could not like her spunk? But she nevah shoulda drank and then gone out like that on a bad night. And to jump off the breakwater, fah chrysakes?"

Nell put one hand over her mouth, her eyes on Pete. His face was beet red, and even from a distance, she could see the throbbing in his temples. He lifted a tight fist and his eyes, unblinking, fastened on Jake Risso's bald head.

In the next instant, Pete was beside Jake, his fist raised and an angry torrent of syllables pouring from his mouth.

Ben thrust his paper cup into Nell's hand and headed toward Pete.

Archie and Sal approached from the other side.

But it was Tony Framingham who saved the day.

Flying from his post against the wall, Tony wedged himself between Jake and Pete. In one swift movement he wrapped Pete Halloran in a grip so tight it would have knocked the air out of a slighter man.

And in the next instant, Tony had pulled Pete across the room and out the side door of Our Lady of the Seas basement.

Cass heaved an audible sigh of relief.

Nell released the air trapped in her lungs.

And before anyone could react, the crowd filled into the space left in the two men's wake, like water spilling into a sand hole, and the gentle Father Northcutt stepped up onto the small platform at one end of the room and announced to everyone that there were more desserts up on the front table. Plenty more.

And Josie Archer, God bless her, wanted everyone to eat up.

Chapter 6

Funerals have a way of sobering towns, especially when the service is for someone beautiful, feisty, and far too young to die. But summer in Sea Harbor wasn't a season; it was a happening, and the sun-drenched streets of Sea Harbor, the small restaurants and shops and smooth sandy beaches, refused to give in to the dourness of death.

Life goes on, Ben had said at lunch that Wednesday. *No matter if we'd like to stop it for a while. Make sense of the senseless. It goes on.*

So it did, Nell thought, as she walked down the winding streets of her neighborhood toward the village shops. And as if to prove it, a gaggle of preteens, towels wrapped around their necks, bicycled by on their way to the beach for a late-afternoon swim.

Nell had taken a pot of chowder over to Josie Archer the night before, and knew that her life, too, would somehow move on, though it would never be the same.

The unanswered questions that plagued Izzy and Nell didn't seem to touch Josie. The whys and hows and incongruities of a strong young woman drowning in familiar water were of no consequence to her mother.

"Angie is with her father in heaven," Josie told Nell. "She never stopped missing Ted. Not for a single minute, not for all these years. And now they're together."

Nell walked past the road where Izzy lived, automatically looking up the hill toward the green-shuttered house that Izzy had turned into a cozy home. The polished hardwood floors, bright rugs, and comfortable furniture suited Izzy far more than the decorator-styled Beacon Hill town home her law firm had helped her find. The town home was status; the Seaside Harbor cottage was Izzy. And it was close enough to the knitting studio for Izzy to walk or ride her bike to work if she wanted to, though she often drove her small car to carry things back and forth to the shop—paperwork and supplies, CDs and fresh flowers for her sales manager, Mae's, desk.

As Nell crossed over Harbor Road, she spotted Cass coming from the other direction. "Are you through for the day, Cass?" she asked as they met up in front of Izzy's store window.

Cass's nose and cheeks were flushed—clear signs of a day on the water. Her jeans were clean, but the bottom edges were dark with permanent saltwater stains. Her sea-blue eyes were tired today and lacked the laughter that Nell was used to seeing there.

"Maybe *through* as in forever, Nell." Cass held the door for Nell and followed her into the shop.

Mae Anderson, Izzy's shop manager, was standing behind the checkout counter with a bundle of receipts in her hand and a pencil held between her teeth.

She smiled a greeting and nodded toward the next room. "Izzy's thataway," she mumbled without dropping the pencil.

Izzy looked up from her spot on the floor as they rounded the corner. A half-empty shipping box of new yarn sat in front of her. "Hi, you two. What's up?"

"I'm here for needles." Nell leaned over and gave Izzy a peck on the cheek.

"And I'm here because I need my friends," Cass said.

Nell looked at the tired lines around Cass's eyes. It seemed way too soon for Cass to have to face a reminder of finding

Angie's body tangled in her lobster warp. "The *Lady Lobster* is back in business?" she asked.

Cass nodded. "I have to, Nell. Lobstering is what I do. I need to be back on my boat. But my stomach lurches with every trap we pull. I keep seeing her—you know? But I have dozens of traps out there—and they need to be checked." She pushed her hands into the pockets of her jeans. "Life moves on, you know?"

Nell nodded. Cass and Ben. Two peas in a pod. But they were right. You had to get back on the horse that bucked you.

Cass leaned against the wall. "It's as if my traps are jinxed, Nell. Someone got into them again last night. I thought maybe, with all that's happened out there, the poachers would move on to another spot—"

Nell slipped her glasses up into her thick hair. "I'm so sorry, Cass."

"It's hard not to take it personally, you know?" Cass ran her fingers through her hair, and black strands fell loose from the elastic band. "I'm sure the poachers don't have a clue whose traps they're pillaging. They don't know me from Adam. But I can't help but feel they've violated me somehow."

"Could it just be a lean season, Cass?" Izzy gathered skeins of periwinkle, celery, and sky-blue cashmere from a shipping box. She slipped them into small cubicles.

"No. Folks farther north have been hauling in plenty of keepers, and my bait bags are empty, so someone's been visiting the traps. But it's not just that. I know when my traps have been fiddled with, even if lobsters haven't been in them. Just like you'd know, Izzy, if someone came in here during the night and messed with your yarn. Someone is definitely doing bad things out at the breakwater. And I swear I'm going to make them wish they hadn't."

Nell's fingers played with the smooth finish of the needles. "Cass—this is a hard time. Finding Angie the way you did was awful. And the loss of lobsters—of income—on top of it. But the police will figure it out soon."

Cass managed a smile. "Maybe. But it's not a pleasant place to be right now."

Nell could only imagine. The image of Angie had stayed with her all week, and she hadn't seen it directly, only through Cass's words and the endless replays in the news.

"Maybe it's selfish to be worrying about my own problems," Cass went on, "but if I don't start selling lobsters soon, I'll have to throw in the towel. But what else would I do?" Her voice cracked with uncharacteristic emotion. "This is what I love. You two know that. This is what I do."

Nell slipped an arm around the younger woman's shoulders and felt the worry in Cass's frame. Being out on the water, driving the boat she had spent her life savings on, was truly Cass's life. She had allowed Birdie, Nell, and Ben to invest a little in the *Lady Lobster,* but she was already well on the way to paying it back with fresh fish and lobster—and cash when the haulings were good. They'd get back every penny, whether they wanted it or not. Nell knew that.

"If there's any crime around here that people won't tolerate, it's poaching, Cass," Izzy said. "The thing is, I think Angie's death has put other things on the back burner, but now that the funeral is over—"

"Is Angie Archer going to dominate our whole summer?" Cass blurted out.

Her abrupt tone jarred Nell and Izzy.

"Sorry," Cass said just as quickly. "That was awful of me. But you can't walk into Coffee's or get a bagel at Harry's Deli without being served up the latest gossip about Angie's life. And people look at me as if I'm somehow connected to it. Let the dead rest in peace. Isn't that what the good padre says?"

"Her funeral was just two days ago," Izzy said. "Angie grew

up here—people are bound to talk about it, Cass. This isn't like you. What's wrong?"

Cass seemed to give the question serious thought. Finally, she said, "I think I resent her. I didn't trust Angie Archer in life, and I don't trust her much in death."

"Because of Pete," Nell said.

"Sure, because of Pete. He's a mess—I don't think he said three words to me on the boat today. A week ago he was bothered to the core about the poachers, but he doesn't seem to care anymore. And who knows, maybe he was just a plaything for Angie. But it's more than that. I may be silly, but Angie had a bad aura about her. She was kind of secretive."

Izzy uncurled herself from the floor. "She didn't talk about herself much, is all."

"Some people are like that," Nell said. "I suppose we all have secrets of one sort or another. But I've known Angie nearly her whole life, Cass. And I don't think she would have intentionally hurt Pete."

Cass shrugged. "Maybe you're right, Nell. Maybe I'm blaming Angie for the black cloud over my lobster traps. I just wish she'd picked somewhere else to go swimming that night."

Izzy brushed sand off her jeans and bent over to pick up the empty shipping box. She straightened up. "Let's face it. Angie wasn't swimming. Not in those fancy boots she spent two months' salary on. We know that."

And not in the exquisite, one-of-a-kind cashmere sweater that Izzy had loaned Angie, Nell thought. The sweater must have crossed Izzy's mind. But it wouldn't be mentioned, not by either of them. Not now. A lost sweater was nothing when compared to a lost life.

Izzy walked down the two steps to the back room, and Nell and Cass picked up the rest of the boxes and followed her.

"Has Pete been able to talk about Angie's death?" Izzy asked. She collapsed the box and set it on the floor. "He wandered in here yesterday, hung around for a while as if he wanted to say something, but we were really busy and I didn't have time to talk."

"Not much. I've asked a few questions, but he doesn't want to go there."

"Give him time," Nell said.

Cass didn't answer. She picked up another shipping box, collapsed it, and placed it on the pile for recycling.

Nell could feel her unrest. Cass would be fine, but probably not until at least one of her issues was put to rest. She picked up a stack of collapsed boxes to take outside to the Dumpster and pushed open the side door with her hip, then stopped still in the doorway. "Did you hear that?" she asked, looking back into the shop.

Nell peered out the door and scanned the narrow alley that ran alongside the shop down to the water's edge. It was empty, except for George Gideon striding down to the waterfront as he began his nightly security stint. Cocky Gideon, as Cass called him. He looked back, nodded a hello, then moved on, his heavy backpack shifting between his broad shoulders.

"What do you hear?" Izzy asked, stepping out onto the small doorstep beside Nell.

"A whiny sound, like a baby crying. There. I hear it again."

Cass stepped past Nell and Izzy and looked toward the water. "I hear it, too. An injured gull?" She frowned and walked over to the green Dumpster pushed up against the clapboard siding.

Nell stepped outside. And then she heard the small cry again, coming from above. She leaned back and her eyes traveled up the side of the Seaside Studio, past the windows of the back room, to the apartment above. "Izzy, look. Up there."

Cass and Izzy stood out on the gravel pathway and their eyes followed the direction of Nell's finger.

And then they saw it.

Sitting on the windowsill inside Angie's apartment, its eyes as big and round as quarters, was a fluffy calico kitten.

Chapter 7

$\mathcal{T}$he three women hurried up the steps to the small apartment above Izzy's shop. Izzy fumbled in the pocket of her jeans for the ring of keys and pushed one into the lock.

Instantly, the tiny kitten flew off the windowsill and landed at their feet. Izzy scooped it up and cuddled the ball of fur to her chest. "Poor, sweet kitty. Where did you come from?"

Nell touched the kitten's soft coat with her fingertips and felt the tiny body purr beneath her touch. It was no bigger than a ball of angora yarn, with lovely red, black, and white markings. "What a beautiful kitten," Nell said. "A true calico. I didn't know Angie had a kitten."

"I didn't, either," Izzy said. "She told me she liked cats, but they made her sneeze, and . . ." Izzy paused, and then her face twisted into a frown as she absently scratched the tiny kitten's back.

"What's wrong, Izzy? You look puzzled."

Izzy lifted her cheek from the kitten's fur and looked at Nell. Concern creased her forehead. "This can't be Angie's kitten."

Cass frowned. "You're sure?"

"The police came up here after Angie died—routine, they said. They had to check for suicide notes, that sort of thing. I came up with them, and I'm sure the kitten wasn't in the apartment that day. I was with them the whole time, and unless the kitty was hiding somewhere, it wasn't here. It must have gotten in later . . . some other way."

Nell's brows pulled together as she looked around the apartment. *It was possible the kitten had been hiding,* she thought. The old cat that she and Ben had in Boston could disappear for days inside their brownstone home. Nell looked around the apartment. Did this sweet ball of fur live up here—without its owner—and no one knew it? And if not, how did it get inside a locked apartment?

Through the arched doorway leading to the sleeping area, Nell could see Angie's bed, made up neatly with colorful silk pillows lined up against the headboard. A book sat on the night table, and alongside it, a bottle of water, as if any minute, Angie would walk in from the bathroom, slip beneath the cool white sheets, and read herself to sleep. Beyond the bed, a closet door was slightly ajar, and Nell could see shoes lined up neatly on the floor and some outfits hanging side by side on the rack above them. Only the shelf above the clothes rack was in disarray, with boxes pulled out as if Angie had been in a hurry the last time she looked for a bag or a pair of shoes. The tops of several boxes had fallen to the floor and tissue paper cluttered the shelf.

There were certainly places for the kitten to hide—but it was so friendly, it seemed unlikely that the lure of people wouldn't have drawn it out from some secret spot. It hadn't been a bit timid when three women rushed in on it today.

"If Angie had a cat, there'd be food," Nell said abruptly, pushing aside the discomforting thoughts and walking into the kitchen. Angie having a kitten no one knew about was a far better option than finding another explanation for how the kitten got into the apartment.

The galley kitchen—with a small refrigerator, two-burner stove, and butcher-block counter—was built into the small alcove at the end of the sitting area. Nell opened the cupboard just above the sink, but it was nearly empty. A couple cans of soup, some granola bars, but nothing that would feed the kitten. The refrigerator held two cups of yogurt and an apple.

"Izzy, you're right," Nell said, a sense of unease taking root. "There's nothing that says a kitten has been hiding here. If this kitten had been alone since last Thursday, there'd certainly be telltale stains and odors."

"So someone has been up here since the police were here," Izzy said, putting words to Cass's and Nell's thoughts. She held the kitten close.

"And the kitten slipped in when someone opened the door," Cass said.

"Angie and I had the only keys," Izzy said.

"Would she have given a key to someone else?" Nell asked.

"I don't think Pete had one," Cass said. "And even if he did, why would he have come up here after she died?" Her tone was defensive.

Nell could think of lots of reasons why Pete might want to come up into Angie's apartment, not the least of which was to simply sit and breathe in the smell of the young woman who was lost to him. Aloud, she said, "I think Izzy is right—someone must have been up here in the past day or so, and the kitten slipped through the open door without being noticed. When that person left, she was left behind."

"Gideon?" Cass asked. "He may have felt it was his security-man duty to check it out. And I'm sure he knows a way to get past locked doors."

Izzy shook her head. "We outlined his duties clearly, what he should and shouldn't do. And the apartment was off-limits, even from his flashlight. I didn't want him scaring Angie in the middle of the night."

Nell bit down on her bottom lip. Sea Harbor was a small

town. And everyone knew the apartment belonged to Izzy. And everyone also knew that Angie lived there, and that she'd died.

Cass cupped the kitten's face in her hand. "This looks like one of the kittens Harry Garozzo had in his deli. He had a basketful that he was trying to give away. Maybe she wandered off."

"When was that, Cass?" Nell asked.

"Monday, Tuesday, maybe? It happens every spring and summer, Harry said. People leave them at his back door. I guess word has spread that the big, goofy Italian has a soft spot for finding kittens good homes. It could easily have strayed up here."

"But the more mysterious part is how it got inside." When Nell looked around the apartment again, she saw things she hadn't noticed at first—slight signs of disarray. A desk drawer open, magazines in disarray on the coffee table. A small television sat on the bookshelf. And on the desktop Nell spotted orange earphones and Angie's small iPod that she'd seen her with often—all easily absconded items if the visitor had been a thief. But if not a thief, then what was he—or she—looking for?

Nell looked up to see her niece watching her, reading her thoughts. Nell brushed them away. "Let's go downstairs and get this pretty little thing some food," she said.

"My thoughts, too." Izzy held the door open for Nell and Cass, the kitten a curled ball in the crook of her other arm.

Nell looked back over the apartment one more time, her gaze lingering on a tall narrow table that she and Izzy had found at an estate sale last winter. They thought it would be perfect against that wall—a good place for a vase of flowers or a small lamp, a place to drop your mail. It looked like that's how Angie had used it, too. A small wicker basket held several pieces of mail—advertising and flyers for the coming Fourth of July picnic. A pack of mints, rubber bands, and some loose change—just like the basket on her own kitchen counter. A flash of red in the puddle of change caught Nell's attention and when she lifted up the basket, a set of keys fell out.

"My apartment key!" Izzy said. She looked at the scarlet A on the knitted swatch. "These are the extra keys Angie returned last week."

"The night she died," Nell said, remembering Angie tossing the key ring on the table.

"I guess we know how someone got in," Izzy said. "But—"

"How did they get the keys?" Cass finished. "Where did you put them, Iz?"

Izzy was silent for a moment, rubbing the kitten's fur while she thought back over that night and stared at the keys, looped around her finger. Finally she looked up. "Nowhere. I never put the key ring away, just tossed it in one of the baskets on the table, along with measuring tapes and spare needles and a mess of knitting gadgets. I remember now because someone pulled it out during a beginners' class last Saturday and admired the way I'd used an old swatch— and the scarlet A for apartment. Everyone laughed at that."

"So whoever came up here took it from your basket," Nell said.

"Next question—who?" Cass followed Nell outside.

"It could have been almost anyone," Izzy said. She cuddled the kitten close as they walked back into the shop. "Everyone from my UPS guy to a class of teenagers knitting sack purses has been in the back room this week," she said. "Even Angus and Pete stopped by. People seemed to want to hang around. Maybe it was a prank, some curious kids wanting to see what was inside. The teenagers loved Angie, thought she was glamorous. Maybe they were curious about where she lived. Whoever did it left the key, so clearly they didn't plan on going back in."

"I don't think so." Nell thought about the desk drawer left open and the disarray in the closet. "I think someone was looking for something up there."

Cass looked over at the big wicker basket in the middle of the table. "Izzy, I think Nell's right. Something was going on with Angie. And I hate it, because it's all tied up with our lives. I want these past few days back. I want our summer back. And that won't happen until we find out what happened."

Izzy walked over to the window seat and sat down, cuddling the kitten. "Well, one thing I know for sure," she said.

"What's that, Izzy?" Nell said.

"I'm going to keep her."

Nell and Cass looked over at her.

Izzy lifted the kitten to her chest and rubbed her cheek against the soft fur. "The kitten. I'm going to keep her. I think she's exactly what we need right now. This sweet little thing came to the Seaside Knitting Studio for a reason, and this is where she will live and be happy."

Cass leaned over and tickled the kitten's chin. "You have a good life ahead of you, little calico—clam sauce fettuccine, grilled tuna, the list is endless."

Nell laughed. The kitten had worked magic, lightening the mood. She lifted the fluff of fur from Izzy's lap and cupped it in the palms of her hands, looking into the kitten's bright blue eyes. The kitten looked back at Nell, steady and calm, its gaze curious.

If only you could talk, little one. Nell smiled into the kitten's unwavering look. *If only you'd share your secrets with me. Tell me how you got into Angie's apartment—and what you saw while visiting there.*

Chapter 8

$\mathcal{B}$irdie Favazza fell in love with the calico kitten the minute she laid eyes on her, but she was dismayed to hear that after twenty-four hours in residence, she still had no name.

"It isn't good for the sweet thing's psyche," she said, pulling a small waste ball of rose-colored yarn from her knitting bag and rolling it along the floor in the shop's back room. Birdie always brought a plethora of projects to the Thursday-night knitting group—she was never sure what the evening's mood and Nell's treats would move her to knit.

The kitten scampered after the yarn, its tiny paws barely touching the floor. In one brief day, she had purred herself into the hearts of Izzy's staff and the dozens of customers who had stopped to stroke and cuddle her.

"She loves it here," Izzy said, pouring Birdie a glass of the Pinot.

"Of course she does," Birdie said.

Nell stood at the sideboard, tossing together a salad of sautéed wild mushrooms, fresh greens, tomatoes, and thin slices of fresh tuna, seared on the grill and pink and juicy on the inside. Pine nuts, lightly browned, and chunks of fresh mozzarella cheese would top off the salad, and it would be perfectly complemented by Birdie's wine.

Beside her, Cass looked for opportunities to pluck out slices of tuna.

Birdie rummaged around in her bag and settled on a soft, nearly finished baby sweater she was knitting for her housekeeper's grandbaby. Birdie loved bright colors and was working up a sweater that boasted a kaleidoscope of hues—bright green raglan sleeves, a bold red border, cobalt blue for the back, and golden yellow and deep green front panels. "Angie's strange drowning and now this kitten showing up in a locked apartment," she said, "might make one think our town haunted."

"I don't think it's ghosts doing these things." Nell wrapped the forks inside four napkins and set them beside the wooden bowl. "I talked to Harry today about the kitten. He said the kitten must have wandered off from the others. He knew one was missing, but figured that some child whose mother had said no to a new kitten had simply slipped it beneath a beach towel and carried it home."

"Was he surprised where she ended up?" Izzy handed Nell a glass of wine and sat across from Birdie. She picked up her half-knit sweater. She was far enough along now that the cables had taken shape and given the sweater definition. Uncle Ben would love it, and it would keep him warm when he walked the beach in the middle of December. Between her and Nell, Ben Endicott would never be without the perfect sweater for any kind of Sea Harbor weather. The kitten jumped up on Izzy's lap and curled up beside her handiwork.

"He wasn't as surprised as I thought he'd be. He comes in early on Tuesday mornings—around four, he said—to bake his sourdough bread. His wife's been encouraging him to walk to work these days—it's good for his heart and the bulge around his middle, Maggie says. As he walked past the alleyway, he saw someone just a few feet from the apartment steps."

"Good grief," said Birdie, looking up and taking off her glasses.

"He said the person had black hair—he thought it was Gideon, even though his backpack was missing. He noticed that because he'd never seen him at work without it. But he was in a hurry, so he went on to the deli, fed the kittens some milk, and busied himself baking bread. He left the door open a crack because of the oven heat, and a kitten could easily have slipped out into the dark."

"Do you think it was Gideon?" Cass asked. "That gives me the creeps."

"Harry wasn't sure—he *assumed* it was Gideon, I guess you'd say. But he didn't actually see anyone go into the apartment."

"But someone did," Izzy said.

"Purl," Birdie declared from across the coffee table.

"Pearl?" said Nell, looking up from fixing her salad.

The kitten stopped in the middle of the floor and looked up at Nell, its head cocked to one side, as if to argue the point if necessary.

"We'll call her Purl," Birdie said. "With a U, of course."

"I like it," Izzy said.

"To Purl," Nell said, lifting her wineglass.

"To Purl," Birdie, Cass, and Izzy repeated, glasses lifted toward the purring kitten rubbing up against Nell's leg.

Izzy leaned over and planted a kiss on Birdie's lined cheek. "It's a perfect name for her, Birdie."

A rapping on the back door startled the group into silence.

All heads turned toward the sound.

"Visitors?" Birdie asked.

"Sometimes my UPS man comes late," Izzy said, brushing away the anxiousness the noise had stirred up in the room. She pushed her knitting to the side and walked over to the door.

On the alley step stood two policemen.

"Hi, Tommy," Izzy said to the awkward young man whose hand was still raised in the air, ready to knock again. She smiled and nodded to his partner, a tall skinny man named Rob who rarely spoke but wore his uniform proudly.

"What are you two doing here?" Nell asked, thinking that the Sea Harbor police were perhaps more efficient than she'd sometimes given them credit for. Perhaps they'd seen the lights, wanted to be sure everything was all right.

"Could we . . . c-come in?" Tommy asked. His cheeks were flushed, and he shifted from one foot to another.

Tommy Porter's discomfort reminded Nell briefly of the summers when he had been unabashedly in love with Izzy. The two had been in the same sailing class one summer, and she remembered Tommy's painful stutter when he'd try to talk to Izzy and the teasing he got from the others in the class. Tommy went on to win every race, shine in every regatta, but he never overcame his awkwardness in Izzy's presence.

"Of course. You, too, Rob," Nell said. "We're just about to eat and knit—two things we do very well."

Izzy smiled at Tommy and tried to ease his discomfort. "How are things for you, Tommy?"

Tommy shifted from one foot to the other. A small sheen of perspiration appeared on his forehead.

Birdie stood and walked over to the two men. She stood as tall as her frame allowed and looked up into Tommy's somber face. "You look very nice in your uniform, Tommy. Your mother must be proud of you." She reached up and touched his shoulder, her voice almost a whisper. "But you might want to stand up a tad straighter."

Tommy immediately pulled his shoulders back, sucked in his abdomen, and took a deep breath. "Miz Favazza," he began, looking down at Birdie. He paused, and then stepped farther into the room. The movement seemed to bring him confidence. He kept his eyes on Birdie, which oddly allowed him to speak clearly and evenly. "We're here because of Angie Archer."

"Her drowning?" Nell said, encouraging him to continue.

Tommy shook his head. "She didn't drown, Miz Favazza," he said, still looking at Birdie.

Rob stepped up beside Tommy and spoke for the first time. "Well, the thing is, she *did* drown," he said. He cleared his throat and looked down at his large black shoes.

Nell followed his eyes. His shoes must be specially made, she thought. They were bigger than Ben's size thirteens. She wanted to talk about Rob's shoes, where he got them, were they specially ordered? Shoes were easy to talk about, and no matter how Rob got his shoes or didn't get his shoes, it wouldn't interfere with the lives of those she loved. But his words, Nell suspected, would do exactly that.

Rob cleared his throat and continued. "She drowned because someone put a drug in her drink and the drug paralyzed her. When she fell into the ocean, she couldn't swim or move a muscle to save herself.

"Angie Archer was murdered."

Chapter 9

*T*he news of Angie Archer's cruel murder spread through the Sea Harbor community with the force of a nor'easter. According to the autopsy report, she hadn't gone swimming or strolling or jogging along a breakwater on a bad night, a scenario most of the town had tried to cling to. Angie Archer had been murdered, and in an awful way.

The *Sea Harbor Gazette*, with a headline bigger than the Sox beating the Yankees, called it a result of a "date rape drug." Although Angie hadn't been molested, the reporter wrote, a drug common in crimes intended to render a person helpless was found in her body. No matter how skilled a swimmer Angie'd been, she wouldn't have been able to move a muscle once the flunitrazepam was dropped in her drink.

Tommy and Rob had told the knitters the apartment would have to be off-limits for a day or two, though they didn't expect to find much up there. The forensics guys would want to do a check, though, Tommy had said. "And, Izzy," he promised her, "I . . . I'll be s-sure they're quick."

And Tommy had kept his promise, Izzy told Nell the next day, though the racket they made that morning was unsettling to customers. "They were noisier than Angie," she said with a sad smile.

Ben and Nell had kidnapped Izzy from the knitting shop

Friday, insisting she take a lunch break and have a sandwich with them at Harry's Deli.

"Is there a lot of talk of the murder in the shop, Iz?" Nell said. Her uneaten pastrami sat in front of her. Nell's phone had rung all morning long, friends and neighbors, Father Northcutt updating her on Josie, board members from the Historical Museum. Everyone was concerned; everyone felt awful; and nearly everyone was sure it was a stranger, an awful person who had committed a terrible, random act of violence.

Izzy nodded and picked at her mushroom sandwich. "The rumors are starting, as you'd expect. Mostly people are talking about Angie's love life. Wondering if there's a connection there. I guess it's the date-rape drug angle."

"As far as I know, Angie didn't have much of a love life, except for Pete."

"And Pete wouldn't hurt a fly," Izzy said.

"Not only that, but he's so crushed at all this bad news that he can barely function, Cass says," Nell added. But he had been Angie's date that night, Nell thought. And she knew that fact would not escape anyone looking into Angie's murder.

"I think mostly people who've come into the shop want so badly to move on that they're calling Angie's murder a random act, a beach bum who's long gone."

Ben took his glasses off and rubbed the bridge of his nose between two fingers. "It makes it all easier, I suppose. If the murderer has moved on, things can go back to normal more quickly. The gossip is exciting for a while. But it's short-lived. Then people want it over, want the beaches safe. Want their summer back."

" 'Murders don't happen in Sea Harbor,' that's what people are saying," Izzy said. "They happen in Boston and New York and Los Angeles, but not here. Never here."

"Except one did," Nell said.

"What did they do in the apartment?" Ben asked.

"Not too much. They looked through everything, but Tommy was with them, and he said he made sure that anything they didn't need to take they put back neatly."

Nell smiled. "He's trying to protect you, Iz."

"I guess it can't hurt to have a sweet guy on the force watching out for my interests. The police mentioned what we noticed, Nell—that it didn't look like Angie really lived there. She hadn't made it her own. They were hoping to find something like a cell phone or a computer, Tommy said."

"Her cell phone was with her, we know that. It was like another appendage—she never went anywhere without it. It's probably rusting and useless at the bottom of the cove," Ben said. "What about her computer?"

"She had a laptop," Izzy said. "But it wasn't in the apartment, Tommy said."

"Maybe at her office at the museum," Nell said. "I'm sure they'll check there."

"Tommy said they'd be through by this afternoon. I guess I can go up this weekend and gather up the rest of Angie's things."

"Not alone," Nell said.

Izzy agreed. "You're right, Aunt Nell. We'll do this together for Josie."

A shadow fell over the table, and they looked up into the ample, perspiring face of Harry Garozzo. He leaned over the table, his waist buckling beneath the bend and his large baker's hands flat on the pocked wood surface. "Damn shame," he said. His voice was gruff with emotion. "Who would do such a horrible thing like this? Not anyone in Sea Harbor."

"That seems to be the sentiment, Harry. Or at least the wish," Ben said.

Harry pulled an empty chair over from another table and sat down. He wiped his hands on his stained bib apron. "I dunno what to think. Angie was a good girl." Harry scratched his bald head. He looked at their plates and frowned. "What, the food's bad? You're not eating? You donna like it?"

Izzy, Nell, and Ben picked up pieces of their sandwiches.

Harry nodded. Then he looked over his shoulder and lowered his voice so the customers lining up to buy roast beef and turkey, chunks of Vermont white cheddar, or his famous sourdough rolls couldn't hear him.

"The thing is," he said in low tones, "Angie came in here a lot. I liked her. She didn't cook much, that one. But, oh my, she liked to eat." His round face broke into a smile. "And she couldn't get enough of my smoked turkey. I'd pile thin slices high on a sourdough roll, then a fat slab of Swiss, smother it with my Russian dressing. She ate those sandwiches like there was no tomorrow."

"And?" Nell prompted, suspecting Harry had more on his mind than Angie's favorite food.

Harry leaned closer. His bushy brows lifted up into his forehead. "Well, here's the thing. I didn't think much of it at the time because it was her business, you know? Not mine. I leave my customers alone with their privacy. But the other day Angie was eating in the back booth like she did. Just enjoying my turkey. And she gets a call on her cell. Her voice got louder than usual, and when I walked by on the way to the kitchen, I could see the look on her face. She wasn't happy, I'll tell you that much. And she told the caller never ever to bother her again. It was only business, she said. I thought that was strange, but that's what she said. 'It was only business.' And she told him she wouldn't be back, that he had the wrong idea. And then she said, and I remember it because her voice got stern, but it was shaking a little, too. She said if he ever bothered her again, she'd tell someone. 'I swear, I'll tell,' she said. 'And then where will you be?' "

Harry looked up and frowned at a waiter neglecting an empty water glass.

"Tell who?" Nell asked.

"Harry, tell *who*?" Izzy insisted, drawing Harry back to the conversation. "You said that Angie was going to tell someone. Who was it?"

Harry paused for effect; then he looked from side to side, checking to see that all his customers were enjoying their sandwiches and the wicker baskets on the tables were filled with bread sticks. He looked over at the deli counter and nodded, pleased that the line was moving quickly and no one had to wait too long.

"Harry!" Izzy said, slapping the tabletop. "Who, Harry?"

Harry looked back at Nell, Ben, and Izzy. He leaned in a little closer. "Angie said, and I heard it as clearly as I hear the dishes rattling in the kitchen . . ." Harry paused to wipe the perspiration off his forehead with the back of his hand.

"Here's what she said, and she said it clearly and sternly and with a voice part frightened and part mad. She said, 'You back off, you leave me alone, or I swear I will tell your . . . your *wife*!' "

Harry stood back up, straight and tall, and pleased with his performance, smiled at Ben, Nell, and Izzy, and lumbered off to his post behind the deli counter.

Chapter 10

*N*ell and Izzy pondered Harry's startling story as they moved into their afternoon. If Harry had heard right, someone was harassing Angie, or at the least, bothering her. It was another chink in the random crime theory, they agreed. Another reason to find out what had been going on in Angie's life those last days, right beneath their eyes, their shop, and their knitting projects. Another piece to the puzzle that was Angie.

Nell considered canceling Friday supper. Angie's murder hung over the town like a heavy cloud and didn't lend itself to friends gathering on the deck on a beautiful summer night.

But Ben thought otherwise. "People might want to be together," Ben said. "Let's light the coals, chill the martinis, and we'll be here if anyone comes."

Ham and Jane Brewster arrived at precisely seven o'clock.

Jane walked into the kitchen and hugged Nell. "That poor Angie Archer," she said. "I can't think of anything else, Nell. Ham and I found ourselves wandering around the studios today, being sad, then mad, then sad again. So we decided we'd come by and if the door was open, that would be good. If not, we'd go back to the studio and wander some more."

"We've brought a friend," Ham said, walking across the Endicotts' kitchen and setting a bottle of wine down on the butcher-block island. A tall, sandy-haired man with a familiar smile followed him across the kitchen. Sam Perry was teaching a photography class at the summer arts academy, Ham explained.

Ben shook his hand. "It's not our most festive Friday night, Sam, but we're glad to have you anyway."

"This town holds its own close," Sam said. "I can see that. A murder is a lot to handle."

Ben held open the French doors leading to the deck, and invited the small group outside. "Sea Harbor is a great place," he said, "but it's hard right now to get past the bad things happening."

"You don't expect things like murder in this calm and peaceful place," Nell said. "But we've weathered lots of storms up here. We'll get through this, Sam." She passed him a martini Ben had just mixed.

The bang of the front screen door announced that Ham and Jane weren't the only ones needing company tonight. Birdie and Izzy walked through the family room and out to the deck, carrying more wine and a sack of Harry's sourdough rolls.

Nell noticed the quieter mood that accompanied people's steps—Izzy usually flew through the house. And Birdie's step was light like the bounce of a ball. But tonight things were heavier, slower, touched with sadness and concern.

Izzy greeted Ham and Jane, gave Nell and Ben quick hugs, then turned toward the man sitting off to the side, one of Ben's martinis in his large hand.

For one second, Izzy stood still, and Nell wondered briefly if she was ill.

Then her mouth dropped open, her eyes as round as Purl's, and she stared openly at Sam Perry.

"Izzy?" Nell said. "Are you all right?"

Sam had gotten out of the chair, his hand extended. Then it fell to his side and a slow smile spread across his face. "Izzy Chambers," he said, "are you stalking me?"

"In your dreams," Izzy said. And then she allowed a small release of air. "It's Sam," she said softly, as if to explain her reaction. She moved toward him then and wrapped the man twice her size in a hug. Finally she pulled away and looked at Ben.

"Uncle Ben, I need a martini."

"I'm taking a wild stab at this," Ben said. "You two have met." He handed Izzy a cocktail glass.

Izzy wrapped her fingers around the narrow stem and took a sip. "I've known Sam almost my whole life—he was my oldest brother's best friend. And for most of that time, I didn't like him much. But tonight"—she looked over at Sam—"tonight I really needed a hug. And I remembered that you were okay at that."

The teasing disappeared from Sam's eyes.

"Angie Archer lived above Izzy's knitting studio," Nell explained. "We all knew her—this murder is very close to home. Too close."

"Knitting studio?" Sam said.

"I bought a little place on Harbor Road, Sam. Nell and Ben helped me fix it up—and I love it. I love helping people create beautiful things in a world that isn't always so beautiful. That's what I do, Sam."

"The law firm?"

"No more law firm," she said.

"Good," Sam said. "You should never have given in to your dad and gone into law in the first place. You were always smart and strong-willed as a mule, probably great lawyer traits, but I never could see you defending bad guys, and from what I hear, you can't always just pick the good ones."

"No, you can't," Izzy said. Her answer was spoken softly and addressed more to herself than Sam. She picked a slice of Brie from the tray and followed Nell into the kitchen to get the pasta ready. Birdie was sitting at the island with Cass, her hair damp from a recent shower, their voices quiet.

"We knew all along she hadn't just fallen off the breakwater," Cass said. "So it's not a complete surprise, right? Why does the official murder news churn my insides this way?"

"The police and television are already spreading the word that the murderer is most likely long gone. If I hear the word 'random' one more time I am going to choke a reporter," Birdie said.

Nell busied herself at the sink, filling a large pot with water. "It wasn't random," she said. "Anyone who knew Angie like we did knows that couldn't have been the case."

"She would never have gone out on the breakwater alone for no reason," Birdie said.

"And the whole evening before she died was filled with question marks," Izzy said. "Starting out with Pete on her arm, then seeing her in the bookstore with Tony, arguing. It was too odd to not be significant. She got a phone call, Pete said. Right there in Jake's. She looked resigned, like it was something she had to do. She told Pete she'd make it up to him. They argued, she left."

"It was Tony?"

"Pete doesn't think so," Cass said.

Nell turned on the burner. "Archie said Tony was leaving the bookstore when Angie walked by. It seemed like a chance meeting, from what Archie could see. Tony stopped Angie in front of the store and said he needed to talk to her. Just for a few minutes, Archie heard him say," Nell reported. "Angie said she had exactly that—a few minutes—and he better make it quick."

"And we know they argued in those minutes," Izzy said.

"So Tony could have followed her to the breakwater," Birdie said.

"But why?" Nell said. "Tony would have no reason to hurt Angie." Nell turned away from the stove and faced the others. "All these incongruities. And they all involve people we've lived with, people we know and care about."

Izzy went on and repeated the lunch conversation at Harry's, filling Birdie and Cass in on the overheard phone call. "Nothing of this reeks of randomness," Izzy said. She set down her martini. "I don't think so."

"Angie's awful death is a cloud over our town, our knitting group, our lives," Birdie said.

And it was. Nell could feel it. Angie's murder was wrapping itself around them like a tight ball of yarn. "It's the not knowing that makes it impossible to go back to the way it was before. Until we find out who's responsible, that cloud will hang there, sucking life out of the summer."

"The only way to put things back in place," Birdie said, slapping her tiny hand down on the island, "is to figure it out. Who did it? And why did they do it? Angelina Archer's death is holding us back from living the days as they were intended to be lived. And if the police want to concentrate on some stranger who has headed north to Bar Harbor or Nova Scotia or the Arctic, that's dandy for them. They'll write it up that way, close their report, and file it on a dusty shelf. And we—ladies—will concentrate on Harbor Road."

The thought was sobering to the knitters. And challenging. And it was the truth.

The strange phone call Angie had gotten in Harry's Deli. The kitten found in the apartment. The way she'd treated Pete the night she died. Harbor Road. Their home.

Nell looked at Birdie and saw that she was watching her, reading her mind. Birdie held up a glass, nodded, and smiled.

"What are we toasting?" Ben asking, walking into the kitchen for a fresh platter of cheese. Sam followed close behind him.

"To better days," Birdie said.

"I'll go for that," Ben said.

Cass looked up and spotted the unfamiliar face. "And who are you?" she asked Sam Perry. Before he could answer, Cass slipped off her stool and looked at him again, her brows lifting in recognition. "I know who you are. You're the guy who was taking photographs down on the breakwater. And Archie Brandley has a book of your photographs in his store window. I looked at it. It's not bad."

Sam grinned at her bluntness. "And I remember seeing you at the breakwater, too—in the *Lady Lobster*, right? I have some shots of you. Great boat, by the way."

Cass nibbled on a piece of Brie, her cheeks showing pleasure at the compliment. Nothing was closer to Cass's heart than the *Lady Lobster*, and a nice comment about her prized possession went a long way.

"Maybe you accidentally caught a poacher in one of your photos," Izzy said. "We're having a terrible problem with poachers down there, Sam. And Cass's traps are among the targets."

"I heard talk of that," Sam said. "Sorry, Cass. It's way too beautiful a spot for bad things like that to go on."

Nell listened peripherally, her mind spinning out in other directions. She thought of the nightly pilfering of the traps—and of the night Angie Archer died. Where were the poachers that night? Stealing lobsters when they could have saved a young girl's life, pulled her drugged body from the water until it could work again?

A brief surge of anger heated Nell's chest and she pressed it away with the palm of her hand. Anger wouldn't bring peace back to Sea Harbor. But answers would.

Nell refreshed the cheese platter and carried fresh salsa and chips to the deck. The others soon followed.

Izzy sat on the deck glider next to Nell and rested her head on her shoulder. "It's good to be here, Aunt Nell. I didn't want to go home tonight, but I didn't want to stay at the studio or hang out with friends and listen to a dozen scenarios of how and why Angie died. Mostly, I guess, I didn't want to be alone. I wanted to be with friends and those I love."

Nell nodded. The unease was all around them. And no matter how the town or the police wanted to push the murder off on a random, crazed person passing through town, none of them would rest easy until they knew the answers. Until they knew the who. The why. Only the *where* was all too familiar.

Ben used a long fork to place the pork chops on the grill and in minutes the smell of sweet and pungent barbecue filled the air, clinging to the overhanging trees, rising to a sliver of moon above them. Conversation was muted and comfortable, friends among friends among tragedy.

"I used this brown sugar and ginger marinade especially for Pete," Nell said to Cass. "It's one of his favorites. Do you know when he'll get here?"

"After we brought the *Lady* in, he was going to shower and then stop at the Gull for a quick beer. I figured he needed to be with his buddies. But he said he'd come by shortly after that."

"Was he okay?" Nell asked.

"As okay as he can be." Cass cut into her plump pork chop. "I think he figured being with his buddies might make him forget what was going on. Those guys talk about the Sox, the Pats, and fishing—easier topics to deal with. Pete can barely talk about the murder. He won't turn on the television or read a paper. But maybe that's good. No reason to go over the gruesome details endlessly."

Nell nodded. That was wise. It had been only twenty-four hours since the autopsy report came back, and the local television channel and radio stations had saturated the airwaves with the news. And even the announcers had adopted the spin of so many merchants and friends and neighbors. "A stranger in our midst?" the noon reporter had crooned. And gone on to talk about the difficulty in finding a murderer who could now be worlds away. A needle in a haystack, she said.

Nell had slipped some Segovia CDs in the player. Soon soft,

easy strains of classical guitar music drifted out over the speakers and into the night air. Jane and Birdie passed around salad, rolls, and grilled sweet potatoes to fill their plates.

"I don't suppose anyone in Sea Harbor ever needs a therapist," Sam said, not resisting the second chop Ben slid onto his plate. "Come sit on the Endicotts' deck, listen to Segovia, and let the sea air clean out your head. Magical." He sat back in his chair and stretched out his long legs in front of him. "Has anyone told Dr. Phil about this?"

"It's our secret," Nell said. "Therapy by the light of the moon. And tonight we need it most of all."

Dessert was passed around a short while later—New York–style cheesecake, the lemony sides straight and tall, with plump strawberries from the market sliced along the top.

"Sam, when do your classes begin?" Nell asked as Ben poured coffee and brought out glasses of water and brandy.

"In a week or so. Jane and Ham suggested I come up early to get the lay of the land."

"Margarethe wanted him here for the art academy benefit next week," Jane said. "She wants to introduce Sam to the benefactors and show them we're serious about this project of giving all kids a chance to do art."

"I met Mrs. Framingham today at the yacht club," Sam said. "She was playing tennis with a much younger woman—in the noon heat, no less—and winning."

"That's no surprise," Ben said. "She's has the best backhand in Sea Harbor. Strong as an ox."

"Her benefit will add some balance to the awful things going on around us," Nell said. "I'm glad you'll be here, Sam. We'll be there."

"How about you, Izzy?" Sam asked. He looked at her over the rim of his coffee cup.

Izzy shrugged. "I'll have to see, Sam. If next week brings as many surprises as this one has, I don't know where I'll be on Saturday night."

"It must be hard to get your arms around all this," Sam said, watching the emotions pass across Izzy's face. "Hard to digest."

"Digest. Believe. Accept," Izzy said. "Move on. They're all hard."

Cass nodded agreement. "The week that was." Her hand slipped into the pocket of her jeans to silence the buzz of her cell phone. She pulled it out and checked the number. Then frowned and stepped inside the French doors.

Nell was in the kitchen, wrapping up three pork chops. She spotted Cass speaking on the phone and walked toward the deck door, carrying the foil-wrapped package in her hands.

Cass folded her phone and slipped it into her pocket.

"Cass, I'm keeping these chops warm for Pete. Even though it's late, he may still be hungry," she said.

Cass looked up at Nell, her tan face filled with weariness and worry. She sighed. "There's only one way to find out, Nell. Let's take them down to the jail and see if he's hungry."

Chapter 11

$\mathcal{S}$am's battered Volvo—too many camping trips in the mountains, he told Nell—was parked behind Ben's car, so he offered to drive Ben and Cass down to the station.

Cass insisted no one else come. "Pete won't want a circus," she had said.

Pete's voice had been slurred on the phone, and Cass knew he'd had more than one drink at the Gull. But that was about all she knew. "There's a part of me," Cass said, "that's tempted to leave him there. I'm just glad he didn't call my mother."

Cass didn't mean it; of course, she'd been worried about Pete, just as they all had been. Nell hugged Cass tightly and sent her off with Ben and Sam, knowing they'd take care of her. If anyone could handle the Sea Harbor police, it was Ben. He'd spearheaded a recent campaign to replace the crumbling old station down near the bridge, and he'd known Chief Jerry Thompson since his teenage summers on the Cape when Jerry befriended him and pulled him into the coveted group of townies.

And Sam Perry? Nell wasn't sure how he fit into the fray, but he seemed comfortable being in the middle of it. And helpful. And without rhyme or reason backing her up, Nell trusted him.

The others had stayed behind, helping Nell clean up. Izzy commandeered the dishwasher while Ham made sure the coals were covered with sand and the garbage taken out. Birdie and

Jane found the drying towels and parked themselves near Nell at the sink.

"Do you think this arrest has anything to do with Angie's murder?" Jane asked, drying one of Ben's martini glasses. "Pete Halloran is such a sweetheart. He couldn't possibly have had anything to do with her murder."

But the others were quiet. They were all crazy about Cass's six-foot-three little brother. Pete was such a softy that he had trouble banding the claws of the lobsters he and Cass caught. But those things didn't matter anymore. Angie had been murdered. Drugged—and murdered. And Pete was one of the last people to see her before it happened.

Nell shivered at the sink and pressed her hands to the bottom of the sudsy stainless-steel basin, staring out the window into the black night. Pete couldn't have killed Angie. Not any more than she or Izzy or Cass or Birdie could have killed her. But he most certainly would be a suspect, along with other people dear to her.

Nell had waited up for Ben to come back, after the others had left, but once he got home and assured her that Pete was fine, that he hadn't been arrested for Angie's murder, and that he was safely back home in his little apartment on the edge of town, she was able to give in to the weariness of the day and sleep, pressed lightly into Ben's comforting length.

The details, Ben said, could wait until morning.

Ben's special coffee was gurgling in the kitchen when Nell came downstairs the next morning. She'd slept late, unusual for her. Emotion had taken a toll. But the strong aroma of the Colombian coffee lightened her step.

"It's strong enough to curl your hair," Birdie often complained as she'd head for the cupboard and a bag of Earl Grey tea.

Ben spotted Nell coming down the back stairs into the kitchen and filled a mug to the top before returning to his spot at the table. A soft breeze from the open windows ruffled the pages of the Saturday *Boston Globe,* already pulled apart into piles—front pages, business, sports, style.

"So fill me in," Nell said, settling herself across from him, her elbows on the table, her chin cupped in her hands.

"Pete got rowdy." Ben stirred his coffee and flattened the business section with his other hand. "Going to the Gull to avoid talk of Angie was a bad decision, it turns out."

"Who was there?"

"The usual Friday nighters—lots of Pete's buddies. But they weren't the problem. There were others there who didn't know Angie like we did, and they were talking about her. 'What kind of girl would be drinking out on the breakwater?' That kind of thing. 'What was she looking for?' Pete heard it. And after a few drinks, he lost it and started a fight."

"So Jake Risso called the police?"

Ben shrugged. "Jake isn't a bad sort. He tried to stop it, apparently. But he couldn't risk getting the place all broken up. It was probably a good thing to do. It protected Pete from himself. He felt mighty sheepish by the time we got him home."

"And I don't imagine Cass held back on letting him know how she felt about it."

Ben laughed. "Nope, you're right about that. Sam Perry was a big help. He got Pete back in his apartment and even stored your pork chops in his fridge. Pete says thanks, by the way. Or at least it sounded sort of like that."

Ben took a drink of coffee and sat silently for a minute, his face growing more serious. "I ran into the chief while we were at the station. He repeated what we'd heard yesterday—that the likeliest scenario is that a stranger killed Angie, someone passing through. They've talked to people like Pete and Tony. But there are no likely suspects who could have been on the dock when they estimate Angie was killed. At least no one they've come up with. And the drug angle changes things, Jerry said. Those kinds of drugs—the ones used to immobilize people for whatever the reason—are foreign to Sea Harbor. It just doesn't fit here. The police found nothing helpful in Angie's apartment. No clues. No personal calendar or notes. There was little of Angie there, they said. It was almost as if she'd never intended to really move in and make it her own."

Nell nodded, remembering the few personal things she'd seen. Some clothes. A picture frame. But the apartment was Izzy's, not Angie's, filled with the things she had found to make it comfortable and cozy for the person who lived there. And Angie had added little to make it her own.

"Jerry said that they'd have to talk to people who knew her, of course. But there were some beach bums who hung around the breakwater and beaches last summer, and Jerry suspected it might be something like that."

"That seems a big assumption, Ben."

"Maybe. The guys last summer robbed a whole string of cottages before taking off for parts unknown. And it presents at least the possibility that someone hanging around for no good reason approached Angie that night."

"Do you think that's what happened?"

Ben didn't answer, but he didn't have to. Thirty years of sitting across from him at the breakfast table had bred its own clear language. A careful look into Ben's brown eyes told Nell his thoughts—and they matched her own.

"There are so many loose ends, Ben. But the most absurd part of that hypothesis is the idea that Angie would have a drink with a stranger—and on a night when she had plans with one of the nicest men in Sea Harbor. And going out on the breakwater on a nasty night? It wouldn't happen. Not 'randomly.' "

Ben rubbed the handle on his coffee mug absently. "No, it couldn't. But there are people who know more about it than we do and hopefully they'll figure all that out."

"We can hope."

Izzy called shortly after Ben left the house for a Sox game at Fenway. "The police are finished looking through Angie's apartment, Nell. Josie suggested I just pack up her things."

Nell had talked to Josie that morning, too. Her neighbors and friends had rallied around her, and she told Nell she was okay—and that it was going to be all right. Angie was at peace, she repeated. And Nell heard in her voice that she believed that to be true. The police would release the body and she would bury Angie quietly—just a few neighbors and Father Northcutt.

"She'll lie down right next to Ted." It was almost as if the news that Angie was murdered was lost to Josie—or wasn't a part of her grieving process.

"I think Josie was thinking more of me than of herself," Izzy said on the phone. "She worried that having Angie's things still in the apartment was uncomfortable for me, and that I might want to rent out the space. Can you imagine?"

Nell could. That would be Josie's way.

"I assured her I wasn't even thinking of renting the apartment for a while," Izzy went on. "That it was the last thing on my mind. But the truth is, I think she wants this over with. Closure. So if your offer to help is still good, I know it'll be easier with you there beside me."

Izzy had suggested around four, when things quieted down at the shop.

Nell filled the back of her car with boxes and some old newspapers, and drove down to the village. From the brief time she'd spent in Angie's apartment, Nell doubted if they would need half the boxes she'd collected.

A parking spot opened up directly in front of the Seaside Knit-ting Studio. *Parking karma, as Birdie would say,* Nell thought, and turned off the ignition. The minute she stepped onto the curb, her eyes were drawn to Izzy's shop window. It was a virtual rainbow of color. A rainbow in the middle of a terrible storm.

Nell stood in front of the window and feasted on the visual effect Izzy had created. She'd filled the space with an ocean of yarn in colors that took Nell's breath away. She pressed her fin-gertips against the glass, as if to touch the dripping skeins. Izzy must have gotten up at dawn to put it all together. Her own little attempt to dispel the gloom. And she'd done a magnificent job of it.

Several old brass-cornered trunks were positioned at different angles in the narrow space, cushioned on a bed of silk petals. Nell recognized one trunk from an antique sale she and Izzy had gone to in Rockport last winter. Another was Izzy's grandmother's—Nell's mother's—steamer trunk. Izzy had cleaned it up and polished the brass fixings to a high sheen.

Draped across the dark surfaces of the trunks, flowing gently over the sides and down to the floor was a waterfall of yarn that reminded Nell of a recent Monet exhibit at Boston's Museum of Fine Arts. The colors were irresistible and only the thick glass kept Nell from sinking her fingers into the hand-dyed strands of mossy green and soft coral, turquoise, and deep, watery blues. One skein, cascading down the center of the trunk, was a rich blend of saffron, goldenrod, and shades of yellow, reminding Nell of Izzy's hair. It was beautiful. *Sea yarn,* the handwritten sign read.

Nell smiled into her reflection in the glass, her cheekbones catching the sun's reflection. And she knew before walking into Izzy's shop that the trip to clean out Angie's apartment was going to be an expensive one. Sea yarn, she suspected, didn't come cheap.

Nell greeted Mae and was told that the store had nearly sold out of the new, luxurious yarn. It was a good thing it was closing time, she said.

"It's a beautiful display."

"Sure it is. The girl has talent," Mae said. She glared at the computer screen. "But this computer doesn't. Darn things. You're damned if you use 'em, damned if you don't." She snatched a calculator from the drawer and began punching in the day's figures.

"Almost sold out?"

Mae chuckled and lowered her rimless glasses down to the slight bump on her nose. "No need to worry. Izzy knew you'd go nuts over those colors. She set aside a stash for you and has clear plans for how you should use it."

"This is a dangerous place, Mae. And where is the temptress?"

"In the back room. She was helping Harriet Brandley finish up some booties for the fourteenth grandbaby. Fourteen! Booties and sweaters for the Brandley babies alone'd keep us in business. Been crazy as all get-out in here today. Even Miz Framingham stopped by to see the display. Izzy talked her into staying for a class she was teaching on making scarves with the new yarn. Izzy could talk an Eskimo into buying ice."

The thought of Margarethe taking Izzy's class made Nell smile. Margarethe knew more about knitting and yarns than all of them put together. And she was used to *giving* instructions, not taking them. But Mae was right—Izzy probably *could* sell ice to an Eskimo, provided they could afford it. If not, she'd give it to them.

Nell found Izzy standing at the bookcase in the back room, sorting through a pile of CDs. Purl was on a knit cushion in the middle of the table, curled into a sleeping ball. All around her, the table was littered with skeins of yarns, needles and scissors, and empty lemonade glasses.

"Sorry it's such a mess," Izzy said, leaning over to peck Nell on the cheek. "We had a class today."

"So Mae tells me."

"Ah, Miz Framingham, as Mae calls her. She almost bought out my supply of sea yarn. I think I could retire off today's sales."

"And she took a class?"

"Yes, though she didn't need to. She's an amazing knitter. She knows more about yarn than anyone I know. I asked her how she knew so much. She was kind of reluctant to talk about it, but finally admitted that she had a grandmother who taught her how to knit. It was the one good thing in her childhood, she said. But anyway, she wanted to experiment with the sea yarn. Mostly, though, I think she needed her mind to be on other things." Izzy scooped up a handful of spare needles and put them in a basket.

"What do you mean?"

"News that Angie's death was a murder upset her terribly. She thought the media was unnecessarily frightening people." Izzy picked up a sack from the table and handed it to Nell. "Here's what I saved for you. Isn't it beautiful? I decided we needed beauty in our lives right now. And I think that's why Margarethe stayed around, too."

Nell opened the sack. It was filled with turquoise sea yarn in differing shades, one melting into another, until it looked like the sea on a perfect summer day.

"I thought you could make a lacy scarf or shawl to go with your sexy black dress for next week's benefit. I threw in a simple pattern—you can easily finish it by next Saturday."

"Dear Izzy. I don't know how I managed while you were off being a lawyer. Thank you. And speaking of the arts benefit—"

Izzy shook her head and held up one hand. "Nope. I won't need your extra ticket, Aunt Nell. I was hoping I'd weasel an invitation out of Margarethe Framingham by inviting her to stay for the class. She seemed pleased that I brought up the event—all the women in the class assured her the town wouldn't let Angie's murder put anything on hold. " Izzy picked up an engraved rectangle of cream-colored cardboard from the bookcase and flapped it in the air. "But for whatever reason, I am now an invited guest."

Nell smiled.

"Maybe Cass would like your extra ticket—she probably can't afford one, especially with all that poaching going on, and could certainly use a party. What do those tickets cost? Three hundred a pop? I'll donate to the artists' fund, but on my own terms, I'm afraid."

"What's all this idle chatter?" a voice floated in behind Nell. "I thought we had work to do." Birdie stood on the step in the arched doorway, nearly hidden behind a pile of cardboard boxes piled in her arms.

"Birdie, give me those," Nell said, taking a box off the top of the pile and setting it on the floor. "There, now I can see you. What are you doing here?" The question was a bit silly, Nell thought. One never knew when Birdie would show up. She didn't miss a beat of the town's pulse, somehow knowing what was going on before things actually happened. Nell suspected she protected more Sea Harbor secrets that Father Northcutt's confessional box.

Birdie set the other boxes down and brushed her small hands together, releasing a cloud of dust. "I saw your car, Nell, and the boxes in the backseat, and decided my visit to Ocean's Edge for tea could wait. Those old ladies aren't nearly as interesting as you two, and I didn't want to miss out on anything."

Those *old* ladies, Nell knew, were a group of wealthy Sea Harbor residents of Birdie's generation who, like Birdie herself, could buy and sell the town if they so chose. And the tea gathering was more likely a date with a bottle of sherry and a platter full of gossip.

"Old ladies, my foot," Izzy said. "You will never be old, Birdie."

"That's true," Birdie said. She brushed a shock of white hair back from her forehead, where age spots and freckles blended together. A maze of tiny lines, like a well-drawn road map, spread out from the corners of her eyes, which lit up her wise, lined face. "But I'm not here to talk about age, sweet pea. I presume these boxes are for Angelina's things and there isn't much else I can do for poor Josie. So let me help."

"Me, too," said Cass, coming in from the front of the store. "Mae said you were all back here. I don't need yarn, but I sure need all of you."

"Well, then, grab a box," Izzy said.

"Izzy Chambers, are you back here?"

"One more minute and we would have missed her," Cass mumbled under her breath.

Beatrice Scaglia swept into the room. Even on Saturdays Beatrice was dressed for a power meeting or luncheon. Her pink summery suit, a size four at the most, Nell guessed, matched her two-inch heels perfectly, and as always, every hair was in place.

"It's that gorgeous yarn, Izzy," Beatrice said, smiling at the circle of women. "I must have it."

"The sea yarn?" Izzy asked. "Mae would be glad to help—"

"Izzy dear, Mae Anderson is a charming woman. You"— Beatrice pointed a long red fingernail at Izzy—"are a fiber artist. I knew that from the start, which is why I helped push your license through for this shop. And I found your class so interesting last week that I may actually take up knitting. The new yoga, my friends call it. So therapeutic, they say." Beatrice's red lips formed a perfect smile.

She probably will be mayor someday, Nell thought, listening to the exchange. According to Ben, that was Beatrice's goal. The diminutive powerhouse already drove nearly every council meeting and knew every newborn, every aging Sea Harbor resident by name. Watching her in action, Nell understood completely why her sweet husband, Salvatore, never said a word.

"Are you moving?" Beatrice asked suddenly, looking at the stack of boxes.

"No," Nell said. "We're cleaning out Angie Archer's apartment."

Beatrice looked up at the ceiling. "Why?" she asked. A strange look crossed her face. "Now?"

"Yes," Izzy said. "But I think Mae has a few skeins of the yarn left if you'd like some."

Nell thought Beatrice looked slightly pale. Tiny beads of perspiration dotted her forehead. "Are you all right, Beatrice?"

Beatrice pushed a smile into place. "Of course I'm all right. But you can't do it alone. I'll help." She leaned over to pick up one of the boxes.

"No, Beatrice," Izzy said.

"Yes," Beatrice answered, and without another word, she walked to the back door and up the back steps.

Chapter 12

It was a strange little cleaning quintet, Nell told Ben as they drove over to Sweet Petunia's the next morning. But having Beatrice there certainly kept cleaning out Angie's things from being the emotional task it might otherwise have been.

Beatrice talked nonstop, Nell said, demanding that she sweep, then dust, then clean out drawers. Midstream, without the others hearing, she had stepped outside and called her husband, Sal, insisting he bring over a bottle of chilled white wine to refresh them. Sal arrived at the door looking sheepish, his thick dark hair mussed and his face quiet and serious as it always was. It was clear to Nell he wanted to be anywhere but in the middle of five women cleaning a murdered woman's apartment. He was embarrassed doing far simpler things, like lighting candles for the Christmas pageant or passing the basket for offerings at church—all tasks, Nell suspected, Beatrice dictated he do. It must have been almost painful for him—Beatrice insisting he come in and help. And Nell understood in a fresh way why Sal Scaglia liked his job at the county offices so much—the paper shuffling and filing required must have provided a pleasant haven for him.

By the time Angie's clothes and books, and a few other personal things—her orange earphones, an iPod, and some photos—were packed and stacked neatly in the closet, Beatrice's pink suit was smudged, one heel broken, and poor Sal had finished off the wine, sitting alone on the back step.

"A Scaglia moment," Ben said, amused at the story. "Beatrice is a character. So the boxes are still up there?"

"Yes. Josie wasn't home, so we'll just wait until there's a good moment."

Ben pulled into Annabelle's parking lot and found a spot at the edge of the lot.

Even though the talk would be of Angie's murder, Ben wouldn't be robbed of breakfast at Sweet Petunia's. Sunday mornings were for Annabelle's, the *New York Times,* and Nell's knitting. They couldn't control gossip about the latest developments in the murder case, he admitted, but they could still enjoy a moist frittata.

Set back from the main road of the Canary Cove art colony, up a short gravel drive and tucked into a grove of pine trees, the small restaurant lured more residents than tourists, and that suited the Endicotts just fine. It was always good to be among friends and neighbors, but especially now.

Annabelle's teenage daughter, Stella, met them at the door, which was propped open and held in place by a stone pelican with a fish in its mouth. Annabelle had tied a daisy-print ribbon around its neck. Over Stella's shoulder, Nell could see that the restaurant was nearly full.

"Like who would have thought this'd ever happen in Sea Harbor?" Stella asked, her green eyes huge behind blue-rimmed glasses. "It's like *CSI*—but better. My mom says I can't talk about it to customers, but, like, you guys are friends." She grabbed two menus from the hostess stand and ushered Ben and Nell through the restaurant and out to the small weathered deck that ran along its side and looked out over the sea. "I'll give you a table out here, where you can talk and knit better."

"It's awful news, Stella," Nell said, sitting down at a small table next to the railing and settling her large knitting bag at her feet. It held the new sea-yarn scarf she had started and hoped to finish this week. She looked up at Stella. "But there's not much to say, is there?"

Stella frowned and bit down on her bottom lip. Her plucked eyebrows arched as she looked back toward the screen door that separated the porch from the inside of the café. Then she leaned toward Nell, her head lowered and her large tinted glasses so close that Nell could see herself in the lenses. "Now, here's what I know," Stella whispered. "Angie was with a guy, like, having a drink. Then *plop*, the little pill went into the glass. And when he pushed her off, it was all over. She had a way of making men mad, you know?"

"No, I don't know that," Nell said. "And you don't either, Stella."

Ben, not willing to engage in Stella's gossip, walked over to the sideboard, drawn by the smell of fresh coffee. He returned carrying a steaming silver pot and filled Nell's mug.

Stella slapped her hand over her mouth. "Sorry, Mr. Endicott. That's my job."

Ben sat down next to Nell. "No problem, Stella. I was a pretty accomplished waiter in my college days." He smiled up at her, then pulled his glasses out of his shirt pocket and unfolded the *Times*.

Nell poured cream into her mug and watched Stella's head swing around again, this time aimed at the red-checked curtain of the kitchen window, hoping her mother was busy over a hot stove and not looking out.

She looked back at Nell. "There's more here than meets the eye, Mrs. Endicott," Stella said in an official *CSI* way. Her brows lifted again and she held her head high, as if balancing a secret that might slide off her head if she moved too fast. She pushed her glasses back into place and pulled a small tablet out of her pocket.

Then, her mind switching to other things, she turned and walked back inside the restaurant.

Ben looked up from the paper. "Did she take our order?" he asked.

"No." Nell watched the screen door to the restaurant swing shut behind the teenager. "I don't imagine life at the Palazolas' is ever dull, especially with Stella around." Nell stirred her coffee and thought about the courage of the Annabelles of the world—single moms raising kids, holding down jobs. Annabelle's husband, Joe, had been a successful swordfish captain until the day his boat and crew were swept out to sea in the middle of a sudden summer storm, leaving his wife with four small children to raise. In the blink of an eye, Annabelle's life was shattered into a million pieces. "I needed to do a one eighty," she had told Nell during those days of shock and forced decision. "The kids had such great needs. And Joe had plans for each one of them—plans that needed money."

So Annabelle buried her grief and took action to honor her husband's dreams. She decided the one thing she did especially well was talk to people and cook eggs. And so Sweet Petunia's was born. Using her family's old Sicilian recipes and ones she made up on the spot, Annabelle and her restaurant became instant Cape Ann favorites, and Nell and Ben found that going more than a week without one of Annabelle's frittatas wasn't a good thing.

"People rebuild their lives in ways we couldn't imagine," Ben said, stepping into her thoughts. "It's what the human spirit is about."

Nell nodded. "It's what Josie is already beginning to do." She looked up and smiled at the Seroogys, neighbors from Sandswept Lane, as they headed for a table at the back of the deck. Her gaze traveled to the table next to them, where Angus McPherron sat alone, as always. His long white hair curled over the edge of a rust-colored V-neck sweater that looked familiar to Nell. It was slightly out of place on the unkempt man whose usual attire was an old army jacket or torn T-shirt. She stared at the sweater from across the deck, bringing the style and stitches into focus. And then she knew where she had seen it. In Birdie's capable hands on several Thursday nights the past spring. In her mind's eye, she could see Birdie working out the pattern and selecting just the right yarn that would be good for chilly mornings. It was a lovely cotton, slightly nubby to the touch but lightweight for the summer. Nell assumed back then that Birdie was knitting it for a nephew or one of her other relatives. But she had guessed wrong. Her diminutive friend was full of surprises—and apparently keeping Angus McPherron warm on chilly mornings was one of them.

Parishioners were starting to stream into Sweet Petunia's from the ten o'clock Mass and Angus was momentarily lost to her view. Nell spotted Father Northcutt sitting down for his usual heaping breakfast of fried oysters and eggs. Nell had talked to him recently about cholesterol, but he had assured her his good cholesterol took care of his bad. "Just like in the celestial realm," he'd said with a wink, and Nell had taken the gentle hint to mind her own business.

Father Northcutt usually ate alone at Sweet Petunia's, too, smiling briefly at passersby but avoiding the eye contact that would welcome conversation. Instead, he focused intently on Annabelle's food, spiced up exactly the way he liked it. But today, absent his usual smile, the good father sat with Margarethe and Tony Framingham. And Nell knew without hearing their words that they were talking about Angie Archer and the horrible way her life had ended. Margarethe was probably offering to help Josie however she could. Tony, across from her, sat still, his head lowered, as the conversation continued between his mother and the priest. Watching him, Nell wished she could read his thoughts. He had been one of the last people to see Angie. Their conversation hadn't been a happy one—and then, just hours later, she'd been murdered.

Beyond the deck, sailboats began weaving their way out of the harbor. The gulls' shrill cries mixed with the sound of motors as two whale-watching boats, packed with people, set out to sea. It was a typical Sea Harbor Sunday, but not typical at all.

Stella emerged through the kitchen door, balancing two heaping platters of herbed spinach frittata in her hands. "Sorry, it got, like, crazy in there. Tommy Porter is here and he's like a rock star, people asking him all sorts of questions about, well, you know, Angie. This is what you ordered, right?" She set the plates down on the table and wiped her hands on a skimpy apron that hung like a hammock from her narrow waist.

Ben looked down at the creamy mountain of eggs on his plate. Thin flakes of parmesan cheese rested on top, and a pile of fresh strawberries, peaches, and mangoes were piled artfully on the side. A thick slice of English muffin with butter dripping off the toasted edges finished off Annabelle's fine presentation. The aroma of cumin and coriander wafted up from the eggs, and Ben assured Stella that yes, indeed, she'd gotten his order just right. Wikked right, he said, using his favorite New England slang.

"There you two are." Birdie came through the swinging screen door and smiled up at Stella. "You look very pretty today, Stella. I think maybe you've added a few pounds to that frame of yours, and it's a good thing. You were too bony, sweetheart. Not a good look." Birdie's words were carried on uneven breaths.

Stella looked at Birdie, unsure whether to thank her or stomp off. Finally she offered a lopsided smile and said, "You sit right there before you fall down, Miss Birdie. You don't look so good. I'll get you some water."

Nell looked up as Stella scurried off. She saw that Birdie was flushed. Her short white crop of hair was damp, as if a fine spray of seawater had cooled her off, and when she brushed her white bangs aside with the back of her hand, Nell could see tiny drops of perspiration above her clear gray eyes.

Birdie poured herself a mug of coffee and pulled out a chair across from Nell.

"You look like you've run a race, Birdie," Nell said, frowning. "Here, have my water." Nell pushed her glass across the table.

"I rode my bike over. And that tiny hill seems to have gotten a tad steeper in recent days." She picked up the glass and took a long swallow.

Nell was relieved to hear that Birdie was riding her bike. Her heart was healthy and strong, according to the doctor, and bicycle riding was just fine. But Birdie's driving didn't merit quite the same report. Even cocky teenagers hugged the inner edge of the street when Birdie drove down Harbor Road in her 1981 Lincoln Town Car. Neighbors stayed out of her way and dogs and cats seemed to flee when the familiar engine revved up and barreled down the hill. But no amount of talking could convince the strong-headed woman to buy herself a small, more manageable car. Ben had tried without success to sell her on the merits of a Corolla or Camry or maybe one of the new hybrids.

Birdie loved her Town Car. It had belonged to Victor Morino, her second husband, and the fragrant, woody aroma of his pipe tobacco still lingered in the leather seat. "Oh, my, if this car could talk, I would be in trouble," she had teased the knitters one Thursday night, her eyes twinkling with mischievous secrets. So Birdie continued to drive all eighteen-plus feet of the long elegant car around the hilly environs of Sea Harbor, and Nell recited a daily prayer that they wouldn't someday regret not taking charge of the situation more forcefully.

Birdie set the water glass down and eyed Nell's eggs. "Annabelle is trying something new, I see."

"It's good, Birdie. Want a taste?"

Birdie wrinkled her nose. "I don't need new and different.

In fact, what I want is the old and familiar. And that means a peaceful Sea Harbor summer. Angelina's murder is changing the texture of the town. It creeps into everything, making people look at one another suspiciously. I know you thought there was something fishy from the beginning, Nell, but I don't like this kind of awfulness in our town."

"None of us do, Birdie," Ben said. "But it will go away. People will move on."

Birdie's smile had disappeared and she waved one pointed finger at Ben, then Nell. "I know one thing for sure. People in Sea Harbor are good people. Angie should never have come here; that's as clear as the nose on your face. She needed a bigger world than this."

"Birdie, how can you say that? This was Angie's town, too. And Josie loved having her daughter back, that much I know for sure."

"You're right, I guess. I just want so badly for it all to go away. And no matter what you say about Angie enjoying her job and liking it here—she never seemed settled to me. Look at her apartment. Was that settled? It looked like she was ready to flee in the middle of the night—just as I predicted. And now this. None of it makes any sense, not the official patched-together scene of what happened that night or anything else."

Nell was silent.

"Well," Birdie said brightly, forking her fingers through her hair, "I think we need to get a little more organized, Nell."

Ben looked up from his paper and frowned. "You're going to let the police do their job, Birdie. This is murder we're talking about, not poachers or lost pets."

"Ben Endicott," Birdie said, her hands flying in the air and her face breaking out in delight. "Are you suddenly becoming a fuddy-duddy? Since when do you have to protect us?"

Stella brought a platter of eggs—over easy—and set it down in front of Birdie, then scurried off.

"Now, if this isn't telepathic service, I don't know what is," Birdie said, smothering her English muffin with butter and strawberry jam. "What if I ever decided to order something different?"

"Annabelle would know," Nell said. "I think she knows all things."

"And that one probably does, too, the way she listens to each table." She nodded toward Stella, who was now filling Tony Framingham's coffee cup, her head leaning just close enough to hear the flow of conversation.

"I guess it's natural to be curious," Nell said.

"It's more than that," Birdie said. "Look at her sweet face. Love-struck. She thinks Tony Framingham hung the moon."

Nell looked over and saw that Birdie was absolutely right. Stella's smile wasn't about her mother's amazing spinach frittatas or the table conversation. It was all about Tony.

And Tony was oblivious. His head was turned toward the water, and he seemed to be looking beyond the white sails and the sleek double-deck whale-watching boats headed out to the open sea. He was oblivious to his mother's conversation with Father Northcutt, and for certain he was unaware that Stella hovered longingly at his elbow.

Nell wondered again what was going through Tony's head. From what Archie Brandley said that night, Tony had been harsh with Angie. And where had he taken off to in that big orange car of his?

"I wonder what the good father is talking so animatedly about," Birdie said, swallowing a forkful of eggs.

"Maybe they're discussing some kind of memorial fund for Angie," Nell said. "That might help ease Josie's grief."

"And make Father Northcutt feel better, too."

"You should talk, Birdie Favazza," Nell said. "You've paid for more pews in that church than you'd have time to occupy in two lifetimes."

"Time or whatever," Birdie said. "We all get spiritual in our own way, that's what I say. But he who asks shall receive. And the padre does a nice job of asking."

"And receiving," Ben said. "But he's a good man. It's part of his job."

"That's right, Ben," Birdie agreed. "And I see it as a part of my job, too, to fill the coffers."

"You're a good person, Birdie—in spite of yourself." Ben said.

"Sometimes," Birdie said, a twinkle in her eye. "Sometimes not."

When they got up to leave a short while later, Father Northcutt was still engaged in conversation with Margarethe. Tony had quit pretending he was a part of the conversation and stood alone at the railing a short distance away, his attention elsewhere.

A short distance from Tony's elbow, Sal and Beatrice Scaglia sat with the Brandleys, platters of frittata and cups of steaming coffee in front of them. Beatrice's small hands played with her pearls as her voice rose and fell in animated cadence. *She's probably telling them how she single-handedly cleaned out Angie's apartment for Josie,* Nell thought. She looked over at Sal—dressed today in a khaki suit and pink-striped tie. Beatrice picked out his clothes, Nell suspected. Somehow Sal didn't seem to be the pink-striped type. He was good-looking in an ordinary sort of way and probably interesting, too. But as usual, he sat quietly next to his wife, allowing her the full stage. He looked sad today, she thought. Sad and a little anxious.

Their eyes met as Nell walked by, and she smiled at him.

But instead of returning her smile, Sal Scaglia put his napkin down, pushed his chair back, and followed Nell to the restaurant deck door.

"Angie Archer's murder . . ." he whispered into Nell's back. She stopped and turned around.

"Yes, Sal?" she said, waiting for the familiar expression of dismay at a beautiful young woman's tragic and cruel death.

But instead of words, Sal Scaglia's long, quiet face was filled with a terrible kind of angst Nell wouldn't have thought him capable of. He opened his mouth to speak.

At that precise moment, Stella Palazola, carrying a glass of juice in one hand and a platter of eggs in the other, hurried through the screen door. The heel of her clunky sandal caught slightly against the doorsill, and before Nell or Sal could move aside, the tall glass of freshly squeezed orange juice tipped from the tray and poured like spring rain down Sal Scaglia's pink-striped tie.

Chapter 13

*N*ell slipped out of her skirt and pulled on a pair of cotton capris and a sleeveless blouse. Her friends joked that surely she'd done something to remove that flap of extra skin that seemed to appear by magic on upper arms when one turned sixty. Nell had her mother to thank, she supposed, for her tight bone structure, prominent cheekbones, and firm upper arms. But she suspected she'd wear what she wanted to, no matter how many flaps of skin waved when she walked. Comfort was usually the determining factor in Nell's wardrobe.

Downstairs in the airy kitchen, all was quiet save for the bugling of the herring gulls on the beach across the back road. Nell straightened up the family room, folding the scattered pages of newspaper and piling them on the coffee table. Ben was a news junky, and the *Sea Harbor Gazette* wasn't nearly enough to satisfy his lust—the *Globe* and *New York Times* cluttered their drive with such regularity that Nell knew Johnny the paper boy's birthday and favorite CDs. She collected her knitting from the couch and slipped it into a large roomy bag.

After the bountiful breakfast at Annabelle's and peculiar encounter with Sal Scaglia, Ben and Nell had left the restaurant, insisting they give Birdie and her bike a ride home. The three spent the ten-minute drive exploring the possibilities of what Sal had meant to say—but the quiet man's motivation escaped them.

"Did he know Angie?" Birdie had asked. Practically every-one in Sea Harbor knew everyone else, but that didn't mean they had spoken or been friends. And Nell could think of nothing that would have put Sal and Angie in the same room at the same time.

"I think Sal is a sensitive man," Nell said. "Maybe he was just expressing the helplessness and dismay so many of us feel. And Beatrice would certainly have been dissecting the crime over breakfast, lunch, and dinner."

The explanation didn't sit well with any of them, but it was enough to allow them to move on with their day.

Ben had plans to help Ham and Jane work on an old Hinck-ley sailboat that they had invested in. And maybe they'd get in a quick sail. "I need to work off that sour cream Annabelle piles on top of her eggs," he said.

Nell agreed. She watched Ben's diet carefully, but Sundays were not about cholesterol, and Nell turned the other way. En-couraging Ben to exercise made her feel better about it. Sailing was therapy for him—the ocean expanse, the breezes and salt air calmed Ben in remarkable ways when worry or concerns began to crowd his chest and mind. "It puts the world right," he told Nell. "At least for a while." Angie's murder didn't escape Ben's thoughts easily, and a sailing trip with dear friends would be a welcome reprieve for a few hours.

"And I'm sailing off to the Studio to get Izzy's help on this scarf she started me on," Nell told Ben.

Nell considered herself a good knitter. Her stitches were steady and even, and her seams not too bulky. And she was fast, sometimes finishing a strawberry hat for a baby during the course of a single board meeting. But she still needed Izzy's help some-times. When it came to knitting, Izzy had that intuitive something, like a photographer who captures magic in a cloud shot, or who knows instinctively when the light is just right over the water.

Izzy could look at a sweater or sock or hat, and in seconds, zero in on the problem—and fix it.

And Nell needed Izzy's help today or she'd never finish this scarf in time for the Framinghams' benefit next week.

But Nell had another reason for walking down to the village shops, one best kept from Ben. There were too many loose ends in this murder scenario to be comfortable.

Just before he left, Ben had talked to the police chief again, and he told Ben they'd found nothing around the harbor except the sighting of two guys who'd been hanging around the yacht club. Some cars had been broken into, and several women had complained of being bothered on the beach. They'd given descriptions of the men and the reports had indicated they'd moved on to Rockport, Newburyport, up into New Hampshire. They were probably up in the wild woods of Maine by now, Jerry had told Ben. But they'd keep looking.

Nell listened to Ben in silence. Angie's murderer was not in Maine. He was probably right here in Sea Harbor. And the sooner they figured out who stole the key to the apartment—and the other inconsistencies of the last few days of Angie's life—the better.

Nell hoped Cass might be at the shop, too. She often spent Sundays around Harbor Road, drinking mochas at Coffee's or sitting on the pier with a book. It was the one day she relaxed, and she certainly needed some of that. Between the lobster thefts and Angie's death, Cass had not had a stellar week. Her talk of spending the night on the beach, trying to catch the poachers—with a murderer walking around—was disturbing to Nell. She hoped to talk to her about it.

The sea yarn was still on display in Izzy's window, and as Nell approached, she saw people lingering in front of it, lured like kids to cotton candy.

Nell passed them by and went in the knitting shop door, held open today to catch the breeze.

Although the Seaside Knitting Studio was open on Sundays during the summer season, Izzy never worked the floor herself. Instead, she left the front counter in the hands of Mae's twin sixteen-year-old nieces, Rose and Jillian, whose giggles spilled over the skeins of yarn and who delighted customers with their teen talk and enthusiasm. Mae had taught them how to knit as soon as they were old enough to hold needles without poking out their eyes, and they were now a surprising resource for the summer people when they needed a project for their television-less cottages or long afternoons at the beach. And, Mae told Nell, it added some needed structure to their summer. She'd heard enough of Izzy's wild stories of summer fun beyond her aunt and uncle's watchful eyes to not be wary.

Nell walked through the front door and smiled at Jillian, whose ears were plugged with tiny white circles connected to her iPod. She was bouncing behind the counter to sounds only she could hear, but managed a quick wave as her head moved back and forth to the music. Nell could see Rose in the baby room, helping a customer pick out pale pink fingering yarn for a newborn-size sweater. Skeins of cashmere in pink and lime green and buttery soft yellow were piled on the table like a rich ice cream sundae, and Nell resisted the urge to wander in and scoop them up.

Izzy was in the back room, sitting cross-legged on the floor, poring over photographs spread out in front of her. The windows were wide open, and a breeze rustled the newspapers spread out on the couch. In the background, soft strains of an old Beatles CD played. And, to Nell's delight, Cass was hunched down beside Izzy, her dark hair falling down over her face as she looked at the photographs.

Izzy had on her dark-rimmed glasses, a sign that whatever she was looking at deserved her full attention. She nibbled on her bottom lip, her face pulled into a frown and her eyes following Cass's pointing finger.

"What're you two up to?" Nell asked. She set her knitting bag on the floor beside the table and walked over to Purl. The kitten, now a comfortable and prized resident of the Seaside Knitting Studio, was curled up on the seat beneath the open window, her fur slightly ruffled by the breeze. "Hello there, sweet Purl," she said, scratching the kitty behind its ears. "This is pretty close to heaven for you, isn't it?" Balls of waste yarn in all colors of the rainbow dotted the cushion and floor.

Purl rubbed her tiny head against the edge of Nell's hand.

"Nell, look at these," Izzy said. She waved Nell over with her hand.

Nell leaned over the top of Izzy's head and looked down at a series of dark photos. She recognized water and lobster buoys—and darkness.

Cass stood up and leaned back against the edge of the table. "I took these last night, Nell, down at the breakwater."

Nell froze. "You what?"

"Don't worry, Nell, no one attacked me. In fact no one even tried to pick me up."

"Cass, what were you thinking? There's a murderer walking around this town and you're spending the night on the beach?" Nell felt the color rise in her cheeks.

"I was safe, Nell. Shush," Cass said. "And I wasn't alone. I planned to do it alone . . . well . . . before Angie was killed. But it's different now. At least until they find the guy. A group of us who have traps in that area got together and we set up some cameras."

Cass pointed to a photograph in the middle of the group. "See?"

"It's a dark night picture," Nell said.

"Oh, look harder." Cass shook her head in exasperation and leaned over Izzy, pointing to one of the pictures. "See that shadow on the left—over near the edge of the breakwater?"

Nell shook her head. "Cass, the whole photo is a shadow. What should I be looking for?"

"The poacher."

Nell frowned. "Someone saw him?"

"We decided to foil the thief—hoist him by his own petard sort of thing."

"And how are you going to do that?"

"Safely, Nell. We waited for a while in the shadows, near the edge of the breakwater where no one could see us."

Nell could visualize that easily enough. The breakwater rose well over ten to fifteen feet up, depending on the tide, and along the base, at the water's edge, there were slabs one could perch on and not be seen from the top—and maybe not from the shore. The top where Angie spent the last minutes of her life.

Cass raked a hand through her thick hair and continued. "We fastened the camera in a crevice between two slabs of granite and went home."

Nell released a small breath of relief.

"I went back at dawn to pick up the camera before joggers or divers came out."

Nell pulled out her glasses and put them on. She looked closer at the photo. It looked like all the others—dark, with small shadowy glimpses of light on the water and reflecting off an occasional buoy. "I'm sorry, Cass, but I don't see anything." She lifted the photo closer and squinted at the dark image.

"There's a shadow, down near the middle of the breakwater, right at its base. I think that's one of them. That's probably where they slip into the water. He probably had a black wet suit on so it's hard to see."

"Did you check your traps this morning?"

Cass nodded that she had. "Not a lobster in sight. Roy Whitford said he got a few—but they were all eggers so he had to toss them back."

Nell looked at the photo again. The shadows took shape the longer she looked at them, but it would take considerable effort to form them into distinguishable humans. She imagined someone—the poacher—hidden down in the shadow of the wall, waiting to slip in.

Cass lifted Purl to her chest, tucking her under her chin. "What are you thinking, Nell?"

Nell rubbed her eyes. So many unknowns. "I'm thinking about your poacher, Cass. Maybe that's him, right there in the photo. And above, on the top, that's where two people stood together and talked the night Angie died. Had a drink. And then one of them fell noiselessly—or maybe with a splash?—into the water. Was that figure there that night? Could Cass's poacher have seen what happened to Angie?"

Izzy and Cass were still and only the sound of Purl's purring stirred the air.

Finally Cass spoke. "The poachers aren't there every night, I don't think," she said, Nell's hypothesis taking root in her mind. "But you're right, Nell. If someone had been there that night, they could have seen something. They *would* have seen something."

"But surely they'd tell the police," Izzy said.

"Maybe they have. And maybe that's why they're concentrating on someone traveling through," Cass said.

"Well, I don't think looking outside Sea Harbor is going to unearth anything but tourists visiting New Hampshire and Maine," Nell said. She sat down next to Izzy at the table and took her needles out of her bag. "I rack my brain to come up with possible motives for killing Angie, and I can't come up with anything. She irritated some people, but that's certainly no motive. But there was something going on in her life that we didn't know about, I'm convinced of that."

Cass scooped up the photos from the floor and pulled up a chair. Purl followed close behind, crawling up Cass's pant leg and onto her lap.

"Angie affected people in so many different ways," Nell went on. She told Cass and Izzy about the odd encounter she'd had that morning at Annabelle's with Sal Scaglia. "I didn't even know Angie knew Sal, yet he was distressed about something," Nell said. "It was strange, not quite right somehow. When Beatrice dragged him over to Angie's apartment while we packed he seemed removed. But today he was emotional."

"Beatrice didn't seem particularly distressed," Izzy observed. "Her concern seemed more about preventing future murders on the breakwater. As if without her help, there'd be one a month."

"That's what she does," Nell said. "She plans for the future of Sea Harbor, so I guess it's not so unusual she approached a murder that way."

"I wonder if the police have talked to the Scaglias," Cass said.

"What would they ask?" Nell wondered. Sal and Beatrice were probably like a lot of other people in Sea Harbor. Decent people who were curious, interested, and even sad about Angie's death, but felt it in a removed way. A protective empathy. *If I feel bad for Josie Archer, then it won't happen to my family.*

Izzy got up from the table and returned almost immediately with a pitcher of ice tea and bowl of lemons. "Sun tea time—and maybe a brief respite from distressing thoughts." She pulled Nell's sea-yarn scarf from the bag and spread it across the table. Shades of greens and blues and tiny threads of gold ran together like a rippling stream lit with sunlight. "Aunt Nell, this scarf is beautiful."

"And very unfinished." Nell sipped her tea and sat back, giving Izzy free rein.

"What's the problem?" Izzy looked more closely and touched the scarf with the tips of her fingers. "I knew this would be gorgeous. I want to use it as an example in my lace class." She picked up the end of the long scarf, now nearly three feet long. "The colors are perfect for you. You'll wear that sexy black dress with the scooped neckline, and wrap this airy piece around your neck. We'll add long strands at the end to give it even more length."

"That's just like you, Izzy. You're seeing the beauty, not the flaws," Nell said. "And that's very nice. But look closely." Nell held the end of the scarf up to the light. "The needle slipped out, and I lost three or four rows. With all those yarn overs, I can't capture the stitches I've dropped. They disappear when I touch them."

Purl jumped up on the table and eyed the scarf. She reached one tiny paw out to survey the damage.

"No, baby," Izzy said, abruptly pulling her back. She slid the scarf from Purl's reach and examined it carefully. Where there should have been a knitting needle, there was a row of scattered stitches and patches of airy space formed from the yarn overs.

"How many rows did you drop?" Izzy pulled her glasses from the top of her head and slipped them back on. She sat down at the table, crisscrossing her legs beneath her like a five-year-old, and picked up the scarf, her fingertips studying the pattern as she surveyed the damage.

She looks like she's reading Braille, Nell thought, as she watched Izzy's fingertips read the pattern and explore the mistakes.

"Don't watch her, Nell," Cass said. "She says it makes her nervous, but I think it's because she doesn't want us to learn her secrets."

Izzy dipped into the basket in the center of the table and pulled out a long darning needle. "Secrets, my foot. I don't want you to watch me because I make things up as I go—and I want you to think it's all carefully planned." She pushed a handful of hair back from her face. "I love the airiness of this, Nell. You'll be the belle of the ball." Her fingers worked quickly, first pulling out one more row of knitting, then carefully working the needle into each stitch and yarn over with the long spare needle.

"You need to put a lifeline in here. It will save you a lot of grief."

Nell watched Izzy replace the narrow darning needle with her number six, then quickly purled a solid row. After that, she slipped a string of dental floss through the darning needle, and through each stitch in the row. *A lifeline.* How she wished Angie had had a simple lifeline.

"There," Izzy said, finishing the row and handed the needles and half-finished scarf back to Nell. "Good as new. Move the floss up every now and then, and at least you won't lose much. This yarn is so silky—and with all the lacy spaces, it's easy to lose your way."

Nell took the scarf back and surveyed Izzy's repair. "You're a miracle worker, sweetie. Thanks."

Cass watched the process from the window seat. Purl had re-joined her and purred contentedly on her lap. "Too complicated for me. I feel very secure in my garter scarf mode. Knit, purl, bind off."

"You better watch your back, Cass," Izzy said. "Birdie is tired of watching you knit scarves. She's threatening a makeover, I guess you'd say."

"Nope, not me. Knitting scarves lets me be here on Thursday nights. That's all I care about. Friends and Nell's amazing food. And I think there are still a few lobster buddies who haven't been blessed with a scarf. I've a long way to go before I have to learn how to work thumbs and sleeves."

"Don't count on it, is all I'm saying," Izzy said.

Nell folded the scarf and put it back in her bag. "How's Pete doing since Friday night?"

Cass shrugged. "He can hardly get his arms around the fact that Angie was murdered, Nell. It eats him up inside."

"He thinks he should have prevented it," Nell said. "Even though that makes no sense."

Cass nodded. "But he went out fishing today, kind of a bus-man's holiday for him, but I was glad he got away."

"By himself?"

"No. He ran into Tony Framingham at the Gull a couple nights ago—I guess the night he drank too much. Tony suggested they go fishing. He has a fancy new boat."

"That's odd," Izzy said. "Somehow I can't quite see Tony and Pete as fishing buddies."

Nell listened to the exchange and rubbed her bare arms against a sudden chill. The expresson she'd seen on Tony's face just a few hours ago wasn't the kind that spoke of a pleasant afternoon with a buddy. He was deep in thought, looking over the sea as if it would relieve him of a burden.

"What would Pete and Tony have in common?" Izzy wondered out loud.

Nell looked around for her purse, then walked over to give Purl a pat before she went to meet Ben for a Sunday fish fry at the Ocean's Edge. She thought about Izzy's question and the answer brought her no peace.

What Pete and Tony had in common was as obvious to Nell as Cass's concern for her brother. What Pete and Tony had in common was Angie Archer—and the fact that they were both with her the night she died.

Chapter 14

*N*ell slipped her knitting bag over one shoulder and left Izzy and Cass to help Mae's nieces close up the shop. She had a half hour before meeting Ben. And that might be just enough time to say hello to Archie Brandley. She wondered if he remembered any more about the night Angie had sat in the loft, arguing with Tony.

Nell paused at the bookstore's open front door and peered into the cool interior. Several customers were standing in line at the checkout counter, and Nell could see several more sitting in the reading area and wandering around the display tables. It was almost closing time, and she could see it wouldn't be a good time to chat—Archie would be busy winding things up for the day. Besides, Nell wasn't at all sure what she'd say to the shop owner. Archie probably didn't hear the whole conversation between Angie and Tony from the lower level, but he heard something, she knew that. And she and Archie had been friends for longer than Angie had lived. They could talk about most anything. Even the night that Angie had been killed.

The night that Angie had been killed. Nell felt a shiver pass up her spine and settle between her shoulder blades. That's what that ordinary Thursday had become. One of those moments in time that freezes and takes on a life of its own. *The night that . . . "Where were you that night?"*

"Those look like serious thoughts, Nell."

Nell looked up into the open face of Sam Perry. He had come from the bookstore and carried Archie's signature blue-and-white-striped bag. A camera bag was slung over one shoulder.

"Hi, Sam," Nell said, slightly startled that someone had been looking at her and she hadn't been aware of his presence.

"That was a wonderful dinner Friday night. Thanks for including me in the mix."

"It didn't end so wonderfully. But Ben said you were a big help with Pete. Thank you, Sam."

"Pete's a good guy. Most people around here are. I never imagined I'd like small-town living, but there's something oddly comforting in having the bookstore owner know what I had for dinner last Friday night."

Nell looked down at the Brandley Bookstore sack in his hand and laughed. Small-town living wasn't for everyone. But the familiarity and sameness suited her and Ben, too. And the pleasurable things about living in Sea Harbor far overshadowed the things that sometimes were difficult, when folks not only knew your favorite meals but when you got a speeding ticket, or in an argument with a spouse, or missed out on a promotion.

"Archie knows everything. I think his store has its own set of ears sometimes. Did you find some interesting reading?"

Sam nodded. "Some books about the area that Ben recommended to me. *Hammers on Stone,* those kinds of books. The more I know about something I'm photographing, the more focused my images seem to be. I'm not sure how all that works, but it seems to be true."

Nell stepped slightly to the side as George Gideon walked down the street, his familiar backpack slung over one shoulder. He turned into the alley next to the bookstore and lifted one hand in hello. His hair was slicked back and he wore a heavy gold chain around his neck.

Nell returned the greeting and introduced the security guard to Sam.

"Gideon tried to keep the Harbor Road shops secure," she said.

Gideon's response was gruff, as if he thought Nell was chiding him. "I don't hear complaints. I work hard. Keep things in order."

Order, Nell knew, meant making sure security lights were replaced and doors stayed locked. Gideon was strong, his arms muscular, and he had a broad chest—but Nell suspected it came from activities other than keeping things secure. "I meant only that with Angie's death, it feels a little less safe around the harbor," Nell said. "And we're glad you're on the job, Gideon."

Gideon nodded but kept his body stiff. He looked up at the closed apartment windows. "She was a looker," he said.

Nell frowned, suddenly uncomfortable.

An odd smile flitted across Gideon's face, his eyes still on the apartment. As Nell watched him, the smile morphed into a smirk. "She had a way about her, little Miss Archer did. I miss seeing her around."

Nell bit back the words that sprang to her lips. Gideon made her uncomfortable. When the shopkeepers hired him, she'd suggested they might find someone less gruff. But she had no real reason, only instinct, to object. She agreed with Izzy that he was better than no one. And he was the only one who applied for the job, Izzy'd said.

Gideon shifted beneath the weight of his backpack. "You don't need to worry yourself," he said to Nell. "I watch over Izzy good."

The words had an edge to them that caused hairs to lift on Nell's arms.

She saw that he was watching her, playing with her, enjoying her nervousness.

"So for now, you can count on me. But maybe not for long."

"Oh?" Nell said.

Gideon looked over his shoulder as if someone might be hiding in the shadows, listening. He turned back to Nell and Sam and lowered his voice. "Yes, ma'am. My ship is comin' in. Not quite here, but it's on its way." He laughed as if he had said something funny, and then, with one large hand, he shifted the weight of his backpack and sauntered down the alley toward the water.

Nell watched him walk away. "He's a strange man," she said to Sam. "I can never quite connect with him. Sometimes I wonder what he carries in that big pack of his. I hope it's not a bottle that gets him through the long night rather than patrolling the shops. Someone got in Angie's apartment quite easily without him knowing it. Frankly, I wouldn't be at all sad if he moved on to another job."

"It sounds like that's what he's planning," Sam said, watching Gideon stop at the edge of the water. "I know you worry about it, Nell—especially with your niece's store being here. But I've seen a million Gideons. Cocky and probably not the kind of guy you'd trust house-sitting or bringing in your mail. But harmless in the long run. And I have to tell you, coming from big cities, this little town seems like one of the safest places I've been."

"I've always felt that way, too. But Angie's murder has changed things."

"But it's a *good* place, Nell. I feel that, and I can see it in my photos. In some cultures, people think a photograph steals a part of the soul. I don't know about that, but I do think photographs glimpse a part of the soul. And the ones I've taken here in Sea Harbor show me that good, decent people live here."

Nell felt some comfort in Sam's words. It was one of the reasons she and Ben had moved here—the decent people. "You're right, Sam. But the disconcerting thing is that someone in the mix murdered Angie. Until we figure out some things, it won't be right."

Sam nodded. "Sure. I can see Izzy thinks about it, too."

"Izzy moves methodically. Her stint as a lawyer taught her that. She's about putting puzzle pieces together carefully, just like the beautiful pieces she knits."

"Yes, that's Izzy. I think my coming to Sea Harbor jarred her methodical ways. Made her a little uncomfortable, a chunk of her childhood coming back."

"Well, she won't hold that against you forever."

"Good to hear."

"But you're right that the unrest here bothers her. And even more so because we knew Angie the way we did. It brings it so close to home."

"So that's Izzy's store?" Sam nodded toward the small shop with the wide green awnings over the windows. "It looks like her. I think I'd have picked it out even if you hadn't mentioned it."

"People love her shop. They walk through those doors and even if they've never held a knitting needle, they sit and stay a while. It's magical and cozy—very much like its owner."

Sam continued to look at the shop, the flowering hibiscus plants on each side of the front door, planted in large earthenware pots, the colorful window display. "Jack said Izzy didn't stay with the law firm long," he said.

"No."

Sam's silence told Nell he was hoping she'd say more, maybe fill him in on the abrupt move Izzy had made that had disturbed her family. Instead, she smiled and said, "And that's another thing about small-town people, Sam. Even if they know your secrets, they don't always share them readily."

The crooked smile she'd seen before came back. "I shouldn't be prying, anyway, Nell, but I always liked Iz." Sam looked up at the windows over the store. They were closed tightly. "I wonder what she'll do with the apartment now."

Nell nodded. "I'm not sure. Renting it helps with the mortgage, but I don't think she's thinking about that right now, not after all that's happened."

"I can understand that. I wonder if she'd consider something less formal than a rent arrangement. Maybe it wouldn't seem so intrusive right now. Like letting an old friend stay there for a couple months. But for money."

Nell was still. She bit back the "of course she would" answer that sprang to her lips. Nell had no idea how Izzy would feel about Sam staying above the shop. And the fact that she herself would sleep better shouldn't play into the decision. *Back off, Nell,* she heard Ben say.

"Ham and Jane are putting me up for the summer," Sam went on. "They're great hosts. But their place is small, and I know a body as big as mine is an imposition on their privacy, though they'd never say so. I looked at a cottage south of town, but this is closer to the galleries and the art academy classes."

"I don't know," Nell said finally, her voice neutral. "You could mention it to her, I suppose."

"I might do that." Sam looked at the knitting studio again, then told Nell he'd better follow Gideon's example and be off to work. He wanted to hit the breakwater before sunset and take some photos of the fishermen and night divers. The light was nearly right. "Lesson plans," he said with a smile.

Nell touched Sam on the sleeve of his T-shirt as he started to turn away. "Sam Perry," she said, "you are the tonic I needed today. In several different ways. Thank you."

"Those are mighty nice words coming from such a lovely woman, Nell. You've added a nice note to my day, too." He tipped his head, shallow dimples forming in his smile, and walked toward his car.

Nell watched him climb into the Volvo. He turned, waved once, then made a U-turn in the middle of the street and headed up the windy road toward the north-end beaches. She watched him until he turned the bend that took him out of sight.

Her eyes moved back to the open parking space. With the Volvo gone, a stone bench in front of the framing store just opposite the Seaside Knitting Studio came into view.

Nell stared. Sitting on the bench, his tie removed and a knit shirt replacing the dress shirt, was Sal Scaglia. His back was bent, his elbows on his knees, and sunglasses shielded his eyes. But there was no doubt that what he was staring at was the apartment above Izzy's shop. Angie's apartment.

Nell lifted one hand, a slight wave, then started across the street to talk to him.

But before she could reach the other side, Sal noticed her approach, rose abruptly from the bench, and hurried down the street in the opposite direction.

Chapter 15

*M*onday dawned gray and rainy on the Cape, the kind of day that blanketed the beaches in quiet and brought bustle and activity into the village. Shopping and eating were the activities du jour—restaurant owners rejoiced and the crews of whale-watching boats stayed home and played with their kids.

Ben Endicott sat at the kitchen table, watching his wife check her calendar for the week. A light rain fell onto the kitchen sky-light, the pings rhythmic and oddly comforting. "Will you miss me?" he asked.

Nell looked up. She was quiet for a moment, as if contem-plating the question, and then she shook her head. But her smile, her eyes, and the lazy look she gave him said otherwise. She and Ben had awakened early when the rain began, and they had come down to the kitchen for coffee and cereal late. Very late. Of course she would miss him.

But in spite of the house seeming twice as big without Ben in it for the week, sometimes dismissing the routine was required when two people shared meals, a house, and a bed. And Nell had a busy week.

"Your brother isn't all that practical," Nell said. "Why he picked Colorado for the company board retreat when everyone lives in New England is a mystery to me. Such a burden—all that travel," she teased. "You'll be back Friday?"

"In time to grill the dinner of your life. Plan on plump sil-very trout." Ben got up and refilled Nell's coffee mug. "*Colorado* trout."

"Of course," Nell said. "All work and no play."

"And you know we Endicotts are never dull." Ben kissed Nell on the top of her head, still damp from her shower. "And now I need to pack, my love," he said, and headed for the stairs.

After Ben drove off in the airport limo, Nell looked at her cal-endar in earnest. She kept a Sierra Club calendar hanging in the kitchen, with squares big enough to hold all their events. "Use your computer calendar," Izzy had said. "Or get a BlackBerry. Or an iPhone. Be cool, Aunt Nell. You certainly have enough meet-ings to warrant an organizing toy." But though her computer was well used and she'd be lost without e-mail, Nell liked seeing the dates written in her own handwriting and knowing at a glance where she was supposed to be. She didn't want to power up her laptop each time or discover she'd forgotten to recharge the bat-tery. And she considered the handheld devices as simply intru-sive. The thought of something in her pocket sending her e-mail messages as she jogged along the beach or hiked in Ravenswood Park was not appealing. Sometimes aloneness was good.

Nell checked meetings and appointments, then started her daily to-do list. The week held board meetings—the arts council and Historical Society—meetings that would allow her to speak her piece, guide grant endeavors, but mostly to sit quietly, lis-ten dutifully, and work on her sea-yarn scarf. Today's meeting over in Gloucester was with another child advocacy group that needed some advice, and then she'd come back and drop in on Izzy's Frogging with Friends class. "The enthusiastic ripping of stitches" was how Izzy described it on her Web site. Nell was de-termined to learn how to pull herself out of her mistakes and not have to depend on Izzy each time.

But mostly she needed to talk to Izzy or Cass about Pete.

A phone message from Cass the night before had disturbed Nell, but it had been too late to return the call when she and Ben got home. Hopefully Izzy would have more details.

After his fishing trip, Pete had spent a few hours at the police station, Cass had said. And it hadn't been by choice.

Nell's meeting in Gloucester was over shortly before noon, and she walked out of the building feeling invigorated and proud—and for a few hours she pushed thoughts of Angie's murder to the back of her mind. Cape Ann was a good place with good people, and groups like this were a testimony to that. The child advocacy group was planning an after-school enrichment series for children in low-income families. Seed money had come from several grants Nell helped funnel through the system, and planning was in full force.

Nell found herself smiling as she walked down Main Street toward her car and the short drive back to Sea Harbor. And people passing her smiled back.

A tapping on a storefront window startled Nell. She stopped and looked toward the sound.

"Nell, darlin'," a round, flushed face in the window of Sugar Magnolia's Café mouthed to her. And the small hand beside the face beckoned her in. It wasn't a choice, as was Mary Halloran's way. *Come in now,* was what she was saying.

Nell checked her watch. She had plenty of time before Izzy's class, and seeing Mary Halloran was something she'd been wanting to do for days anyway. Cass and Pete's worries would have passed to her by now, no matter how they tried to protect their mother. Besides, she had settled for coffee and a banana earlier in the day, and her body was more than ready for something substantial.

Nell smiled, nodded back to the bobbing silver head in the window, and turned into the restaurant.

The Gloucester breakfast and lunch restaurant always seemed to be crowded, and today was no exception. But somehow, Cass and Pete's diminutive mother had commandeered the choice window table with a view of everyone who went up or down Main Street. A table that easily held six. And there was one of her.

"Sit, Nell," Mary said.

Mary Halloran was a small woman, but her lively Irish eyes lit up rooms. Today she sat alone, and her smiling face was pinched, her eyes tired. A pineapple fritter and platter of eggs Benedict sat in front of her, untouched.

"Have you seen Pete or Catherine?" Mary asked before Nell had completely settled herself in the chair.

"Not today, Mary. But I got a message from Cass last night." She shook out her napkin and put it on her lap. How much Mary knew about Pete's troubles wasn't clear.

"So she told you that Pete may be in trouble," Mary said. "They don't want me to know, of course. But how could I not know? I am Pete's mother. They made him come down to the police station, Nell. My sweet Pete, who wouldn't hurt a slug."

"Mary, they're talking to people who knew Angie, that's all," Nell said. "That's normal in a situation like this." Nell knew her words lacked conviction. She wished now that she had called Cass back, no matter what the hour. At least she would know firsthand what she was talking about.

Mary picked at her fritter with the tip of her fork. "You're right. And Pete doesn't have anything to do with Angie's death."

"Of course not, Mary. Pete is one of the gentlest, kindest young men I know." The thought of Pete doing anything with date-rape drugs was so ludicrous, Nell couldn't hang on to it for more than a second.

The waitress appeared and scribbled down Nell's request for the quesadilla Magnolia and a glass of ice tea. "Don't worry about

Pete, Mary," she said as the young girl walked off. "He'll be fine. That's how you raised him."

"I know that. Deep down I know that. But it's disturbing, Nell. You have to know it is."

Nell nodded. It was disturbing to all of them. They needed closure to Angie's death. And that meant figuring out who murdered her. It was simple in its enormity. Just find out who did it. Until they knew that, the suspicions and innuendoes would creep into their lives and hurt people she cared about. And that simply wasn't acceptable.

"I didn't have anything against Angie Archer," Mary said. "Pete liked her. I know that. And how could she not love my Pete? But it wasn't a forever kind of thing, and Peter knew that. He knew her job wasn't going well, and he knew she'd soon be leaving here."

"I thought she was doing a good job at the Historical Society," Nell said.

"I don't know for a fact that she wasn't. But Angie told Pete she'd be leaving soon. She wanted him to know that." Mary took a bite of her eggs. "The girl was at least honest."

Nell was glad she had run into Mary like this. Mary clearly needed to talk. And she shouldn't be sitting here alone worrying about her son.

Mary swallowed her eggs, took a drink of coffee, and continued. "So I thought, Nell, that maybe Angie thought she was going to get fired."

Nell sat back in her chair while the waitress set down her quesadilla. It was a perfect golden tan, steamy and aromatic, with small pieces of green apple, red onion, and grapes swimming in melted Monterey Jack cheese. Enough, Nell thought, to see her though the day—and maybe evening, too.

"If that's true, Mary," Nell said, "it's the first I've heard of it."

But it wasn't the first time she heard rumors that Angie might be leaving town. Jane had mentioned it, and Birdie, of course, had always suspected Angie wasn't home to stay. But telling Pete that she'd be leaving soon somehow added a new dimension to the rumors. For all Cass's doubts, she was convinced Angie, at the least, considered Pete a close friend.

"Did Pete know where Angie was going?"

Mary shook her head. Her hoop earrings jingled with the movement. "But I suspect he was hoping she'd ask him to go with her. That wasn't going to happen. I knew that. Mothers just know."

"Pete wouldn't have left Cass in the lurch with the lobster business," Nell said. Though she wasn't entirely sure that was true. Pete's feelings for Angie were intense.

"Catherine certainly needs Pete now, especially with these awful poachers creating havoc. I have half a mind to try to catch them myself."

"Well, they aren't making Cass's life easy, that's for sure." Nell suspected that no one had dared mention to Mary that her daughter had spent late hours out on the breakwater trying to do that very thing. A wise decision not to tell her, she thought.

Nell worked her way through the quesadilla. She liked all of Sugar Magnolia's specials, but this was her favorite. And now Mary was eating, too. The pineapple fritter had disappeared, and the eggs Benedict were on their way.

Mary wiped the corners of her mouth with her napkin and looked over at Nell. "Nell, darlin', you were just what I needed today. Your company and a pineapple fritter can make almost anything right."

"You have lovely grown children, Mary. Don't forget that for a single minute in the middle of this ugly mess."

Mary took the check from the waitress and put several bills on the table. "My treat. And in return, you will keep an eye on my darlings."

Nell got up and retrieved her purse and knitting bag from beneath her chair. "With pleasure. They both have your grit, Mary Halloran. Cass and Pete are going to be just fine."

"Sure and they will be," Mary said as they walked out the door together, then turned in separate directions toward their own cars. Nell had almost reached hers when she heard Mary calling her from down the street.

"And one more thing, darlin'," Mary called out. She stood beside her pale green Chevrolet, standing on tiptoe to peer at Nell over the roof. "If you know a nice young gentleman wanting to settle down, I think it might help Catherine forget about those nasty lobster thieves. I surely do."

Izzy's frogging class had already begun when Nell slipped through the archway of the Seaside Knitting Studio's back room. At first she thought she had made a wrong turn and ended up in a Pilates class at the Gloucester Y. The crowded room was noisy and upbeat. And rather than sitting on the couch and chairs with yarn in their laps, the women were standing all about the room—in front of the bookcase and the back door, over near the windows, and they all had their eyes on Izzy. Dressed in shorts and a T-shirt that sported a frog in sunglasses and a pair of knitting needles at her feet, Izzy stood with her back to the alley windows, moving her arms as if pulling air into her lungs. The rhythmic sounds of an old Marvin Gaye CD pumped music into the room.

Nell found a spot near the ocean windows. Curled up on the window seat showing total disinterest in the movement shaking the room, sat Purl. She meowed a greeting to Nell, then closed her eyes and blocked out the activity. "I'm with you, Purl," Nell whispered. She watched the women follow Izzy's movements— sucking in huge gulps of air, then releasing the air slowly, while all the while their hands moved in and out, fingers curling and touching together in front of their chests, as if pulling taffy. In the front row, barely visible over the bobbing heads, was Birdie, her short-cropped silvery hair bobbing to the music.

Izzy waved at Nell without missing a beat. "Okay, friends," she shouted over the beat, "that's step number one to successful frogging. Breathe deeply, relax, get ready to join in the dance—and laugh whenever the spirit moves you." With her hands pressing down in a graceful movement, she urged people to sit.

"The second step—and a very, very important one—is to be with friends." Izzy's wide smile blanketed the group and her voice softened. "And so we are."

Nell noticed how crowded the room was, as if people needed to be with people. The rainy day had lured Laura Danver off the beach. And Jane Brewster was there, too, her blouse smudged with signs of clay. She'd told Nell that the feel of the soft cushy yarn and brilliant colors in Izzy's shop were a tonic for her. Therapy, she called it.

Several of Izzy's friends, professional women taking a day off and young moms in tank tops and jeans, their lean bodies still moving to the beat of the music, lined up near Izzy. And around the back, Nell spotted Margarethe Framingham sitting next to Birdie, her lap filled with a crimson cashmere shawl she was knitting. There were new faces, too, that Nell didn't recognize. Probably people from the cottages north of town or bed-and-breakfasts that dotted the windy roads of the Cape. Cecelia Cascone, the tiny Italian grandmother who knit hundreds of hats for the Sea Harbor winter clothing drive, sat happily next to Mae's niece Jillian, sipping ice tea. Friends, vacationers, people who lived up the street or over in Gloucester or Rockport or Manchester-by-the-Sea. A community of knitters. Izzy's dream come true.

Nell noticed Beatrice Scaglia in the front row. Odd to see her in the shop again. Izzy had mentioned that she'd attended a class last weekend. She somehow didn't seem the knitting type, but then perhaps that was what was so wonderful about yarn and needles. It was everywoman's—or man's—craft. Seeing her made Nell think about Sal, who'd wandered in and out of her thoughts all day. He had clearly avoided talking with her when she spotted him yesterday. Yet hours before seemed to want desperately to say something. If she had a chance today, perhaps Beatrice would shed light on how well the Scaglias knew Angie.

"And the third step is to make frogging *fun*," Izzy was saying from the other side of the room. "Do it with gusto. Have a glass of wine or ice tea—" She waved to the wide bookcase where a wooden tray was heavy with snacks, a bottle of wine, and a pitcher of tea.

She pointed to the perky frog grinning out at the group from her T-shirt. "And what does our mascot say?" she asked.

"Rivit, rivit," Birdie obliged, knowing the routine.

"Which sounds like?" Izzy prompted.

"Rip it," Birdie said, and Izzy lifted a half-finished angora sweater sleeve from a chair at her side. With happy gusto and to the gasps of people in the front, she pulled out several rows of yarn, winding them steadily around her elbow and hand.

Izzy continued, explaining the fine points of pulling stitches and the do's and don'ts of repairing a single row, two rows, three, or even a dozen, without losing the bulk of a project and throwing it away in tears.

The hour passed in a flash, with Izzy weaving through the room, picking up unfinished shawls and sweaters, admiring the fine, lovely knitting and convincing each knitter that once she had that one dropped stitch or misplaced hole taken care of, all would be right with the world.

Nell sat on the sidelines, her own knitting in her lap, the rows lined up and mistakes finessed under Izzy's artful direction. She noticed Beatrice Scaglia moving about the room, talking to people, asking about sick relatives. *Always the politician,* Nell thought. But her hands were free of knitting. *Odd,* she thought. She leaned over and picked up a dropped ball of yarn, and when she looked back up, Beatrice was waving, smiling, and slipping out of the room. Nell frowned. Well, she'd catch Beatrice soon.

"And Wednesday," Izzy announced, as people began to pack up their knitting, filling tote bags and backpacks, "Margaret Elliot is coming over from Rockport for our summer intarsia class. Don't miss it—she's wonderful." She flopped down on the window seat next to Nell and Purl and kissed her aunt on the cheek.

"Izzy, have you talked to Cass?" Nell asked when things quieted down. She kept her voice low, not wanting to fuel the rumor mills.

Izzy smiled good-bye to a friend, her smile fading as she turned her attention back to Nell. But before she could answer, Birdie and Margarethe Framingham walked over from the other side of the room.

Birdie's usual smile held worry and disapproval.

"Margarethe told me the police questioned Pete yesterday," she said without greeting.

Margarethe sat down on the couch. "This is foolish and meaningless, Nell," she said. Her level eyes moved from Nell to Birdie to Izzy, and back to Nell.

"It's routine, of course," she continued, "but the police are grasping at straws. They need to move on to solving real town problems—like the poachers who are creating havoc in the north bay and the fishing regulations. Whoever did this random act is in Nova Scotia by now."

The use of a drug to paralyze someone didn't sound random to Nell. It sounded planned and calculated. And *real,* to use Margarethe's own terminology. But even in casual conversation,

Margarethe's words came out as definitive. It was probably from years of being the town's matriarch, the imposing figure who led meetings and determined new directions for the city. Even the mayor deferred to Margarethe. Nell wondered if Margarethe would like to just let her hair down sometimes, sit and gossip and have a glass of wine. Perhaps they'd encourage her to drop in on their knitting group some Thursday night. With Birdie's Pinot, Izzy's upbeat music, and a platter of escargot, she'd have no choice but to let go of her school-marm demeanor. Aloud she said, "Why do you think it was a stranger, Margarethe?"

"Chief Thompson said as much. And it makes sense. Angie was out on that beach by herself. And she was so attractive. It fits. It all fits. But reports need to be written and loose ends tied up. And that's why they talked to Pete. Procedures."

Birdie wedged her small body down between Izzy and Nell, nodding. "That poor sweet Pete. No one can possibly believe he had anything to do with this."

Izzy fiddled with a stray piece of yarn left on the couch. "But he was with Angie that night. Questioning him makes sense."

Margarethe frowned. "Pete and Angie were together that night?"

Izzy nodded. "They had a date that night."

"Apparently Angie got a call on her cell while she was with Pete," Birdie said. "We don't know who called her—and of course the phone is gone. But it doesn't seem likely it was a stranger. Angie wouldn't have agreed to meet a stranger on the breakwater, leaving sweet Pete behind, now, would she?"

For a moment, Margarethe seemed uncharacteristically flustered. "Chief Thompson thinks it was a stranger. The phone call may have been inconsequential, not related at all to her going to the beach. Surely, the police have an explanation."

"The explanation is that they want it to go away, Margarethe," Nell said. "Just like so many in this town. I want it to go away, too.

So do Izzy, Cass, and Birdie. But it won't disappear until we know what happened that night. Pete needs that closure. We all do."

Nell hoped the conversation would end there. She didn't want to get into the fact that Tony had also been with Angie that night. Another complication. Tony could tell his own story, surely. And enough people saw him with Angie that the police must know.

As if reading Nell's mind, Birdie said, "It's good to see Tony around town, Margarethe. You must be happy to have him back."

Margarethe sat straight, her spine not touching the couch back. She seemed to be giving Birdie's words exaggerated attention. Nell watched expressions flit across her handsome face. Margarethe probably worried about Tony just like Nell worried about Izzy and her brothers. It was what you did, no matter your children's ages.

Finally Margarethe's face softened with a smile, and she said, "Yes, Birdie. You're right. Tony is a good son. It's always good to have him here."

"It's nice when the young folks move back."

"Tony hasn't moved back, Birdie. He's just visiting. He has business in New York and Boston, a life there. He'll stay for the benefit Saturday night, of course, but then he will be on his way." She rose from the couch and slipped her bag over one shoulder. "I'm happy that the three of you are coming. It's for such a good cause. And that talented Sam Perry tells me that he is an old family friend of yours, Izzy. How delightful."

Izzy nodded. "Sam was like a brother to me. With all the baggage that brings."

Nell watched her niece's expression. She couldn't tell if Izzy felt delight or not. But Nell suspected a level of comfort came from having an old familiar friend around during a rough time.

Margarethe began to walk toward the front of the store, then stopped just as she reached the archway and turned back. "What was Beatrice Scaglia doing here?" Margarethe's words snapped like a rubber band.

Izzy frowned. "She was here for the class, just like the other—"

"Curious," Margarethe said. "Beatrice doesn't knit. Never has. Never will." With a slight look of disdain flashing across her face, Margarethe turned and walked through the store.

Chapter 16

"Well, dear, wait for me." Birdie scuttled after Nell as she stepped through the back door of the Seaside Knitting Studio. "I need a ride, and since Ben Endicott seems to have appointed himself my chauffeur—and he's utterly derelict in his duties by fishing in Colorado—I think you, my dear, must pick up the slack."

"My car's just across the street, Birdie—it will give us a chance to catch up."

Birdie nodded. "My sentiments exactly."

Nell and Birdie stepped out into the alley, squinting against the glare of the late-afternoon sunlight. It was a few seconds before Nell spotted the figure standing at the foot of the steps, still as a statue.

She stopped on the step, startled for a moment. "Gideon, you frightened me."

George Gideon stood next to the open shop window, leaning against the weathered building. He pushed away from the side as Nell and Birdie stepped onto the gravel.

"Sorry, ma'am," Gideon said, his fingers touching the bill of his baseball cap. "Didn't mean to scare you."

Music from Izzy's CD player filtered through the window, the sound carrying into the alley, and Nell wondered if Gideon had been listening to their conversation. She shook off her suspicion. *He'd surely have no interest in listening to a bunch of women talk.*

"It looks like you're still keeping us safe," Nell said. "You mentioned you might be switching jobs."

"I didn't say that exactly, now, did I?" Gideon grinned. "I'm thinking of buying a business. Maybe a bait shop or a bar. The Gull isn't as high-class as it used to be."

Birdie's eyebrows lifted into her silver bangs. "A bait shop? A bar? Those things cost money, George Gideon. Did you rob a bank?"

Gideon looked down at Birdie, and a tinge of discomfort flashed across his face. "No, ma'am," he mumbled.

"Well, good," Birdie said. Her eyes lowered to his bare arm, muscular and tan with a fish tattoo on the bicep. Her eyes widened. "Gideon, what in heaven's name did you do? You look like you've been in a cat fight."

Nell looked at the back of Gideon's hand and forearms. They were crisscrossed with scratches, now crusted over and forming a tiny roadmap of red marks across his weathered skin.

Gideon looked down at his hand and arms as if they belonged to someone else. He looked up, then nodded slowly. "Cats," he said. Then, without further talk, he turned and for the second time in as many days, walked away from Nell and down to the water's edge.

Nell and Birdie drove through the center of town, past the Ocean's Edge Restaurant and Lounge, over the small bridge that gave sailboats entry to the river and fine homes west of town. Nell turned onto a hilly street in the oldest neighborhood in Sea Harbor, once home to sea captains and merchants, and entered a wide drive, flanked on both sides by a thick stone wall that marked the one boundary edge of Birdie's property. The ocean marked two other sides, and a thick woods on the south side separated her land from the neighbor's. Built a century earlier by Captain Antonio Favazza, Birdie's three-story stone home sat above the water on the south end of town. The Favazza place was a landmark—the Stone Castle, some called it—and though it could easily have been turned into an inn or high-end condominiums and was an unlikely dwelling for a woman just this side of eighty, Birdie had made it clear to anyone who dared broach the topic that she would never leave her home, not while her heart continued to pump blood through her body. Topic closed.

For the brief time they were together, Sonny Antonio Favazza became the true love of Birdie's life, and though she married four times after his untimely death nearly forty years before, Bernadette Favazza never changed her name again nor moved from Sonny's home. The home and the name stayed, she told each subsequent suitor. A package deal.

Nell turned into the estate and drove around the parking circle, parking near the heavy wooden front doors. Off to the right, back near the woods, was a long garage and above it, accommodations for help. But Birdie didn't like live-in help, except for Harold Sampson, the gardener, and his wife, Ella. Harold was nearly as old as Birdie, but he dutifully worked each day, trimming bushes, planting flowers in season, and mowing the lawn on the John Deere tractor that Birdie had bought for him.

Nell knew not to scrutinize or talk about what Harold actually did. After fifty years of service to the Favazza family, Birdie felt she owed it to him and Ella to keep a roof over their heads and food on the table. And that was that.

"Turn this thing off and come inside," Birdie said with a wave of her hand. "And I have an exquisite Pinot uncorked and waiting for us. We need to talk, to catch up."

A half hour later Nell and Birdie were seated on the stone patio that circled out from the house on the harbor side, high above the water. Soft gaslights cast shadows across the granite floor. The two old friends sat in ocean-liner chairs, refurbished and polished until the teak arms were slippery beneath their touch. On a low iron table sat a platter of cheese, crackers, and warm rosemary herb bread, thin slices of smoked turkey, and two glasses of wine that Ella had quietly carried out.

Nell took a sip of wine, then sat back in the chair and pulled her knitting onto her lap. She looked out over the sea. "It's a perfect night," she murmured.

Across the harbor, flickering lights reflected off the black water like fairy dust. And where the land snaked out farther, the lights of Canary Cove art colony outlined the galleries and cafés. Music from a small combo on the deck of a bar near Ham and Jane's traveled across the water to where they sat.

"You can see everything from here," Nell said. And she knew Birdie did just that. A well-used telescope sat in its sturdy mounting below the patio awning.

"Margarethe and I were talking about that today. I anchor the land on the south, and Framingham Point reaches from here to forever on the north end."

They both looked northeast, beyond Canary Cove to a chunky piece of land that jutted out into the ocean, surrounded by water on three sides. And at the end of the thumb was the magnificent Framingham home and grounds.

Nell checked her scarf and counted the stitches to be sure she hadn't lost any. She took a bite of cheese and rested her head back against the cushions. "At times like this, sitting here beneath the sky, the world is soft and peaceful. Safe. Angie's murder seems so very far away."

"But nothing's far away, of course. Everything is still here, hidden in the darkness." Birdie pulled a shawl around her shoulders.

"I think I dislike the suspicion most of all—these are our friends and neighbors, Birdie, and one of them killed Angie." Nell looked up at the sky. It was a bright night, with a wash of stars that swept across the blackness like a lacy knit scarf. "We are all looking at one another, wondering, trying to patch together a picture that explains Angie's murder."

"We both feel it—that sense of forboding?"

Nell nodded against the back of the chair. "Everything bothers me right now. Things I wouldn't have noticed before have become ominous somehow—like Gideon and the way he lurks around Izzy's shop. Tony's behavior. And all this talk about Angie leaving as soon as she finished a 'project.' We need to find out more about what Angie was doing. She lived and walked and talked right in the middle of us, Birdie. And look how little we knew about her."

"You're right, Nell. My point exactly. That phone call at Harry's for example? Now, I don't mean this in a bad way—I don't snoop—but there isn't much that I don't hear about from someone or another. And if there'd been something going on with a married man, I think I'd have known it."

"I don't think she was involved with anyone, Birdie. So don't worry. Your radar is still intact. From what Harry said, someone *wanted* to be involved with her. Maybe was obsessed with her. But it clearly wasn't reciprocated."

"It's certainly motive for murder, telling a wife."

Nell sipped her wine. Yes, that was true. A motive wasn't very helpful, though, not without a face or person to put it with.

"Everyone has secrets, I guess," Birdie said. "I think Gideon has a ton of them. And Angie. Tony." Birdie took a sliver of cheese, put it on a cracker, and handed it to Nell.

"We only know what people let us see."

"True. Look at Margarethe. She's as visible as Father Northcutt's church in this town. But what do you really know about her? She's powerful. She's kind and generous. She's rich."

"And she protects her son, just like we all would."

"But she has a past, too. Sonny knew her when she came to Sea Harbor—she was young, eighteen or so. She ran away from home, Sonny said. She told him once the only good thing that ever happened to her before she moved to Sea Harbor was a grandmother who taught her to knit. Knitting saved her life, she said. I tried to ask her about it once, but by then her past was off-limits. It wasn't worth talking about. She preferred to live in the present with the respect her role called for."

"She's like Josie. And Annabelle. Women who have survived, in spite of what they were dealt."

Birdie poured them each another inch of wine. "I talked to Tony today," Birdie said. "I saw him go into Coffee's so I followed him."

Nell smiled at the image of Birdie traipsing into the coffee shop behind the Framingham heir.

"I asked him what he and Angie were talking about that night in the bookstore. He said Angie was nosing around into things that were none of her business. But the instant he said it, I could tell he wanted to take the words back."

"So he was telling her to stop whatever she was doing."

"Yes. He said she wasn't going to make anything better for anyone, so why hurt people. And then he launched into a short lecture about people making saints out of the dead, no matter what they had done in life. That's what we were doing with Angie, he said, and we didn't know what we were talking about. 'A damn shame,' he said. And then he pushed back his chair and stomped off like the spoiled boy I remember from years ago."

"I don't think we've made Angie into a saint, Birdie. But it's only natural to put the good memories in place when someone dies before you dig up the bad ones. If for no other reason, the family needs that."

Birdie nodded. "That's true. But, Nell, darlin'," Birdie said, "I think Tony may have said one thing right. For good or for bad, we need to know more about what Angie did besides planning an exhibit for the Historical Museum's fall show. Maybe the time has come to dig in the dirt."

Chapter 17

$\mathcal{N}$ell's board meeting at the Sea Harbor Historical Society was scheduled for noon on Wednesday. The small group would have chowder and salads from Elm Tree Catering, the reminder e-mail had read. And they made wonderful chunky chowder. Sweet, with a touch of wine to brighten it up.

But chowder or not, Nell would have attended the meeting. She'd had lunch with Josie Archer on Tuesday and promised her that she'd pack up some pictures Angie had on her desk at work. And if there was anything else personal, she would take that to Josie as well.

But maybe there'd be more than pictures at the museum, she thought. There might be some answers, too.

Nell and Birdie had sat beneath the stars way too long Monday night—but the deep quiet had helped them line up the planets, as Birdie put it. Get their ducks in a row. And Birdie was right. They'd been looking all around Angie for some answers. Now it was time to look at Angie herself and see what she could tell them. And since she'd spent more time at the Historical Society than probably anywhere else, it seemed a good place to start.

Nell walked across the square, pausing at the gazebo where she half expected to see Pete Halloran sitting on a bench, feeding the pigeons while he waited for Angie to take her break from work. His absence was more striking than his presence had been, a stark reminder of recent events.

Pete was still feeling the assault of being questioned by the police, Cass had told her last night. "It's churning around inside him like a storm," she had said. "It will spill out eventually."

The questioning in a stark room at a metal table had almost made that happen, Cass said. He'd been so angry. And it wasn't because of the questioning. It was because someone had murdered Angie, and no one seemed to know what to do about it.

Nell crossed the street and hurried up the steps to the Historical Society and adjacent museum. Hearing her name called, she turned and looked through her large round sunglasses into the eyes of Margarethe Framingham, dressed today in a knit suit and large hat to shield her face from the sun. The suit was knit of an expensive wool silk blend in a deep rose color. It reminded Nell of the balloon flowers that lined her neighbor's drive on Sandswept Lane. She resisted the urge to reach out and touch the finely knit garment. Small cables, barely visible, ran up and down the fitted skirt and were repeated in the shawl-collar jacket. She had seen Margarethe working on pieces of the suit at meetings, and the finished product was a work of art.

"Hello, Margarethe," Nell said. "You look wonderful. I'll be distracted through the whole meeting, trying to figure out how you managed to knit that gorgeous suit."

Margarethe smiled. "Izzy played detective to find me this yarn. I don't know how I survived before her shop opened." She touched the edge of her jacket. "Fine woven yarn is something to be cherished. It needs to be cared for like a fine piece of art."

Nell looked again at the fine stitches in the suit, even and not too tight. Margarethe attacked her knitting projects the same way she did civic causes. Sometimes Nell found her energy and purpose a bit obsessive and overwhelming, but she got things done.

And if she herself needed to be obsessive to knit a suit as unique as Margarethe's, she just might consider it.

"I've missed a few meetings recently," Margarethe said, "but it's time to get back to my responsibilities. It's been a sad time for us, but our lives go on."

Nell nodded and followed Margarethe up the steps. Margarethe was right, she thought, but not completely. Moving on fully only came with answers; dust swept under a rug was bound to come out at a later date.

Although several men had joined the board in recent years, today's gathering was all women, and they gathered around the oval table in the board room where papers and pencils had been neatly spaced, right next to napkins and soup spoons. Beatrice Scaglia sat at one side and, noticing an empty chair next to her, Nell walked around the table and sat down.

The first half hour was routine, the reading of minutes and the treasurer's report, an update from Nancy Hughes, the director of the museum. It was only after those so inclined had filled their bowls a second time with clam chowder and a platter of lemon bars was passed around the table and emptied in record time that Nancy brought up new business.

Nell cleared her place of food remnants and took out her knitting, scooping up the long tail of her scarf and settling it into her lap. She reached for the second needle and then settled in to listen. The scarf was coming along nicely—nearly four feet of lovely knit sea yarn. A few more feet and she'd be able to wrap it around her neck, as Izzy suggested, and let it flow down across her dress.

"It's lovely," Beatrice whispered, pointing at the scarf.

"And I hear you are taking up knitting, too, Beatrice? It's wonderful therapy."

Beatrice smiled brightly. "Once I work some more hours into my days, I will consider it," Beatrice said.

"But you took Izzy's frogging class."

"Yes, I did," Beatrice said. Her tone of voice indicated that the topic was complete.

Nell tried a different one. "Beatrice," she began, her fingers working the yarn and her tone friendly and conversational, "did you and Sal know Angie Archer well?"

"Of course not," Beatrice said sharply.

Nancy tapped her water glass with a fork then, and Nell sat back in her chair. She looked sideways at Beatrice. She had slipped on her glasses and her serious-meeting look and was examining the agenda with exaggerated attention. Her voice had been sharp, indicating the discussion of both her knitting interests and Angie Archer were over. Finished.

Beatrice was a conundrum, she decided. For someone so organized, so involved, it seemed quite odd she'd devote time to a class on ripping out stitches before she'd learned to knit and purl. Perhaps it was the calisthenics Izzy had added to the class that intrigued Beatrice. As for Angie, maybe Beatrice didn't know her, but Sal was another story, and Nell wouldn't let that one go so easily.

Nancy began speaking and Nell pulled her thoughts back to the meeting.

"I'd like to suggest something today that we haven't done before, but it seems appropriate," Nancy said. "We would like to do something to recognize the dedicated work of the late Angie Archer." She looked up and down both sides of the table and rested her palms on the smooth surface, leaning slightly forward. "I think you all met Angie at one time or another—many of you knew her growing up. This is a terrible tragedy for her family and friends—and for us here at the museum. The staff and I thought a small gesture would be appropriate, if you all agree."

Nell paused in her knitting. "What a nice idea, Nancy," she said.

"It's well deserved, Nell. Angie worked hard."

The others at the table nodded.

Beside her, Beatrice Scaglia held her smile, but Nell thought her body stiffened slightly.

"Oh, yes. Angie worked hard and was so sweet," Lillian Ames, a museum volunteer and board member, said. "I would watch her at her computer, listening to her music through those earphones, and researching like a little beaver. I teased her that the earphones would make her go deaf—like me." Lillian laughed and pushed her thick brown-rimmed glasses up to the bridge of her nose. "But then she would show me all the things she was gathering up, the list of deeds and pictures and things for the exhibit."

Nell remembered the music that filled Angie's apartment the night she died. Music was a part of the Seaside Knitting Studio, and even though Angie's was sometimes too loud, it was at home there. Some people worked better to music, Izzy said, and her iPod and CD player were well used. And it sounded like Angie's were, too.

Nancy smiled. "Angie was unique, that's for sure. But a hard worker, and her efforts have left us with a better and more organized library than before she came, not to mention the work she did for the fall exhibit."

"What exactly was she working on?" Lucy Stevens, a neighbor of Nell's on Sandswept Lane, asked.

Nell listened for the answer carefully. She knew Angie was hired because of her research degree in library science, and that she was helping Nancy with a special exhibit.

"She was cataloging everything she could find on the stone quarries—stories, deeds, photographs," Nancy said. "Then pulling it all together for an exhibit we have planned for the fall."

"Was Angie going to help with the exhibit?" Nell asked.

"You know how we are around here, Nell. Everyone helps with everything."

"I heard that Angie might not be working here much longer," Nell began.

"Oh, no," Nancy said. "We were hoping Angie would stay a good long time."

"So she wasn't going to be losing her job?"

"Angie?" Nancy laughed. "Nell, you've seen us go through a lot of staff over the years. Part of that's the nonprofit handicap— we can't always pay people what they're worth—and other times it's because we may hire unwisely. But Angie didn't seem concerned about the pay, and she was most definitely not an unwise hire. She was good at what she did. Hard working and conscientious. In fact, she went above and beyond the call of duty."

"And she seemed to like it here, what with the other young folks coming back to town," Lillian offered, wanting again to be helpful. She looked over at Margarethe and added, "I saw your handsome son come in here the other week to see Angie. They sat out back and talked so seriously, like they were sorting out the world's problems."

Nell saw a look of surprise pass over Margarethe's face. This was news to her as well.

But Nell remembered what Birdie had said. For some reason, Tony thought Angie was up to no good, that her time in Sea Harbor had more sinister motives than helping with a museum exhibit. Tony had even threatened Angie the night she was murdered, so whatever he thought she was doing was serious—at least to him.

"Tony and Angie grew up together," Margarethe said to Lillian. "They were probably catching up on news of old friends. You know how they do." She smiled and turned back to the group. "The idea of something to recognize Angie is a wonderful one. Let's do it."

The conversation shifted in an instant. Margarethe was a master at it, and Nell admired the gracious way she had of switching topics without Lillian being embarrassed for bringing up a personal subject at a board meeting. But the thought of Tony bothering Angie at work—if that's what he had done—stayed with Nell.

Margarethe went on. "I think we should buy that walnut display case that we've been wanting to exhibit our ship models. We will put a tasteful brass plaque on it that says it's in memory of Angelina Archer. And her mother will see it every time she comes into the museum."

"And it will bring her such joy," Lillian said, clapping her hands.

The Historical Society didn't have the money for the expensive case that Margarethe Framingham was talking about. Nell knew that from numerous budget discussions. But she didn't doubt for one single minute that the next time she came into the library for a board meeting, the case would be in the center hall, polished and oiled—and completely paid for by Margarethe Framingham. Fastened to the top would be a shiny brass plaque with Angie's name on it—a gesture that would, indeed, inject a moment of pleasure into Josie Archer's grief.

The board meeting ended by two. As the others filed out into the front hall, Nell followed Nancy into her office. She explained Josie's request.

"Of course, Nell," Nancy said. "And thank you. I've been meaning to call Josie and do it myself, but you know how that goes. The phone rings, someone comes in, and on and on."

Nell knew it to be true. Nancy Hughes was the best director they'd had since she'd been involved with the museum. She was sharp, energetic, and personable, and her instincts in museum direction had been right on target. Nell liked her very much. "Are you going to hire someone for Angie's position?" she asked.

Nancy took a key from her desk drawer and motioned for

Nell to follow her to the back of the building. "I'm going to try, Nell, but she'll be difficult to replace. The project she had been working on, though, was nearly completed. I was starting to talk with Angie on what we should tackle next."

They walked through a wood-paneled library, open to the public like the museum in the east wing, and to a back room that housed the research staff.

"So Angie was ready to do another project for you?" Nell asked.

"Well, let's say I was ready for her to start a new project. Now that you've brought up the question of her time here, it makes me wonder."

"What do you mean, Nancy?"

"Well, I never questioned that she would stay on after the quarry project ended. We had just given her a raise, and I know she liked working here. But when I talked about a new project, she was evasive. Noncommittal. I didn't think much of it until you mentioned today that there was talk of her leaving."

"It was just talk, Nancy. Little things she said that made people think she wouldn't be around long." Nell stopped at a wooden desk that she knew to be Angie's. The top was littered with scattered yellow pads, a pencil holder, and a desk calendar. There were few personal things marking the area—a makeup case in a tote bag beneath the desk, but not much else. It wouldn't take long to pack this up, but there was something decidedly sad about a workspace that was nearly neutral.

"The police looked through it, hence the mess. They declared it 'inconsequential.' That made me sad, that they would cast it off as not important. It's a part of Angie. It's important."

Nell nodded. "I brought a couple sacks. And that's probably more than I need. It doesn't look like Angie had many personal things here."

Nancy didn't answer. She stood on the opposite side of the desk, her hands on her hips, frowning. "Something's missing, Nell."

"From the desk?"

"Her computer, that's it," Nancy said, snapping her fingers in the air. "It's not here." She pulled open the deep desk drawers, then checked the bookcases. "It's a small laptop. White, I think. She liked it better than our clunky old models."

"Maybe the police took it. That would make sense. There'd be e-mail, and maybe something of interest to them."

"No, I'm sure they didn't. I was back here with them. It wasn't here that day."

Nell looked around the room. Bookcases lined the inner wall, and windows looked out onto the small back parking lot. "I don't see a computer."

Nancy waved one hand through the air. "Of course it's not here. She always took it home. I forgot. I guess all this mess has me rattled."

But Nell knew the computer wasn't at the apartment. The police had looked, Izzy said.

Nell shook out the shopping bag and set it on the chair. "We all are a bit rattled, Nancy."

"Hopefully, it'll be behind us soon. Margarethe mentioned that the police think it was a random act. Awful, but random, someone seeing a beautiful young girl and trying to force her into something she didn't want to do. I guess Sea Harbor isn't immune from unsavory people passing through now and then."

Nell was silent. A random act. The words had become a mantra. People were going to start believing it. "Nancy, was most of Angie's work done on the Internet? Is that why she used the computer?"

"Oh, no. That was some of it, of course. It's amazing what

you can find on the Web. But she did a lot of work in the library here—looking up old histories, pictures, deeds. And she spent hours over at the county building."

"What did she do over there?"

"Looked up old deeds, information about the land around here and the quarries. She said it was an amazing place to find things. She'd come back excited, like someone who'd just found a buried treasure. The two of us would go through her pile of photocopies as if it were Christmas morning. She was a brilliant researcher, Nell."

"I'll pass that along to Josie. She'll like hearing it."

Nancy walked over to the door. "You won't get anything done with me yakking, Nell," Nancy said. "I'm going back to my office, but please call if you need me."

Nell listened to the click of Nancy's shoes on the hardwood floor, fading into silence. Then she dug into her task, filling the paper sack with the few personal things Angie allowed to enter into her work realm. She picked up a framed picture of Angie with her mother and father, standing near the Fisherman's Statue in Gloucester. Nell looked at the smile on Ted Archer's face, his arm looped around Josie's shoulders on one side, and the little red-haired girl on the other. Angie was about five in the photo and was looking up at her dad with an expression of pure joy. Ted's smile was filled with pride and love. He was a good man. And even when hard times hit, he tried his best to take care of Josie and Angie.

Nell wrapped the picture in some newspapers and slipped it into the sack, then continued with the few remaining items. A coffee mug from the Life Is Good store in Gloucester. Inside the top drawer she found some elastic hair bands, a box of tea.

Nell slipped it all into the bag with the other things—a few pens and pads of paper. Several old postcards of the quarries,

Dogtown, the barn-red wooden fish warehouse in Rockport, and a beautiful sunset off Good Harbor Beach. Nell shivered in the warm air.

She'd collected a large part of Angie's life in Sea Harbor—and it barely filled a Filene's shopping bag.

Chapter 18

*N*ell tossed and turned in the bed, which was wider by a mile without Ben lying in it beside her. He was having a fine time, he'd told her when he'd called. The skies were blue and sunny, breezes cool, and the trout in the Colorado River were lining up for his bait. He missed her. He'd be home in a day.

Sometimes Nell went with Ben on company trips like this, and hiking a Colorado fourteener would have lured her to his side. But fishing she could easily forgo. She'd enjoy the trout once cleaned and filleted and basted with dill and lemon butter. Not before.

Finally, with sleep beyond her reach and the day brightening, Nell gave up and slipped out of bed. She pulled on a pair of lightweight warm-up pants and an old clambake T-shirt, tugged her pink Sox cap on her sleep-scrunched hair, and headed out the back door. She hadn't been jogging for a few days and her body was feeling it. Some stretching and a short jaunt would clear her head and her achy back—and bring the world back into focus.

Some days Nell headed to Sweet Hollow Park for early-morning exercise—the thick trees offered a protected trail up through the piney woods. But today a southern breeze warmed her face, and she headed, instead, through the narrow windy path behind her home that led to the packed sand of Sandpiper Beach.

A short distance north of the harbor, Sandpiper Beach was a gentle curve of land protected by the distant breakwater. Mothers and babies found it a perfect spot to swim on warm days, but early in the morning it was a choice stretch of sand for joggers, strollers, and dog walkers.

Nell crossed the road, stretched her limbs on the rough wooden fence that marked a small parking lot, and began a slow jog down the beach. Slim, firm bodies passed her by, and she waved at familiar faces—some of Izzy's friends, a young man she was on a board with, Mae's teenage nieces running in tandem. She was happy in her slowness, and felt the aches disappear from cramped muscles as her body moved to its own rhythm.

"Nell," a voice from behind carried forward on the wind. Nell slowed as Izzy ran up beside her, her hair a mass of wet waves sticking to her cheeks and neck. She slowed her stride to match Nell's.

"Want company?" she asked.

Nell smiled her answer, and the two jogged in comfortable silence for a while, Izzy accommodating her strides to Nell's pace.

"How has your week gone?" Izzy asked.

"Yesterday was busy," Nell said, her words coming out in puffs. She told Izzy about cleaning out Angie's desk. "There was little there that spoke of a life at all, much less Angie's."

"No notes, letters? Did you check her e-mail?"

"She used her laptop at work," Nell said. "And it was gone. Nancy said she always took it home at night."

Izzy pumped her arms, her forehead wrinkling. "Are you sure? The police looked for a computer."

"And didn't find it."

"No. They took very little, and not a computer. But Tommy said they hurried through things. I'll look again. I think I may have someone staying up there for a while."

"Oh?" Nell turned away from the water and jogged toward a

wooden bench. Jogging was one thing. Jogging while carrying on intelligent conversation was another thing altogether.

Izzy followed her up the sandy incline and stopped in front of the bench, bending her body at the waist and grabbing the toes of her tennis shoes. Her eyes were focused on the sand, and strands of damp hair fell over her face. "Don't give me that look, Nell," she said without looking up. "I don't have to see it—I can feel it as clearly as if I were looking directly into those all-seeing eyes of yours."

Nell sat down on the bench and stretched her legs out in front of her. She pulled the baseball cap from her head and shook out her hair, all the while smiling at the back of Izzy's upside-down head. "So I think it's a good idea, Izzy, that's all. So does Ben. But I didn't instigate it."

Izzy straightened back up and sat down next to Nell. "What I don't get is why a guy would want to live above a knitting store when he could be in a cottage right by the ocean."

"Izzy, the Seaside Knitting Studio is about as close to the water as you can get."

"You know what I mean."

"Well, for starters, Sam isn't here to sit on the beach and get a summer tan or party it up. He's here to teach at the Canary Cove Arts Academy and to take photographs. If he wants to learn about Sea Harbor, living above your shop is a much better place to be."

Izzy brushed her hair from her eyes and looped it behind her ear. "I'm just being stubborn. Sam's not so bad—he's grown up nicely."

"And he'd probably say the same about you," Nell said. She held back a smile.

"Seeing him was a surprise—good and bad. One tiny part of me resented that somehow my past was moving into my present. I like having it separate, controlling it. Sam was around, you know, during some of those times when Dad made it clear that my love for art was a great hobby. But law—" Izzy's voice dropped an octave and she tucked her chin into her chest. "Law, my lovely, smart daughter, law is a *career*."

Nell patted her hand and laughed at Izzy's imitation of Craig Chambers. Nell loved her brother-in-law dearly, and Izzy loved her dad, but she also knew Craig had placed some of his own formidable hopes and dreams on his daughter. And it had caused much angst for the young Izzy Chambers.

"But about the apartment," Izzy went on. "Though I hate to admit it, you're right, Nell. Every little noise I hear overhead sends shivers through me. It's just the wind or the fact that the shop is older than Methuselah, but it jars me. Having Sam up there will be a good thing. Especially now."

"You're saying that in a tone that scares me a little, Izzy."

"I don't mean to scare you. But if I don't tell you, you'll hear it from someone else."

"Hear what?" A familiar pang squeezed Nell's chest, an uncomfortable feeling that she'd had before when Izzy was reluctant to talk to her about something. She remembered the phone call after Izzy's big court case nearly two years ago. Izzy had called from the courthouse, happy and buoyed by the compliments of the lawyers in her firm. "Way to go, Izzy Chambers," they had cheered loudly. "You're on your way to the top."

But when Ben and Nell pulled up beside Izzy's town house later that evening, with congratulatory flowers and champagne in their arms, the curtains were pulled and reporters blocked the front steps. They slipped around to the back, unnoticed in the commotion, and found Izzy in the kitchen, alone, her face damp with tears. And Nell had the same squeezed feeling when Izzy looked up at her, not wanting to speak, but needing to explain.

Izzy's court case hadn't been a difficult one, but it had been her first. A young man, not much older than Izzy's brother, Jack, had been accused for the third time of armed robbery. Through keen reasoning and logic, Izzy convinced the judge that her client was innocent—and he got his life back. A third conviction would have meant a long sentence. He hugged Izzy tightly, and the television cameras dutifully filmed the embrace for the six o'clock news. But a short while later, in a neighborhood shopping area not far from Izzy's place, the newly freed man quietly held up a deli and shot the owner and his wife dead.

Izzy went back to Sea Harbor with Ben and Nell that night. And not too many days later, after long discussions with the Elliot & Pagett law firm, all came to an agreement, and Izzy finished up her current cases, sold her brick townhome, and bought the Seaside Knitting Studio on Harbor Road. Nell had suffered Izzy's pain during those difficult days, then welcomed her to Sea Harbor—and a life that fit Izzy like a well-knit pair of socks.

"Tell me, Izzy," Nell said now, knowing she might not like what Izzy was going to say.

"You know that Tony and Pete went fishing the other day. I don't know why, exactly, since they aren't friends, but they did."

Nell nodded.

"They stayed out late, apparently. They'd gone out to the island, drank a few beers. According to Pete they spent a little time fishing, a lot of time talking. Tony pumped him with questions about Angie. That was the whole reason he'd invited him, Pete said. What was their relationship like? How did they meet? What did they talk about? Did she talk to him about her work? When was she leaving? And on and on. Pete had a terrible time, he said. Tony didn't seem to give a hoot about Angie. He acted as if Angie had told Pete some kind of secret. And Tony was trying to get Pete to tell him what it was. But Pete didn't have a clue what Tony was getting at. So everything went sour and they ended up mostly drinking beer."

"And?"

"They pulled into the harbor late and saw lights behind my shop as they brought the boat in. Just in the back—you could only see them from the water. They thought they saw a shadow, too, but they were too far away to be sure of that. They were sure of the light, though."

"Maybe it was Gideon's flashlight."

"It could have been. It's probably no big deal," Izzy said. "Pete went by and checked on his way home and he said someone was sitting on the bottom step and ran off as soon as Pete drove up. By the time Pete got out of the car, the person was gone."

"Izzy, isn't it Gideon's job to see that things like that don't happen?"

Izzy shrugged. "Nell, it's probably nothing. I know from my teenage summers here that kids sometimes go into empty cottages to drink a six-pack or smoke a cigarette. It's for the thrill of it. The danger. But no harm intended and once Sam moves in, no one will think twice about shining lights in my shop."

Nell knew Izzy didn't believe her own hypothesis any more than she did. A second-story apartment in the middle of the village wasn't exactly a cottage. And it wouldn't even be thrilling.

"Nell, look over there—" Izzy whispered, and nudged her gently in the side. Nell looked up and saw Angus McPherron standing just at the edge of the water, looking at her and Izzy. He stood still, his heavy shoes barely visible as they sank beneath his weight into the sand until the tide formed a frothy cuff around his ankles. He wore black baggy pants and an old cap pulled down until it nearly touched his bushy eyebrows. But his eyes were clear and focused.

Nell lifted one hand in a wave and smiled at him.

Angus nodded, then slowly made his way across the narrow stretch of beach, the wet sand sucking at his boots and their imprints forming a trail of smooth wet holes behind him.

"Good morning, Angus," Nell said.

Angus nodded again at both of the women, his gnarled fingers playing with his beard. It was soft and white, a Santa Claus–type beard that seemed out of place on Angus's weathered skin.

" 'Morning ladies," he said. "I'm thinking it's a nice day to walk in the water."

"Yes."

"I know you were her friends. I used to walk along the water with her."

"With Angie," Nell said, instinctively knowing whom Angus was talking about. She wondered, briefly, if Angus had been able to hear their conversation, but just as quickly, she dismissed the thought. The sound of the sea made most conversations private, and even if the wind had been carrying voices, Angus's hearing, she knew, was not as sharp as it had once been. "You and Angie were friends, too," Nell said.

He nodded and a smile softened the serious look on his face. "Angie liked my stories. We'd sit on the village pier or out on the breakwater. We both liked to do that. We'd let the breeze cool our faces. And we would talk about the old days."

Angus looked north as he spoke, as if seeing Angie out there on the breakwater, waiting for him. "People don't fool me. I tell them my stories, but I know they aren't usually interested." He shrugged. "Some are, some aren't, I guess. But I like to talk to people, and if they don't want to listen, my feelings aren't hurt. Half the time I make the stories up. But the ones I told Angie were true. She liked those better."

Nell slipped strands of loose, damp hair back over her ear. "I like your stories, Angus. A lot of us do."

He shook his head. "Thank you, Nell. Angie was my best audience, though, and I don't mean for you to take offense at that." He smiled, a sad, enigmatic smile. "She breathed in my stories, and then she remembered them, word for word. Sometimes she even wrote down things that I said. And she always asked questions. She liked me, you know. And I liked her very much."

Nell listened to the old man talk and remembered times she'd seen Angie with Angus, sitting on Pelican Pier, or out at the breakwater or here on Sandpiper Beach. Seeing them touched her somehow, the unlikely pair, with Angie hanging on Angus's words and making him feel important and relevant.

"You must miss her, Angus," Izzy said. "I do, too."

Angus looked out over the water and his face was long and sad. He frowned and squinted against the bright rising sun. "Sometimes my thoughts get mixed up, my head gets foggy," he said. "You have to excuse me. I'm an old man. Angie helped me focus. I miss that most of all. Indeed I do." He looked out over the ocean and smiled. "*Indeed*. She'd always say that. *Indeed*, as if she were British. *Indeed*, *Angus*, she'd say."

He smiled again, a small, sad acknowledgment. Nell could see the confusion in his eyes. It fell softly and peacefully over his face like morning fog.

"Good morning to you, ladies," Angus said again. "You be safe. Keep Angie safe." He paused, looking down at the tips of his wet, sand-coated boots. When he looked up, a tear was sliding slowly down his cheek.

"She loved me, you know," he said, his voice hoarse. "Anja loved me." Then he turned slowly and walked back toward the water, his broad, bent back casting odd shadows on the sand behind him.

"Anja?" Izzy said to Nell as they watched Angus lumber down the beach.

"Anja was his wife," Nell answered. "I wonder if Angie and Anja became confused in his mind. Two women who cared about him enough to listen."

Birdie called Nell at noon, telling her that she was bringing both wine and fruit, and Nell could skip dessert for the Thursday-night knitting group. Sweets would make them sleepy, Birdie said. And they had things to knit and serious topics to discuss.

Nell considered Birdie's logic while she unpacked her grocery sacks, but only for a moment. Wine, she knew, would never be considered a soporific in Birdie's mind; there'd be no convincing her. It was the stuff of living. Not sleeping.

Nell pulled mixed baby lettuce from her bag and put it in the sink. The day had turned warm, as Cape Ann weather could do without notice. The open windows brought a breeze, and her shaded yard and nearness to the ocean allowed Nell to keep the house open and the air-conditioning off, but it might still be warm in Izzy's shop tonight. So a light tuna and snap pea salad would fit the bill. She'd sear the fresh tuna that she'd picked up in Gloucester, then slice it in thin strips. Crisp wontons, a lime and ginger dressing, sliced avocado, and some early cherry tomatoes from her garden would make it a fine meal for a warm summer night. An enticement to knit. And heaven knew what else.

Birdie's phone call and hint of serious discussion had only added to the concern that lingered with Nell after her morning run, though life and summer plans in Sea Harbor were going forward—signs were up around town seeking volunteers for the Fourth of July fireworks, animated talk at Harry's Deli was all about the fancy Saturday-night benefit at Framingham Point, and the smell of wet beach towels and coconut oil lingered along the village streets.

But no matter what visitors and vacationers might see in the postcard-perfect town, the rhythm was off-kilter. Like the eerie, warm quiet she had felt as a child just before a Kansas tornado ripped across the plains. Or the tranquil lull, the sunny sky, before a perfect storm gathered its energy and rained down havoc on the lives of good and solid people.

Chapter 19

*N*ell checked her watch. She'd run out of balsamic vinegar, the only thing missing for the salad. She had plenty of time before knitting club—hours in fact—an unusual respite in the busy week. She might even get a hot bath in before heading over to Izzy's.

Later, at the Thursday-night knitting club, she wouldn't be able to tell Cass, Izzy, and Birdie exactly why she had done it. It just happened, a sudden impulse as she left Shaw's parking lot with her balsamic vinegar in the grocery sack beside her. Maybe it was her unconscious, telling her that this was what she should do.

She turned her car in the opposite direction of her home and headed a few blocks west on Stanley Avenue, then pulled into the packed parking lot of the county offices building.

Nell looked up at the big stone facade, then walked inside. She couldn't remember ever being in the building before, though she knew Ben had been there many times, getting property deeds and copies of family papers. It was an old building with narrow hallways and a musty smell that reminded Nell of the old library in Kansas City where she'd spent half her life. She paused inside the entrance, looking for the office in which Angie Archer had reportedly spent so many of the last hours of her life.

Registrar of Deeds, she read on the wall directory. Room 114. That would have to be the place.

"Nell Endicott," a voice behind her called out, and Nell turned to the smiling face of Rachel Wooten.

Rachel and her husband had moved into Nell's neighborhood a few years before and sometimes ended up on the Endicott deck for Friday martinis. Nell had forgotten that Rachel worked in the county building. "We've missed you on the deck, Rachel," Nell said. "You and Don need to come over soon."

Rachel smiled. "Thanks, Nell. The days slip by way too fast. We'll come by soon. In the meantime, though, can I help you find something here?"

"Maybe you can. I think I want the property deeds office. Angie Archer was working on a project for the Historical Museum, and Nancy Hughes said she got a lot of information here."

"Yes, she did. Angie was here often. I'd see her breezing down the hallway, that beautiful head of red hair flying in the breeze. It's all so awful. I sure hope they find the guy soon."

"I do, too, Rachel."

"Come." Rachel looped her arm through Nell's. "The Registrar of Deeds' office is right next to mine. I'll walk you there." They started down the hall and Rachel's voice grew quiet. "It hit us hard when we found out Angie was murdered. Someone you see often, you know. It was especially hard on our registrar, who rarely says a word. But somehow Angie worked her magic on him. He'd light up like the sun when she came in—and when Angie was here, he'd talk a blue streak."

A coworker of Rachel's walked up then, smiled at Nell, and reminded Rachel of a meeting.

"Oops, I'm sorry, Nell. I need to go. But it's that next office, right there." She pointed to a frosted glass door.

Nell thanked her and walked on in. She stood for a moment, looking around at the computers, the long tables, and banks of filing cabinets. And then she turned toward the quiet man sitting behind a wooden desk.

"Nell Endicott," the registrar said, looking up from his computer. "Well, hello."

Nell's eyes widened in surprise. "Sal Scaglia. Well, of course it's you. It hadn't dawned on me that if I visited the deeds office, it would be your office. How silly of me. My mind is too full of things these days, but this is a happy coincidence."

Sal leaned over his cluttered desk and shook Nell's hand. "Do you need help finding a deed?" He gestured for her to sit down.

Nell sat on the chair in front of his desk. She took in Sal's short-sleeved shirt and glasses, the pens in his pocket, his navy blue pressed pants. He wore brown-rimmed glasses today and looked like a shy professor. "No, Sal," Nell said. "I don't need a deed. I need information. And I think you are just the person to help me. I'm glad you're here."

"What kind of information?"

"That's what I'm not sure of, Sal. It's about Angie Archer."

Sal took off his glasses and pressed his back against the chair. He blinked several times, and Nell thought for a minute that a piece of dust had landed in his eye.

"Are you all right, Sal?"

"Yes." Sal put his glasses back on. "What about Angie Archer?"

"I understand she spent a lot of time over here," Nell began.

"A lot of time?"

"In your office."

"Why?" Sal looked down at some papers on his desk and frowned. He pressed his fingers against his temples as if Nell's questions had given him a headache.

Nell was puzzled. "I think she came to look up some old deeds for a project she was working on for the museum exhibit."

Sal's chest moved as he released some air. "Oh, yes, I remember now. She was working on a project. She worked over there." He pointed to the table with the computers.

"Did she ever talk about her work?"

"No, no. She worked hard while she was in here. She came in to work."

"I was just wondering if she might have come across some information that someone else might not want her to know about. Something that might put her in danger."

"What would that be?" Sal pushed his chair back a foot, as if putting distance between himself and Nell.

"I don't know. I was hoping you might know, Sal."

"Many people come in here, Nell. Angie Archer was just one person. Lots of people come in to research old deeds. Lots of people. I didn't really know Angie all that well."

Nell nodded. She was making Sal nervous, but she wasn't sure how to put him at ease. Perhaps a change in conversation. "It was so nice of you and Beatrice to help us with the packing the other day."

Sal's face hardened. "We shouldn't have messed with those private things. Beatrice shouldn't have done that."

"I think she was just trying to help, Sal."

Sal was silent. He took off his glasses again and looked at Nell. "I'm sorry I haven't been more of a help. But I'm afraid I have to get back to work now." He pointed to a stack of papers on his desk. "As you can see, I have a lot of things to do, a lot of responsibility."

Nell nodded. She stood and reached for her purse. "Well, if you think of anything, Sal, just let me know. I thought, well, when we met at Annabelle's, I thought you wanted to say something to me about Angie."

But Salvatore Scaglia had moved on to other things, and Nell's comment went without a response.

She'd been dismissed.

Chapter 20

$\mathcal{N}$ell was rarely the last person to arrive for Thursday-night knitting, but her confusing conversation with Sal Scaglia and a rash of last-minute phone calls had put her behind schedule. She parked her car on Harbor Road and hurried across the street, her basket of food in tow.

Ahead, she saw Gideon lumbering along the sidewalk. She quickened her step, thinking she'd say hello. Perhaps familiarity or knowing Gideon better would somehow ease her mind about the man, though she doubted it. Ben had taken her fears seriously when she had shared them with him the night before on the phone. Her instincts had always been keen, worth heeding, he said. But this time he thought she needed to back off. Izzy didn't spend much time at the store after hours, so she wasn't around the guy. Now Sam would be moving in. And if Nell had heard the man right, he was about to win the lottery or get a better job or take off on a fool ship—so he'd likely be moving on anyway. "Let it go, Nell," he had said. "Izzy will be okay."

When he reached the knitting store, instead of heading down the alley as he usually did, Gideon headed across the street.

That explains it, Nell thought. Gideon wasn't reporting for security duty early after all; he was heading toward the Gull, fortifications for his night of duty.

Nell watched him walk down the street until he disappeared

into Jake Risso's bar. "I hope he limits his intake," she murmured. The shops on Harbor Road needed his full attention, not one blurred with alcohol.

"Nell Endicott, what is this? Are you talking to yourself now?" Father Northcutt stood in front of her, a heavy sack from Brandley Bookstore in one hand. He wore his usual summer attire—a knit shirt and long walking shorts. He saved his collar and black suit for official visits, and claimed a knobby-kneed clergy with summer duds was much easier to approach, should anyone need a priestly ear.

Nell smiled at the priest. He'd been pastor at Our Lady of the Seas for as long as she'd been coming to the Cape with Ben—back when the elder Endicotts entertained the Sea Harbor church hierarchy on a regular basis—and he knew everyone in town, whether they came to his church or not. He was a bit preachy sometimes, Nell thought, but she supposed there were some who liked that. But no matter, underneath it all he was a teddy bear—a kind and gentle man.

"I was just hoping that Gideon was heading to Jake's for a hamburger or two," she said.

Father Northcutt looked down the street as Gideon disappeared into the tavern. "Jake tries to keep an eye on him, Nell. He knows that Izzy, Archie, and the others along this street depend on him, but . . ."

"But?"

"I don't know, Nell, it's not for me to say, of course. But Gideon may be better suited for other work."

"You're always the diplomat, Father. But I agree."

"I think he could be easily distracted, you know? Responsibility, diligence, and Gideon aren't three words your little knitting group could weave together easily. And he's a little too interested in the ladies, for one thing."

Nell thought of Angie alone in that apartment all those weeks. Did Gideon find her interesting? He had said as much.

"You know what I mean, Nell," the priest went on. "He's not a bad sort. And he comes to the eleven o'clock on Sunday semiregularly. He brings his mother, a strong, rather domineering little woman, if you'll excuse my brass assessment, but nevertheless, she's a faithful parishioner. But I'm thinking Gideon might be coming to watch the young summer ladies with their tans and little sundresses more than to hear the homily." He shrugged and his chins wobbled slightly above the open collar of his knit shirt. "Perhaps I'm not bombastic enough from the pulpit. What do you think, Nell?"

Nell touched the older man's arm. "I think you do just fine, Father. And it's nice to know Gideon comes around your way. You can ask the powers that be to keep an eye on him for me. With you in charge, I'll be happy."

"And I'd be happy being invited to dinner," Father Northcutt said, eyeing her bag and leaning toward it. "I haven't smelled anything that good in weeks, Nellie."

Nell laughed. "If you practice up on your knitting and purling, we might consider having you join us."

Father Northcutt laughed, a deep, throaty sound, and sauntered on across the street and the short walk up Pine Avenue to the rectory. Nell could hear him, still chortling, as the elderly priest disappeared around the corner.

Nell hurried into the shop, later than ever now. She waved a hello to Mae, and headed directly toward the back room.

"I've just had the strangest conversation," Nell said, hurrying down the steps to the knitting room.

"I haven't had a decent meal in days, and you're having conversations," Cass said, hurrying over to help Nell with the sacks. "The thought of you not showing up nearly sent me over the edge."

"I'd never abandon you, Cass, you know that."

"I hope to heaven it's true." She pulled open the thick paper sack and breathed in the smells.

"Your wine is poured and waiting, dearie," Birdie said, and smiled up at Nell. Purl sat curled in a calico ball on her lap. "I would get up, but as you can see, my lap is nicely occupied."

"I went to see Sal Scaglia today," Nell said. She set the wooden bowl on the table, then poured the lime, balsamic vinegar, and cilantro dressing on the fresh greens. The marinated tuna went on next, followed by slices of avocado and tomatoes. Next was a sprinkling of crisp wontons and goat cheese.

"Sal?" Izzy walked over and handed her the glass of wine. "Why did you go to see Sal?"

In minutes they'd all filled their plates and gathered around the low coffee table. Between forkfuls of salad and sips of wine, Nell poured out the story of her afternoon visit. "Nancy said Angie had spent hours over in that tiny deeds office. And Rachel Wooten confirmed it. She said that Angie'd had quite an impact on Sal. A good one, they all thought—he was animated and conversational when Angie was around. But when I mentioned Angie's name to Sal, it was as if I were talking about a total stranger. And he made it very clear that he had more important things to do than talk to me about Angie Archer."

Izzy munched on a sourdough roll, her forehead wrinkled in thought. She wiped the butter off her fingers and set her plate down. "Maybe Sal was just being his quiet self. He never talks, Nell."

"Because Beatrice, bless her, talks for him," Birdie said. "The oddest couple I've ever met, but they say opposites attract."

"I know Sal is shy," Nell said, "but there was more going on than shyness. He was nervous, I think. But I can't figure out why he wouldn't admit that he knew her."

Purl jumped from Birdie's slacks onto Nell's lap and eyed her salad.

"You're welcome to curl up, Purl," Nell said, "but that's the best I can do."

"I agree, Nell. This thing with Sal doesn't make sense. But I think we're at least making some headway."

"Do you think Beatrice's coming over to help us clean out the apartment has anything to do with it? That was odd, too. She's never set foot in my store before, and suddenly she's taking frogging classes and helping us clean out Angie's apartment." Izzy cleared her plate and took out a basket of knitting.

"Well, that's an interesting thing, too. According to Margarethe, Beatrice has never knitted anything. Yet she took a class in frogging."

"A little backwards," Birdie said. "Maybe she wants to be sure she can fix her mistakes before she makes them. That's a little how she approaches city problems at the council meetings."

Cass laughed. "Birdie, what would we do without you?"

"Well, you, young lady, have asked just the right question. Without me, you might spend the rest of your knitting career on scarves."

Cass frowned. She looked at Izzy, then Nell. "This doesn't sound good."

"It's all good, Cass. We've got lots to do tonight, and now that we're fed, we'll have a toast."

"You're getting kind of bossy, Birdie," Cass said, collecting the rest of the plates and putting them on the bookcase.

"Shush, Cass. Raise your glasses, everyone."

Four glasses of Birdie's Pinot were raised into the air in unison.

Birdie sat forward on the couch, her back straight and her eyes sparkling. "Here's to friendship," she said.

"To friendship," they chorused.

After a moment, Birdie raised her glass again. "And take a big gulp this next time." She paused, then said dramatically, "Here's to Cass's shawl."

Three glasses were lifted. One remained on the coffee table.

"Shawl?" Cass said. Her dark eyebrows shot directly into her bangs. "Birdie, sometimes I think you're truly batty."

"Shame on you, Cass. Respect your elders and lift your glass. To Cass's shawl," Birdie repeated.

Izzy nudged Cass's elbow. "Come on, Cass. Be a sport."

Cass frowned and lifted her glass a few inches off the table.

When the toast was completed, Birdie picked up a sack from beside the couch and pulled out a ball of yarn. "Izzy helped me pick this out, Cass. It's a lovely silk and wool blend—"

"Silk?" Cass yelped. She glared at Izzy. "Izzy, I catch lobsters. I don't knit with silk. I can't afford it, for one thing. And I don't wear shawls." Cass walked over to the table and refilled her empty plate.

"Don't fuss so, Catherine. The shawl is for your mother. Mary will love it. And it's time. Scarves alone do not a knitter make."

"It's beautiful yarn, Cass," Izzy said. "And you can do it. It's a little Faroese shoulder shawl, something to keep Mary warm without it getting in her way. The shoulders are shaped so it won't fall off, even for an arm waver like Mary. She'll love it. And this yarn is so soft and scrumptious, you'll want to eat it."

"The tuna will do fine. But thanks," Cass said. She wiped the corners of her mouth with a napkin and watched Birdie pass the skeins of yarn to Nell, who fingered it as if it were a tiny kitten, like Purl.

"I've picked the pattern and the needles," Birdie said. She handed them to Cass along with the pattern.

Nell leaned over and looked at the picture. The shawl hit midarm, shaped nicely at the shoulders, and had a lovely, lacy design running along the back. The pattern might be a little difficult for Cass, she thought, but she'd have plenty of help.

"It's perfect for Mary," Nell said aloud. "The beginning is easy. Just cast on, Cass—you like to do that."

"And while you're doing that, Cass dear, Izzy will pour us another glass of wine," Birdie said.

Izzy disappeared into the studio's galley kitchen for a chilled bottle, taking the empty plates with her.

Cass picked up the needle and began to cast on stitches. The silky yarn sat in a heap on her lap, and her forehead was knit as tightly as her cast ons.

Birdie leaned forward and looked down through her glasses at Cass's stitches. She touched her hand and whispered, "Make these looser, dear. Casting on is your one chance to be a loose woman."

A thump from above stopped Cass midstitch. The room was silent as the three women stared at the ceiling.

Izzy came back into the room. "Don't worry. It's a good thump. Sam Perry doesn't wear boots, but he weighs more than Angie did. He's thinking about renting the place for a month or so. At the least, Aunt Nell can stop worrying when I'm here after closing and get some sleep."

"Well, now," Birdie said, "that's good news, Izzy. I approve."

"Coming from you, Birdie, that's a real coup for me. But back to business. Now that Cass's shawl is underway, I want to go back to Sal. And Angie. I think we are just an inch away from figuring this out." She sat down next to Birdie and pulled her sweater from the basket beside the couch. "Who would want to hurt Angie and, more important, why? A lot of gossip accompanies lost stitches and baby booties, and things said about Angie that I didn't know, even though she lived a floor away."

Nell nodded. "I've heard things, too. People see different things. People saw Tony Framingham with Angie at the museum, for one thing." She looked at Cass. "Did Pete say anything about that, Cass?"

Cass finished her cast-on row and began the garter stitch. She shook her head. "Pete knew Angie didn't like Tony. He wasn't sure why Tony showed up sometimes, but Angie insisted she couldn't stand Tony Framingham."

"That fits what we saw the night she died," Izzy said. "They had a shouting match in the bookstore. And Tony threatened Angie, according to Archie. I don't think he liked her either."

"If we're making a list," Cass said, "don't forget the old man of the sea. I like Angus well enough, but he should be on the list."

"Angus?" Birdie lifted her head. "That gentle old man? He couldn't kill a mosquito."

"He used to follow Angie. I'd see them, down at the harbor where she'd go running. The old man would be nearby, watching her, just biding his time."

"They were friends, Cass," Nell said. "That's all." But she thought of the old man's reaction the other day on the beach. It was odd, not quite right, somehow.

"He thought Angie was his best friend," Izzy said. "And she did spend a lot of time with him. I'd see them together around the Ocean's Edge. In fact, the night Angie died, I had drinks with some friends at the Edge, and they mentioned that Angie and Angus had been talking outside earlier that night. They were laughing about it because Angie was dressed up for a date."

"Which we know was Pete."

"So Angie had a date with Pete that night, left him because she got a phone call. But Angus was across the street, and he stopped her when she left the bar," Cass said.

"Do you know that, Cass?" Nell asked.

She nodded. "Pete told the police as much, though they said there was no use talking to Angus because you never knew what you'd get. I guess we all know that's probably true, but when Angus was clear-minded, he knew so much about this area. He was helping Angie on a project she was working on."

"It makes sense," Nell said. "Angie was collecting information on the land around here, and who would know more about that than Angus?"

"And we know Angie ended up in Archie's bookstore with

Tony that night," Izzy said. "They came in together. Archie said he saw them meet right outside his door—Tony seemed to be looking for Angie. They had a few words, then walked upstairs in the shop to continue the conversation in a more private place. At least that's what Archie assumed."

"But we don't know what happened between the bookstore and the breakwater," Birdie concluded. She leaned over and picked up a pen and the yellow pad and began to make her list.

"Right." Izzy put down the alpaca shawl she was making for her mother. "So we have Angus—who might have had an irrational love for Angie. We have Tony who threatened her."

"And though we know our sweet Pete could never harm a fly," Birdie said, "we need to put his name with the others if we are making a complete list." She added notes to the paper in her distinctive handwriting.

Cass looked up. "That's fair. And you're right—Pete is about as confrontational as a butterfly. Sometimes I think he'd be better off if he were a little less trusting."

"What about George Gideon?" Birdie asked, looking over the rim of her glasses. "He's always hanging out in that alley."

Izzy walked back to her chair and settled into the cushions, her plate balanced on her lap. "Gideon, absolutely. Except we hired him to hang out around here, Birdie."

"I know, I know," Birdie said. "A foolish decision if ever I heard one, Izzy. The man is a womanizer, and he drinks on the job. He never worked an honest day in his life. And my guess is that all he's protecting around here is himself."

Nell looked over to the open window, suddenly wondering if their words were traveling farther than the room. And those windows seemed to be a favorite spot of Gideon's these days.

"Angie didn't like him," Izzy said. "She thought he was creepy."

"Archie thought he spent more time watching Angie's windows than checking doors. He thinks Gideon was infatuated with Angie," Birdie said. "I think I'll talk to Gideon."

Nell frowned.

Birdie looked at her. "Murder's a serious matter, Nell, and no matter what you're thinking, I'm not a foolish old woman. I don't put myself in danger."

Nell smiled. "Can't a person think in private around here anymore?" she asked.

Birdie refilled Nell's wineglass and looked up into her face. "No," she said. "That's what friends are all about."

Nell thought about Gideon and her encounters with him over the past couple weeks. He'd been quite adamant in telling her that the murderer had moved on. Too adamant, perhaps. How could he possibly know that? Could he have approached Angie that night? Tried something, maybe. The thought made her shudder.

"And don't forget your conversation with Sal," Birdie said. "He's on the list. And maybe Beatrice, too."

"Where was Gideon the night Angie was killed?" Cass asked.

"He should have been right out there behind the shops." Izzy took a sip of her wine.

"I think we're missing something important. Something about Angie herself. She was worried those last days, yet Nancy said her work at the museum was going well. She'd done a great job."

"She was angry, too," Izzy said. "She stopped in here one day just before she died, just to talk. We sat and had coffee together. I had the feeling something had happened to her. She talked about people lying. She hated it when people lied, she said."

"That's an odd thing to say," Birdie said. "Did she explain herself, Izzy?"

"No, but she looked genuinely sad. As if she truly wanted the world to be different—but couldn't do a thing about it."

"Pete said she was like that. Upbeat and fun-loving one minute, then sad the next. But Angie would never tell him what was making her sad." Cass smoothed out two rows of knitting and looked at the beginnings of her shawl.

Birdie nodded. "You're doing fine, dear. Now make sure you don't tense up toward the end of your rows."

"I think that's what we need to find out," Nell said. "What was making Angie sad—or mad. And why she was leaving Sea Harbor soon. The police look for things like blood and evidence. But I think if we look into Angie's heart, we'll be closer to finding the truth."

A slight tapping on the back door brought Nell's words to a halt. Izzy stood and walked over just as it opened a crack, then wider, and Sam Perry stepped inside, his tall figure filling the doorframe and his camera bag swinging from a strap around his neck.

"Hi, ladies. Hope I'm not interrupting."

"What do you think, Sam?" Izzy asked.

"It's perfect, Izzy. What a great place. I sure appreciate your doing this for me."

"My friends here would tell you that it's for all of *us*, Sam," Izzy said.

"And that would be the truth," Birdie said. "It will be nice to have someone other than George Gideon keeping an eye on our knitting studio."

Sam dropped the keys on the table. "I've met him once or twice and understand what you're saying, Birdie. I took my students up to North Beach today to take some shots and we ran into him. He seemed to be moving from beach towel to beach towel, grazing the ladies, so to speak."

"Ugh," Izzy said, wrinkling up her face. She glanced at the window, then looked at the clock on the wall. "He should be coming on duty soon. But enough about Gideon. When do you want to move in?"

"Now," Sam said. He smiled. "But I guess the weekend will suffice. How about I come over tomorrow after class and I'll help take the boxes of Angie's things over to her mother's? Then Saturday I can bring my meager belongings over. I don't have much."

"Sam, it's good of you to do this," Nell said.

"Well, the least I can do is help clean up my new home. And I told Izzy I'd look into having the locks changed." He looked over at Izzy. "So it's a date?"

Izzy frowned for a moment, the words sounding unfamiliar. She cleared her throat. "How about an appointment?" she said finally.

Izzy could control her voice and mannerisms, Nell thought, like any good ex-lawyer. But she had absolutely no control over the slight blush that spread down her neck. Perhaps summer was coming to Sea Harbor after all. Or at least it was just around the corner.

Chapter 21

$\mathcal{B}$en arrived home on Friday afternoon. To Nell, it seemed he had been gone a month.

"I should go away more often," Ben joked. He walked out onto the deck where Nell had placed a platter of cheese and crackers and a carafe of sun-brewed mint tea. Nell's hand rested on the small of his back, and her body leaned nicely into his side as they stepped into the late-day sunlight.

"It's been a long week," Nell said. "I'm glad you're back, Ben."

"So fill me in," he said, drawing her down beside him on the swing. "We've a little time before Ben's Colorado fish fry." He leaned forward and poured them each a glass of tea.

Nell sipped the tea, looking over the tops of the trees toward the ocean. "I don't have much to tell that I haven't told you over the phone, Ben. It's more a collection of emotions. Uncomfortable ones. Do you remember the summer that we went out to the ranch for the Fourth of July?"

Ben nodded. "The summer of the tornado."

Nell nodded against his shoulder. "Yes, that one. Remember how we stood outside that day and looked up at the sky while the warning sirens went off in the distance? How the air got heavy and still, and the birds went crazy, chattering and flying in circles."

"I do remember. It was my one and only Kansas tornado. That early part was fascinating and foreboding."

"It was almost like a spell, holding us in suspension. That's what it's been like here, Ben. That eerie calm that you can feel deep down inside. But you know it's not right, and you know it's not going to last. It's going to explode in an enormous black flurry and rip things apart."

Ben touched her hair. "Far as I know, there are no tornadoes scheduled for Sea Harbor, Nellie."

Nell nodded, her head rubbing against his shoulder. Not one tracked by Doppler radar, maybe. Not that kind.

When the phone rang, they both looked toward the house, thinking for a minute they'd not answer it, savor this time alone. But when Ben got up and walked into the kitchen to answer, Nell knew before he called her in that it was a call they needed to get.

"That was Izzy," he said, grabbing the keys to his SUV from the counter. "She needs us."

Nell had been right. A tornado had struck Sea Harbor. Or at least one small part of it.

"What a mess," Ben said, looking around the small apartment that was once Angie's apartment.

Sam and Izzy stood in the center of the living room, sur-rounded by debris. The books that Izzy had piled on the shelves to warm the apartment were scattered across the floor, some open with their pages bent where they hit the floor. A desk drawer hung awkwardly at the end of its groove, ready to fall. Two small area rugs were rumpled, kicked aside, and cushions from the cor-duroy sofa had been pulled up at odd angles and left that way, leaning against the back or sides.

Nell picked her way across the room to Izzy's side. She looked at Sam. "You found it like this?"

"We came up to check the door for new locks," Sam said.

"And take the boxes of Angie's things over to her mother. This is what we found."

Izzy and Nell walked back into the bedroom area where they had stored the boxes of Angie's things, and Sam and Ben followed.

It mirrored the living room, drawers emptied, bedclothes pulled back, and the mattress was pulled partway off the bed. Izzy walked over to the open closet door where they had stored the boxes of Angie's things. The boxes were ripped apart, clothes and shoes and cosmetics thrown all over the closet floor and trailing out into the bedroom.

Nell's heart sank.

"I should have taken Angie's things to Josie right away," Izzy said, her eyes brimming with tears.

Nell wrapped her arms around Izzy's shoulders. "We'll pack them again, Izzy. It will be fine."

"I wonder if they found what they were looking for," Izzy said, her voice soft. She bent down and picked up a jean jacket that had been Angie's, held it for a moment, then folded it carefully and set it on the bed. She picked up a small cardboard box in which she'd carefully packed a few of Angie's personal things—some photos, CDs, a few pairs of earrings. She frowned, then fingered through the messy contents.

"What's wrong, Izzy?" Nell asked.

"I packed Angie's iPod in here. It's gone."

"You're sure, honey?"

Izzy nodded. "Positive. And those orange earphones are gone, too."

"Someone did all this for an iPod and earphones?" Ben said. "Doesn't make sense."

"Maybe the intruder didn't find what he was looking for," Nell said, "and he took the iPod for a consolation prize. So silly. So unfortunate."

Nell glanced into the kitchen area and noticed that even the refrigerator had been searched and the freezer door left open. A small pool of water had collected on the floor. Several of Izzy's plates had fallen from the cupboard and lay cracked on the counter.

Izzy's eyes were huge, taking in the chaos that had been a clean, tidy apartment the day before.

"Have you called the police?" Ben asked.

Sam nodded. "There's a bad accident out at the rotary that they're taking care of first. And because no one was living here, it's not a priority, I'm afraid."

"The police probably can't do much," Ben said. He looked over at Izzy. "There's not much damage, Iz. Mostly just a mess." Ben rubbed his hand along the wall. "My excellent paint job is still intact."

Izzy offered a small smile.

"We can clean this place up in no time," Sam added, sounding more enthusiastic than any of them felt. "It already looks better than a lot of places I've lived."

The concern on Izzy's face was obvious. Nell hugged her. "It's okay, sweetie," she whispered. But it wasn't okay—and all four of them were well aware of that. The earlier intruder had done nothing, just let in a sweet little kitten. It had bothered Nell, but there hadn't been much upset and no aftermath that they knew of. But this destruction and disregard was truly frightening. Nell walked across the room and absently picked up some magazines from the floor, her thoughts disjointed and moving in several directions at once. She hoped Izzy couldn't feel her fear.

What if Izzy had been in here? If someone had been here, she wondered, would they have been as carelessly thrown aside as the books and dishes and bedclothes?

"Someone was looking for something," Sam said. "Something that could have fit in a drawer or beneath a mattress or behind a row of books, from the looks of the mess."

"Or in a freezer," Nell said.

"Which narrows it down to a million things," Izzy said.

Sam picked up a plastic garbage sack and walked into the kitchen area. "Well, I'm claiming this room," he said over his shoulder. "The rest of you are on your own."

Nell watched him begin to sweep up the broken pieces of pottery and dump them into the garbage bag, then look around under the sink for other cleaning supplies. She didn't know much about Sam's family, but someone had definitely done a fine job of raising him. And for right now, in this place and time, she was awfully glad he was here.

The trout didn't reach the hot coals of Ben's grill until much later that night. But by the time Nell, Izzy, and Sam walked out of the Seaside Knitting Studio apartment a couple hours later, the rooms smelled of soap and lemon oil, the bed was stripped and the refrigerator emptied out. Once Eddy McClucken from the hardware store had finished putting in the new lock and after they'd stashed seven boxes of clothes, books, and personal items in the back of Ben's SUV, the tired crew called it a day.

"I think showers can wait," Nell announced, not leaving room for arguments. "It's time to go home and feast on Colorado trout. I called Birdie to say we'd be late, but we'd be there. She's in charge."

As sometimes happened at the Endicott home, friends arrived before those who lived there, making themselves at home, and when the bedraggled foursome arrived, Ham had cleaned the fish, Birdie had lined up the martini mixings, and Cass had swept the deck clean of pine needles, lit the gas lanterns along the railing, and put a Norah Jones CD in the player. Archie and Harriet Brandley showed up with a loaf of sourdough bread and an enormous bowl of Harriet's spinach pasta, and Jane had mixed together her special mayonnaise herb sauce for the fish. And Rachel and Don Wooten had come, too, reminded recently that Friday nights at the Endicotts were a fine ending to a long week.

Nell sank into a chair and gratefully accepted the glass of water Birdie offered her, along with the promise that once Ben got mixing, she'd have something better.

"What could Angie possibly have had that someone wanted so badly?" Jane asked after the story had been told and retold. "It doesn't make sense to me. Could she have been in some trouble? Drugs?"

"Angie was honest, almost to a fault," Ben said. He stood at the grill, an old checkered apron covering his shirt and shorts and a basting brush in one hand. The trout sizzled as he basted it with dill butter. "And she was plenty tough on anyone who wasn't."

"That's the truth. I remember when Ted Archer lost his manager's job at the Framingham plant," Birdie said. "It was one of those layoffs to save money, so Tony's grandfather took the higher-paid men and pulled their jobs right out from under them. No warning. It was right before Christmas, I remember. Angie was just a child—twelve or so—but Josie thought she was going to personally take out the old man's eyes. She hated him."

Archie nodded, remembering the story and the people affected by the layoff. "I think Angie held Tony Framingham personally responsible for his grandfather's sins. She didn't have much use for him, that's for sure. And if Angie didn't like you, you darn well knew it."

"Tony?" Jane said, surprised. "He was a cocky teen, but I thought he'd grown up all right."

"Unless you crossed him," Archie said.

"And Angie crossed him?" Ben said.

"She did something he didn't like. I don't know what, exactly, but Tony told her she'd be sorry she ever came back to Sea Harbor."

"But why, exactly?" Izzy asked.

"Well, now that's the question of the hour, isn't it? Tony

never finished his threat because yours truly showed up to escort him out of my bookstore, as you yourself personally witnessed, Izzy."

Nell listened to the chatter, but none of the scenarios played out. Not tales of Angie's childhood, her emotional response to injustices, unrequited lovers. None rested comfortably in her mind, nor held a motive for murder. Not even Tony's threat. Although that was something she wished she knew more about.

Gideon, though, frightened her. Everything about him seemed darker since Angie's death, and there didn't seem to be any reprieve. Had he been that dark and sinister before, and they just hadn't noticed? Or was Angie's death creating a cloud over everyone, deserving or not?

By the time the trout was passed from grill to plates and the crispy bread and salad passed around, the only thing in the whole day that made much sense to Nell was the cool breeze, the deck full of lovely friends, and the thought that tomorrow was another day. She felt fairly certain that Tony wasn't the kind of person who could ever hurt anyone, but then, she realized with some surprise, there wasn't anyone in her town she thought capable of killing Angie Archer. But someone most definitely had.

Nell walked the Wootens to the door a short while later and thanked them for coming.

"Did your talk with Sal go okay, Nell?" Rachel asked. "I know he can be difficult to talk to. I think he's so scared of his wife he avoids talking to most women. Angie was an exception."

Nell paused, unsure of what to say. She didn't want people who worked in the same building with Sal to think poorly of him. She chose her words carefully. "Actually, he didn't have much to say. I think his mind was on other things. He seemed very busy."

Rachel looked puzzled. "Sal? I don't think Sal ever gets really busy. There's an administrative assistant who works in the next office, and I think she does the bulk of the work. I don't know if it's entirely fair, but people think Sal was appointed to that job because of Beatrice's connections with the city council and the chamber. She wields a lot of power over there. And she likes the title, Registrar of Deeds."

"Well, he had a stack of papers on his desk and I think he was anxious to get back to work, for whatever reason. But basically he said he didn't know Angie well. So he wasn't the best person to talk to anyway."

Rachel's brows lifted and she looked up at her husband, Don, then back to Nell. She hesitated for a moment before she spoke.

"I don't know how well Sal really knew Angie, Nell, but just between you, me, and a whole bunch of people who work at the county offices, Sal Scaglia was head over heels in love with Angie Archer."

Chapter 22

*T*his would be the last night he'd be dressing up like this—he was beginning to feel like a fool eel in the rubber suit, and it pulled on his crotch in a miserable way.

The man, cold and damp, ran one hand through wet, stringy hair. Seaweed, he thought, pulling out a greenish brown strand. Crap. He hoisted the heavy rubber sack over his shoulder and pulled himself up on the uneven outcroppings of the breakwater until he reached the top.

It was hard work, but truth be told, it hadn't been all bad. He'd gotten it down to a system. Not a bad job. Slipping down into the cold water late at night in his wet suit, finding the traps on the muddy bottom. Then pulling out those feisty red-crusted gals. It had its moments for sure. He could even understand why some folks did this for a living. And legally, to boot.

Hell, maybe that's what he'd do—buy himself a fleet of lobster boats. Get a place in Gloucester or maybe up in Maine. He wouldn't stick around this town; he'd said he wouldn't, and he was a man of his word. As long as there was money attached, anyhow.

He'd torn that whole apartment apart for nothing, a darn shame. But finding the computer in the hot chick's apartment would have been gravy—a bonus—he'd been told, just in case it pointed the finger at anyone. He'd still collect the money and hightail it out of town. That's all that poor excuse for a human being wanted anyway.

He thought about the apartment and the white sheets that he'd found on the bed, the silky underwear in the boxes. He should have made a trip up there while she was alive, that's what he should have done. But no matter now. Miss Hotty Totty was worth more to him dead than alive. Not often he'd say that about a woman.

A huge moon filled the night with light, reflecting off the water and lighting his way along the breakwater as he headed back to the truck. On rainy, cold nights when the world was asleep, poaching was a breeze. But on nights like this, with the moon so big and round and people out late, strolling and doing whatever, teens on the prowl, looking for trouble, it was a challenge. And that was the part he liked best of all—the danger, the chance of besting everyone, sneaking those lobsters into his sack with no one knowing any better. That and the once-needed extra cash.

And damned if he wasn't good at it. No one ever saw the black slinky figure as he slipped off the lower ledge of the breakwater and into the water. He was too slick for them—he'd never be caught. He'd hear them talking in Harry's Deli or at the Gull, planning how they'd catch the poachers, fry 'em in hot oil if they could. And he'd sit right next to them, perched up on a bar stool at the Gull, and help them plot and plan how they'd do it. Jerks.

But tonight was sayonara. This last one was pure gravy. He'd promised his buddies a huge lobster bash and they'd get it. He could have bought the lobsters, had the whole shindig catered with the money he'd gotten so far. But he was smart. There were plenty more, more than he'd dreamed of. He'd soon be eating lobster for breakfast if he wanted. Have someone bring it to him on a silver tray. But for one last thrill he'd get them the old way. Slip on down there to lobster heaven—or was it hell?—and get them for free.

He laughed out loud and made his way along the breakwater to the beach, watching his steps so he didn't trip. Wouldn't it be a fool's luck to fall and break his neck tonight, just when things were finally falling into place?

The heavy sack caused him to lean forward beneath its weight. Maybe he'd taken a few more than he needed, but better too many than not enough. He sucked in a lungful of air, straightened again, and made his way slowly across the beach. When he reached the dead-end gravel road, he turned toward a weedy parking lot near the boarded-up lighthouse. Folks had abandoned old cars in the lot and his truck fit right in, not noticed in the heap of rusting iron. No one would know he'd been there.

The sound of wheels on loose gravel made him shift the weight of the sack and quicken his pace. From behind him, a truck screeched and skidded as it came barreling down the empty road. Some fool teenagers out for a joy ride, he thought.

He moved to the edge of the road as the vehicle came closer, spitting gravel in all directions.

At first he thought it was the headlights, filling him with a blinding light so fierce his whole body filled with fire. Then, in the next instant, the light turned into moonlight, bright and glorious, and his whole being soared toward it, thrashing, and spinning, and whirling in the black night.

And then, abruptly, the night melted into nothingness. The air was still, the night dark and empty.

And the only sound left on the old lighthouse road was the frantic scurrying of dozens of crustaceans seeking release.

Chapter 23

$\mathcal{A}$t first, no one knew who the dead man was. His body was smashed up against a pole on a narrow gravel road north of town. He had no wallet on him and his face was badly disfigured, making identification difficult.

But what was of greater interest wasn't the man's name or his address. What grabbed the attention of the early beach-bound joggers who found him and the policemen and ambulance driver who were called to the scene were the scurrying lobsters emerging from the thick rubber sack.

"He h-h-had a whole rubber sackful of 'em," Tommy Porter told Izzy as they stood in line at Coffee's early Saturday morning. "Must have been a dozen keepers trapped in that sack."

Nell and Izzy stood in line waiting for their order, listening to Tommy talk, and to three other conversations going on simultaneously in the busy coffee shop, most about the strange man who was found dead on Lighthouse Road.

"Do you think he was the poacher?" Izzy asked.

"Sure wasn't dressed like a lobsterman. And there wasn't a boat a sight," Tommy said, in a feeble attempt at humor. His excitement seemed to ease the stuttering, and it was only an occasional word that came out in stops and starts. "We don't know who it was yet. Sometimes those poachers move around from one little town to another. Probably no one we know."

"How did he die, Tommy?"

"Someone slammed into h-h-him. His own fault, probably. H-he had on a black wet suit. No one could have seen him, not on a dark road in the middle of the n-n-night."

"It was that old lighthouse road near the breakwater?"

Tommy nodded.

"Who hit him?" Nell asked.

"Don't know. Whoever it was didn't stay around. Maybe somebody who doesn't like poachers, which would be about the whole town."

"Is that what people think?" Nell asked.

Tommy shrugged. "Don't know. Maybe a fella with a few too many pints under his belt."

"Nevertheless, it's an awful way for someone to die."

"Maybe. But it's b-been a rough time for Cass and Pete and the others. At least they can get back to lobstering."

"I guess that's right."

"Two decaf lattes," the girl behind the counter called out.

Izzy looked over Tommy's shoulder and held up her hand. "That's us."

Tommy looked crestfallen, as if his big chance in life had been crushed by a decaf latte. "See you, Izzy."

Izzy smiled brightly and picked up the lattes. She and Nell wove their way through the crowded store and out the door.

"I can't imagine anyone would intentionally kill someone for stealing lobsters," Izzy said. "People talk that way, but they don't mean it."

Nell drank the steamy latte, then brushed a line of foam from her lip. Of course people didn't mean it, at least not Cass, who'd been very vocal in her threat to string the poachers up by her own pot warp if given the chance. But who knew what one might be capable of if a livelihood was being threatened? Sometimes you had to walk in those shoes, she thought, before answers were crystal clear.

"Lots of gossip around Coffee's today," Izzy said. "The poor guy who was killed, Margarethe's gala tonight. The horrible and the extravagant. But at least it's kept people from talking about the break-in above my shop."

"I think the consensus was that some beach bum wanted a place to bunk for a while, and an empty apartment was fair game." Nell took the paper cup from Izzy and the two began to walk down Harbor Road.

"That's ridiculous."

"Yes," Nell said and sipped her latte. The news of the hit-and-run victim had served as a distraction, but not enough to block out Rachel Wooten's parting words the night before. "Izzy," she asked suddenly, "did you ever notice Sal Scaglia hanging around the shop?"

Izzy thought for a minute. "Well, there was the other day when his wife insisted he come over to clean Angie's apartment—"

"But not while Angie was alive?"

"I don't think so, Nell. Why?"

Nell told her what Rachel had said.

"Nell, that's so surprising, that shy man, in love with Angie?"

"Rachel seemed sure of it. Or at least he was infatuated with her. But somehow Angie made quite an impression on Sal Scaglia."

"What do you make of it?"

"I don't know, Izzy. But I think it's something we all need to talk about. It throws another person into the picture, for better or for worse."

"Nell, now that you mention it, I guess I did see Sal across the street a couple times, but I never thought anything of it. If you look out my shop windows long enough, you'll see just about everyone in Sea Harbor."

"Speaking of people hanging out around your shop." Nell paused and pointed across the street to the front door of the knitting studio.

Izzy started to laugh, and then she and Nell crossed the street to the shop.

"What are you doing here at this hour?" Izzy asked.

Sam Perry sat on the front step, two duffel bags, a cardboard box of books, and several camera cases piled on the step beside him. His long legs were stretched out across the sidewalk, and his elbows rested on the step above. Orange Top-Siders brought attention to a pair of long feet, and an angled Sox cap and sunglasses kept the early-morning sun out of his eyes.

"Good morning, ladies," Sam said, his face breaking into a smile. "I thought you'd never get here. Shouldn't a knitting shop be open by now?" He glanced at his watch, an exaggerated frown creasing his forehead.

"Geez, Sam, it's eight a.m.," Izzy said. "I'm only here because Nell and I are going to finish up her scarf before the store opens."

"Well, here's the thing. You told me I could move in today." Sam lifted himself up from the step and stood beside her. He pushed his sunglasses to the top of his head.

"*Today* has barely begun, Sam. Hold this." Izzy thrust her coffee cup into his hand and fumbled in her large bag for a set of keys.

Sam took a drink of the latte and wrinkled his nose. "Don't they have just plain coffee around here?"

Nell sighed. "You and Ben. Give him a Dunkin' Donuts coffee any day. He's hopeless."

Sam held the door open for Izzy and Nell, then grabbed his camera bags and followed them inside. "Just give me the keys, Iz, and I'll be out of your hair."

"Don't be so macho. We'll help you get that stuff upstairs."

Together the three of them collected Sam's belongings and made their way out the back door and up the steps to the apartment. Nell paused at the top step, suddenly afraid to move. She'd found too many surprises on the other side of that door since Angie died. And she didn't want to face another.

But Izzy didn't hesitate, and turning the new key in the polished brass lock, she pushed the door open and stepped inside. She and Nell had left the windows open a crack, a gesture Ben and Sam had not understood and protested loudly. But Izzy and Nell felt an intense desire to rid the rooms of any scent or reminder of the unknown person who had torn the rooms apart with such abandon.

Fresh air helped enormously.

Nell smiled. The rooms were clean and airy, and ready for Sam. She and Izzy had made the bed before leaving last night. Except for refilling the refrigerator, all was ready.

Sam set his camera bags down near the couch and walked around the room, opening windows. "I love this place," he said. He walked into the kitchen, opening the refrigerator door and peering into the empty interior as if he'd lived there for years. Then he closed it and smiled. "I feel good about being here, good vibes. Thanks, Izzy."

Izzy stood still, holding the ring of keys. She smiled.

Nell could read her niece's thoughts as clearly as if she had shouted them out loud. Izzy was happy, too—happy and relieved that someone safe was going to be above her shop. Relieved that the bad karma, from wherever it had come, might be on its way out of her store—and out of her life.

Chapter 24

$\mathcal{N}$ell picked up an edge of the long, narrow scarf that she had finished just hours ago. It was beautiful, a long, lacy blend of all the colors of the sea. The slender fringes created even more length to the scarf, and as Izzy had planned, it would float gently in a breeze as Nell walked or danced.

Nell held the scarf up and looked at the hundreds of intricate stitches that held it together—the holes in the scarf were lovely, the substance of lace when surrounded by the stitches. But the holes in their lives right now were not nearly so lovely. And the stitching around them loose and uneven.

Nell and Ben were greatly relieved that Cass and Pete's traps were now secure. But the gruesome death of the poacher was disturbing. He had been pushed against a pole, his face smashed beyond recognition. And by late afternoon, rumors had picked up all over town about who might have done it. Someone had crushed a man to death—and didn't even stay around to see if he was alive or if he needed help. Ben said the police didn't have much incentive to do anything about it, though there would be a cursory investigation, he supposed. And they still didn't know who the man was, though dental records would be checked.

Nell rubbed her bare arms. It was a lot to deal with. Angie's death, the damage to Izzy's apartment, a man killed for stealing lobsters. Or for being on a road late at night instead of home in bed. But she knew they were getting close.

Tonight, though, they had a party to attend, and if the stars were lined up right, as Birdie would say, for one lovely evening, they'd eat and dance and forget about the things that were twisting their lives uncomfortably. Some things could wait until tomorrow.

Nell wrapped the scarf around her neck twice, as Izzy had suggested, and walked over to the full-length mirror. She slid her hands down the sides of her black, summery dress. It was simple and elegant, and one of Ben's favorites. The dress was cocktail length, and slightly uneven as it dipped midcalf. And the sea silk scarf looked like shimmering jewels around her neck. Except for a pair of dangly blue sapphire earrings that Ben had given her for their anniversary, the scarf was all the jewelry she needed. Nell smiled at her reflection in the mirror, pushed a stray hair back in place, and headed downstairs to a waiting and patient Ben.

Izzy had turned down their offer for a ride to the arts benefit, but Ben had insisted that they pick up Birdie.

"You look like a lovely jewel tonight, m'dear," Ben said to Birdie as she settled into the back of their car. "How did I get so lucky? Not one, but two of you?"

"I guess you're just fortunate, Ben Endicott," Birdie said. "But I could have gotten myself over to the party quite nicely, you know."

"And deny me the pleasure?" Ben said, eyeing her in the rearview mirror.

"You do look lovely, Birdie," Nell agreed, staving off the argument about Birdie's driving before it gained any momentum. Ben was convinced Birdie would drive herself directly into the ocean one of these nights. "That's a truly elegant dress."

Birdie's long silvery dress was a perfect fit for her. Nell admired her friend's composure and elegance, both of which belied her age. She wore a butterfly shawl over her shoulders to ward off the ocean breeze. Nell knew the shawl well. It had taken Birdie a good chunk of last winter to knit—in between a dozen scarves and hats—but it was worth every stitch, they all assured her.

At the edge of town, Ben turned onto Framingham Road, a windy, tree-lined lane that went only one place, and that was the elegant Framingham estate.

Nell opened her window a crack and ocean air filled the car. "Margarethe seems to have the power to determine all sorts of things, including what kind of weather she'll have for parties. It's perfect." Cape Ann evenings were unpredictable. Sometimes the heat lingered after the sun went down, and other times it could be damp and chilly. Margarethe's evening was nicely couched in between—cool enough for light wraps, but not too breezy for strolling along the beach.

Ben drove slowly, and they watched the lights along the ocean's edge flicker in the crisp breeze. On the other side of the road, small gravel pathways wound through thick stands of pine and willow to the Framingham quarries, once alive with the sounds of hammers pounding on granite as men worked the motions. But now they were as quiet as the night, the deep quarries filled with water and surrounded by scrub bushes and wild flowers.

And straight ahead, even from this distance, they could see the lights that marked the Framingham home. Parties on the point were always an event, but tonight Margarethe had pulled out all stops. Tiny Christmas lights decorated clusters of small trees along the property, and a long line of candlelit torches lined the enormous circle drive. Parking areas off to the side were already filling up with cars, and an army of uniformed valets stood at attention, ready to relieve drivers of keys. Ben pulled to a stop and helped Birdie and Nell out of the car.

"It's beautiful," Nell said. "A fairyland."

Sally Goldenbaum

In addition to the main home—a three-story wood and stone home that Sylvester Framingham Sr. had built years before—were guest cottages, a boathouse, pool cabana, and staff homes. And tonight they were all outlined in tiny, sparkling lights.

"I remember my dad's stories about coming out here years ago when he was a kid, back when some of the quarries were still being mined," Ben said. "The main house was here—but a fraction of the size of this one. There wasn't much else but a couple shacks. But things took a turn once old Framingham took over. He wasn't the best-loved man in town, but he knew how to turn a buck and build his own little empire. And once the quarry era ended, he seemed to turn granite into gold and opened that food-processing plant out on Rainbow Road. When Margarethe applied for a job, the story is told that the old man was ecstatic. He was crazy about her because she was strong and smart."

"I think the old man threw Margarethe and his son together, just to keep her around," Birdie said.

"That's the story. She filled the gap—Tony's dad was quiet, hated business and the social responsibilities it required. Margarethe was the opposite."

"It's hard to imagine Margarethe married to anyone like that," Nell said.

"They seemed to work it out. She was genuinely sad when her husband died."

"She's done an amazing job of handling the family fortune," Birdie said. "The old man got the last laugh."

Ben took Birdie's arm and looped the other behind Nell as they walked up the wide fan of steps to the front door.

At the front entry, Margarethe stood tall and stately, welcoming guests. She looked like a queen, Nell thought. Her broad shoulders were covered with a filmy lace stole, and the long, heavily beaded dress must have taken a whole crew to sew on the tiny crystals.

Nearby, Jane and Ham Brewster and a coterie of artists from Canary Cove greeted guests and thanked people for their generous contributions to the Arts Academy. The evening would include a silent auction of art works donated by the artists, and along with the tickets, they predicted there would be enough money generated to support the academy and scholarships for the next year, at least.

"Nell, that scarf is exquisite," Margarethe said, admiring the gentle, fluid wrap. "I knew it would be."

"I had trouble visualizing the end product," Nell said, "but I trusted Izzy's eye."

"A wise decision," Margarethe said. "Izzy knows her yarns." She urged them all to make themselves at home out on the back veranda or the tent just beyond. Appetizers and drinks were at every turn, and dinner and dancing would follow.

Nell handed her wrap to the outstretched arm of Stella Palazola, Annabelle's daughter, and smiled her thanks. Mae's twin nieces were doing the same on the other side of the room, the young teenagers earning a few extra dollars while they ogled the beautiful dresses and enjoyed being a part of the summer gala.

"Has Izzy arrived yet?" she asked Jane as they walked into the spacious entryway.

"Oh, yes—Izzy certainly has arrived," Jane said, a mischievous glint in her eye.

"That sounds mysterious," Nell said. "Is she all right?"

"*Very* all right. I think they headed for the martini bar on the veranda." Jane pointed through the round entryway, to open French doors at the back side of the house. "Ham and I will join you shortly."

"They?" Nell looked at Ben, then Birdie.

"She came with Sam," Birdie said. She handed her butterfly shawl to Stella, who eyed it with outright envy. "Just be sure your hands are clean, sweetie," Birdie said, her brows lifting up into her bangs in warning. She turned back to Nell. "When I went to retrieve my wrap at Margarethe's Christmas party, I walked in unexpectedly on the little helper bees. The sweet young things were having a grand time trying on the mink stoles and assorted finery. I think they shall have a grand time tonight with my shawl. I hope they like it best."

"What would we do without you?" Nell said, hugging her impulsively.

"I don't intend to let you find out anytime soon," Birdie answered briskly. "Now, where's the martini bar?"

They spotted Izzy before they saw the bar. And instantly Nell understood Jane's smile.

Izzy Chambers commanded center stage. Izzy, in a word, looked spectacular.

Her streaked hair was pulled back tightly from her face, fastened behind with a tiny silver ribbon that allowed her eyes and high cheekbones to take over her face. But what caused Ben to take in a quick breath and Birdie and Nell to catch their breath was the strapless cobalt-blue dress wrapped around Izzy's shapely body, with the two sides fastened in a knot between her breasts. Silky waves of fabric flowed over her curves in a waterfall of shimmering blue until they collected in a puddle at her feet. Nell had never seen her niece look quite so lovely.

"There you three are," Izzy said, walking toward them. "Well?" she spun around. "What do you think?"

Birdie's head swiveled back and forth and a smile spread across her lined face. She tiptoed up and kissed Izzy on the cheek. "Oh, to be your age again, sweet one," she whispered in her ear. "I'd have myself a dress exactly like that."

Birdie looked over Izzy's shoulder at Sam Perry, standing just behind Izzy, an amused grin on his face.

"And I'd take one of those too," she said, poking an index finger in Sam's direction.

Nell and Izzy laughed.

Birdie pulled away slightly, and then she added quietly, "And that little bit of cleavage is quite nice."

"Birdie!" Izzy said. Her hands flew up to the top of the gown.

"Sweetheart, there's no reason to hide God's gifts under a bushel basket. Let them shine, I say."

Nell looked over at Sam, hoping for a change of topic. "It was nice of you to bring Izzy, Sam."

"I brought Sam," Izzy corrected. "I thought he'd probably get lost coming out here and end up in a quarry. Since he was an honored guest, it was the least I could do." She looked at Sam. "And he doesn't look half bad, does he?"

"Izzy was afraid I wouldn't lock up the apartment to her satisfaction. She's a little squirrelly about that these days. Or I might not feed Purl the right amount. Purl's attached to me, by the way—drives Izzy crazy. So that's why I got picked up," Sam said, nicely skirting talk of his attire.

"That, too," Izzy agreed.

Ben shook Sam's hand and nodded toward the walnut bar behind him. "Sam, seeing all these beautiful ladies has put me in serious need of a martini. Shall we?"

"Excellent idea," Sam said.

"Izzy, you look radiant," Nell said.

"Thank you, Aunt Nell. I decided I'd had it with all the bad things going on around me. I needed to step out of it all—at least for one night—and be someone else. So I did. The dress is borrowed."

"But nonetheless perfect for you," Birdie said. "You look ravishing, Isabel. And I agree. Life is short. Enjoy."

"Thanks, both of you. I just wanted to have fun, you know? And Sam, well, he's so safe. He's like a brother, I've known him so long."

Nell looked over at Sam. He was standing next to Ben, waiting for the bartender to finish shaking their martinis. But Sam's eyes weren't on the martinis or the bar or on Ben Endicott. They were glued to the woman in the shimmering cobalt-blue dress. And as far as Nell could tell, his thoughts were far from brotherly.

But Izzy was right—he was safe and trustworthy. And that's what mattered to Nell.

Ben and Sam returned with the martinis just as a jazz ensemble began playing in the background. A cool breeze came in off the water and they moved over to the edge of the veranda to watch a small group of dancers move onto the portable floor set up just inside the white tent. When Ben's cell phone rang, Nell looked over, surprised. She and Ben had a pact to always turn their phones off at social gatherings.

"Sorry. I forgot," he said to Nell, and glanced down at the screen. Ben looked closer, then whispered to Nell that he'd be back in a minute, and he walked away to a quiet corner of the veranda. She watched him go, wondering what minor emergency was requiring her husband's attention tonight. Nearly all their friends were here.

Without intention, Ben Endicott had followed in his father's footsteps, becoming Sea Harbor's godfather, as Izzy liked to call him. He was the person neighbors called when a loved one died or a son or daughter was having trouble passing the SAT, or a small loan was needed for a sick relative. People called at odd times and for odd reasons—and Nell wondered briefly what it would be tonight. But whatever it was, Ben was the person to call. Sometimes with just a few calm words, he could push anxiety or worry away.

When Ben hadn't come back by the time dinner was announced, Nell gathered the others and suggested they go into the tent and find their table. Ham and Jane joined them, and Cass and Pete. Ben would be along soon, she said, and it would disrupt the schedule of events if diners dallied. But as she followed the others into the tent, she turned and scanned the nearly empty veranda. Ben was nowhere in sight, and a dollop of worry worked its way into her thoughts. If he had left, he would have told her, she thought. There was a large contingent of people who had come up from Boston for the arts benefit. He had probably run into an old friend and found a quiet place to talk. That, too, would be typical.

Once inside the cavernous tent, the evening's festive mood took over, and by the time the group found their engraved name cards and seated themselves at the round, white-clothed table, Nell's concern had slipped to a back corner of her mind and her attention drawn to the centerpieces. Each table featured a black-and-white photograph taken by Sam Perry—signed, matted, and set in a smooth and simple maple frame. Some were from his new book, others shots he'd taken on his travels—a child sitting by a stream in India, an old man walking across a New York street— each an expression of life in the unique way that was making Sam Perry's work noticed by collectors and publishers.

"Sam, how wonderful," Nell said, looking closer at the photo. "Margarethe certainly twisted your arm."

"She's persuasive, I'll admit," Sam said. "But she took care of the hard part—the matting and framing. I was happy to provide the prints."

Two waiters circled the table, pouring champagne and placing crisp salads with chunks of lobster in a nest of romaine lettuce at each place.

"Tony Framingham is entertaining quite a group," said Birdie, lifting her flute by the slender stem.

Nell followed the nod of Birdie's head. Two tables away, Tony sat with a group of people his age, mostly unfamiliar faces— probably friends from New York whom he had brought in for the evening gala. Tony's polished good looks seemed artificial to Nell tonight. Perhaps it was the tuxedo. But as Nell watched, he re-minded her of an actor on a stage. Saying the right words. Smiling at the right time. But she sensed an underlying current beneath his words and his smile. And when the attention turned to oth-ers at the table and he wasn't in the spotlight, a somber look fell across his face—an expression that didn't match the lighthearted party mood surrounding him. *Full of sound and fury,* she thought. A dark cloud. But did it signify nothing, as in Shakespeare's play? Just then, Tony turned his head. Before Nell could look away, he caught her eye.

But the social, polite smile didn't return to his face, acknowl-edging Nell with a friendly nod. Instead, Tony looked back at her, long and hard, without a hint of welcome. It was Nell who finally turned away, uncomfortable.

The movement of the chair next to her brought her atten-tion back to the table. "Ben, it's about time." Nell reached up and touched his hand, smiling. "Come, sit. Let me have the waiter bring your plate. Where've you been?"

"The waiter is already on it." Ben sat down and touched the fringe of her silky sea-yarn scarf. He looked around the table. "Sorry to be so late, folks. Sometimes cell phones are more a curse than anything else." He took a swallow of the scotch that the waiter had placed in front of him and forced a smile in place.

"Ben, what is it?" Nell asked.

Birdie, Izzy, and Ham caught Nell's question and looked at Ben. Jane and Sam stopped their conversation midstream. The table grew silent, an island in the middle of music and animated conversation and loud bursts of laughter.

"It's about the man who was killed last night," he said.

"The poacher?" Cass said.

Ben nodded. "It was George Gideon," he said solemnly.

Chapter 25

"*G*ideon!" The word was a hushed chorus, eight voices colliding in the center of the elegantly decorated table.

The police chief had called him, Ben said, hoping he'd find Father Northcutt for them. They knew Margarethe had urged him to come to the party to give the blessing. The police said old Mrs. Gideon was in a horrible state and asking for the priest.

Ben found the good father just as he was about to be seated at the head table, and the older priest immediately excused himself to help out his parishioner. His job was not a nine-to-fiver, he politely told his hostess. Duty called.

"I don't know too much more," Ben said, "except that it didn't seem to be a one-time excursion for Gideon. He knew what he was doing."

"So he had been poaching all these weeks?" Cass said. "And smiling our way when he'd see us on the street."

Ben nodded.

"And he did it at night, while he was supposedly on duty, patrolling our shops," Izzy added.

"While all of you were *paying* him to patrol your shops," Jane said.

"Now we know what was in that backpack of his," Izzy said. "Probably his wet suit."

Ben took a swallow of scotch. "Probably so. The police talked to one of his buddies, who confirmed that Gideon seemed to be in the lobster trade of late—not getting rich off it, the guy said, but making enough to make it worth his while. But he didn't know much more. Oh, except one thing," Ben said, remembering the brief conversation he'd had. "The guy said that they were planning a farewell party at Gideon's tonight. He was planning to move away from Sea Harbor."

"He said as much to us, too, in an odd way," Nell said, remembering Gideon's talk about his ship coming in.

Around them people were finishing their meals, waiters and waitresses were scurrying around removing empty plates and pouring coffee, and when the band began to play, several couples moved onto the wooden dance floor.

"Ben, do you think Gideon's death was accidental?" Nell asked, moving closer to him so he could hear her above the music.

Ben shook his head. "I don't think a hit-and-run accident would have been so violent, Nell. It might have killed him, sure, but this collision left no doubt that the victim would end up dead. Someone had finally had it with this guy."

"Well, don't look at me," Cass said. "I had no idea who the poacher was, and even if I had, my murderous thoughts don't usually leave my head."

Nell smiled. The thought of Cass murdering anyone, despite her proclamations, was ludicrous. Especially the way she looked tonight, so elegant and lovely. A red sleeveless dress set off her deep tan, and her hair was loose, not gathered in the back with a rubber band like she usually wore it. Thick, shiny black waves hung loose to her shoulders, framing a lovely face. It was a far cry from the yellow slicker or jeans Cass usually wore as a part of her trade.

"We don't even know if that's why he was killed," Ben said to Cass. "Gideon was a shady guy, from what I've heard. He may have been into more than poaching. The police aren't saying it was intentional. They're considering a hit-and-run, though that doesn't make much sense to me."

By the time the dessert plates were removed from the tables, people were moving freely about the tent, greeting friends and chatting animatedly. Above them, wide paddle fans moved the air and cast shadows across the room.

Ben looked around at the flurry of activity. "Something tells me I wasn't the only one who got a phone call," he said.

Nell followed Ben's look and suddenly felt the buzz as the news traveled from table to table, from waiter to passing guest. The name "Gideon" could be seen on people's lips, then dropping off and eyes opening wide with surprise. And Nell knew that by the time the trays of brandy appeared, everyone at the party would know that the poacher now had a name. And a name they all knew.

But what Nell wasn't expecting was the news that greeted her as she and Ben left the others on the dance floor and walked back into the main house to place their bid on a piece of art work.

Birdie met them at the open French doors, a puzzled expression on her face. "It's amazing what one finds out in the ladies' room," she said.

"What's that, Birdie?" Nell said.

"Word has it that maybe Gideon killed Angie," Birdie said.

"What reason would he have had?" Nell asked. She had to admit that the rumor didn't completely surprise her. She'd had her own uncomfortable suspicions about Gideon. But a motive escaped her.

"Lust, or so spoke the sweet young thing handing me a towel in the restroom," Birdie said.

"I don't think so," said Ben. "Gideon was a cocky fellow, but murdering Angie? Why?"

Just then Margarethe Framingham walked through the French doors and onto the patio. She spotted the threesome and walked over immediately, her face grave. "I don't know whether to be relieved or horrified," she said.

"You heard about George Gideon?" Ben asked.

"Yes. Father Northcutt told me before he left."

"Esther Gideon must be devastated," Nell said. Another Sea Harbor mother left without her grown child in such a short period of time. And all George Gideon's faults wouldn't erase the pain of losing him.

Margarethe nodded. "She's a devout person, a good member of the parish, Father said. And she worried considerably about her son. But at least we can finally put all this behind us."

"Well, the lobstermen in the cove will be able to be about their business again," Ben said. "It has been a difficult few weeks for them."

Margarethe nodded, her fingers playing with the diamond bracelet on her wrist. "And that was the same cove where Angelina Archer was killed. There's a connection, I feel sure."

The group fell silent. It was a comfortable leap to make, to knit up the summer's tragedies in one neat package and move on. For that brief moment, Nell wanted terribly to believe that what Margarethe was suggesting was true, that in one blind moment, Gideon had committed a crime that he lived—and died—to regret. And as tragic as it all was, they could move on now into their summer, without worry and suspicions clouding their days and evenings.

"And there's one more thing," Margarethe said. "I don't know if you've heard, but Father Northcutt called me from Esther Gideon's."

"What's that?" Nell asked.

"They found those atrocious orange earphones that Angie wore in Gideon's backpack. And an iPod that had her name programmed into it. Gideon had them with him the night he died."

The group fell silent. Nell knew Ben and Birdie were sharing her thoughts. Their unspoken suspicions had been right—Gideon had torn apart Angie's apartment. But stealing a pair of earphones certainly didn't explain the damage that had been done. Gideon was looking for something other than Angie's earphones when he ravaged her apartment, of that she felt sure.

"Sam Perry will be signing his books in the library in a few minutes," Margarethe said, changing the subject and trying to push aside the somber mood. "Do stop by—and the art auction is going on inside as well."

"Of course we will," Nell said, aware of Margarethe's efforts to salvage the festive spirit around them. "It's a wonderful party, Margarethe—far too lovely to be tarnished by rumors."

"Nell's right," Ben said. "You've done a terrific thing tonight. People are having a good time. And I, for one, would like to check out Ham Brewster's painting of the Gloucester schooners. I think it's just what my den needs, or so Ham tells me."

Birdie laughed and rested one hand on Ben's tuxedoed arm. Diamonds sparkled from her fingers. "Come, Ben, let's just see how high we can raise the ante. You and I could do some serious damage, I daresay."

"I think you two need a chaperone," Nell said, as Margarethe waved them all off and turned her attention to a group waiting to speak to her and pour more effusive praise on the summer's grand event.

Birdie and Nell moved into the spacious dining room, where pieces of pottery, watercolors, matted photographs, and wooden sculptures were displayed. Pads of white paper at each piece held names and amounts and Birdie and Ben set to work, jotting down bids on their favorite pieces. As she watched them move around the room, Nell knew that the car would be a bit more crowded on the way home than it had been earlier in the evening as they drove out to the Framingham estate.

Across the wide entryway, Sam sat at an antique desk in the

formal living room, a pile of his books in front of him and a line of people waiting for their special inscriptions. Nell watched him as he graciously looked up at each person, made a connection, asked about their lives.

Sam spotted her over the shoulder of a guest, managed a quick wave, then ducked his head and scribbled onto the front page of a book.

"There you are, Cass," Nell said, moving to a chatting group in the living room doorway. "Do you know where Izzy is?"

"I left her on the terrace," Cass said, carefully balancing a glass of wine in one hand and Sam's book in the other. "I think they were going down to the dock to check out the Framingham yacht collection." Cass wrinkled her nose, indicating there wasn't a vessel in Sea Harbor that could hold a candle to her *Lady Lobster*.

Nell thanked her and walked through the house and onto the terrace. The air was brisk now, but Margarethe had thought of everything, and large heat lamps warmed the terrace. Beyond the terrace steps, well-tended pathways wound down toward the dock and boathouses. Over near the wide fan of steps leading down to the green lawns, Nell spotted a familiar couple. Beatrice Scaglia had a bright yellow gown on—a designer dress, Nell felt sure. And beside her, Salvatore Scaglia stood dressed in a black tuxedo, looking oddly out of place and uncomfortable. Nell walked over to say hello.

"You look lovely, Nell," Beatrice said. "That scarf is a work of art."

Nell thanked her and suggested that once she took another class at Izzy's, she'd be making scarves like this herself.

Beatrice laughed lightly and went on. "And this news tonight is music to our ears. We finally have closure. Sal and I were just saying that at long last Sea Harbor can feel safe again, weren't we, Sal dear?"

Nell looked over at Sal. He was shifting from one shiny black shoe to the next. Small beads of perspiration dotted his forehead. He looked at Nell with a pleading look—almost childish, Nell thought—and she could read his thoughts as clearly as if he'd spoken them aloud. *Don't mention our conversation. Don't ask me any questions. Please.*

Nell stood still for a moment, feeling Sal Scaglia's pain. At that moment she knew that what Rachel Wooten said was true. Sal Scaglia had loved Angie Archer. But, she thought, looking at Sal's long, sad face, love was sometimes the most potent motive of all for murder.

A group of people walked down from the house then, and Beatrice latched on to them, urging Sal to join her.

He looked back at Nell briefly, then hurried along after his wife.

Nell moved on. It wasn't the Scaglias she'd been looking for. And it wasn't the time or place to talk with Sal. Not tonight, anyway.

She looked across the patio and deck, and finally, her gaze extending to the water, she spotted Izzy down on the dock, her blue dress highlighted by rotating spots. The ocean breeze made the folds swell and settle around her body like billowy sails. Small lights along the dock turned the dress silver, then deep blue, and against the black night, there was an ethereal look about her. Next to her, Tony Framingham was an imposing figure in his black tuxedo.

As Nell moved closer to the dock, she noticed that Izzy's head was held in place tightly, her back and shoulders tense. In front of her, Tony Framingham leaned toward her, his eyebrows pinched together. The closer Nell got, the more defined Tony's features became—his wide brow creased and hard angry lines outlining his jaw and cheeks. He was pointing a finger at Izzy as if she had done him an irreparable wrong. As Nell stepped onto the dock, he lifted his other arm, his hand open, his palm wide.

"Tony!" Nell shouted, the single word shooting out over the water like a dart.

Tony's hand dropped, and he and Izzy turned as one, staring at the woman moving along the pier toward them.

"Aunt Nell," Izzy said, her word a warning to Nell to stop. She forced a smile to her face. "It's okay."

Tony stepped back, his eyes boring into Nell. "What did you think, Nell? That I was going to push Izzy off the dock? The summer's favorite activity, right?" He snapped his fingers. "First she's here, then, poof! Gone."

Nell stared at him. "Of course not, Tony," she said. But for that instant, that's exactly what she had thought—that Tony Framingham was about to harm Izzy in some terrible way.

"We were having a discussion, that's all, Nell," Izzy said. "There's no need to worry."

"From outward appearances, not a pleasant one," Nell said.

"And not a secretive one, either," Tony said. "We were talking about Gideon. He was a bad guy. A lady's man, a crook, and who knows what else. He was probably out there that night, stealing Cass's lobster on a lousy night when there'd be no one else around. And when he saw Angie—well, you can fill in the blanks."

"You figure it out, Tony," Izzy said. "Why on earth would Angie be out there alone? Certainly not to meet someone like Gideon." Izzy tried to ease the moment with a teasing tone. "Tony, you're too smart to believe that. Angie wouldn't have wandered out there alone, for starters. And do you suppose Gideon carried drugs around in his wet suit, just waiting for some innocent woman on a pier to give them to? The person who killed Angie did it because Angie knew something or had something they wanted. And once we discover what that is, we'll know who the killer is."

"Izzy, you're just stirring up trouble," Tony said. "You can't mess around with people's lives. Gideon was a mess, everyone knows that."

"I think Tony's right about one thing," Nell said.

"Throwing me a crumb? That's more than your niece will do, Nell. What am I right about?"

Tony had calmed down some, and his manners seemed to be slipping back into place. But Nell still thought it odd that the conversation had elicited such emotion in Tony. He seemed to care too much. He *wanted* Gideon to be the murderer.

"I think you're right that Gideon was near the breakwater that night," Nell said. "It seems he reported for work every night, hung around the shops until they were all closed, then headed for the North Beach breakwater. I suspect it won't be long at all before people come forward who saw him there, or on his way, lumbering along with that black pack of his.

"The part that interests me more than identifying Gideon as the poacher, is that he was *there* that night, Tony, just as you suspect he was. And that means that if he didn't do it himself, he may have been the only person in Sea Harbor who knew who the real murderer is."

By the time Nell and Izzy found their group again, the wind had whipped up along the shore, turning the night air chilly and sending strollers into the main house or back onto the dance floor.

Izzy pulled Nell aside as they walked into the living room. "Tony argues for argument's sake, Aunt Nell, that's all. He's always been opinionated, and he hates being wrong. I admit, he got a little carried away, but he'd had a few drinks. He seems to think that our nosing around in a case that the police are anxious to put to bed is going to disrupt life in Sea Harbor. Make people uncomfortable."

Nell nodded, but not because she bought Izzy's explanation. She simply didn't want it to ruin the rest of this lovely evening. Opinionated or not, that wasn't enough to explain the menace in Tony's voice or the look in his eyes.

"I think this is going to turn into a late-night affair," Ben said, pulling them into the conversation. He accepted several snifters of brandy from a passing cocktail server and handed them to Sam's, Ham's, and Birdie's outstretched hands.

"As long as you insisted on driving, Ben," Birdie said, "I might as well take advantage of it." The others settled for coffee and one last circling of the bid sheets.

"I see Ben's name at the bottom of quite a few slips of paper," Nell mused.

Jane glanced down at the names on the long white sheets of paper. "Ben, Margarethe, and Birdie are our hope for the future," she said. "You are generous folks."

"And while we're slinging praise," Ham said, "here's to you, Sam." He lifted a brandy snifter into the air. "The kids love your class. A lot of them have never viewed anything through a lens, and this is so good for them. They see things differently, themselves included."

"It's a good group—a mix of kids from all over town—and everyone helps out, even Izzy," Sam said. "The kids and I are going to invade her knitting studio one of these days—it's the perfect place to play with interior color and shadows and lighting."

"That's a terrific idea," Nell said.

"Once I saw that window with those dripping hanks of color, I knew I needed an excuse to get in there to photograph them. I figured Iz couldn't say no to the kids."

"He's absolutely right," Izzy said. "No way I'd let Sam in the studio without a covey of kids around him."

"Some of the kids' photographs might look nice in the shop," Nell said. "Maybe you could have a kids' art showing, Izzy."

Izzy's brows lifted. "Good idea. We might as well use Sam to the fullest while he's here."

Ben walked up, announcing that his bus was about to leave. "Call me what you will—but Cinderella and I are on the same schedule." He glanced at his watch. "And my chariot is about to turn into a pumpkin. Any riders?"

Nell touched Birdie on the arm. "Birdie, what do you say we leave the younger set to the final brandy toasts and head out?"

Birdie protested for effect, but took Ben's outstretched arm when offered.

Ham and Jane went off to thank Margarethe, and Nell watched the others heading for the tent and some late-night dancing. She watched them walk off, then followed Birdie and Ben out to the car.

It wasn't until Ben had sent for their car to be brought around that Nell and Birdie realized their wraps were still upstairs.

"I'll just be a minute, Ben," Nell said. "You and Birdie wait for the car and I'll pick up our wraps."

Birdie agreed, admitting, for once in her life, that her body was a bit weary and if saved that long flight of stairs, she'd be grateful.

Nell hurried up the outside steps and into the house, looking for Stella or one of the other young women who had taken their wraps hours before.

But the music in the tent had picked up its tempo, pumping a beat across the yard and into the house that Nell could feel inside her chest. There would be no hope of finding any of them now, Nell thought. She suspected the whole coterie of teenagers hired to help were now in the tent, enjoying the late-night crowd and the music. *Well, good for them,* she thought, and headed up the circle of steps to the second floor. After a decade or two of parties at the Framinghams', she could surely find her own wrap.

Nell peered into a large, open suite opposite the top of the staircase and spotted the pile of coats and shawls neatly positioned across the beds and divan. She spotted her own black shawl immediately, just inside the door and folded nicely on the back of a loveseat. Birdie's was next to it, the elegant red butterfly shawl draped over a mountain of silk pillows as if on display.

Nell smiled, wondering how many youthful bodies had modeled it in the course of the evening.

She draped both shawls over her arm and turned to leave when a series of high-pitched giggles stopped her just inside the doorway.

Nell looked back. The two rooms of the suite were connected by a short hallway, lined on either side by mirrored closet doors. In the mirrors' reflection, Nell spotted Stella Palazola and two friends, each one twirling like models, their shoulders covered in guests' lacy shawls and silk brocade jackets.

The teenagers hadn't seen Nell. Their full attention was given to the whirling, elegant images looking back at them from the mirrors.

Nell smiled, remembering Birdie's story. She'd have to tell Birdie they thought hers was the prettiest. As she turned to leave, not wanting to disturb their fun, a bright flash of color in the mirror caught Nell's eye. She paused, then took a step back into the room. And in the next moment, Nell's body froze. She took a slow breath and focused on the image in the mirror.

Stella was draped in a lacy cashmere sweater, her reflection a flash of brilliant color. It wasn't an ordinary sweater or shawl, but one Nell would have recognized from miles away.

Before Nell could collect her thoughts, Nancy Hughes and several other friends from the Historical Society board walked into the room, chatting and laughing.

"Nell, I haven't seen you all evening," Nancy said effusively, hugging Nell. "And here we all are, the older generation, heading for our coats and off to bed."

"You don't exactly fit the description of older generation, Nancy," Nell said, pushing a calmness into her voice that her body failed to absorb. Her back was to the closets, but she could feel the movement behind her.

"Well, older than the generation still tearing up the dance

floor," Nancy said. "Alex claims we haven't danced this much since our wedding. He's collapsed at the front door, waiting to take his weary wife home."

Nell nodded politely as they chatted about the party, the food, and the piles of money raised for Canary Cove and the Arts Academy, while searching for their wraps in the neatly arranged piles.

When they finally left, Nell turned toward the closets. The hall was empty, just as she knew it would be. The voices would have sent the teenagers scurrying out the other side of the suite. She walked through to the small sitting room at the other end. It was empty as well, except for more coats and wraps arranged neatly on the back of the chairs and couches.

Nell walked over and began picking through the piles of garments. They wouldn't have left with the sweater, surely, but there was no sign of the brilliant cashmere wrap.

"May I help you, Mrs. Endicott?"

Nell turned and looked into the smiling face of one of Mae Anderson's nieces.

"Hello, Rose," Nell said, standing straight. "I think I'm fine. I thought maybe I had picked up the wrong wrap, but I must have been mistaken."

"Okay. Sure. Some of us are going swimming, if you want to come," Rose said. Her eyes twinkled, and she held up a tiny swimsuit. "Miz Framingham said we could use the pool before we go home. She doesn't need us to help anymore."

"Well, good. You have fun, Rose. Would you believe I forgot my suit?" Nell forced a smile and left Rose her privacy to change.

Nell's heart fluttered as she hurried down the steps and out to the waiting car. Ben reached across the seat, opened the door, and Nell slid in beside him, handing Birdie her shawl and snapping her seat belt in place. She looked straight ahead, collecting her thoughts as Ben maneuvered the car around the circle and out onto the road.

"Nell," Birdie said, leaning forward from the backseat and tapping her on the shoulder, "What's the matter with you? You look like you've seen a ghost."

Nell took another slow breath, forcing her heartbeat back to normal. She looked over at Ben, then twisted her shoulders to look back at Birdie.

"Birdie, that's exactly what I've seen," she said. "I've seen a ghost."

Chapter 26

$\mathcal{I}$t was hours later that Nell finally turned out the light and fell into a light sleep, one punctuated by dreams of mirrors and falling skeins of yarn, and glistening golden threads tangled and misshapen.

"It was the sweater Angie was wearing the night she died. I would stake my life on it," she told Ben as they lay side by side, unable to sleep. "The Chinese yarn in that sweater was unique and the saffron shade exquisite. And Izzy had designed it herself, so it couldn't be a copy. It was a work of art," Nell said.

"You're sure the mirror didn't distort it, Nell?" Ben asked.

"I don't think so, Ben." Nell knew Ben wanted to understand, but it was hard to explain to him that she *knew* that sweater intimately. It wasn't like any other sweater. During those days and nights when they fixed up the shop, she and Izzy would take time-outs to knit and talk and plan. She had watched the spun cashmere fibers turn into a soft luxurious wrap beneath Izzy's expert fingers. The sweater became a part of those special months when aunt and niece renewed their relationship, shared intimate thoughts, and together looked ahead to Izzy's new life in Sea Harbor.

When Izzy had loaned the sweater to Angie—good advertising or not—Nell had had to bite back her disapproval. But Izzy had promised it was just a short-term loan and it would come back soon.

But it hadn't come back. It had been looped in a soft knot around Angie's shoulders the night she died.

There was only one explanation, Nell told Ben. Someone invited to the Framingham arts benefit had murdered Angie. Or if not, knew who did. Nell was sure of it. And Izzy's saffron-colored cashmere sweater was the key.

Sunday's skies were cloudy over Sea Harbor, with a gusty, warm wind tossing the waves and luring sailboats out into the waters. Ben suggested they get out in the fresh air and have a taste of Sweet Petunia's Sunday special.

Though they had eaten enough the night before to last several days, Nell was determined to talk to Stella Palazola. And Annabelle's restaurant was the one sure place of finding her on a Sunday morning. She didn't want to embarrass Stella by letting on that she'd seen her trying on guests' clothing—she would have to go about it delicately—but she had to find out more about the sweater—Izzy's sweater—that had grabbed the teenager's fancy.

On their way over to Annabelle's, Izzy called. "Sam and I are coming, too," she said.

Sam and I. Nell snapped her cell phone closed. That had a nice ring to it.

Izzy and Sam had already claimed a table in a far corner of the deck when Ben and Nell arrived at Annabelle's. The smell of fresh herbs and rich coffee greeted them as Izzy waved them over.

"I thought the whole town—including you two—would be sleeping in this morning," Nell said, sitting down next to Izzy. "Did you stay late?"

"Way too late," Sam said. "I felt like an old fogy when I collapsed around two. I didn't think I'd ever get Izzy out of there— she's a dancing fool."

"I think it was the dress," Izzy said. "Kind of like Dorothy's red slippers in *The Wizard of Oz*. I couldn't stop. I was asleep before my head hit the pillow. But it seemed all of five minutes later—though it was actually more like nine this morning—when Cass called and woke me up."

"Is everything okay?"

"Fine. Cass goes to Coffee's early on Sundays—she's afraid she won't get a good seat. And she ran into Birdie . . . And Birdie told her about the sweater." Izzy shifted in her chair and tilted her head to one side. "*And* the earphones they found in Gideon's pack—a double whammy. So we know Gideon ravaged Angie's apartment. Tell me *everything*, Aunt Nell. I can't believe the sweater is somehow still around."

"And here I thought it was our company that brought you to brunch," Ben said.

"That, too, Ben, but I can't believe my sweater is still alive. I haven't talked about it because it seemed so selfish. A lost sweater—even *that* sweater—is nothing compared to Angie's murder."

Nell nodded, understanding Izzy's conflicted emotions. She repeated her jarring encounter in the coat room the night before, explaining the history of the sweater to Sam, and looking up now and then to be sure Stella wasn't close by. She hadn't seen the young waitress yet, but Stella had a habit of appearing out of thin air if she sniffed news or gossip. Nell needed to talk to her, and *soon*, but she didn't want to frighten her, either. The fear of Stella clamming up and denying there ever was a sweater was real if the teenager thought she'd get in trouble.

"Could the sweater have been left on the breakwater and found by someone the next day?" Sam asked. "Maybe they realized its value—or just liked it—and decided to keep it?"

Nell had considered that same scenario, then dismissed it. "That seems logical, Sam. It certainly could have slipped off her shoulders. Or Angie could have set it down while talking. Or, if she fought off someone, it could have slipped off." She took a drink of her coffee and then continued. "All those things are possibilities. Except that the sweater would never have survived the night."

Ben looked up from the *Times* and took off his reading glasses. "Why not, Nell?" He looked down at the lightweight cotton sweater that Nell had knit for him when they still lived in Boston. "This one has lasted a long time."

Izzy was about to repeat Ben's question, when her eyes suddenly widened and she slapped the tabletop with one hand. Coffee sloshed against the sides of the mug. "Of course it wouldn't have survived. It rained that night, that's why," she said. She turned sideways to look at Nell. "Nell, you're brilliant."

"Not only did it rain, we had high winds that night," Ben added. "You're right, Nell."

"And if by some miracle the sweater hadn't been blown out to sea," Nell continued, "it would have been drenched with salty sea water and muddy debris. It would have been destroyed. The sweater I saw last night was in beautiful shape. It was perfect."

"But why would someone wear the sweater to an event where it could be recognized?" Sam asked.

"That's puzzling," Nell admitted. "Unless it had been a gift—whoever murdered Angie gave it to someone. Maybe someone who isn't from Sea Harbor. There were people from all around the Cape, from Boston, too, invited to the party."

"Like all of Tony's friends," Izzy said softly.

From across the room, Ben spotted Stella and waved her over to take their orders. "I think Stella is avoiding us. Do you think she knows you saw her last night, Nell?"

Before Nell could answer, Stella walked over to the table, her glasses fogged from the steam in the kitchen.

Noticing her glasses, Nell realized that Stella hadn't had them on last night. It would have been a miracle if she had recognized her in the softly lit room.

"Hi, guys," Stella said with a wide grin. "Cool party, huh?" Stella wore a skimpy T-shirt today, and over it, a small tank top that ended just above her waist. Her hair was pulled back into a ponytail. "I had, like, such a cool time."

"You and your friends work hard at those affairs," Nell said.

"Oh, geesh, that's not work. Work was, like, getting up this morning," Stella said. She looked at them through her tinted glasses, her lips turned up in a mysterious smile.

"How about some more coffee, Stella," Ben asked, holding up his cup. "And I think we're ready to order."

Stella poured coffee all around, then pulled a pad and pencil from the pocket of her shorts. She turned to Sam. "My mom's Sunday frittata special is, like, awesome. Today she put salmon in it. Cheese, mushrooms. Potatoes. Sour cream."

"Then that's what I'll have," Sam said.

Stella grinned again, this time only at Sam, and disappeared.

"I think she missed your orders," Sam said.

Ben laughed. "Sometimes Stella asks, sometimes not. Fortunately, Annabelle doesn't cook an egg we don't like."

When Ben and Sam began talking about the Sox–Yankee game, Nell turned toward Izzy, but her niece's attention was somewhere else. She was looking beyond the deck railing, over the treetops and galleries, to the robust waves lapping against the rocky shore in the distance. Izzy seemed intent on something that Nell couldn't see. She looked younger than her years today, Nell thought. And worried.

Izzy turned back and took another drink of her coffee, playing with toast on her plate. "I really had a good time last night. I think it's the first time since Angie died that I was able to put it all aside for a few hours. And I'm glad I didn't know all this then. The sweater. Gideon breaking in." She paused, and looked up into Nell's face. "I want so badly for all this to end, Aunt Nell. It's too close, you know? It's *touching* us." She pressed a finger into her arm.

Nell wanted to reach out and wrap her niece in a hug like she used to do when Izzy was a little girl and would beg Nell to make the world fair and right. "Just do it, Auntie Nell," she'd plead when a friend's parents were divorcing or her dog got sick or a baby bird fell out of a tree. *Just do it.* She wanted to promise Izzy that she would, that the suspicions and cloud hanging heavy over her shop would go away—poof!—as easy as erasing a headache with an aspirin. Instead, she touched Izzy's hand where it rested on the tabletop and said, "Me, too, Izzy."

Stella returned with heaping platters of frittatas and placed them down in front of them, poured more coffee, and hurried off. Nell watched her go, wondering when she'd be able to get her alone. The restaurant was packed and Stella hadn't stood still since they arrived.

"Was there any more talk of Gideon last night?" Ben asked.

"Some," Izzy said. She picked up a piece of toast from her plate and smothered it with blueberry jam. "It came up a few times, but no one liked Gideon very much, so news of his death wasn't as jarring as it might have been. Some people thought he got what he deserved. He was a poacher. But still . . ." Izzy paused.

"Still . . . ?" Ben asked.

"Well, it was a horrible way to die, no matter what people thought of him. And I can't imagine how someone could have hit him so forcefully and not stopped to see if they could help. People in Sea Harbor aren't like that. Besides, that road is a dead end. Why would anyone have been on it?"

Ben had proposed the same inconsistency the night before, and Nell wondered how the police explained it. "I suppose someone who'd been drinking might have made a wrong turn, but with all the debris and rusted trucks at the end of that road, it seems they would have hit other things in addition to George Gideon."

"It's a little too coincidental," Ben said.

Nell sipped her coffee. *Coincidental or intentional*? she wondered.

Ben directed the conversation on to other things—sailboat races and explaining to Sam the upcoming Fourth of July party held on Pelican Green, the park that stretched down to the harbor. "Lobster rolls, fried clams, plenty of beer—and the best fireworks on Cape Ann. It's a good time for all," he said.

"And this year they'll unveil the statue Margarethe has commissioned of her father-in-law," Nell said.

"I think she's trying to compete with the Fisherman Statue over in Gloucester," Izzy said. "Jane said it's huge."

"What did the grandfather do?"

"The family ran quarries," Ben said. "The Framingham quarry wasn't the biggest, but it was productive, very lucrative. At one time the family employed hundreds of men to work their motions. That's how the Framingham fortune was made, but it was good for the town, too."

"So the monument will honor Tony's grandfather?"

Ben nodded. "Margarethe really admired the old man. He was tough to work for, but at least he provided jobs."

"Working in the quarries was hard, grueling work," Nell said. "I was looking at some of the photographs at the Historical Society Museum. Imagine the wear on a body—smashed hands, splinters of fine granite that could pierce an eye."

Izzy grimaced at the thought. "Maybe the statue should honor the workers. Angus came from a family of quarry workers, Angie said. And his father worked the Framingham motions."

Nell nodded. "That's right. Angus has quite a history—some happy times, but tragedy, too. I remember Ben's parents talking about the family."

"I think Angus is one of the most fascinating people around here," Sam said. "He let me follow him around the other day, and

I took enough photos to fill a book. His face is a map—filled with stories and emotion and a long life well lived."

"I'd like to see those photos sometime," Ben said. "Angus's father-in-law used to own a Cape Ann quarry around here somewhere."

Nell set down her fork, realizing she had finished nearly the whole plate of frittata. "That part of Angus's life is a sad one. Angus's wife, Anja, was very close to her father. One day, not long after the wedding, Anja and her father were out at the quarry when a dynamite blast went bad. Both Anja and her father were killed. It was a very difficult time, and people say Angus was never the same after that. I think his mental lapses are his protection. When he starts to remember, he escapes into his own world."

"That somehow fits the man I've gotten to know through his face," Sam said. "There's definitely tragedy in those deep lines."

"You guys ready for me to take your plates?" Stella asked, appearing at Ben's elbow.

"Stella, you are ever vigilant," Ben said.

"While you take care of that, I'm off to the ladies' room," Nell said. She didn't want to talk to Stella at the table, but she might be able to catch her on her way back to the kitchen.

Izzy excused herself, too, and followed Nell into the restaurant. Over to the side, at a long table near the window, Tony Framingham sat with the group of friends he had brought to the art event the evening before. Tony looked up, caught their eyes, and waved.

"He's in a much better mood this morning," Nell said.

"He wasn't so bad, really. Tony and I have always argued. We were just falling back into old grooves."

"He seemed angry, Izzy. Not just argumentative."

"He has something on his mind, I agree about that. He seems almost too determined to close the book on Angie's murder. And he hates that we're asking questions, keeping it open and alive."

Just then Stella walked back into the main restaurant and headed for the kitchen.

Nell touched her arm as she passed. "Stella, do you have a minute?"

Stella glanced around, checking her tables, and nodded. "Just a minute though—Tony's table is one of mine and they may need me." She beamed as she looked over at the Framingham heir.

"I'll be quick," Nell assured her. "It's about last night at the benefit. When I went to get my shawl, I noticed a beautiful golden cashmere sweater—"

Stella's hand flew to her mouth. "Oh, Miz Endicott—"

"No, no, Stella, it's okay. I just got a glimpse of it, and I can completely understand that you may have noticed it, too. It was so unique. Really beautiful. I just wondered if you knew who the owner was."

Stella's face colored, a deep, sunburned red that spread from her neck to the top of her head. "Belonged to?" she choked.

"Which guest wore it," Nell said. "It was so beautiful, I wondered where she got it."

"Got it?" Stella repeated.

Nell noticed tiny beads of perspiration on the waitress's forehead and regretted cornering her while she was on duty. She seemed distraught. "Stella, please, don't worry. I didn't mean to embarrass you."

"You won't tell Miz Framingham, will you? She wouldn't let us come back if she knew we tried things on."

"Oh, Stella, it's not a big deal," Izzy said. "I used to work those summer parties when I was your age, and we did the same darn thing."

"And Izzy never got fired, sweetie, so don't worry."

"So—so you won't tell what I did?" Stella stammered.

"Of course not. I just thought if you remembered who wore that gorgeous cashmere wrap, I could talk to her about it. Find out where she got it. Never mentioning you, of course." Nell looked at the teenager with a look she hoped would engender trust. "It's very important to me, Stella."

But Stella didn't seem convinced. She fidgeted and pawed her small paper pad into a damp wad. Finally, her eyes focused on her sandals, she mumbled, "A guest. How would I know who?"

Then, without looking at Nell or Izzy, Stella spun around and hustled over to see if Tony Framingham or his friends would like more coffee, never looking back.

"Now, that's downright weird." Izzy bunched her hands on her hips and watched Stella cross the room.

"Stella doesn't seem the type to be flustered over such a little thing. If that was the worst thing you ever did all those summers you spent with Ben and me, Izzy, I would have lit vigil lights at Our Lady of the Seas in thanksgiving."

Izzy laughed. "Someday I'll fess all, Aunt Nell. But not now. Now is for getting back to the shop. Cass is actually working on her mom's shawl and I told her I'd help with the shoulder shaping. What are you up to today?"

Nell waved at Ben and Sam, who had come in from the deck with car keys in hand, carrying both their purses. What was on her schedule? She had a long list of things to do. A talk to prepare for the arts council in Gloucester. Boxes of flowers she had picked up at the market that needed immediate planting. Bills to pay and e-mails to return. A short article she was writing on grant applications and several birthday gifts to wrap for mailing. She turned back to Izzy.

"I think I'll take some pots of marigolds over to Josie Archer. I bought too many, as always, and I'm sure she could use some color on her front porch."

Chapter 27

$\mathcal{J}$osie Archer lived in a small square house on the edge of town, close to the bridge that separated Cape Ann from the rest of Massachusetts. Josie was one of those Cape Ann residents who claimed she never set foot over that bridge. It wasn't true, of course. Nell knew that for a fact because she and Ben had driven Josie to Angie's graduation from Simmons College in Boston. Josie had sat in the front row of the auditorium, prouder than a parent had a right to be, she told Nell and Ben. She had insisted they leave a chair empty for Ted, so wherever he was, he would join them in spirit to see his beautiful daughter receive her diploma.

But for the most part, Josie did, indeed, stay close to home. She and Ted had lived in this Sea Harbor neighborhood all their married life. Willow Road was a pleasant, modest street, home to neighbors who knew one another and who stopped by the grocery store for milk and bread if someone was sick. It was a perfect place for Josie to live, Nell thought, but far too confining to have held the free-spirited Angie. Her teenage years spent in this close-knit neighborhood and tiny house must have been a challenge for Josie. And certainly a challenge for Angie as well.

Nell pulled into Josie's driveway and got out of her car. She knew several people who lived on Willow Road—one of Archie's sales clerks had just redone the white cottage on the corner, and

Janelle Harrow, who cut Nell's hair, lived directly across from Josie.

Josie was in good hands, Nell thought. If she was lonely or needed someone to talk to, all she'd need to do was walk out her front door.

Nell took the clay flowerpots from her trunk and walked up the steps to the neat front porch. She set the pots down, but before she had a chance to knock, Josie swung the door open.

"I've been waiting for you ever since you called, Nell. What beautiful marigolds." Josie bent over and touched the bright blooms. "These are exactly what this plain little porch needs." She set one pot at each side of the steps. "Now, get yourself in here, Nell, and let's visit."

Josie wore a flowered blouse and yellow linen slacks that were slightly baggy through the hips. She had lost weight these weeks, Nell could see. She should have brought food instead of flowers, but she could certainly do that next week. Or maybe she could convince Josie to come for a Friday dinner on the deck. Sometimes grief required alone time, but eating with friends might help the healing.

"I've made us some tea," Josie said, ushering Nell into the living room off the entryway. The room was clean and neat, with the couch pillows plumped up for company. And all around the room—on the bookshelves and mantel, the side tables and hanging on the rose-colored walls—were family photographs.

Josie noticed Nell looking at the photos. She smiled. "My Ted and my Angelina. They were so much alike. Sometimes I felt like the outsider—their feelings and thoughts were lined up like two peas in a pod." Josie pointed to a framed photo on the mantel of Angie and her dad. "He took her everywhere when she was little. Angie missed him so—but they're finally together. Now, come sit, Nell, and tell me about you," Josie said. She pointed to the couch.

Nell sat against the velvet cushions in front of an oval-shaped coffee table, and Josie took a chair opposite her. On the table was a tray with a plastic pitcher of tea, two tall glasses, and a bowl of sliced lemons.

Josie poured Nell a tall glass of tea. A plate of sugar cookies sat next to the tea, and Josie had set out two lace napkins, one for each of them, with a tiny A embroidered in the corner of each.

Nell could see new, deep lines in Josie's face, and her faded red hair was streaked with gray. But her smile was warm and her eyes soft and sincere. *Josie will survive even this,* Nell thought. *The most difficult thing a mother can ever face, the murder of her child.*

"How is Ben?" Josie asked. "Ted thought the world of that man. His parents, too. The Endicotts were such good folks."

"They thought the same of the Archers, Josie. Your Ted helped Ben and his parents out of many jams—leaky roofs, frozen pipes. Ted could do anything."

Josie sipped her tea and smiled over the curl of steam, the good memories playing across her face. "When Ted lost his job out at the factory, Ben Endicott and the good Lord saved his life."

"How was that, Josie?"

"Ted was depressed. No job, not much money. Angie was young, and I was pregnant with her baby brother."

"I didn't know that, Josie."

"You didn't live up here permanently those days," Josie said. "I suppose that's why, because everyone knew. It just wasn't meant to be. I got sick, and Ted insisted on staying home to be with me. I knew he shouldn't have—they needed him at work. He didn't have vacation. But he wouldn't hear of it, and when he went back to work, his job was gone."

"And the baby?"

"The good Lord took him. It was God's will, though Ted didn't see it that way. He was sure that losing his job made me lose the baby. Of course it wasn't true, Nell."

"I'm so sorry. You've suffered more than your share of loss, Josie."

"We're given what we can handle."

"Well, you are an inspiration. The whole town is distraught over Angie."

Josie set her cup down in the saucer. Her eyes looked intently at Nell. "I don't think it's my place to always understand the Lord's ways. But my Angelina—why anyone would ever want to harm my baby is something I won't ever understand."

"None of us understand that, Josie. It's an awful thing."

"It was a gift when Angelina came back home. She wasn't going to be here long—she told me that when she came back—but she was here for a while, anyway, and she stopped by almost every day."

"She was leaving again?" Nell asked. Coming from Angie's mother, the rumors and innuendoes that had been circulating the past days took substance. Apparently Angie *had* been planning to leave Sea Harbor—but she hadn't shared it with her employer or her landlord, or even close friends like Pete, as far as Nell knew.

"She was going back to Boston. The college had offered her a job. Imagine, my Angelina, working at a college." Josie leaned forward and picked up a bound leather book from the coffee table. She handed it to Nell. "Angelina's master's thesis," she said proudly. "She had a copy bound for me so I could put it on my coffee table."

Nell ran her hand over the pebbled leather surface. She felt that tinge of regret again, that there was so much about Angie she hadn't taken the time to know. She looked down at the title: "Research Methodologies in Land Deeds: Use and Misuse."

Josie smiled at the book. "Angelina loved the history of land. She was intrigued with the early days of Cape Ann and this enormous pile of rock that we built our lives on. Even when she was young, she loved all that, but it became a passion when she went off to college. She'd come home for holidays and go snooping around the museum and the courthouse, looking up deeds and things. I told her those old papers made me sneeze, and she would laugh. She said it wasn't just old paper. It was people's lives."

"That explains why she liked her job at the museum."

"Oh, yes." Josie nodded and handed the cookie plate to Nell. "But it wasn't a permanent job. She was working on that exhibit for Nancy and when it ended, she would leave. She was moving back to Boston in a week or so." Josie picked up one of the embroidered napkins and wiped the corners of her mouth. "A week or so," she repeated.

Nell could read the "if only" in Josie's mind. But she wouldn't say it out loud, Nell knew. If this had been preordained, she would somehow accept it and bury her "what ifs" and "if onlys" in her faith.

"Angelina asked me if I'd like to move with her," Josie said, her voice lifting slightly. "I think she meant it, too, but she knew I wouldn't leave Ted's house."

"But it was a lovely thought," Nell said.

"Yes." Josie offered a small laugh. "A sweet gesture. But no matter, I couldn't have lived with Angelina, as much as I loved her. She saw the world differently than I did. She was so much like her father. People were good or bad. You did right or wrong. Such clear lines. I told her life wasn't like that, not black and white. That's why we had confession, to acknowledge weaknesses. God forgives, I told her. But she would have none of it. And she couldn't forgive. Not ever."

Nell watched the emotions play across Josie's face. And at that moment Nell knew that Josie Archer would find a way to forgive her own daughter's murderer. No matter what. "Josie, I hope you will call me if you need anything. And Ben, too."

"Oh, Nell, of course I will. You were always so good to my daughter. And Izzy, too. Angelina loved that little apartment of Izzy's. She always wanted to live at the edge of the sea, and thanks to you two, she got her wish. I think her time here was very special to her."

Nell nodded. She was glad Josie could see it that way. What Nell saw was that the time in Sea Harbor—and whatever that time held for Angie—in some way led to her death. And that wasn't special. It was tragic. She stood and collected her glass and napkin, setting them back on the tray. She gathered her bag and looked again at the pictures lined up along the top of the mantel. It was a timeline of Angie's life in small, framed photographs—Angie as a baby; Angie without her two front teeth, sitting proudly on her father's lap; Angie holding up a shell at Good Harbor Beach.

Josie came up beside her. "I love looking at these. The memories are such a salve for my soul. Everyone isn't so blessed, you know, with such a wonderful family, such amazing, loving memories."

Nell swallowed hard. What a remarkable woman. She concentrated on the photos to hold back a rush of emotion that tightened her throat. There was one at the yacht club—a group of gangly kids in swimsuits standing with arms wrapped around one another. She spotted Izzy in the front and Angie standing tall in the back, her red hair making her easy to see. "The summer swim team," she said aloud.

"Angelina was a strong swimmer. Ted saw to that. 'Can't live by the sea and not be a swimmer,' he told her."

Nell moved on. The high school pictures showed Angie in school plays, receiving an award, and there was one shot of a group of young people in formal dress.

Josie picked up the picture. "Prom court," she said proudly. "Angie was on the court."

Nell looked closely. There was a king and queen in the center of the photo, and several attendants. Angie stood just behind the queen, her red hair floating around her shoulders. Her expression was of discomfort. A somber look.

"Angelina didn't like things like dances, big school events, but she loved to dress up. So when she was elected to the prom court, she reluctantly agreed to go." Josie shook her head. "I remember it so clearly. It wasn't her best night."

Nell looked again at the picture. She recognized the queen, a sweet gal whose family lived on Sandswept Lane. She looked at the young man with the crown on his head. "Isn't that Tony Framingham?"

Josie nodded. "And that was the problem that night. Tony Framingham. At first Angie refused to be in the picture, but they made her—told her it would look strange in the yearbook if she wasn't in it. What would they say in the caption?"

Nell looked at Tony's broad smile and black hair. "Tony was a problem? Was he Angie's boyfriend?"

Josie laughed, but without humor. "Oh, no. Tony was not her boyfriend. Sometimes I think Tony was why Angie left Sea Harbor."

"I don't understand, Josie."

"Nell, my daughter hated Tony Framingham with a terrible fury. Sometimes it swallowed her up. Having to stand that close to him in a picture ruined the whole night for her."

Nell frowned, staring at the picture. "Why?"

"Angelina was convinced that Tony Framingham's family killed her father. That's why. She hated Tony Framingham in a way no person should hate another human being."

Chapter 28

$\mathcal{A}$fter leaving Josie Archer's house, Nell stopped at the Historical Museum on her way home, knowing Nancy would still be working, even though public hours ended at four on Sundays. Nancy used that time, she'd told Nell, to ready herself for the busy week ahead.

"Nell, what's up? You look surprised. A good surprise, I hope." Nancy welcomed Nell into her office and pulled out a chair.

Nell forced a smile to her face. "Surprise" didn't begin to describe how she felt about Josie's revelations. The different pieces to the conversation had spun around in her head all the way to the museum. She tried to make sense out of them, order them. Angie's dislike—*hatred*, Josie had said—of Tony Framingham was too strong to have come from Angie, even though Pete had claimed she'd said as much. Coming from Pete, a jealous boyfriend, it didn't have the same substance. But what surprised Nell more than the fact, was the reason.

It was a giant jigsaw puzzle, waiting for someone's keen eye to put the pieces in the right place. But Nell felt quite certain that there were pieces of the puzzle still missing. "I need a clear mind, Nancy," she said. "Someone to help me sort this out. This horrible happening with George Gideon, and occurring so soon after Angie's death, has me wondering how many other things have gone on in our safe little town without us noticing."

Nancy sat behind her desk, her elbows bent and her chin resting on her hands. "You don't think it was a hit-and-run?"

"No." It wasn't until she said the word that Nell knew what she thought. Gideon was killed. And before he died, he had ransacked Angie Archer's apartment. For what? And did he die because of it? "I think someone killed Gideon."

Nancy frowned. "The police don't."

"No. They're under so much pressure to put this to rest. But I think someone killed him, Nancy, and I think it's connected to Angie's death."

"Do you think it's connected to her work here?"

"I don't know." Nell told Nancy about her conversation with Sal Scaglia, leaving out Rachel's observations. "Did Angie ever talk about Sal, Nancy?"

Nancy thought for a moment, and then she remembered something that happened the week before Angie died.

"Sal called here," Nancy said. "Angie was out to lunch. He said to tell her that he had some more information for the project and she should pick it up. When I told Angie, she got a strange look on her face, and she let me know quite clearly that she had all she needed from the Registrar of Deeds. That was it. And I don't think she went back."

Nell listened and tucked away the information. It was making more and more sense. "I also wanted to tell you I talked to Josie Archer. She told me Angie said she was hired for a limited project, and she'd be moving back to Boston next week. She had a job at the college. Why would she tell her mother something totally different than what she told you?"

Nancy looked down at her desk, pondering the question. "I don't know, Nell. But it explains why she was evasive whenever I'd try to set up a time for us to talk. Why she took the job in the first place, knowing from the get-go that she wasn't going to stay long, is the real question."

"But she worked hard while she was here, right?"

"Absolutely. Angie did everything we asked of her and more. Actually, now that I think about it, there was only one thing that Angie refused to do for me the whole time she was here, and that was to give a report to our board about the quarry exhibit she was working on. Absolutely refused. It struck me as odd, because she was so articulate. I thought she'd enjoy the opportunity to speak in front of all of you."

"You would think so. I always thought that Angie had some theater in her blood." Nell pushed back her chair and stood up. "And there're some powerful people on that board—good connections, if Angie cared about that."

Nancy looked at her watch. "Speaking of the board, I'm meeting Margarethe at the Edge to finalize the display case plaque for Angie. I can't believe she's making time the day after that amazing party—but she is adamant that we do this soon, so we're meeting for a sandwich to work out the details. At least this is something positive we can do—a bright spot in these uncertain days."

Nell left the library not feeling any bright spots at all. Instead, the afternoon weighed heavily on her shoulders. She felt burdened, as if she were wearing a heavy metal jacket and couldn't figure out how to take it off. Her head ached from trying to pull together the scattered pieces of Angie's life. And her heart ached for the lovely woman who had a lost a daughter far too early.

Nancy's mention of Margarethe made her remember something she'd meant to do since Saturday night: call her and ask about the sweater. Maybe Margarethe had seen who was wearing the cashmere wrap. She wouldn't go into the fact that Angie had it on that night—there was no reason to spread more gossip.

Nell took her cell phone from her bag and dialed. Almost immediately Margarethe's gracious recorded voice came on. Nell left a message—a thank-you for hosting the grand arts benefit and a question at the end about the beautiful sweater she'd spotted in the bedroom. Just a casual inquiry about the gorgeous knit garment. She didn't mention Stella, of course. The teenager was right—Margarethe probably wouldn't invite her back if she knew she'd tried on the guests' coats.

When her cell phone rang as she crossed the small square to her parked car, she looked down at the caller's name. It wasn't Margarethe, but an even more welcome caller. Someone to listen, to help sort out the puzzle. And Birdie was one of the best puzzle solvers she knew.

Nell sat down on one of the benches, and for the next half hour, poured out her scattered thoughts, the random facts, her unformed suspicions—relying on her friend to help pull it all together. Or to tell her to go fly a kite.

But Birdie did none of that. Instead she called Cass and Izzy and said to be at her house at seven sharp. "New developments," she told them, in her new Sherlock Holmes manner. Nell was bringing enough of her creamy crab soup to go around. And she'd already put the Pinot on ice.

"And don't forget to bring your knitting," she said before hanging up each call. "It helps us think."

Nell picked up Izzy, then Cass, and they drove down Harbor Road, past the shops now closed for the night. Summer visitors strolled the village area, looking in store windows, and stopping in the coffee shop or bars that dotted the harbor, while they waited for their dinner reservations at Ocean's Edge.

As they drove up the hill that wound through Birdie's neighborhood, Cass pointed out the window. "Isn't that the old man of the sea?"

They looked over to the side of the road and spotted the hunched figure headed toward town, his head bowed, and a bright red knit scarf around his neck.

Izzy laughed. "That's sweet. He's wearing one of Birdie's knit scarves. She knit a big fancy A and M on the ends."

"But it's summer," Cass said, and they all laughed. Angus did as he pleased. Seasons didn't really matter much.

"I wonder where he's going," Izzy said.

"It's Sunday," Nell said. "He's probably headed for the Ocean's Edge."

Cass turned and watched him disappear around the bend. "But where's he coming from?"

"You never know with Angus," Izzy said. "He seems to be everywhere."

"He seems sad these days," Nell said. "He misses Angie, I think."

"A strange relationship, though, don't you think?" Cass said. "He was obsessed with Angie."

Izzy shifted against her seat belt and looked back at Cass. "I think that sometimes, too, Cass. He followed her home one night and sat out on the ledge behind the shop for a long time. Archie saw him out there and gave him some coffee, then told him to go home. But other times I think they were genuinely friends. He liked having someone listen to him. Angie listened."

"And why, exactly, did she do that?" Cass asked. "I mean, we all listen to Angus when we have the time, but Angie listened beyond the call of duty."

"Maybe she just had a soft spot for him," Izzy said. "He's a sweet man."

"But I wonder how Angus interpreted it. Could he have thought Angie liked him? I mean romantically?"

"Oh, heavens, no," Nell said. But as soon as the words left her lips, she wondered what right she had to speak so forcefully about Angus McPherron's feelings. He was sweet and odd at once, a harmless nice person with a sad past, she'd always thought. He'd wandered the harbor for years and never caused anyone a bit of trouble. And yet—

"Sometimes he's charming. A gentle man," Izzy said. "He comes into the shop sometimes because Mae gives him slices of her banana bread, and he's the only person on earth who likes my coffee. But one day after Angie died he came in demanding to see her apartment. He said there were things there that belonged to him."

"Izzy, you didn't tell me that," Nell said. She frowned and turned into Birdie's drive.

"I guess I forgot. I remember it, though, because we were really busy that day. Sydney Hill had come up from Boston to teach her Snow Socks class. Margarethe was in the studio buying a stash of silk mohair in this fantastic bubblegum color—she wasn't sure what she wanted it for, but she had to have it, she said."

"A woman after my own heart—Ben is threatening to have a yarn garage sale." Nell pulled around the circle drive and parked the car. "So Angus made a scene?"

Izzy nodded. "But it wasn't bad. Mae was busy, so Margarethe went over and coaxed him outside. Mae saw her giving him a wad of bills and then she sent him over to Harry's Deli for some food."

"Margarethe can convince anyone of anything," Nell said. She opened the door and walked around the car to take the soup tureen from Izzy's lap.

Birdie met them at the door. "Come, come." She waved them in. "For a minute I thought you were going to spend the evening sitting in your car. Did I miss anything important?"

"We were talking about Angus," Nell said. "We saw him walking down your hill."

Ella Sampson stood just behind Birdie, smiling at the guests. She took the soup from Izzy and disappeared.

"Angus goes down to the Edge every Sunday like clockwork," Birdie said.

Nell smiled. "Yes. I see him eating on the patio sometimes. Charlie—that nice young chef—makes sure he gets his fresh vegetables."

"Why was he coming from this direction?" Cass asked. She followed Birdie up the wide windy steps.

"He stays here sometimes," Birdie said simply.

"What?" Nell stopped at the top of the steps and stared at Birdie.

Birdie pushed away Nell's surprise. "Well, not all the time. But that carriage house has two apartments, and Ella and Harold didn't mind a neighbor. He comes and goes—and this gives him a place to get his mail and keep the few things he owns. That little cabin he had on the way to Rockport had frozen pipes and God knows what else. Probably all sorts of vermin. No heat. So when it got too cold last winter, I told him he could use the carriage house. He's not here much, Ella says. Especially not in the summer."

"Birdie, I have known you almost thirty years, and you still pull out a surprise now and then."

"Keeps you young, Nell. Surprises are good for the soul."

Not all surprises, Nell thought. There'd been a few these past weeks that were doing anything but keeping her young.

They all followed Birdie down the hallway to a room that Nell loved—a cozy den filled with books and a curved wall of leaded windows that overlooked the entire harbor and beyond. Sonny Favazza—Birdie's greatest love—had added the room on as a wedding gift for Birdie, so they could sit there together at night and watch the world settle down. And it was Birdie's favorite place to knit, to listen to music, and to be with her friends—but only very special ones.

Nell sat on a leather love seat facing the windows and watched a long line of pleasure boats coming in for the night. Lights in the restaurants blinked a welcome to diners, and in the distance, protruding out into the ocean, the fat thumb of land that was the Framingham estate was still lit up like an enormous Christmas tree farm. From here, the main house rose tall and stately on the rise of land. Even though it was miles away, from Birdie's den it looked close enough to toss a Frisbee across the water and have it land safely on the front lawn.

"The party seems eons ago," Izzy said, following Nell's glance.

Nell nodded. In some ways it seemed like a long, long time ago, but in other ways, she felt like she was still out there on Framingham Point, watching Stella Palazola twirl in front of the mirror, her arms wrapped in Izzy's cashmere sweater.

Birdie settled on another love seat across from Nell, her knitting basket at her side, and Izzy and Cass curled up in large overstuffed chairs. Between them was a low wooden coffee table on which Ella had piled napkins and spoons, a bucket holding a chilled bottle of wine, and a platter of warm bruschetta and spiced nuts.

"Birdie, how did you put this together so quickly?" Nell asked.

Birdie flapped her hand in the air. "Magic. It's all smoke and mirrors," she said. Then she nodded toward the hallway and added, "And Magic's first name is Ella."

"Cass, how are you doing on your mom's shawl?" Izzy asked, and pulled out her own half-finished sweater from the bag. It was a floppy, loose cardigan with a hood, a perfect hanging-around-the-house or -studio sweater that she knew she'd wear until it fell off her body. The soft, cushy mohair came in a pistachio green, a bilberry shade, and a deep blue-black that reminded Izzy of a stormy sea. She had immediately slipped several of the pistachio skeins behind the counter for herself.

"Amazing color," Birdie said, reaching over and touching the cloud-soft fiber.

Izzy smiled. "I love it. Come in tomorrow and I'll find some for you, Birdie. A soft winter hat to pull over your ears." She lifted her brows into slivers of bangs that spiked across her forehead. "Or perhaps for Angus?"

Birdie laughed and leaned forward to pour wine all around. "Now, about Mary's shawl?" She looked over the top of her glasses at Cass.

Cass took a swallow of wine and set her glass down, pulling her backpack out from behind the chair. "I brought it, Birdie, so don't panic. But before you all start offering me advice on the neckline or lace edging or how to finish the seams, let's talk business."

Nell pulled out her needles and a ball of camel-colored alpaca and began to cast on for a throw. She had made the same pattern at least a half-dozen times—but it was a perfect project when she didn't want to count and worry about dropped stitches. And a perfect elegant gift for anyone who lived through cold New England winters. "Cass is right," she said. "We've got catching up to do, a puzzle to solve."

"Murders," Izzy corrected. The harsh word hung out there in the middle of the room, quieting the group for a moment.

Murder.

"The police are pretty much through with it," Cass said, breaking the quiet. "Tommy Porter told Pete it was all wrapped up—George Gideon killed Angie. And Gideon was killed by a hit-and-run. And the town's safe again at last."

"Does Pete believe that?"

"None of it. But he's so relieved they're leaving him alone that he doesn't say much. And I think he's finally starting to come back to life."

"Time will help," Birdie said.

"Time and Angie's mother."

"Josie?" said Nell.

Cass took a bite of bruschetta and chewed it slowly. "That sweet woman—in the middle of all her grief—she called Pete and thanked him for making Angie happy the last few weeks of her life. Angie told her wonderful things about Pete, she said. I think it was the best present anyone could have given him. With all the rumors floating around that Angie was using him, or playing with his emotions, or that she was seeing other guys on the side, he was beginning to wilt away. He needed his good memories of Angie back to help him deal with her death, but people were trying to rip them to shreds." Cass paused. She pushed her hair back from her face and fastened it with a band. Her cheeks were flushed with emotion and her dark eyes were sad. She looked around at the group. "But, you know, he really cared about her. And I think she cared about him, too. No matter what I may have said in the past, I'm happy about that."

"Bless Josie," Nell said.

Cass nodded. "Right."

"That rumor of her dating Tony is definitely an urban legend. Tony was never a threat to Pete."

"People saw them together," Birdie said.

"Yes, but it wasn't for pleasure." Nell repeated the conversation she'd had that afternoon.

"Hate is a pretty strong word," Izzy said. "Angie *hated* Tony?"

Nell nodded. "Reading between the lines, I think Ted Archer had no use for the whole Framingham family, and Angie adored her dad. What he thought, she thought. Josie was far more forgiving."

"I remember when Ted Archer lost his job," Birdie said. "It was sad. The company needed to save some money, and they did it ruthlessly. The Archers had been a part of the Framingham company forever—Ted's grandfather and dad worked in the quarries—and when the quarries closed and they opened their plant, Ted stayed with them. He'd been there so long that he was paid more than the other managers, so it made good financial sense to let him go. They used his absence as an excuse."

"That's horrible. A man with a child, a sick and pregnant wife."

"Ted thought so, too," Birdie said. "He was quite vocal in his dislike for the family—Ben will tell you as much, Nell. His parents spent a lot of time up here during that time and they stepped right in and gave Ted work. He did carpentry work for us, too. And others followed, feeling bad for the unfortunate treatment he got. But Ted always felt violated, somehow. And he had already started to drink to ease the pain. Truth be known, I think that's what killed him."

"How could Angie have blamed his death on the Framinghams?" Cass asked.

"Maybe they were kind of a secondary cause, at least in Angie's mind," Izzy said.

The group fell silent and Ella brought up the heated tureen of soup. The smell of fresh oregano and thyme rose up with the steam and filled the room.

Ella set it on a hot plate on a side table along with bowls. "Help yourselves, ladies," she said. "I kept a taste back for Harold and me." Ella slipped out the door and they heard the fading sound of her slippers on the steps.

"She's superstitious," Birdie explained. "It's good luck to wear slippers in the summer or some such thing."

"Maybe we could all use a pair of slippers," Cass said.

Nell walked over to the tureen and began scooping the creamy soup into bowls. Large chunks of crab meat floated in the pungent broth and sprigs of parsley, sliced onion, and broccoli added color to the mix.

"I talked to Archie Brandley at the party last night," Birdie said. "He's happy Sam has moved into Angie's place."

"Along with the rest of us," Nell said.

"He thinks Angie had an ax to grind here, and that's why she came back."

Nell listened carefully. She was convinced of that. And that reason was enough to get her killed.

"That would explain the fact that she never intended to stay," Izzy said.

"But she didn't realize the danger in whatever it was she was doing."

"Or maybe she did and didn't care," Cass offered. She got up to refill her bowl.

"So whatever it was threatened someone so terribly that he needed Angie dead."

"And Gideon knew about it," Izzy said.

"I think Gideon saw the whole thing. He didn't kill Angie— he'd have had no reason to do that. But he was at the breakwater— people have already come forth saying they saw him headed that way."

"He was headed down that way to steal the lobsters," Cass added.

Nell nodded. "He was probably down on the ledge where he couldn't be seen. He seemed to have mastered his side job. Maybe he didn't know Angie died, not until it hit the news. But he could have put two and two together," Nell said.

"So he may have been blackmailing someone," Izzy said.

Cass nodded. "That makes sense. And whoever he was black-mailing killed Angie. And that someone was . . ."

"Angie wanted to hurt Tony. That may be an important part of this," Birdie said.

"And then there's Sal." Nell filled them in on the conversation with Nancy. "It's quite odd. When I went over to the county offices, Sal acted like he hardly knew Angie, which wasn't at all true. And the phone call Nancy got adds more mystery to it."

"He loved her, according to Rachel Wooten," Izzy asked.

The four women pondered the thought of Sal Scaglia and Angie while finishing off their soup. "It's hard to imagine Sal in the position of a Romeo. I don't know," Birdie said. "He's so shy."

"What is it they say about the shy ones?" Cass asked. "Still waters. Aren't they the ones to be careful of?"

"What if Sal told Angie how he felt about her? And Sal was afraid she would tell Beatrice?" Izzy said.

"Beatrice's wrath would be awful to face," Nell said. If Sal was bothering Angie, and she threatened to tell Beatrice, it could make Sal's life awful. But murder?

"I think Sal is hiding something," Birdie said. "We need to find out what." Later, after the soup tureen was bone dry and Ella's key lime pie had disappeared, Birdie suggested a cup of decaf before they all headed home.

Izzy stretched her arms and slipped her knitting back into her bag. "I think I may skip the coffee, Birdie," she said. At that moment her purse jingled, and she reached in for her phone, checking the number. She frowned, then checked her watch. "It's Sam—and it's late. I hope Purl is all right—"

Izzy clicked on the phone, said hello, and then fell silent.

Nell read her expression as it moved from curiosity to surprise to dismay. "We'll be right there, Sam," she said, and snapped her phone closed.

"It's Angus," Izzy said. "He came to the apartment above the shop disoriented, looking for Angie. And then his body folded up, and he collapsed on the floor right at Sam's feet."

Chapter 29

By the time they reached the Beverly Hospital, Angus had been admitted to the intensive-care unit and hooked up to monitors and tubes. Sam and Ben stood outside the swinging doors, their faces drawn and fingers wrapped around paper cups of cold coffee.

"Ben had just stopped by the apartment to invite me out for a beer," Sam explained.

"Angus came up the back steps, mumbling something we couldn't understand," Ben continued. "His face was ashen, and he was asking for Angie. But before we could get him to sit down, he collapsed right at Sam's feet."

"The medics arrived in minutes. Heart attack, they said. And a bad one."

Nell looked through the pane of glass separating them from the still figure. Angus lay unmoving against the white sheets. He looked peaceful, she thought. But the tubes connecting him up to machines told a different story.

Nurses scurried back and forth, checking vital signs and the sacks of liquids hanging from metal posts. Finally a woman in a white jacket pushed through the doors and smiled at them. "Are you here for Mr. McPherron?" she asked.

They nodded and moved to a small alcove of seats, where the doctor explained that the next twenty-four hours were the most critical.

"But I think you all should leave. There isn't anything you can do, and he needs his uninterrupted sleep more than anything."

"But you will call?" Nell asked.

"Of course." The doctor looked down at the chart to check her notes, then back at the group. "We found an envelope in his pocket with an address crossed off and *Favazza, One Ocean View Drive* scribbled in. Is that the correct address?"

Birdie lifted her hand. "That's my name and my home. Angus is staying with me for a while. There isn't any other family."

The doctor nodded. "Then you will be our contact, Ms. Favazza."

"That's fine," Birdie said, brushing a trace of moisture off her cheek.

The doctor checked a message on her pager, then disappeared, her heels echoing along the white-walled hallway.

Birdie got up and walked back to the window in the door. She stood up on her toes, peering through the window and spoke to no one in particular. "I'm not going anywhere until I know the old guy is out of the woods." She looked back at the group, huddled in a semicircle behind her, and pulled her gray brows together in a stern look. "But you go on—all of you. Scat. I'll call if there's a change."

There was no arguing with Birdie, and every single one of them knew it.

"Birdie's right," Ben said. "She'll call us with news, and we can't do anything here but get in the way."

They hugged Birdie good-bye, then headed out into the summer night. Ben climbed into Nell's car, and Cass and Izzy followed Sam to his Volvo. With promises to spread news as soon as it arrived, the two cars pulled out of the hospital parking lot and headed home.

Ben and Nell drove in weary silence, their mutual thoughts not needing expression. A short while later, they drove up the hill of their sleeping neighborhood and into the garage at 22 Sand-swept Lane. "We've been up after midnight two nights in a row," Ben said. "Think we'll make it, Nellie?"

"I think we will," Nell said. "The question is, will Angus McPherron?"

Birdie called Nell early the next morning to report that there hadn't been any change. Angus was still alive. And that was about all the doctors would say. Harold had picked her up and taken her home to shower and get a few things done. She'd go back to the hospital later.

Nell knew there was nothing she or Ben could do. Just wait. And hope that the phone would ring. Her day was full—but nothing that she couldn't drop in a second if Angus needed them.

A long shower brought life back into her bones, and after a quick cup of coffee with Ben, she drove down to the village to give Izzy an update on Angus—and then over to a committee meeting at the museum.

The Seaside Knitting Studio was bustling with customers when Nell walked in, but Izzy wasn't anywhere in sight.

"You won't find her here, Nell," Mae said, speaking over the head of a customer. A curious smile lit the sales clerk's face.

"Is she sick, Mae?"

"Maybe so. She sure doesn't do this when she's feeling normal," Mae said. "Prying her out of here is harder than nails out of granite." Mae's words lacked most R's and Nell held back a smile. Ben lapsed into Boston-speak sometimes, too, but years of schooling and traveling had softened the effect. Mae's dialogue held a bright tough color that Nell loved.

"So where is she, Mae?"

"Took the day off," Mae said, relieving the next customer of an armful of yarn that she was cradling like a newborn.

"On a Monday?" Nell asked.

"I know—miracles happen. This one's name happens to be Sam." Mae waved at a group of regulars who were on their way into the back room to knit and gossip.

"What's up?"

"Sam wanted to explore those old quarries on the Framingham land—see if it'd be a good place to take his class for a photo shoot."

"That's a great idea. What made Izzy decide to go?"

"She called Tony and asked him if he'd show Sam around, but he had some business meeting. So he told Izzy to go ahead and show Sam where the trails were. Seems she and Tony used to sneak their friends in at night to swim in the quarry pools when they were teenagers."

"There's a reason we don't know those things while they're happening," Nell said. The quarries were beautiful for photo ops—but very deep for night swimming and teenage antics. "Margarethe would have had a heart attack if she'd known they did things like that."

"And speaking of heart attacks," Mae said, "how is our Angus doing? Sure surprised me when I heard the news at Coffee's. Angus told me he had the heart of an ox."

"I guess you never know. He's still holding on and we're hoping for the best," Nell said. "I'm off to a meeting, but please tell Izzy to give me a call."

"Oh, I almost forgot this," Mae said. She thrust an envelope in Nell's hand. "I opened it because I thought it was a bill for the studio. Property tax or some other kind of tax. They slap us with all kinds. The return address was the county offices. Had it clean open before I realized it wasn't for the shop a'tall. You might want to ask Ben what to do with it. Shouldn't have read it, I suppose . . ." Mae picked up a stack of receipts and began putting them in order.

Nell looked curiously at the envelope—a white, legal-sized rectangle, with a typed shop address, but before she could examine it, the phone rang, pulling Mae's attention away, and a noisy group of tourists crowded into the shop. Nell shoved the envelope in her pocket to read later and hurried off to her meeting.

Nell crossed the street, dodging a young boy on a bike and waving at Mary Halloran as she walked up the hill toward Our Lady of the Seas. *Probably lighting a few more candles for Cass,* Nell thought and smiled at the thought. Cass was such a together young woman—and whether she married or not, she would have a good life, just as Nell felt sure Izzy would. And though she wouldn't trade her own life with Ben for anything on earth, she admired Izzy and Cass and their friends who carved out lives they chose to lead, and not necessarily ones their mothers and grandmothers had accepted as the way things were. The world accommodated this generation differently, she thought. Not better or worse necessarily. But differently.

When Nell's cell phone rang, she glanced down, expecting Izzy or Ben's name to pop up. It was Birdie.

With bad news.

Nell listened carefully, then closed her phone and slipped it into her bag. She walked slowly up the brick steps to the museum, the lump in her throat growing with each step.

"Nell, you're a bit early," Nancy said, calling out from her office just inside the entrance.

Nell turned toward her voice.

Nancy took one look at Nell's face and rose from her desk. "Nell, you look awful. What's wrong? Come in here and sit down."

Nell walked into Nancy's office and sat down on a chair near the desk. "I just heard something shocking, Nancy. And I thought I was about shocked out."

"Is Angus all right?"

"No." Birdie's words circled around in Nell's head, finally settling into the right order. Heavy and solid and awful. "Nancy, Angus McPherron was poisoned."

Now it was Nancy's turn to sit down. "No, Nell. That's impossible. I talked with him just last night, not long before he had the heart attack. He was fine."

"Where did you see him?"

"At his usual Sunday-night spot—the patio at the Edge. Angus is the most faithful diner they have. The hostess sets her clock by him. It wasn't long after you and I talked."

"How did he look?"

"Worried. Margarethe and I were meeting there to talk over that display case, and we watched him sit down. He wasn't sick as far as I could see, though Margarethe remarked how pale he was.

"He left before we did, and shortly after, we heard the sirens, and soon after that the news spread. A heart attack, we heard—in Angie Archer's apartment. That caused quite a stir, as you can imagine. But poison, Nell? That doesn't make sense."

"Could he have eaten something?" Nell wondered out loud.

"He has the same thing every Sunday. Clam chowder and pie. That sweet chef who came over from Rockport makes it just for him."

"Did you talk to him?"

"Just for a minute. The place was crowded—all Tony's friends from Boston were there with him, so we chatted with them. Margarethe must have a sixth sense—she didn't think Angus looked well, so we went over to say hello, like I said. I chatted with him while Margarethe went to check on his food—it hadn't come yet and he seemed agitated. He was distracted the way he gets sometimes. Tired. But nothing unusual that I could see. Once his food came, we went back inside to finish our meeting. And that was that until we heard the sirens. A heart attack makes sense. Poison doesn't."

"According to Birdie, a heart attack *didn't* make sense. That's why they checked further into the cause of Angus's illness. At Birdie's insistence, Angus had had a complete checkup just a couple weeks before. The doctor said his arteries were as clear and clean as a new pipe and his heart muscles as strong as a much younger man's. Angus was in great shape—I guess it's all that walking he does. His weary mind was an emotional thing, the doc said, not a sign of senility. The only bright note in all this is that he isn't dead. And there's a good chance, Birdie said, that he might survive."

"Thank God for that. But surely you don't think anyone in this town would poison Angus, Nell. Everyone knows him—he's a fixture in Sea Harbor. And I can't imagine him having an enemy. He's sweet and gentle."

And maybe that's the problem, Nell thought. Sometimes sweet and gentle isn't good. Being slightly aware, cautious, standing up for yourself—those traits have a part to play in life, too.

"Do you think there's a connection between Angie's death and this awful news about Angus?" Nancy asked.

Nell nodded. "Yes, I do. It doesn't all make sense yet, but I think all of these things are connected. I think they were started by Angie's desire to right a wrong, and they have to be stopped before anything else happens. Dear Angus is the last straw."

Nancy moved the papers around on her desk and checked her watch, then looked at Nell, a worried expression on her face. "I guess we'd better move into the meeting room, Nell. But please let me know if you hear more about Angus." She reached out a hand and squeezed Nell's. "And, Nell?"

"Yes?"

"Be careful."

Nell followed Nancy through a door in her office that led directly into the boardroom. Nearly all the chairs were filled, and Nell hoped the meeting would start quickly to avoid talk of Angus. Though news passed quickly in Sea Harbor, she suspected the heart attack was now common knowledge, but not the poison. And she hoped it would stay that way, at least for a while.

"A glorious party!"

"A perfect night."

"The auction brought in enough to support the Arts Academy for two summers."

Nell took the one empty chair. The swirl of chatter allowed her unnoticed silence. Nell sat still and listened. Party talk. That she could handle without her heart aching.

It was a minute before she realized that she was sitting next to Margarethe, who had taken a half-finished shawl out of her bag. It was oversized, more a blanket than a shawl. A TV wrap, as Izzy called them, made out of soft natural mohair.

Nell touched the edges of the shawl. "Is it just we knitters who do that, I wonder? We see a beautiful yarn and our fingers are lured to it instantly."

Margarethe offered a smile, but her eyes were tired. "Maybe so," she said.

"As you can hear, the party was a grand success."

"We raised more than expected. I'm happy for the academy. Sam Perry was a draw. He's been a wonderful asset to the faculty this summer."

"Your son was also a draw, Margarethe. I enjoyed meeting his friends from Boston."

Margarethe's face remained still, but the mention of Tony and his friends seemed to freeze her features, and the look that had controlled boards and swayed business decisions replaced the weariness in her eyes. She nodded carefully. "Tony has many friends," she said.

Nell felt suddenly awkward, unsure of what to say next. Margarethe's look was one of controlled disappointment—and sadness. Suddenly Nell felt an urge to comfort her, though she had no idea why. Clearly Tony was causing his mother distress. Nell took a sip of her ice tea and attempted to lighten the mood. "Tony was nice to take Izzy and Sam Perry hiking out at the old quarries today. Sam is so curious about the area, and it's a perfect day to take a short hike."

"Excuse me?" Margarethe said. Her forehead wrinkled severely. "You must have misunderstood. Tony had a business meeting and is picking me up afterward," she said.

Nell felt unexplainably chastised. "I'm sorry, you're right, Margarethe," she said quickly. "My mistake. Tony said he was busy, but he generously gave Izzy permission to show him around herself."

Margarethe leaned forward in her chair. "No, he wouldn't do that," she said sternly.

"I'm sorry, Margarethe," Nell said. "Is it a problem?"

"It's dangerous out there, Nell." Margarethe's voice was low and calm, but beneath the calm was an edge of steel. "Tony is just like his father. No sense. Those quarries appear without warning. The water can be a hundred feet deep. He's put them in danger."

Nell took a deep breath and tried to calm the sudden wild beat of her heart. For one brief moment she imagined Izzy and Sam at the bottom of a deep blue quarry. But almost immediately, she realized the folly of that thought. Sam and Izzy weren't foolish kids. They were smart, sensible adults. Any danger for them would be imposed on them, not something under their control like being careful around the edges of a quarry. Besides, though she wouldn't mention it to Margarethe, the quarries weren't unfamiliar terrain to kids who grew up in Sea Harbor or spent their summers there.

"I think they'll be okay, Margarethe," Nell said aloud. "And they'll probably not get close to the quarries anyway. They just wanted to see if it might be a good place to take Sam's students for a photo shoot."

"No, it certainly would not," Margarethe said. "I won't put children in that kind of danger. Tony should have known better."

Nancy's tapping of her water glass was a relief, and Nell settled in to follow the meeting's agenda and block out the unpleasant thought of Izzy and Sam wandering into a place that could in any way present danger to them, however irrational she knew those thoughts to be.

When the meeting ended a short while later, Nell scooped up her notes and her knitting and slipped them into her bag. She waved good-bye to Nancy and stepped out into the bright sunlight.

At the curb sat the metallic orange Hummer that, in just one month, had become as familiar to Sea Harbor residents as the sound of the foghorn on gray days. It signified Tony Framingham. Nell watched as Tony leaned across the leather seat and opened the passenger door for his mother. She wondered briefly how many off-roads Tony encountered in Boston and New York with that big car, and then pushed her judgmental thoughts to the back of her head. He may not be doing much for the environment and fuel conservancy, but the Framinghams certainly contributed their share to society. Things balanced out.

Before she had settled into the seat, Margarethe confronted Tony. Her voice rose as she talked, floating through the car window and up the steps. Nell tried not to listen. But Margarethe's voice was strident and clear as she accused her son of putting people's lives in danger.

"What were you thinking, Tony Framingham?" she said. "You don't deserve the name given you. You're foolish, just as your father sometimes was. We've had enough death in Sea Harbor."

Chapter 30

*N*ell knew it was foolish, but she called Izzy's cell as soon as she got to her car. "Just to say hello," she told herself. That was all. Then she'd head to the market, pick up some things at Mc-Clucken's, and go home. She and Ben hadn't had a quiet moment in days, and she wanted to tap into his logical, well-ordered mind to help straighten out her own thoughts.

Nell remembered her graduate school days when she'd have a complicated paper facing her—and two days left to pull it all together. She and Ben would walk the campus, going through her many note cards and scraps of paper. She would talk. Ben would listen. They'd end up outside the deli in Cambridge Square, where Nell would spread her thoughts and facts across the table while they drank copious amounts of coffee and ate sandwiches piled high with turkey and cheese and brown mustard. When she was finished, Ben would sit back and clasp his hands behind his head, his chair tilted back on two legs and his eyes focusing on Nell in the way that made her shift on the hard metal chair and wish they weren't in a public place.

And Ben'd say, "Here's what you do, Nellie—" And then he'd dictate a perfectly ordered outline, Nell's facts and thoughts and digressions filtered into Roman numeral items that followed one from another and made perfect sense.

So maybe you can work your magic on all these awful happenings around us, my love, Nell thought.

Izzy didn't answer her phone, and for a minute Nell sat still, an uncomfortable paralysis coming over her. She didn't know what to do next. Should she drive out to the Framingham property? But where would she go? There were several different quarries on the huge piece of land. And unlike her niece, she hadn't been swimming in any of them in her youth. Besides, what would she say when Izzy and Sam strolled back to their car, smiles on their faces and maybe a relaxed look about Izzy that had been missing for days—"I came out here because I thought you might have drowned in a quarry? Been pushed into a quarry?"

It was early afternoon. Izzy and Sam were probably still hiking the woods around the quarries, and Izzy had left her phone in the car. Or it had run out of batteries, which happened often to Izzy. All was fine. Surely she would know it if it weren't so.

Nell turned toward the village and found a place to park near Coffee's. A frappuchino while she finished her phone calls might put things into perspective. The patio was nearly deserted, and when her name was called, Nell carried the icy-cold drink outside and sat beneath an umbrella and made her next call.

Birdie was about to head back to the hospital, she told Nell. "Angus has no one else but us, Nell." Ella and Harold were going with her, she said, having formed an odd attachment to Angus as he came and went from the Favazza carriage house.

"They're keeping him sedated," Birdie reported. "But he's getting stronger. Detecting the poison as early as they did will probably save his life." And that was just damn luck, Birdie had gone on to say, her voice with an angry edge to it that Nell rarely heard her use. Someone had meant to kill Angus, and they would have done exactly that, if the doctor hadn't remembered seeing a healthy, robust man in his office just days before.

Good news was a rare commodity these days—and Nell silently rejoiced in the report. She hadn't thought about the man's aloneness before—no family or even remote relatives as far as anyone knew. He had been a loner as long as Nell had known him, the old man of the sea. But he did have a family, in a sense. He had Sea Harbor. The town cared about Angus—and people like Birdie would be there to be sure he was warm and fed. Family had many different meanings, she thought, and she punched a button on her phone to check the remaining messages.

There was only one message that had come while she was in the meeting. Father Northcutt had called, saying he'd been up to see Angus, too. And things looked better by the hour.

Nice of him to call, Nell thought. He certainly kept his finger on the pulse of the town.

The message went on to report that George Gideon's funeral was over. A brief service with himself, Esther Gideon, and an uncle from Boston, followed by a quick, no-frills burial. It was what Esther wanted. She had then made a sizable donation in Gideon's memory to Our Lady of the Seas. Money, Esther had confessed to Father Northcutt, that she had found in Gideon's rented room, stuffed beneath his mattress like a daft old lady would do, and she wanted none of it.

"Give me a call," the priest had said at the end of the message.

Nell punched the return call button, and Father Northcutt answered on the second ring.

"How much money, Father?" Nell asked.

"A lot, Nell. Nearly fifty thousand dollars," he answered. "In cash." He explained that Esther wanted it used for parish upkeep, a new roof or statue, and for the daycare center they'd set up for children whose parents couldn't afford to pay. "We can certainly use it," Father said. "Sometimes the Lord works in strange ways."

"Esther Gideon is generous."

"She thinks that using the money for good somehow sanitizes it. She doesn't think it came to Gideon in honest ways, but there's no proof of that, so the police aren't confiscating it."

"Esther doesn't have any idea where it came from?"

"No. But she knows he didn't have it a month earlier when he had to ask her for rent money. She also dropped off a couple boxes of his possessions that your husband kindly picked up for me. He said he'd sort through them and give anything worthwhile to the shelter. That's what Esther wanted. But it's the money that has me stymied. That's a lot of money for someone who couldn't pay his rent the month before."

"Someone was paying Gideon for something, Father."

"Yes, Nell. It appears that way."

"And now he is silenced for good."

"It seems that way, dear, and I believe caution and prudence are called for in these situations," Father Northcutt said, winding up the conversation. And then, in his inimitable way, he added, "And just maybe, Nell, I'll see you next Sunday at the ten o'clock?"

The money was a shock to Nell. Nearly fifty thousand dollars. But it explained so many things. The money was Gideon's ship. It had finally come in. So he had been down at the breakwater that night, and he saw who murdered Angie. It was a quick ticket to wealth for the security guard. Why work when you had blackmail at your fingertips?

Maybe he was asking for more. And the answer to that came on a lonely road by a speeding truck.

Nell reached in her pocket for some change. Her fingers touched paper and she pulled out the envelope Mae had given her hours before.

Mae was right; it looked like a bill, very official, a tax receipt or property tax notice. But on closer look, Angie's name was above the Seaside Knitting Studio words, not Izzy's or Mae's. And when Nell looked at the folded paper inside, she realized it was as far removed from a bill as it could be.

Nell thought about calling Ben, but dismissed the idea quickly. She knew he had meetings and a golf game. Besides, what could be dangerous in a crowded office building in the middle of the afternoon? Nothing.

Nell approached the frosted door slowly, organizing her thoughts, then knocked once and walked on inside.

Sal was standing over at the windows, staring down into the parking lot. "I saw you get out of your car," he said without turning around.

Nell waited quietly until he turned and faced her.

"I knew you'd come back," he said sadly. "I didn't mean to scare her, you know."

"You petrified her, Sal. You harassed Angie with your phone calls and protestations." She held up the envelope.

Sal stared at it. "I shouldn't have sent that. It was like the e-mails. I knew I shouldn't, but I couldn't help myself. I loved her, Nell." Sal walked over and slumped down in the chair. "So I wrote her the letter, begged her to run away with me. I'd have given her the world, you know."

"It might not have been yours to give, Sal. Did Beatrice know? Was Angie going to tell her?"

Sal rested his elbows on his knees and held his head in his hands. He nodded into his palms. "Angie didn't tell her. She said she would if I didn't stop the e-mails. But Beatrice . . . Beatrice didn't need other people to tell her anything. She checked my e-mail, found out about it all on her own."

Nell heard the hardness in Sal's voice when he talked about Beatrice. And then it grew soft and sad.

"But I didn't kill her, Nell. I'd never have killed her. Why would I kill such a beautiful light? Beatrice said you'd all think I did unless . . ."

"Unless what, Sal?"

"Beatrice said if I didn't get Angie's computer before the police did, they'd read all the e-mails I sent—and they'd think I killed her. She said her reputation would be ruined. How could she run for mayor if her husband was in prison?"

Nell shuddered. Sal's last words were utterly sad and desperate. "So Beatrice got the apartment key from Izzy's shop?"

He nodded again. "She'd been hanging around there, trying to figure out where a key might be. Beatrice can find anything, solve anything. That's what she does."

"And then she had you go into the apartment in the middle of the night to take the computer?"

Sal nodded again. "I had dropped one of my pens in the apartment." He looked down at the pocket of his shirt, filled with a neat row of pens. "They all say Registrar of Deeds on them."

"That explains why Beatrice wanted to help us clean Angie's apartment." Nell thought of Beatrice insisting Sal bring them drinks that day. She was probably inflicting some kind of sad punishment on him. He had hurt her, and she was finding ways to hurt him back.

"I loved her, Nell. That's all. She came to see me a lot. I was able to help her with the work she was doing at the museum, help her find the deeds she needed, the photos and all for the exhibit. I didn't want to hurt her."

"You need help, Sal. That's not love, not when you frighten someone. And not when they tell you to leave them alone, and you keep coming back."

Nell looked down at the letter she held in her hand—a frantic desperate outpouring of love. She folded it and put it on Sal's desk.

He looked up, surprised.

"I don't want this. I don't want to hurt you, Sal. But I want you to promise me that you'll see someone—get some help."

Tears streamed down his cheeks and Nell had to look away. She walked toward the door, then stopped, suddenly realizing what she'd forgotten.

"Sal, where's Angie's computer?"

"Beatrice threw it over the railing of our sailboat. It's at the bottom of the ocean."

It was nearly six when Izzy finally returned Nell's call. "How's Angus?" she asked, and Nell breathed a silent thank-you for the sound of her niece's voice. She gave Izzy the updated report. Relieved at the news, Izzy suggested she and Sam come for dinner.

"We've had an interesting day," Izzy said. "Sam took some great photos of the place. And we'll bring dessert."

Sam and Izzy arrived around seven with six different flavors of Scooper's homemade ice cream. "In my next life, I'm going to be a photographer," Izzy declared. "It was such fun, and you see things so differently looking through a lens."

They were sitting in the family room with the doors open to catch the breeze. Ben stood at the kitchen island chopping onions and tomatoes for fish tacos.

Nell filled them in on the letter and her time at the county offices and they were all suitably surprised.

"So it was Sal calling Angie at Harry's," Izzy said. "The phone call he overheard when Angie threatened to tell his wife."

"But Beatrice already knew."

"There goes the motive for murder," Sam said.

"Sal didn't kill Angie. He's a lonely, sad man," Nell said.

"What about his wife?" Sam asked.

They were all silent for a minute.

"It doesn't seem likely," Nell said finally. "I don't think Angie would have gone to meet Beatrice that night. Though Sal scared her, Angie would know there were easier ways to make him stop."

"Maybe, Nell," Ben said. "But I don't think she can be completely overlooked."

"The whole thing with Angie and Sal is so sad," Izzy said. "Angie talked to him because she was friendly, and she needed his expertise. Probably no one had ever relied on him like that before."

"And he mistook it for affection and fell in love with her kindness," Nell said.

"I guess we'll never know what else was on Angie's computer," Ben said.

"Maybe that's all right. Maybe there was nothing on it," Nell said. "The e-mails were definitely there, and definitely a threat to Sal and Beatrice. But other than research notes, Nancy didn't think there would be much on the computer. She said Angie left it out in the open, loaned it to coworkers. And she'd have been more careful if there was something on it she didn't want anyone to see. She was doing a lot of photocopying, Nancy said, that sort of thing, for her job. I think it was the fact that it was missing that made it seem important. And now we know where it went."

"On a brighter note," Izzy said, "Sam and I had a great time out at the quarries. With a bizarre sort of encounter at the end."

"That's a great place," Sam said. "The light was perfect. No wonder there are so many artists up here—you never run out of inspiration. Izzy turned out to have a flare for it."

Nell sipped a glass of white wine that Sam had brought and wondered if she should mention her conversation with Margarethe about the quarries. She certainly wouldn't mention her own irrational fears, but they needed to understand Margarethe's feelings if they had any intention of going back for more photos.

"And then an odd thing happened on the way back," Izzy

said, as if she had tapped directly into Nell's thought. "We had just gotten to the end of the trailhead where we'd parked when Tony's orange chariot came barreling down the road toward us."

"Well, not exactly," Sam said. "Though when we saw Tony's expression, barreling seemed apt. He wasn't happy and seemed to be taking it out on the poor car."

"Margarethe was beside him, and if looks could have killed Tony right then, he'd be out flat on the quarry trail."

"So they stopped?"

Izzy nodded. "Briefly. Margarethe was gracious, but it was clear she was furious at Tony for 'sending us into danger,' as she put it. It almost seemed as if she thought Tony had meant to harm us. She seemed genuinely worried, and was clearly relieved when she saw us."

"What did Tony say?" Ben asked from across the room.

"Basically nothing," Sam said. "He barely looked at us. I think Margarethe had made the drive rather unpleasant for him."

"Rather unpleasant," Izzy repeated. She looked over at Sam. "You are a master of the understatement."

"Did you tell Tony or Margarethe about the photographs you took?" Nell asked. "She might want to see them—maybe it'd ease her anger at Tony for letting you go in."

"We didn't mention taking any pictures," Sam said. "But that's a great idea. I know from talking to her that she loves that land. She's an interesting woman—and so proud of her Framingham name and what it stands for. Tony seems an okay sort, too, though a little distant. His mother seems to worry about him a lot. A little odd, at his age."

"That's what mothers—and aunts—do. Age doesn't matter much," Nell said.

"And you do it so well, Aunt Nell." Izzy tapped her hand. "Tony must have done something awful to make Margarethe so upset."

Or done something awful that would ruin the Framingham name—like pushing a young woman to her death? Nell hated to give any credence to such a thought, but there was something about Tony, about his temper, that Nell thought needed consideration.

They gathered around the kitchen table and ate Ben's tacos, smothered in his special pineapple and garlic sauce. The big, old kitchen table, set against a bank of windows overlooking the deck, was Nell's favorite place to sit. It was gauged and pocked from years of use, and had been in the Endicott family since they bought the land a hundred years before. The hardy piece of furniture had been the gathering place for meals, games, paperwork, and family talks for as long as Nell could remember—and years before that, she suspected. Nell rebuffed Ben's periodic suggestion to refinish it. Each of those marks is a memory, she told him. You don't sand away memories.

"It's amazing you two aren't huge, the way you both cook." Sam wiped the sauce from the corners of his mouth. "Great tacos."

Behind them, the summer light faded into night and the deck lights blinked on.

"It's mostly healthy food, though I sneak in my pat of butter or two when Nell isn't looking," Ben said. "And speaking of health, I stopped by the station today on some business and heard some talk about Angus's situation. The police were quick to check out the kitchen over at Ocean's Edge, trying to figure out what happened. But they didn't find anything. And no one else had gotten sick, though plenty of people had the same meal. Since Angus went directly to Sam's after eating, whatever happened to him either happened at the restaurant or the few short blocks in between."

"Margarethe thought he looked a little pale at the restaurant," Nell said.

"That young chef loves Angus," Izzy said. "He watches out for him—Angie used to tell me that—and I don't think he even charges Angus half the time."

"Well, they are still probing, trying to figure it out. For now, I think we need a diversion," Ben said. "How about a Sam Perry showing?"

"Yes," said Izzy. "That's a good idea. You'll love the shots we got today."

While Ben, Nell, and Izzy rinsed the plates and got out the ice cream, Sam hooked his camera up to the television screen. "Those quarries are magnificent," he said. "I thought of this summer as kind of a hiatus—a little break from my work with some teaching tossed in for fun. But I'm finding that everywhere I look there's something that draws out my camera."

They settled on the couches and leather chairs near the television, and Sam clicked onto the first digital image. It was on the trail, leading into the quarry. Wild flowers, sweet fern and bay bushes hugged the path and in the distance was a blue opening, clear and beckoning. But the spectacular images were of the quarries themselves, dropped down in the middle of the land, clear round bowls of water with jagged granite rock in oranges and pinks and grays forming the sides. On the outcroppings of rock, flowers and bushes grew, masking some of the stone beneath. The water was so clear that it mimicked the scene above, reflecting the flowers, granite slabs, and bushes so that it was difficult in some photos to tell what was real and what was a mirrored image.

"These are wonderful, Sam," Nell said as the images played across the television screen.

"The first two quarries we came to were pristine like this. But there was one—we should come to some photos of it in a minute—that still had tools around, as if the men had just stopped for lunch and might be back soon. It was fascinating—not visually as appealing, but really interesting."

Sam clicked to the next photo, and they could see the metal tracks in the ground that once carried rail cars in and out. An old chipping tub rested against a tree, filled now with weeds and spindly ferns. The path was wide and firm enough to carry cars.

"Izzy decided next time we would drive in," Sam joked.

"Except there probably won't be a next time," Izzy reminded him. "Unless you can charm Margarethe into letting us come back."

"Would you please go back a photo, Sam?" Nell asked.

Sam clicked back. It was the same quarry, but the water-filled bowl was more in focus, and a narrow path ran along the side. Granite outcroppings coated with brown pine needles poked through the vegetation. "What's that?" Nell asked, pointing to a flash of light up in the left corner of the picture.

"That was me not minding the sunlight carefully enough," Sam said. "There was an old truck nestled near the trees, and the sun bounced off the front of it, making a flash."

"But it has an interesting effect."

"That quarry was especially interesting, though. I'd like to go back to it. On one side there were polished steps, almost like you'd find in a grand old house. It was an interesting sight."

Sam clicked through the rest of the slides, then moved on to a few he had taken of Izzy, her hair blown about her face by gusts of ocean air. Her cheeks were flushed and her eyes bright.

"I think I want this whole last set," Nell said, loving the smile on Izzy's face. "Would you mind putting them on my computer before you leave?"

"Sam's photos are worth lots of money, Aunt Nell," Izzy said, rubbing her fingers together. "Better watch out or you'll get a whopping bill."

"Anyone who feeds me like the Endicotts do can have as many of my photographs as they want," Sam said. "Don't pay any attention to your saucy niece, Nell." Sam turned off his camera and followed Ben into the den to transfer the photos to Nell's computer.

"Nell, I've been thinking a lot about why Angie came here to work. And the fact that she didn't plan on staying long. I think we are definitely missing something."

Nell nodded.

"And there's something else I was reminded about today at the quarries. One day when Angus came into the shop for coffee he told me how smart Angie was and that she knew all about land. She even knew about his own father, he said. I thought that was kind of odd."

"Well, Angus's father was a quarryman, just like he was, and Angie was working on that exhibit for the museum. So maybe she came across something about the McPherrons. That might explain why she spent so much time with him, too."

By the time the dishes were done and photos downloaded, Izzy declared it a day. "Playing hooky has its consequences," she said. "I need to go back to the studio and finish some paperwork while I'm still awake."

As they said their good-byes on the driveway, Nell's thoughts turned back to Sam's photographs. There was something odd, something that seemed a bit incongruous in the beauty that graced the Framingham quarries. But she couldn't quite put her finger on what it was. Perhaps she'd look again tomorrow when she was fresh.

When Nell got back inside, Ben was sitting on the couch. In front of him, on the floor, were two cardboard boxes. He looked up as Nell walked into the room.

"Gideon's things?" she asked.

Ben nodded. "I've gone through them all. Mostly old clothes that I don't think anyone would want. Here's a whole stack of travel folders. Seems he was planning a trip." Ben picked up a folder and handed it to Nell. "Tahiti, Grand Cayman. Gideon had some dreams."

"With the money they found in his apartment, he could easily have gone to any of those places several times."

Ben nodded. "Father Northcutt said the money was in small bills—twenties, fifties, some hundreds. Someone was paying Gideon for something, and it wasn't his lobsters. He couldn't have made this much as a poacher."

"That's exactly what I think, Ben. Gideon was blackmailing Angie's murderer. He was there that night, and he saw someone kill Angie. I feel sure of it."

"And it was someone who apparently could afford to pay the blackmail money." Someone like Tony Framingham, Nell thought, but she kept the thought to herself. She could come up with no reason that Tony would do anything like that. He didn't like Angie, and she certainly didn't like him. But murder? And yet she couldn't shake the thought that Tony knew more about Angie's death than he was letting on. And he had been at the restaurant last night when Angus was poisoned, too. So many coincidences. So little motive.

Ben picked through the rest of the box, but besides the clothes, all Ben found were a few raggedy old paperbacks and girlie magazines, some cracked coffee mugs, and dirty fish line. The box didn't reveal much about Gideon. And it certainly wouldn't help out any of the shelters, either.

Ben leaned back against the couch and put his feet up on the coffee table. "Tell me Nellie, what are we missing here? We have a dead young woman."

"Who started out on a date that night with a lovely young man and ended up at the breakwater. She went there for a reason—and it must have been important to her, or she wouldn't have left Pete the way she did."

"She was meeting someone. Someone who had a bone to pick with her, maybe."

"Josie said Angie was on a mission—she was in Sea Harbor for a reason," Nell said. "A 'project.' Josie assumed it was the job at the museum, but I don't think so. Angie had another agenda."

"Next, Gideon is killed, but not before he received a fistful of cash."

"And not before he ransacked Angie's apartment. Looking for what?"

"I would guess it was the computer," Ben said. "If someone killed Angie because she had something on them, or knew something, or found something, a computer could easily have clues. E-mails, scanned documents, even Web sites. Computers reveal more about ourselves than we know."

"Or it could have nothing. But whether it was true or not, the murderer probably wanted that computer—just to be safe."

"And Gideon was the kind of guy who could have been easily manipulated. Someone may have told him to go to the apartment and get it. But Sal got there first."

"Maybe Gideon asked for more money. He never struck me as being prudent," Nell said. "And the murderer decided to just end it all. And in a horrible, grisly way."

"The police say he was hit by a truck," Ben said. "They found some traces of fender near the road and were able to identify that much."

Nell winced. "Imagine, hitting someone that hard. Someone clearly wanted Gideon dead."

"And someone who knew where he went at night. It was a well-chosen location."

They fell silent then, both of them thinking of Angus. How did this sweet man fit into such an awful series of events?

When the phone rang, Nell jumped, startled at the intrusion into her thoughts.

Ben reached for the phone and Nell watched his face carefully. Good news or bad, she'd know in an instant—Ben's feelings appeared on his face sometimes before he had acknowledged them himself.

A slow smile appeared, then the shake of his head. He ran one hand through his hair. "Well, I'll be," he said. Then, "Thanks."

"Well?" Nell said when he hung up.

"It was Birdie. She said Angus woke up while she was there. He asked her to bring him a Sam Adams. Then asked if he had any mail."

Chapter 31

$\mathcal{N}$ell got up early the next morning and headed for the beach. Ben had a breakfast meeting, he said, and he'd see her later at home. They could tackle Gideon's other boxes then.

Running helped clear Nell's head, and today she desperately needed a head clearing. She ran north along the beach, passed vacation homes and cottages, then over the smooth beach of the yacht club. In the distance was the breakwater, the sun lighting up the huge slabs of granite that formed the barrier.

The breakwater was a beautiful structure in the morning, Nell thought, not treacherous, not a scene of something awful. Sunlight reflected off the smooth planes, pulling out the colors of the stone. Fishermen were already on its back, silhouetted against the morning sky as they cast their lines into the sea. On the near side, in the protected cove, lobster buoys vied with sailboats, their naked masts waving like trees in winter, stripped of leaves.

Nell slowed her pace to a walk, looking back at the yacht club, then out to the breakwater. In a small area on the edge of the club property, across a short span of beach from the breakwater, two stone benches and a table sat in shadows. A perfect meeting place for someone who didn't want to be seen by anyone inside, Nell thought. A private place to have a drink maybe, then walk out on the breakwater. Is that what Angie did that night? Meet someone for a drink, a talk. Then walk out along the stone where no one could hear the conversation. Where only the gulls and the lobsters would be their witnesses? Or was she becoming paranoid, jumping at thin straws that would break under scrutiny?

Nell walked from the table to the breakwater and out onto its wide expanse. She smiled at the fishermen, then stopped near the end and sat with her legs hanging over the side, the stone cool against her thighs. She looked down at the outcroppings leading down to the water and a narrow ledge, visible at low tide. If she were thirty-eight, like Gideon, she'd have no trouble climbing up or down. And none of the fishermen sitting at the top would even know she was down there. She sat for a while, thinking of Angie. Trying to think her thoughts. Did she sit out here, in this same spot, having a drink, talking, arguing maybe? And then the drug began to do its deadly work. Did she feel it, notice that her arms didn't work, her legs, her voice? Was the push gentle? A silent slide into a noisy sea?

Nell pulled herself up and walked slowly back toward the beach. She looked north, across the public beach and the small parking area. She could see the dead-end road from here, the one that ran up to the shamble of old cars, the road no one used. But Gideon had used it, headed that way with his sack of lobsters, toward his car. Probably happy. His life was good. And maybe it was going to get better, he'd be thinking.

Nell turned and began to jog back the way she came, along the clubhouse beach. Just on the edge of the yacht club property, she saw a familiar figure coming toward her. She picked up speed. She'd give a quick wave, a polite, "sorry, can't stop" kind of wave, and that would pass for politeness.

But Tony Framingham, in running shorts and his T-shirt stained with perspiration, came to a full stop several feet before Nell reached him. "Nell, we need to talk," he said.

Nell slowed, then came to a stop, her breath coming in jagged spurts. Sometimes the urge to be polite, no matter what, was a curse, she thought. Birdie would have been fine moving right past him, and she wouldn't have given it a second thought. Maybe she should take lessons.

"Good morning, Tony," she finally managed to say.

Tony's voice was even, unaffected by his fast-paced run. "We need to talk about Angie Archer," he began. He looked at the ground as if planning his words carefully. When he looked back at Nell his brows were pulled together, his voice unfamiliar, forced, as if he were negotiating a tough business deal. "You have to stop this crazy Sherlock Holmes bit. You and Izzy and the others have been asking questions all over town, making people uncomfortable, creating a bad vibe. It's over, Nell. The police know what happened. Mrs. Archer has accepted her daughter's death. Don't make it worse. Let it be."

"But I don't know what happened, Tony."

"Read the police report. I have. It makes sense."

"We all want it to be over, Tony. The police, all of us. Not knowing the ending is the worst thing of all. We can try to go on, but we won't really be able to do that. Not until we know for sure who killed her. And there are still too many missing parts. Things that don't add up. What happened to Angus, for example." Nell took a quick glance at the groups of children and moms unfolding their blankets on the sand and a smattering of runners soundlessly running along the shore. She could say what she liked here. She was completely safe.

Tony frowned. "He had a heart attack. That happens to old men."

"He was poisoned, Tony."

Tony took a step back. For a minute he stood in silence, staring at her, his feet planted apart as if Nell had hit him and he was striving for balance. He took in a lungful of air, then let it out slowly, his composure in place. "I think the town will be a better place if you mind your own business, Nell. You're going to hurt people. And I know you want Izzy safe, don't you?"

Before Nell could answer, Tony turned and began again to run down the beach. He ran faster and faster, beating the ground with his running shoes, bits of sand spitting up in his wake and his arms pumping against the sides of his body until he rounded the curve beyond the breakwater, and Nell couldn't see him anymore.

Nell turned and began her walk back home. Her heartbeat was fast, but not from running now. This time it raced from Tony Framingham's veiled threat.

A brisk shower calmed Nell and brought normalcy back into her thinking. By the time she was through, she wasn't sure what Tony had actually said to her. Had she imagined a threat? For a moment she thought of calling Margarethe and talking to her about it, then quickly squelched the thought. That's what you did when your second-grader was hit by the biggest kid in the class. How did you tell a mother her son might be involved in something sinister?

Nell toweled off, rubbing the blood back into her limbs, and pulled on a T-shirt and slacks. The threat, if it was a threat, was vague, ill-formed. She would forget it and rejoice in the news that Angus McPherron had a fighting chance.

The morning allowed Nell little time to think more about Tony. Or Angus, for that matter. With three back-to-back meetings, she would have to wait until later to think any more about Tony.

It was well after lunch when Nell managed to slip into Harry's Deli for a turkey-pastrami on rye. The news of Angus's waking up was circling Harbor Road. There was genuine joy moving from table to table in the small room, and Nell watched it with surprise and pleasure. People cared, and she wondered if Angus knew that. She wasn't sure she herself was aware that the town considered the old man of the sea *their* old man of *their* sea. Sometimes it took something bad to bring out the very best in people, she thought. On impulse, she ordered a couple extra sandwiches. She'd stop by the knitting shop and, if there were no takers there, Ben had never in his lifetime turned down one of Harry's spicy concoctions.

Birdie was standing at the counter with an armful of yarn when Nell walked in the door. A project for the hospital waiting room, Nell supposed. The studio hummed with activity.

"There you are," Birdie said, spotting her. "I tried to call you." She spoke in a voice that made Nell feel she had done something frightfully wrong.

"We need to talk," Birdie said. "Izzy's in the back." She gave Rose her credit card and told her not to lose it, then cupped Nell's elbow in her hand and ushered her into the back room.

Izzy and Cass sat on the window seat, legs folded up beneath them. Cass's shawl was spread across their laps and Purl was nestled in the center of Izzy's crossed legs. "We're already on the shoulders," Izzy said. "Mary will be so pleased."

Birdie crossed the room and pulled a bundle of letters from her backpack. She dropped them unceremoniously on the coffee table.

"Are you working at the post office now?" Nell asked.

"When Angus asked for mail I thought he was slipping back into that private world of his. But Ella told me he actually did get mail at our place recently, though she'd never known him to look at it. So she stacked it neatly on his dresser when she cleaned his rooms and it usually went untouched. I went through it last night and pulled out the obvious junk. There wasn't much else, a few credit card applications and letters to resident. Except for these." She pointed to two letters bound together with a rubber band. "They're from Angie Archer," she said.

"Angie?" Nell picked up one of the envelopes and looked at the typed address. *Mr. Angus McPherron,* it said.

"The postmarks aren't right. One came yesterday, one last week,

Ella said. Angie didn't know Angus lived with me, so she sent them to his place outside town. By the time the post office figured out where Angus was and passed them on, time had passed."

Across each envelope was the word "Personal" printed in block letters. And at the bottom it read "Important," as if Angie were pleading with Angus not to throw the letters away. The return address was the small apartment above the Seaside Knitting Studio.

"You need to take these to Angus," Izzy said. "You go. I need to be here this afternoon."

"And I'll be out checking traps," Cass said. "But you'll call?"

Angus had been moved to a private room and his doctor was coming out as Birdie and Nell approached his door.

"Great old guy, strong as a stone cutter," she said, smiling back into the room. "He's weak, but he's going to be okay."

Nell and Izzy walked in to find Angus resting against the pillows, his white beard clean and combed and his eyes open.

"Well, ladies, will you look at this?" Angus lifted one hand and pointed to the walls and the windowsills, filled with baskets of fruit, cards taped to long ribbons and pinned to the walls, and stacks of magazines. His finger shook slightly as it moved.

"You have lots of admirers, Angus," Nell said.

His head moved on the pillow. "It seems so," he said. His voice was so soft Nell could barely hear him.

Birdie walked over and pulled a chair up to his bed. She took his hand in hers and smiled into tired eyes. "Well, you do, you crazy old coot. Believe it. And get better. You owe it to us."

He closed his eyes briefly, and when they opened, Nell and Birdie pretended not to notice the tear that rolled down his wrinkled face to the sheet beneath his chin.

Birdie rummaged around in her backpack and pulled out the envelopes. "I brought your mail," she said.

Angus rolled his head on the pillow and focused his eyes on

the letters in Birdie's hand. Without lifting his head from the pillows, he read his name on the envelope, the return address. Angie Archer. "She said she would write," he mumbled. "Indeed." And then his lids fell again, heavy against his pale, tired face.

"Do you want me to read these, Angus?" Birdie asked. She held up the envelopes again.

For a minute he didn't answer and they thought he had fallen asleep. But a few seconds later he opened his eyes briefly. When he spoke, his voice was soft but definite. "Read them and save them for me. Go home now."

Then sleep took over his frail body, and Nell and Birdie slipped out of the room, looking back through the door just once to see a still figure, peaceful against the white sheets.

By the time Nell and Birdie picked up some supplies for Angus, dropped them back at the hospital and returned to Sea Harbor, daylight was fading, giving way to the gentle light of evening. A soothing light, Nell thought, looking through the window of her car. Even in the midst of all this turmoil, a Cape Ann evening could bring peace.

When they arrived at Nell's, Cass and Izzy were sitting on the couch, a plate of cheese and bowl of grapes in front of them. A pitcher of Ben's martinis was on the kitchen island.

"You didn't call," Izzy said, frowning at her aunt. "Is Angus all right?"

"He's much better," Nell said. "So much better today. The doctor thinks he'll be back to normal soon." She looked around. "Where's Ben?"

"He had to help Father Northcutt finish his financials for the church committee tomorrow. He said to tell you he'll be back as soon as he can." Izzy stood and gave Nell a hug. "What happened with Angus's mail? Cass came by when I was closing the store and since neither of us had heard, we came over."

Birdie set the legal-sized envelopes on the island and repeated Angus's request.

"So Angus wants us to read his mail?" Cass asked.

"That's what he said," Birdie answered. "He seemed to be expecting the letters. Angie must have told him she was sending them and that they were important."

The four women sat around the coffee table and Nell ripped open the first envelope. Down in the corner she noticed a small note. *1/3*, it said. Certainly not the date. Maybe the post office had coded it somehow. She pulled out several old newspaper articles, something Angie must have found while doing research at the museum.

The stories were about Angus McPherron and Anja Alatalo, Angus's beautiful Finnish wife. There was a faded picture of the two of them, toasting each other at a long table in a clearing filled with flowers. Behind the festive group, in a circle of rosebushes, a white-draped table held a wedding cake six tiers tall. The article was chatty and personal, in the way of small-town newspapers. It told of the handsome cutter Angus falling in love and marrying the rich Finnish quarryman's daughter. The reporter detailed the extravagant wedding Anja's father had given his only daughter. Nothing was overlooked, not the huge arrangements of flowers, the elaborate food and drink.

A copy of a legal document was stuck in the same envelope. Birdie unfolded it and read the ornate script at the top. *Certificate of Marriage*. It was a copy of Angus and Anja's wedding certificate, signed at the bottom in elegant script by the husband and wife, the witnesses and minister.

Nell smoothed the papers out and put them on the coffee table. She opened the other envelope, slightly bigger than the first, with neat, careful numbers on the bottom in small print: *2/3*.

There was one document inside, an old yellowed deed. Nell

looked at it carefully and passed it to Birdie. "It's a land deed granting rights and ownership."

Birdie slipped on her glasses and looked at it carefully. The name "McPherron" was written on the top of the yellowed piece of paper, and a description of the small plot of land out near the highway where Angus had lived all these years.

Nell looked at the envelope again and the small notation on the bottom. *2/3. Two out of three?* A reminder to Angus that he'd be getting three envelopes in the mail. "Was there another envelope?" she asked Birdie.

"Not that I could find. But these are postmarked a day or so apart. I suppose there could be one still to come," Birdie said.

Nell looked again at the land deed, similar to many that the museum had compiled for exhibits of early Cape Ann settlers—stories of fishermen and cutters from around the world who made Cape Ann a rich ethnic blend of nationalities.

Izzy read parts of the story of Angus's wedding to Anja Alatalo out loud. She was a beautiful young woman, the reporter wrote, with wavy brown hair that fell to her waist.

Nell listened, and thought of the still body lying in the hospital bed. His life with Anja, however short, must have been a wonderful one, she thought. As she lifted the envelope, another article slipped out. Nell slipped on her glasses and read the story slowly. It was the tragic tale she'd heard from Ben's parents, the sad story of Anja and her father being killed on his land. A dynamite explosion gone awry, Ben's mother had told them.

Nell looked again at the old photographs, remarkably preserved—Anja and Angus, Angus and her father, and pictures of the quarries that Luukas Alatalo had worked with his father. She held the clippings beneath the table lamp and squinted to bring them into focus. There was something familiar about the photo, a view she had seen before, maybe in her hikes around

Rockport, Halibut Park, perhaps? Nell tugged at her memory, but clarity stayed at the edges of remembering, nudging her, irritating her, like a pea beneath the mattress.

The growling of Cass's stomach indicated it had been a while since any of them had eaten, and she and Birdie headed for Nell's refrigerator.

"Whatever you find is fair game," Nell called out from her chair.

Birdie took out some leftover pasta and grilled vegetables and heated them in the microwave. Cass helped, heating up a platter of Italian sausages and sautéed mushrooms.

"There're some sourdough rolls from Harry's Deli on the counter," Nell said, her attention still on the photos.

They filled their plates from the bowls and platters on the center island and gathered around the kitchen table, elbows propped up on the wood surface, the yellow papers scattered across the tabletop, and their thoughts on Angus McPherron—and Angie Archer.

"Why do you suppose Angie sent these to Angus?" Birdie asked. "She saw him all the time."

"I think it was safer to send them," Nell said. "Angie knew better than any of us that Angus didn't always tend to things. If she had handed these things to him while they sat down at the harbor or walking along the beach, they probably would have ended up in a refuse heap—or tossed to the wind."

"And maybe she knew she was in danger," Cass added.

Nell nodded. "That's a possibility, I guess, but I hope not. The thought of Angie in danger and not asking for help would be hard to live with."

"I was tough on Angie, especially that last night." Cass's high cheekbones were flushed with emotion as she spoke.

"We all may have misjudged her some, Cass," Birdie said. "But that doesn't change anything. Angie was trying to do something, probably something good."

"And it cost her her life." Nell poured a cup of tea. The room had grown suddenly chilly. The mood somber.

"Okay," Izzy said. "So what's missing here?" She looked down at the array of papers on the table.

"We're missing the third piece. *The three of three*," Nell said. Yes, that had to be it—it was an Angie kind of thing to do, keeping track of the documents in order, helping Angus order his life.

"I don't understand why she sent the deed," Cass said. "We knew that the land Angus lived on was his, so this deed doesn't really tell us much. It's nice for Angus to have, just in case he wants to see it someday. But that's about it. And why did she send the wedding license—and the articles?"

Nell looked at the newspaper clippings again. "Maybe Angie was putting the pieces of Angus's life together for him because it was hard for him to do that himself. She was reminding him of this beautiful woman who loved him." Nell looked again at the photograph of Angus and his bride, unable to let go of the sweet young couple sitting at their wedding table.

"Yes," Izzy said, excited. "That's it, Nell! Angie was putting together the pieces of his life. But there's one piece missing."

"Did Anja have other family?" Cass asked.

"No. Her mother died in childbirth," Birdie said. "That's probably why she was so close to her father. He lived for Anja, I've heard people say."

"So Anja and Angus would get everything when Anja's father died?" Nell asked.

Izzy looked up from a forkful of pasta. She frowned, reading Nell's mind. "But Anja died, too. So Angus would have been the only remaining relative."

The room grew quiet as they thought about the deeds and marriage license and the tragedy that separated this couple so early in their life journey.

Nell placed the contents of the envelopes on the table and

put the envelopes to the side. *1/3, 2/3.* An old deed. Newspaper clippings. A marriage certificate. She thought of the conversation she and Izzy had had with Angus on the beach. *Indeed,* Angie had said to him, he'd told them. *She would send mail, indeed.* A deed. Angie had told him she'd send him a deed.

"A will," Izzy said suddenly. "We're missing a will. And another deed? The license tells us that Anja and Angus were married. The deed tells us about Angus's property. But—"

"The father's will—or Anja's—would tell the rest," Cass finished.

Birdie pushed back her chair and her hands flew up. "And I think I know exactly where it is," she said. She looked at Nell. "The nurse at the hospital—"

"The coat pocket of Angus's jacket. The envelope that gave the hospital staff your address. Angus had it with him when he was admitted."

"Let's hope it's still there."

Birdie got up and picked up her purse, rummaging around inside. "Drats. No car. Izzy or Cass, I need a driver."

"Why don't you both go?" Nell suggested. "Just in case—" *In case of what?* Nell wasn't sure. But she didn't want Birdie to make the trip alone.

"Good idea. And I need to stop by and check on Purl on our way," Izzy added. "Sam had to go into Boston for a meeting and she's all alone."

"I'll wait for Ben," Nell said. It wouldn't take four of them to retrieve an envelope, she thought. And she might be far more useful tying up a few loose strands of yarn right here.

After the others drove off, Nell cleaned up the kitchen, made a pot of coffee, and sat back down at the kitchen table, staring at her laptop. Outside a breeze slapped the top of a pine tree against the side of the house.

Nell pressed a key and brought the computer to life, its familiar humming filling the kitchen. And seconds later, Sam's photographs filled the screen, and Nell clicked through them absently while her mind played with the scattered pieces of Angus's life.

And then she saw it. The intriguing shot of the quarry that had caught her attention earlier. She zoomed in, saw the flash of sunlight on glass captured by Sam's camera. And the amazing, crystal-clear quarry—with the old truck, so close to the granite edge that a nor'easter could topple it into the water with a mighty blast. She zoomed in again and she could see the front windshield, a maze of tiny cracks that caught the light like a prism. And the broken bumper, hanging on by a thread. It was incongruous—and oddly beautiful. The still, perfect quarry opening up the woods, the sunlight, and the old, rusted truck. Nell stared at it. And then her breathing quickened and she put on her glasses and looked again.

The photograph filled the small screen, and Nell's mind cleared. And she knew that if the resolution of the photograph were higher, if she could get just a millimeter closer, she would find blood and tissue coating the rusted bumper of the old truck.

Nell pressed the print button and the photos slid out of the printer on the nearby desk. She folded them and shoved them in her purse. No one would be back for a little bit—the drive to the hospital and checking on Purl would take at least an hour or more.

She had just enough time for one quick trip. And if she was right, there'd be one more piece to add to the puzzle.

Chapter 32

$\mathcal{N}$ell checked her watch as she drove toward Canary Cove. After years of pleading, Annabelle had finally given in to the artists' pleas and kept Sweet Petunia's open until eight o'clock one night a week—but only on Tuesdays—the one night she didn't play bunco or have restaurant paperwork to do, or a television show she couldn't miss. She kept the same breakfast and lunch menu, but no one seemed to mind, and eggs for supper on Tuesdays became a standard among the Canary Cove artists and others privy to Annabelle's schedule, which was never advertised.

Though it was already after eight, Nell knew it took a while to wash down the kitchen and empty the trash. And often diners stayed on, gossiping and catching up on news. She and Izzy had spent many Tuesday evenings at Annabelle's while planning the Seaside Knitting Studio, knitting and talking and filling the small shop with Izzy's dreams, and the friendly owner never urged them to leave. She always had something to do, she said.

Nell turned onto the small gravel road that led up to the restaurant. The parking lot lights were on, and the restaurant was still well lit. She spotted several cars parked in the lot—an old Corolla that Annabelle had let Stella use when she'd turned sixteen. Annabelle's car was there, too, and a few late diners, their cars parked on the other side of the lot. Nell pulled up close to the kitchen door, debating whether to go in or stay put, waiting until all the diners were gone. Just then, she spotted Stella Palazola walking out the kitchen door, dragging two sacks of scraps for Annabelle's compost pile.

Nell dropped her car keys and purse on the front seat and jumped out of the car, hurrying to catch up to the young waitress.

"Stella," she said, stopping the young waitress just as she reached the compost pile behind the restaurant.

Stella spun around, dropping one of the sacks. "Miz Endicott, you scared me."

"I'm sorry, Stella." Nell leaned over and gathered up the sack. "I need to talk to you. Please, just for a minute?"

Stella looked back at the restaurant and Nell kept her eyes on Stella, hoping she wouldn't flee again.

Stella's eyes darted back and forth—to Nell, the kitchen door, then over to the parking lot where the last diners were finally leaving, going out to their cars. In the distance, Nell could hear their footsteps, car doors slamming, distant chatter, and then the sound of cars leaving the parking lot.

Nell held Stella with her eyes.

"What?" Stella asked.

Stella looked defeated, Nell thought, as if she had known Nell would come back. She had become Stella's bad penny. "It's about that cashmere sweater, Stella—"

"I told you, I'm sorry I tried it on. I'll never do it again. Does it matter so much? Who cares about a stupid old sweater?"

"I do, Stella. I care very much. And I promise you that I will never do anything to get you in trouble. But you need to tell me about that sweater."

Stella took off her glasses and rubbed her eyes.

"I know this all seems silly to you."

Stella picked up a sack filled with coffee grounds and dumped it into the compost pile. She wiped her hands on her apron.

"Miz Endicott—" she began.

"You can trust me, Stella. I promise you. But I need to know the truth."

Stella nodded. She picked up her last bag and dumped it into the pile.

And then she turned back to Nell, and she told her the truth.

Chapter 33

$\mathscr{I}$t was late when Nell finally returned home, her mind numb and her heart heavy. Stella had said what she knew she would say. The truth had been there, hovering at the corners of Nell's mind for days now, but she wouldn't allow the suspicions to become fact. She didn't want them to be fact.

Ben was waiting at home, worried. "Don't do this to me, Nell," he said.

"Ben, you're not the worrier. I am."

"You're right, I'm not. So don't turn me into one." He was sitting at the island, drinking a cup of tea and he forced a lightness into his voice. Nell walked over to him and dropped her purse on the floor. She rubbed his neck.

"Birdie, Cass, and Izzy came by."

"And they brought the envelope?"

Ben nodded. He picked it up from the island. "They filled me in about the other documents. I've checked them over."

"And the third envelope?" Nell asked. But she knew before Ben answered what was in it. Izzy had been right. It contained a will. A deed. A fortune. Angus's fortune.

Nell told Ben about talking to Stella. And about the photos she had printed off from Sam's shoot at the quarry. The photograph that held the key to Angus's life—and Angie's death.

Nell reached for her purse, digging inside for the printouts she'd made.

"That's odd," she said. "I slipped the pictures in my purse. I'm not even sure why now. Habit, I guess. But they're not here." She rummaged through it again, but the large bag held her wallet and cosmetic case. Her cell phone and pens, a pad of paper and tissues. But the printed photos she had tucked into the bag were gone.

She mentally retraced her trip to Annabelle's. She'd left her purse sitting on the car seat with the windows wide open while she talked to Stella. Her purse and her keys. She frowned, remembering the voices and click of heels behind her as the last diners left the restaurant. She remembered the sound of footsteps that had come close to where she and Stella were standing, and then faded away. Car doors slammed; then the vehicles drove off until they couldn't be heard anymore.

"Someone took the photos from my purse," Nell said. "And I think I know who." She checked her watch. It was too late to call Annabelle, and she didn't want to explain it all. But she suspected she knew at least one of the diners who had enjoyed Annabelle's Tuesday-evening eggs a few hours before.

Ben and Nell drank hot tea, talking quietly, and finally went up to bed.

"It's too late tonight to do anything," Ben said. "And to what good end? No one is running away. Let people sleep. Tomorrow will come soon enough."

They would call the police in the morning and deliver the deeds and the wedding license and the photos. Angie's hard work to make things right, all tied up neatly in a rubber band.

The phone call from Birdie came early, just before the sun slipped up out of the ocean.

Birdie had been unable to sleep, she said, so she got up and sat at the windows in Sonny Favazza's den, a place she always found comfort. She could see the burst of color from the windows, but the telescope took her even closer. At first the light was small—a flash of light against the black sky. And then it grew larger.

Birdie called 911, then dialed Nell and Ben.

"We're on our way," Ben said, and Birdie assured him that the fire trucks were, too.

Ben drove as fast as he could along the narrow Framingham Road, lit by a lingering moon that seemed reluctant to give way to dawn. Nell's heart was wedged tightly in her throat, not wanting to see what she knew they would find at the end of the road.

They arrived before the fire trucks and police, before Cass and Pete, who had gotten up early to prepare their traps and had seen the fire from their boat. Before Izzy, unable to sleep, who was on her way to the point.

Margarethe Framingham stood at the edge of the drive, dressed incongruously in a suit and heels, as if she were going to a board meeting at the museum. She stood calmly, watching the enormous house that had been the love of her life light up the night. The crackling flames traveled from one room to the next, lighting up from the inside as if a party were about to begin. The old walls created a furnace, sucking in the air, fueling the dancing flames as they played with curtains, crackled exquisite chandeliers, and melted fine books into black lumps of coal.

"Margarethe," Nell called out to her. "Don't."

But the woman put up her hands and took a step closer to the burning house. "Don't come near me," she called out. "If I can't have this house, no one will."

"Why, Margarethe?"

"I tried to talk to that girl, but she wouldn't listen to me," she said. "She wanted to take it all back and give it to an old man who didn't care, didn't need this, didn't want it. This is mine," she said, her voice turning steely. "I worked for it. I became someone because of it. I am important—and you want to take it away. You will never have it. Never. None of you ungrateful people."

In the background, faint and still at a distance, the sounds of cars, sirens, and fire trucks racing over the granite ground toward Framingham Point marred the silent beauty of dawn.

"Margarethe, the land didn't belong to the Framinghams. Not ever. And now two people are dead."

"She didn't have to die. I gave her choices. Life is all about choices. I was worth nothing and made the choice to marry into this family and control it. Angie made the wrong choice. I made the right one. She used her research skills on the wrong thing. Just to settle a silly score."

"I don't think she would consider her father's death a silly grievance, Margarethe."

"He drank himself to death. And being fired from our company was incidental. But no matter, Angie Archer should never have pursued this—she was not hired to dig into the Framinghams' past. This town would be nothing without me."

Without me. The steely arrogance in Margarethe's voice startled Nell. This was not the person she sat with on boards, the generous woman who spearheaded Sea Harbor causes. It was a power-hungry woman who came from nothing—and would never go back to that.

"Margarethe, we can make this right," she said, not believing her words, just as she knew Margarethe would not believe them, but trying desperately to hold her attention.

Ben slowly moved around the circle drive while Nell talked.

"Gideon was a fool, you know," Margarethe said, her voice rising to an unfamiliar level. "He saw us that night as he was stealing the lobsters, foolish, horrible person. No one could ever blackmail Margarethe Framingham."

"You kept Izzy's sweater, Margarethe."

The light of the fire illuminated an odd smile on Margarethe's face. "It slipped off her shoulders. It was the most exquisite yarn, an unusual perfect weave . . ." Her voice trailed off as if she were picturing the saffron-colored cashmere, feeling it with her fingertips. "I kept it safe in my closet. One should care for beautiful things, Nell."

"Angie talked to Angus about this land," Nell said. Out of the corner of her eye, she saw Ben circle the statue in the center of the drive, moving closer to the tall figure at the foot of the steps.

Margarethe looked off into the distance. "Angus told me Angie was giving him proof. But she was dead. He didn't know what she was talking about half the time, fool man. All he wanted was to clutter up the harbor front telling tales. But when he was lucid—"

Nell wrapped her arms around her body, warding off the chill of dawn. "Then he knew, didn't he? Knew that this land belonged to his beloved Anja. And when she died, it belonged to him. And that somehow Angie had put things in place for him."

"Belonged?" Margarethe stepped closer to the house. "What do you know about belonging? I was nothing, nothing! And now I am something. And no one will ever, ever take that away." She turned and looked around the circle, spotted Ben not fifty feet away. She put up her hands in front of her, stopping him, her tall figure a silhouette against the burning backdrop.

And as the fire trucks screeched and whirred, their lights spinning around and casting eerie shadows against the trees, Margarethe smiled back at Nell, nodded politely to Ben, turned as if on a stage, and walked back into her house.

Chapter 34

The *Sea Harbor Gazette* said it all: *Sea Harbor's old man of the sea—a millionaire benefactor.*

And farther down, a headline read: *Fall from Grace.* And the sad, awful story of Margarethe Framingham was detailed in chronological exactness. Nell noticed that Margarethe's accomplishments were listed as well, but they paled in the light of her motivation and awful, murderous compulsion to maintain a name and a fortune. That couldn't be explained away so easily.

When Izzy and Nell visited Josie a day later and carried the boxes of her things into the back bedroom, Josie pulled out one of Angie's graduate school papers and showed it to them. Angie had gotten an A on it, Josie said proudly. She'd chosen Sea Harbor for her paper that semester and discovered unusual land transfers that didn't fall on the grid. So she had come back home after graduation to pick up the trail. It had been a lottery win for Angie, Nell realized now—she'd found a way to extract justice from Sylvester Framingham Sr. for her father's death—and she'd help a very nice man in the process.

Tony Framingham returned to Sea Harbor the next day, as soon as the news reached him. He'd been in Boston, visiting friends.

A blessing, Nell thought when she took a look at the bedraggled figure standing in her doorway that afternoon. No good would have come from seeing his mother die.

Ben and Nell were both home when the unexpected visitor arrived, and they sat with him on the deck, a glass of untouched ice tea in front of him.

"You were the last to see her," he said. "I just want to know . . . I don't know what I want to know."

"The fire chief said she didn't suffer, Tony. She was knocked unconscious when the ceiling caved in. She didn't feel any pain."

"Maybe not at that moment," Tony said. He sat on the bench, his head low and his elbows braced on his legs.

"Did you know what was going on, Tony?" Ben asked.

Tony looked beaten, a handsome man, crushed beneath a sordid history and grief for his mother—and for her deeds. "I knew she wasn't right lately. I got strange phone calls from her saying that people were out to destroy the Framingham name. Things that didn't make sense. That's why I came home.

"I always suspected my grandfather stole the land and the quarries—I talked to my dad about it once and he admitted as much. His old man was a shyster, but he had friends in all the right places. When both the Alatalos died—father and daughter—there was no one to stop him. He was able to come up with a document, have it signed and sealed. Angus was probably overcome with grief at the time, and he may not have even known about the will that stated the Alatalos' fortune, the land, and the quarries belonged to him. It was easy.

"My dad handled the fraud by being distant. Mother knew, and coveted the secret to keep her standing, her power—the only things in life that really mattered to her. I handled it by getting away from here, not taking a cent from my family, finding my own way."

"You knew Angie was up to something, though."

Tony nodded. "She told me as much. Angie always disliked the whole family, ever since her father lost his job. She had a right to, frankly. But I always kind of liked her, believe it or not. Angie saw things in black and white though, and I was definitely a part of the bad guys, even when we were teenagers. When I came back to help my mother, I tried to talk with Angie, tried to get her to back off, to bribe her, if I had to. But she wouldn't listen to me."

"Did you know that your mother . . ." Nell paused.

"Killed Angie? I don't know if I knew or not, Nell. I guess I thought if everyone let the police report stand, moved on, it would all go away—and I wouldn't have to know.

"I was rude to all of you, I know. I thought if I played tough, you'd all back off, forget about it, buy into the town's thinking that the guy who did it was long gone. And then maybe I could convince myself that they were right, some stranger killed Angie."

Tony's face was so raw with sadness that Nell had to keep herself from looking away. He sat in silence for a moment, breathing in and out as if to stabilize his shaken world. When he finally looked up at Nell and Ben, his voice was shaky and his eyes filled with remorse.

"She was my mother," he said at last. "And I loved her."

Birdie dressed Angus up in summery Brooks Brothers slacks and a silky shirt for the Fourth of July ceremony. She slipped a rose into the pocket of his shirt.

"This is your day, Angus. Now, behave yourself."

"Miss Birdie, I just love it when you talk dirty." Angus smiled. He had lost weight, but his mind was clear and though the doctors couldn't explain it, he had maintained a reasonable clarity since his release from the hospital.

"I think he always thought he was alone," Birdie said. "Ever since he lost Anja, he wandered, always on the edge but never really being a part of anything. When he was in the hospital, Sea Harbor showed him he still has a family."

The doctors listened politely and nodded appropriately. But, as Birdie told anyone who would listen, they couldn't seem to come up with a better explanation, now, could they?

Nell waved at Angus as he walked onto the stage. It was set up in the middle of the park near Ocean's Edge. When the skies turned dark, fireworks would go off over the ocean and little children would run around the grass with sparklers in their hands. Already blankets covered the grass, the smell of hotdogs and hamburgers filled the air, and a small band played John Philip Sousa marches to the delight of romping children. As the drums rolled, the mayor stepped up to the podium and blew ceremoniously into the microphone. A shrill ring brought the crowd to attention.

"Ladies and gentlemen," he began, "a happy Fourth of July to you!"

The crowd squealed and several helium balloons floated up in the air above the mayor's head.

They all sat in the first row, just in front of the stage—Nell and Ben, Cass, Pete, Sam and Birdie. The Brandleys were just behind them, Archie outfitted in a red, white, and blue striped shirt with a silly little beanie that had stars and stripes on the top. Ham and Jane slipped in just before Angus came to the microphone.

And Izzy sat on the end, next to Sam, with the cashmere sweater that wouldn't die wrapped around her shoulders. Shortly after the night Margarethe died, a package arrived at the Seaside Knitting Studio, mailed the day of the fire.

Purl had found the package first, just inside the back door, and pawed and pulled until the string fell free. She seemed insistent Izzy open the package then and there.

When Izzy opened the cardboard flaps, she gasped.

"She must have planned that day," Izzy told Nell. "She knew

we were putting the pieces together. Angus was recovering. It was just a matter of time."

Nell had added, "And I think she was at Annabelle's when I went to see Stella the night of the fire. When Margarethe was leaving, she saw us talking—and she'd have known that Stella would finally tell me the sweater didn't come with a guest. It came from Margarethe's closet. She rummaged in my car and found Sam's photos of her truck, the one that killed Gideon, sitting so openly on the quarry edge. It was all closing in on her."

"She didn't cover her tracks well," Ben said.

"She didn't think she needed to—she was Margarethe Framingham."

Nell had touched the sweater with her fingertips, as knitters do. "And Margarethe Framingham would not have let so beautiful a sweater die in a fire, though she didn't think so carefully about her own life."

"So she mailed it to me," Izzy said.

The mayor introduced Angus, and the crowd laughed because there was no one in the whole town of Sea Harbor who didn't know *their* old man of the sea, as they had begun calling him.

But when Angus started to speak, they hushed and listened. The old man looked out at the crowd and at the ocean beyond, and for a minute, Nell thought he wouldn't be able to get through this. They were asking too much of someone who had been through so much—who hadn't regained all his strength and was still weak and frail.

But just as Nell was about to get up and suggest the mayor speak instead, Angus cleared his throat, motioned to Nell that he was just fine, and began to speak.

"Friends—" Angus looked out over the crowd of people filling Pelican Park. Then he looked down at the first couple rows of chairs and coughed slightly, as if he had a lump in his throat. He continued to speak, slowly, hesitatingly, but with the conviction of someone who had something he wanted to say.

"Friends and family—thanks for coming," he began. "I tell stories pretty good, but I'm not much of a speaker. So if you don't mind an old man's whimsy, I'll tell a little story:

"Once upon a time, there was a beautiful Finnish girl who lived on this land with her father, a good man. She met her prince, a plain fellow—a granite cutter—and she stole his heart dead away. Anja was her name, and the stone cutter loved her ferociously. She lit up his day and brought peace to his nights. And when she became his wife, the plain man's life was filled with a kind of happiness he'd never imagined would come his way.

"When his princess died, the man's mind and soul died some, too, even though his old body went on. And then a young woman named Angie Archer became his friend and brought some things back to him—reminded him of his love for Anja. Angie listened to a million stories about Anja. And she even gave the old man back a piece of his princess—her family's land. Big and glorious, jutting out into the sea like a place of honor. So now that old man wants to give some of what he has to you. And the mayor here"—Angus pointed to the man sitting on the stage—"well, he says it's okay."

The crowd laughed.

"See that out there?" Angus pointed to the former Framingham estate, where construction and fire crews had worked around the clock to clear the land of fire debris. The crowd turned as one on their white chairs, shielding their eyes, and looking at the farthest point of Sea Harbor. "It's gonna be a park for all of us. Anja Angelina Park. There's a cabin for me if I want it." He looked down at Birdie and grinned. "It'll be my summer home because I have a fine winter place where they take in your mail and make good soup.

"But y'all come," he said. "It's yours."

When Angus left the stage, there weren't many dry eyes around. Josie Archer was a puddle, and Nell hugged her close.

Izzy came up to Nell then, and soon Cass and Birdie joined them. The four unlikely friends stood close, knit together as surely as the sweaters and scarves and socks that they gave birth to every Thursday night.

Together, they looked out over the harbor and the Anja Angelina Park in the distance.

"Geesh," Cass said. "I'll never be able to remember the name of that park."

The others laughed, a rippling sound that was nearly drowned out by the sound of the first fireworks, crackling and lighting up the sky.

"Just call it Angus's Place," Izzy suggested.

They didn't need to say more. The Seaside knitters had begun falling into one another's thoughts as easily as Purl fell into baskets of cashmere yarn.

Nell looked out over the ocean into a black sky, lit with the bright burst of fireworks, every color of the rainbow lighting up the night. She swallowed hard against the emotion that rose up like the tide.

Angus's Place. Or Anja Angelina. It all meant the same.

Family and friends.

Summer had begun at last.

Nell's Sea-Silk Scarf

Size: One size

Materials:
1 skein Handmaiden Yarns Sea Silk (70% silk, 30% Sea Cell) 400 m/100 g per skein in Ocean (or the color that looks prettiest against your skin).

Size 8 straight or circular needles (Izzy recommends a sticky needle like bamboo or rosewood as the yarn is quite slippery).

Gauge:
Thank goodness for lacy scarves where gauge doesn't matter! This diamond pattern makes a very airy, loopy stitch so that your scarf can drape elegantly over evening finery. If the pattern looks tight, increase needle size until you see the loose sideways diamonds (the "waves") forming in your work. If you'd like to make the scarf wider and more substantial, just add multiples of six to the original pattern.

Pattern Notes:
KW2: Knit Wrap 2.
Knit normally, wrapping yarn twice over right needle before

pulling needle through original stitch. Essentially a YO in the middle of your Knit stitch.

KW3: Knit Wrap 3.
Knit, wrapping yarn three times over needle before pulling needle through.

Wave Pattern:
(multiple of 6 + 1 stitches)
Row 1: K1, *KW2 [KW3] twice, KW2, k2*; rep from start to end.

Row 2: Knit one in each *stitch*, dropping extra loops as you come to them (31 st. on needle using pattern below).

Row 3: KW3, KW2, k2, KW2, *[KW3] twice, KW2, k2, KW2; rep from start to last 2 stitches, KW3, K1.

Row 4: Rep Row 2.

Repeat these four rows to make wave stitch.

Pattern:
Using long tail CO, CO 31 sts.

Set-up row (WS): K 1 row.

Work rows 1–4 of Wave Pattern until scarf measures desired length or 80 inches, then work rows 1 and 2 once more.

Bind off loosely Kwise.

For fringe: Cut 10-inch lengths of yarn. Using a crochet hook, fold two lengths in half and loop folded end through hole made by pattern at end of scarf. Pull loose ends through loop to attach fringe; pull snug. Continue working from edges inward until all fringe is attached.

Tie knots at each fringe end for extra weight. Repeat on second edge of scarf.

Weave in any remaining ends and wear to your next gala event.